TANGLE OF LIES

TANGLE OF MAGIC
BOOK ONE

J.E. NEAL

Copyright © 2023 by J.E. Neal

All rights reserved.

No part of this book may be reproduced in any form or by any electronic or mechanical means, including information storage and retrieval systems, without written permission from the author, except for the use of brief quotations in a book review.

This is an original work of fiction. No AI was used in its creation or in the generation of ideas represented in this work.

To my husband—

I couldn't have written any of the books I've created without him, but this series in particular would never have come to be without his insight, guidance, and help. He's my biggest cheerleader, my greatest inspirer, and my tech guru.

CONTENTS

1.	Fortitude	1
2.	Images	17
3.	The Pillars	29
4.	Guilt With a Side of Guac	41
5.	Diversions	47
6.	Rules and Riches	53
7.	Wants and Needs	63
8.	Confessions and Counter Intelligence	71
9.	Faulty Facts	79
10.	Words	91
11.	Wounds	101
12.	Overdose of Hospitality	109
13.	Admiration and Accolades	117
14.	Energy of Intention	131
15.	Consequences, Confirmation, and Cheeseburgers	143
16.	Hostile Negotiations	149
17.	Home	159
18.	Complications	167
19.	Suites and Sweets	183
20.	The Refrain and the Bridge	193
21.	Portwood and Proposals	197
22.	Gunshots	209
23.	His Father's Son	221
24.	Ioses / Oil on Gypsum	229
25.	Pandora's Box	235
26.	Catwoman, Confusion, and Course Correction	245
27.	Life Can Be Leaky	255
28.	Coffee With Cream and Wisdom	259
29.	Sam	267
30.	Fix the Foundation	273
31.	Effort and Errors	279
32.	Fingo-Nubby Finger Foods	285
33.	Innocent Indiscretions	295
34.	Repercussions and Receivers	305
35.	Duality Dichotomy	311

36. Constants   317
37. Windows and Mirrors   323
38. From the Outside   329
39. Looking In   339
40. Dollars and Sense   345
41. Remains and Remnants   353

About the Author   359
Also by J.E. Neal   361

CHAPTER 1

FORTITUDE

Dan Vindico panicked as tears welled in his wife's eyes again. This was the third time that morning Fionna had choked back emotion. They'd just waved goodbye to their precious baby girl as she climbed onto the school bus for the very first time.

"No more tears. Please. It kills me. I can't leave you like this." He wrapped his arms around her the best that he was able. Her bulging belly, which contained their next addition, prevented him from embracing her fully. It also deeply impacted her emotional fortitude.

"Someone is going to be mean to her. Because kids are mean and… and you're going to be with hot academy girls all day long, and I'm just here and…*pregnant*. I can't even see my own feet."

"Fi." Dan willed patience and tried not to scowl about her worries. "Listen to me, please. You are beautiful, the most beautiful woman in the world and this,"—he rubbed his hands tenderly over her swell—"this is my tiniest baby girl. You're doing a lot of hard work in there. Take it easy today. If someone is mean to Aida, I will personally make certain that Iodex haunts their parents with parking and speeding tickets constantly." That earned him a small grin.

"Hot girls are still going to be hitting on you all day long." Her tone bordered on pouting. Given the fact that she was six and a half months pregnant and that their life had changed rather dramatically in the last year, Dan didn't mind, but he worried.

"*Children*. I will be with children all day." He shuddered but went on with what he knew would actually calm her. "No one is going to hit on me. First of all, the entire Realm knows I married Fionna Styler, the most perfect woman in the universe. Second, you are my whole entire world. No one will ever turn my head because you're it, sweetheart. You are all I'll ever want and all I'll ever need. Without you, I am nothing." That did it. She swooned and seemed to draw resolve from the air around her. "Third, by academy standards, I am ancient. Really, truly old because they are children. But I *do* have to go to work." He braced, not certain how she would respond.

"You are not old, but okay,"—she smirked—"when you get home and we put Aida to bed, we get to play mentor and teacher's pet, right?" Her rapidly changing moods often made him a little woozy, but her sweet giggle let Dan know that she was coming around.

"Hell yeah," he growled as the fantasy flashed through his mind. "I'll be thinking of all the ways you could earn extra credit." He waggled his eyebrows, delighting his wife.

"And you'll text me between your classes, and you'll fail any girl that flirts with you."

Dan noted that it was more of an order. "Yes and yes." He would certainly text and call her as often as he could, but he couldn't fathom being flirted with by students at Venton Academy.

Their marriage wasn't exactly a secret. He was the *former* Chief of Elite Iodex, the highest trained, most dangerous, most vicious, peace-keeping police force in the Gifted Realm. She'd been a nationwide phenom for The Arlington Angels. Their engagement, marriage, adoption, and pregnancies had been analyzed, scrutinized, and discussed ad nauseum in every Gifted paper and all over every Internet news source. Plus, he was thirty-three, so by academy students' standards, he was practically fossilized.

After grabbing his laptop case and the lunch Fionna had packed for him, he pulled her close. "I love you, Maylea." He kissed her heatedly. Though Fionna was her given name, Maylea was the name her mother had called her from the time of her second birthday. It reflected her Hawaiian heritage, and *Maylea* described Fionna perfectly.

His beautiful wildflower, filled with light that illuminated the darkest of places. Her warmth, gentility, her class, her wit and understanding, her grace and intelligence, all filled the empty voids Dan's life had been for so many years. And there, in the deep wells of her sienna eyes, resided that part of her that was wild. The part that Dan would eat his way through fire to feel, the part that coursed so copiously through her veins, the part she granted no one else access to save him. He wished their baby girl hadn't robbed her of her confidence because looking at her swollen full and ripe with his baby drove him mad with need. Nothing else would ever compare.

"You're sure you don't want to come for lunch today?" he asked again.

"I'm still trying to get everything unpacked after Kauai, and I've got to get started on Halia's bedding. In another week or two, I'm not going to be able to get close enough to my sewing machine to sew. I'll come tomorrow."

"Whenever you want. You know where I'll be."

Fionna laid her head on his chest. "I'll miss you."

"Me too." He tried not to see the clock on the ovens as he planted a kiss on the top of her head.

She closed her eyes and drew a deep breath. "I'll be okay. I'm just… you know…pregnant…and sensitive because I'm a Receiver, and I'm crazy, and everyone's leaving me."

"You are not crazy, and I am not leaving you. I'm just going to work. I'll be back before Aida gets home, and we'll spend the whole evening together, okay?" Halia moved against his own stomach. "She knows you're upset."

Fionna ran her hands over her belly again. "I'm all right, or I'll be all right. I just need to get it together. Pregnancy is making me insane."

"I'll be back as soon as my last class leaves." He kissed her again and rushed out the door.

As he racked his brain to think of any way to make this easier for his extremely hormonal wife, Dan knew why she was feeling abandoned. They'd spent every moment of the summer together. They'd worked her family's farm in Kauai in the mornings, napped together on the swinging porch bed on lazy afternoons, and spent hours on end with Aida, inhaling the contentment of family as if their lives depended on it. Dan was certain they had.

They'd prepared delicious food and visited the stunning shorelines of the island with their little girl. It had been a heavenly paradise, one they'd desperately needed in order to heal. The idyllic serenity their sanctuary had offered them had steadied his growing family. There was nothing more he could've asked for, but reality called and he had a job to do.

As much as he missed those long, leisurely afternoons with Fionna's growing curves tucked safely in his arms, jobs, kids, *life* was there in DC to be lived, and he'd spent enough of his merely existing.

The metallic roar of his Ferrari 812 GTS brought a grin to his chiseled features. It fed his soul. He'd missed his Ferrari almost as much as he'd missed his custom Agusta Brutale motorcycle. The day after they'd returned, he'd gone for a long drive on his bike.

At one time, he'd used the Agusta as a message to the world that he wanted to be left the hell alone. Now, he drove the Agusta to feel the raw power and enjoy his body slicing through the wind as the world flew past.

He lamented the forty-minute drive to Venton Gifted Academy almost as much as he regretted taking this damned job in the first place. When he'd purchased his home, he'd done so because it was a seven-minute drive to the Senate. When he was Chief of Iodex, he'd wanted to be able to get to the office in record time. Each marked second was the difference between catching the bad guy and letting him get away. Life and death hung in the balance. Before he'd met and fallen in love with Fionna, he'd rarely left his office.

He'd taken the job at Venton, his alma mater, because he owed the American Realm something. It was a job he was certain he was going to hate. He was a cop. He was born to be a cop. He would always *be* a cop. A shudder worked through his ample musculature. What if he lost his skills? What if he rotted away, locked up in this godforsaken school?

He should be in prison for what he'd done. This self-imposed sentence had to be better than jail.

While reviewing his schedule in his mind and recalling all of the things he needed to tell the five classes he'd be teaching, his cell rang. Smiling, he brought it to his ear. "Hey, sweetness, you okay?"

Fionna had never been overly clingy before. He was concerned that she was calling so soon after he left.

"I'm good now." Just the sound of her voice had his heart beating disjointedly for a moment. "I broke down and made more of my coffee. I hope Halia doesn't mind the extra caffeine, but Mommy needed more Kona this morning."

Dan grinned. "She's your daughter. I'm fairly certain her blood type is at least part Hawaiian coffee."

Fionna's laugh did more to convince him she was well on her way to normal than anything else. "Your mother called right after you left."

Dan ground his teeth. "And what did Marion want?"

"A few things. Mostly, she wanted to *remind* me that this Sunday is Grandparents' Day."

"There's a Grandparents' Day?"

"Apparently, there is. She wanted to make certain that we would be celebrating her on her special day."

"Oh, I'm sure she did."

"She wants everyone to go over to their house for dinner." Fionna was clearly enjoying whatever was coming next.

Delighted that she sounded so much more like herself, Dan found himself longing for her to keep talking no matter what she was going to say. "Great," he sighed. His mother was the worst cook in the Realm.

"Listen to me, because I saved your butt, Vindico."

"Yes, ma'am."

"I told her since it's Grandparents' Day, I really thought she and the governor should come over here, and I'll cook. You know, because I don't want her to put herself out on a day designated just for her." Fionna giggled.

"You are such a hot, sexy, devious little vixen." He let the lust and love he felt for his wife spill heavily into his tone.

"Aww," she cooed, "you say the sweetest things. But listen, there was more, and the next part goes with my weird feeling this morning."

"Weird how? You didn't tell me you had a weird feeling." Panic churned low in his gut. His wife's feelings weren't flippant notions. She was one of the most powerful empathic Receivers in the Realm. She could feel the emotional energy of everything and everyone around her. Despite what anyone else might believe, Dan knew emotion drove the future. Rebellions were built on hope. Greed and power propagated wars. Fear was the root of all prejudice. And love healed the damned. Emotion drove everything. It was the gravity that cemented the web of nature and all of humanity. If she felt odd, something was up.

"You're trending on social media."

The breath Dan had trapped in his lungs escaped. He rolled his eyes. "Of course. I'm back in DC. I'm sure they're just vomiting up the same garbage they went on about last spring."

"No, this has nothing to do with Wretchkinsides or me. It's mostly about your dad, but it's all from Gifted gossip rags. Clickbait titles about you going to Venton to save your dad's job."

"What the hell?"

"He's the Governor of Education, so I guess that's the angle."

"Let them say whatever the hell they're going to say. My old man can handle himself, and so can I. Tell me more about your weird feeling."

"I'm not on campus so I'm struggling to get a clear read. Maybe when I'm there tomorrow I can pinpoint what's wrong. You're not in danger, obviously, or I wouldn't have let you go. But something is wrong. There's deception over the whole campus. It's just still dark for me right now, but please be careful. I never felt like this about Iodex specifically. This is new."

"I promise I'll watch my step and my back. I'll call you after my first class. Take it easy for me today, and stay the hell off social media. You know it gets to you."

"I know. I know. I have lots to do anyway. Let me know if you pick up on anything weird."

"I am not a Receiver, baby doll, but I'll do my best."

As he turned down Venton Drive, the memories washed over him in waves. How many times had he driven that road? Every weekday for six years. Venton Academy had been the backdrop of his youth. It had chiseled the chip on his shoulder he'd worn for years. The one that had been summarily knocked off when Amelia had been kidnapped, and he hadn't been able to rescue her.

The cherry trees that lined the street reached out their branches as if to snare him inside academy grounds. They were caught somewhere between the lush green of summer and the golden hues of fall. They seemed just as confused about their current state as Dan felt.

Consciously remembering to drive past the administration buildings and upperclassman dormitories to access the faculty parking lot, instead of turning into the student lot, he willed this day to go by quickly. This day, the next, the one after that, and the whole damned year. June first he would see all of his girls back in Kauai for another summer of restoration.

"Mentor Vindico," chirped from somewhere nearby as soon as Dan exited his car. He raised his eyebrows and tried to get used to answering to that title. He'd been *Chief* Vindico for many, many years, and that was a title he vastly preferred.

"I'm Aaron Fitzpatrick." The eager looking young man rushed toward him.

"Hi, Aaron." He offered a slight smile to the young man who was grinning at him stupidly.

"I'm in Ioses order."

"Great." Dan summoned his brilliant green energy shield with his hand. The ball of energy grew in size as he drew from the ample storehouses of energy deep within him.

Aaron's mouth hung open as he stared at the fiercely pulsing orb. "What…are you doing?"

Chuckling, Dan gestured his head to the Ferrari. "Making certain no one touches my car."

"Oh…right." Relief eased the panic from Aaron's features. "I'll walk in with you."

Dan released the shield cast onto his car. The black car gave a brilliant green glow as it absorbed the energy.

Sincerely wishing the kid would find someone else to annoy, Dan reminded himself that he was supposed to help guide the students into adulthood and set an example, especially for the members of Ioses Order.

"Sure…I guess. I'm heading to my office."

"Great."

With a nod to his own defeat, Dan led the way.

"My dad says you're this amazing hero that took down Wretchkinsides and the Interfeci and everything, and that you are gonna be a great mentor. My mom doesn't think so, but we're all stoked you're here. She's a Receiver, so you know she's sensitive about everything all the time. Are you going to tell us how you ended him?"

A round of self-hatred roiled through Dan's ample musculature. His fatal mistake tensed in his shield. It was one of the many things he could never take back. It was the reminder that he would forever carry a fragment of energy from the man who'd killed Amelia, his childhood sweetheart. He'd also murdered his first child with Fionna. No matter how hard he fought the blackness, Dan was still aware of its existence. It had marred his soul. He was damned to carry it until he drew his final breath. He didn't have to guess why Aaron's mother didn't think he'd be a good mentor.

"We won't be going over that."

"Oh." Disappointment broadcast from Aaron's features.

That was the most revolting part about having every fucking detail of your life laid out for the entire Realm to see. His and Fionna's pain had been chopped into eye-catching, clickbait headlines, full of half-truths and outright lies. But the way he'd ended Wretchkinsides's life was the truth no matter how much emotion had been vacuumed from the black print on white paper. Fionna had been pregnant with their first child, and she'd lost the baby because of him. Yet another thing Wretchkinsides had taken from him. Yet another thing he would never forgive.

Dan valiantly fought the images resurfacing in his head of staring into the black soulless abyss of Dominic Wretchkinsides's eyes as he'd pulled the life force from his body.

"My sister is in your History of Defense class. She's just a freshman though. I'm a junior. Anyway, she's all, 'I hate Mentor Vindico because he forced Fionna Styler out of Summation and made her have him another baby.'"

Rage rocketed up Dan's spine. "I did not force my wife out of Summation."

"Right, I know. My sister's an idiot. I figure they're all wrong anyway. I'm pretty sure I know why they hired you. I mean, why else would they hire the former Chief of Elite Iodex to be a teacher? Seems weird, right?"

Never one to resist speaking his mind and more than done with this conversation, Dan's jaw unhinged. "They hired me because I'm the best damn officer there ever was or ever will be. Past, present, and future. Training under me will create better-educated, highly skilled officers which is precisely what this Realm needs."

Aaron's smirk only served to rub salt in the fresh wounds of being forced to resign and having to take this job in the first place. "Yeah, I figured you were the shit, or at least *you* think you are. Here's the thing, though—I don't think that's why they hired you. I figure they hired you to clean up all of the stuff that's been going on here. What else could they possibly want you to do here? You said it yourself. You're the shit. If anyone can clean up Venton, it's gotta be you."

"I'll see you in class, Aaron." Dan had never been so thankful to see his office door at the other end of the corridor. He had no idea what Aaron had been prattling on about. Why in God's name would the school governing board want to hire him if not to train better officers? Mentor Sullivan, the teacher who'd trained Dan, had insisted that the school needed him to take this job, but he'd only been trying to help Dan get back on his feet after all the hell he and Fionna had been through.

"Yeah, I can't wait, and if you need anything or you need help, I'm your man."

"Great. I'll keep that in mind."

"Hey, did you hear about the—?"

"I'll see you tomorrow, Aaron."

With a halfhearted wave, Dan edged toward his office door. When his left shoulder gave its customary twitch that said something was off, Fionna's warning echoed along with Aaron's prediction on his hiring. *If anyone can clean up Venton, it's gotta be you.* Then Mentor Sullivan's parting words at the wedding last spring joined the ranks. *They need you up there, Daniel.*

~

Fionna Vindico

Clutching the mug in her hands, Fionna summoned heat from the air around her and let her palms rewarm her coffee. The soothing liquid gave her peace. For the first time in months, she was alone. Alone with her own feelings and no one else's. Alone with things she didn't want to think about, things she certainly didn't want to feel.

Halia moved in her stomach, reminding her that she wasn't entirely alone. Fionna smiled and ran her hands over her bump. She wished she could feel Halia's emotions, but the baby was so thoroughly a part of Fionna herself she couldn't distinguish anything different.

She would've given anything in that moment to feel anyone else's emotions. She considered going shopping, drowning her worries and her pain in the assault of feelings that came whenever she was in a crowd, but her rhythms were already ragged and worn. Adding more weight to her overtaxed energy strains wasn't going to help. She had to stop hiding in Aida's feelings, and as much as she didn't want to, she had to stop letting Dan shield her from everything.

The swirl of elation over the life they were finally living was severed with her guilt. She was so thankful for Halia but terrified that something would go wrong, that the gunshot wound hadn't healed. She worried that her elation over Halia somehow meant that she didn't mourn their first baby the right way. She didn't know what to feel. What was allowable when you'd been through what they'd been through?

Closing her eyes, she tried to tap into the energy of Kauai, the pure pulse of her, but it was too far away. She couldn't access it.

She longed for Dan to come back and wrap her safely in his shield, the only time she couldn't feel anything but his love for her. She cursed her own perceived weakness and turned on the television to distract herself. One of the Gifted news networks was on.

Her father-in-law, Governor Vindico, was trying to get inside the Pentagon. Her heart ached for him. He'd tried so hard to protect Dan and love him through his insurmountable losses. When she and Dan had stepped out of the limelight for a moment of reprieve, it seemed the press had decided to turn their sharpened claws to his father instead. It was so unfair.

Couldn't they understand what the governor had been through? He'd lost a grandchild he hadn't even known he was to have. For a decade, Dan had cut him out of his life just like he had everyone else. She could always feel the governor's pain when she was near him, and now, she could feel it through the television screen.

"Governor Vindico, care to comment on the pictures of Chancellor Dean Wilshire the Realm has seen this morning? Is that why your son was placed at Venton Academy? Can Dan clean this mess up for you, Governor?"

She was so focused on the worry tensed on the governor's features and the way his energy hardened at the edge of his orb she almost missed the questions they were asking him.

Governor Vindico's jaw visibly strained before he unhinged it. "Stay away from my son."

Fionna's eyes closed. He was still trying so hard to protect Dan, and she was overwhelmed with love for that action alone. Halia kicked and Fionna wondered if she really was picking up on her emotions. "I'm all right, baby," she soothed to her stomach. "And Daddy is all right too. I hope."

Her phone rang again, offering her a reprieve. She smiled when she saw who was calling, but worry clouded her happiness in an instant. The duality of her emotions since the miscarriage, the yin and the yang, was exhausting. She allowed herself to wonder if even her emotional range had been widened to the point of pain in the last year. Could she feel such all-encompassing loss if she didn't also feel overwhelming joy? "Why are you up so early?" she asked her grandmother. "Are you okay?"

Tutu's calm, easy chuckle soothed her soul. "I'm up worrying about my granddaughter."

Fionna started to assure her that she was fine, but that was a lie and one could never lie to Tutu. She knew far too much, sensed everything. Fionna was simultaneously envious of her grandmother's wisdom and afraid for what her grandmother must have to feel each and every day. The dichotomy struck another blow. But she'd been quiet too long.

"Maylea? Tell me what you feel."

"A little lost maybe. I don't know what to feel." A harsh swallow tensed her neck. "I'm not sure what I'm allowed to feel."

"You are allowed to feel anything that comes to your heart. You know this. You will only hurt yourself if you try to suppress it. Breathe them out. Let them exist before you try to let them go."

"I don't want to let them go," she choked. "I want them."

"Maylea," her grandmother soothed. "Letting the pain go does not mean that you are letting your child go. Believe me. I know."

"I know. I'm sorry. I shouldn't have said that." She'd been so bogged down in her own fear, she'd let Dan shield her to the fact that when she'd lost her mother, her grandmother had also lost her daughter.

"There is no need to apologize for how you feel or for what you fear, but let me help you. I miss you."

"I miss you too. So much. I don't remember how to be here. I want to be there with you. The last time I remember being here alone I was…"

"Pregnant and more frightened than you've ever been or will ever be."

She told herself to take solace in her grandmother's all-encompassing knowledge and her predictions. At least she'd never be that terrified again. "I've got to stop thinking about it. I'm acting insane. I practically suction-cupped myself to Dan this morning before he left. I don't like feeling so clingy." There. At least she was woman enough to admit that out loud.

"A powerful Receiver seeking her Shield is not a sign of weakness. It is the way things were meant to be."

Fionna needed to argue. She needed to rage. "You don't have a Shield, and you're much more powerful than I am."

Tutu chuckled again. "Do I not?"

"Papa isn't a Shield. He's an Occamist."

"This island is my Shield. My husband is my creator. My Shield longs for my granddaughter to return to the safety of her shores. Why can't my granddaughter long for her Shield to come home as well?"

"I wish I could come home. Believe me."

"And you will in good time. But your Shield will return to you long before you return to me."

"It's nine whole months before we'll be back for the summer."

"This year will hold many things. None of them exactly what you're expecting. You will return here before summer."

"Dan said maybe we could come for Christmas, but I don't know with the baby."

"Maylea, you are exhausting even me. Where is your breath? Find it and fill your lungs."

She did as she was told and drew a deep, restorative breath.

"Again," her grandmother guided, and again she complied. "Good. Now, explain to me why you continue to believe that requiring a part of yourself makes you weak? If someone removed your arms, would you believe yourself weak for not being able to carry the world?"

"I guess not."

"None of us were meant to carry anything alone. You longing for Daniel doesn't make you weak. You admitting that you need him shows your strength. I need my island. I need my husband. I need my granddaughter. I need my great-granddaughters, all three of them even though one exists in spirit. None of those are signs of weakness."

"Okay, then how do you deal with the fact that we can't be there right now? Because Dan can't be here always."

"Strength is born only when we face things we aren't certain that we can. What did your mother used to tell you to do when the feelings of the world were more than you could bear?"

Fionna considered the wisdom of her mother. She struggled to hear her mother's soothing intonation when she was away from Kauai. "To use my energy to create something beautiful instead of worrying that the world isn't."

She could almost hear Tutu's smile from five thousand miles away. "What can you create today?"

"I could start on Halia's bedding. I could make Aida's favorite cookies since it's her first day of school. I could cook something for dinner that Dan loves."

"That sounds like a lovely day. What can you create to remind yourself of your own beauty?"

Fionna considered that. "I'm…not sure. Maybe that's why I feel so lost."

"I've always told you that you get your smarts from me. That is precisely why you feel the way you feel, but you are not lost, Maylea. You are right there with yourself. But you have loss just as we all do. Your Shield spent his entire summer using every ounce of his might and his muscle to keep you from feeling the loss. As admirable as that was, you must feel it."

"It's easier not to. It's easier to let Dan keep me from it." A harsh shiver quaked through her as she fought the tears, fought the feelings.

"It's not the child that you mourn, although that must be carried as well. It's that she took part of you with her when she went, just as Elizabeth did for both of us. But I know this—they are together. And they are happy. Feel that, Maylea. They want you to be happy as well. You can have both the loss and the happiness. You can be whole without pieces of yourself. We all must be."

"I'm scared," she choked. "What if I start crying and I can't ever stop? I have so much to be thankful for. I shouldn't cry. I shouldn't be sad."

"Often times tears are the very things that we create to remind ourselves of our own beauty. There is almost as much healing in the salt of your tears as there is in the ocean. Tears don't mean you aren't thankful. They mean that you are capable of multitudes, and you, my precious kekei, are capable of anything. The strength that you're convinced you can't find might just be at the bottom of the well of tears."

"I don't feel very capable lately."

"The woman who just told me that she can create so much beauty in this world doesn't feel capable?"

Fionna shook her head. "I don't think sewing a baby quilt and making cookies is going to change the world."

"Isn't it? Is there anything more important than creating love in this lost world? Reminding you how much you love yourself will give you the power to love all of those in your care."

"Okay, I'll try." Her phone beeped, and she pulled it away from her face to check who was calling. "Garrett's calling me, Tutu. Let me make sure he's okay."

"My granddaughter is so powerful she requires two Shields."

"I only require one of them, but the fact that I have both is another reason I shouldn't be sad. I'm so lucky."

"You say that as if your Shields require nothing of you, when you and I both know they require everything you have to give. Go talk to Garrett and then make some of the lemongrass and lotus flower tea I sent back with you. Then go sew your quilt. You are not lost. The pieces are all there. You just have to sew them back together in a new pattern."

"Thanks, Tutu. I love you." She switched calls quickly. "Hey. Sorry. I was talking to my grandmother."

"What's wrong?" Garrett Haydenshire demanded. Fionna grinned. She'd missed his terse demands almost as much as she missed laughing with her best friend.

"I'm just…hormonal." That wasn't at all a lie.

"How lucky for Dan." He laughed. "I just got called down to the Pentagon to keep the press away from Governor Vindico. What the hell is going on at Venton?"

"I have no idea. Dan told me to get off social media."

"Listen to your husband. I'll find out what I can while I'm down there. I get off at noon. Want me to pick up some lunch and bring it out there?"

Fionna grinned. "Did you miss me?"

"Hell yeah."

"I missed you too, and that sounds perfect."

"Any cravings?"

"You are *the* best."

"I am aware."

"Will you get me some of those barbacoa tacos from Chevy's?" Her mouth watered from the thought.

"Of course. Guac to go with?"

"You've known me entirely too long to even have to ask that."

Garrett's easy chuckle soothed her soul. "Just making sure. You stay off social media, and I'll bring you tacos in a little while."

"You are mighty bossy today."

"Hey, you haven't been around all summer for me to boss around, and Dan would whip my ass if I didn't take care of you."

"I don't deserve either of you."

"Not true. Hey, I'm pulling up now. Good God, it's a fucking madhouse. I'll see you in a little while."

CHAPTER 2
IMAGES

GARRETT HAYDENSHIRE

Garrett slammed the door to his squad car and stepped out into a nightmare. Not his own. No, his own were vastly different than this. This appeared to be Governor Vindico's nightmare, and Garrett had to figure out some way to protect the man from the demon press all while making absolutely certain that Fionna didn't experience any of the fallout of whatever this was. She'd been through enough.

He saw his older brother, Will, trying to get through the onslaught and into the building.

"Move," Garrett commanded a guy who was half the size of the camera he had strapped to his chest. The guy took a half second to study Garrett before he decided it would be in his best interest to comply. He backed up, and Garrett continued to ease the press back as he made his way to Will.

"What the fuck is going on?" he demanded when he arrived.

Will shook his head and pulled his phone from his pocket. "This." He showed Garrett a Gifted news site. "Only instead of gathering the pitchforks for the guy with his hand on the thigh of a woman who's not his wife, they turned them on the governor."

Garrett's eyes closed in defeat. "You know who they really want, and it isn't the governor."

Will nodded. "There are a lot of people who are pissed Dan's not in jail. Him becoming a mentor at Venton didn't help. The press is furious that Dan and Fionna stepped out of the limelight so they're not readily available to be profited off of anymore. Angels' fans are not happy that the strongest Receiver of our generation is no longer challenging for their team. So, apparently, they all decided to make Dan's dad the sacrifice on their altar of whining. The fact that they're here instead of at Venton should tell you everything you need to know."

~

Dan Vindico

Students and mentors were clogging the corridors discussing their schedules. Dan had less than fifteen minutes to gather the things he would need for his first Defense of the Realm class and to be in the auditorium for the ridiculous back-to-school ceremony. He'd hated the damn thing when he was a student. This was a college. The students needed to get to work. They shouldn't require being patted on the back for knowing their Predilect and being able to state their purpose when prompted.

Distracted momentarily from his ire, he hung back when he saw the latest issue of the Angels' Season Program hoisted upwards to display a picture of Fionna that spanned two pages.

As one of the Angel team owners, Dan knew they'd decided to include a relatively long article along with numerous photos of Fionna celebrating her seasons on the Angels and to gloss over the actual reasons for her retirement from professional Summation—she wanted a family and hadn't fully recovered from the loss of their first child or the gunshot wound that caused the miscarriage.

He and Fionna had posed for several shots bringing attention to their newest endeavor. They had agreed to be the spokesfamily for the Auxiliary International Adoption Program, and the interview had given them an opportunity to bring attention to children that were in desperate need of being adopted, just like their little Aida.

But the picture the young man was currently displaying was one of Fionna from three seasons before. She was posed with a come-get-me grin and wearing a pair of knit short-shorts with Angel written across her luscious ass. Her top half was barely covered by an Angels zip-up jacket with nothing underneath it. The zipper was pulled down to expose her enviable cleavage. Rampant desire and possessiveness fought for dominance in Dan's shield. He narrowed his eyes.

"So, Vindico's gonna be our new mentor, which obviously means that Fi-onn-na will be up here on the regular. And that means that I will be hanging out around Vindico's office…often," the guy holding the photo drawled pompously to his admiring friends.

"Spencer, you're such an idiot. Look." One of his friends grabbed the magazine that also included photos and stats of all of the current Angels and this season's schedule. He flipped the page and revealed the next full-length shot of Fionna.

While trying to remain behind them without being seen, Dan ground his teeth. His shield pulsed through his veins, tinging the air around him dark green. As every person in the corridor was also Gifted, his energy shift wasn't noticed. "She's huge. He ruined her."

The photo he used as his illustration had been taken a week before, right after they'd returned home from Kauai. Fionna was posed in a side silhouette of her entire body. She had a delicate white linen shirt buttoned just to the top of her baby bump. It hung open revealing her very pregnant belly. Dan was posed on his knees in front of her with both of his hands partially obscured under the shirt. He was tenderly kissing her bump. It was his favorite photograph. He'd purchased several copies from the photographer. It was intimate and tender, and not only showed their precious little Halia, but showed just how much Dan adored his wife and babies.

"Nah, that's just a temporary problem," Spencer assured his friend. "She's an athlete. She challenged for years. She'll get rid of the kid, get her smoking hot body back, and then I'll just see if she'd like to become my own personal mentor." He waggled his eyebrows before continuing, "Bet me a Benjamin by the end of the year, I'll be getting myself a piece of that fan-freaking-tastic ass."

Vomit swirled in Dan's gut. His biceps tensed of their own accord.

Fury stormed through his veins. With two long strides, he was behind the idiots in question and jerked the magazine up over their heads.

"What the hell do you think you're...?" Spencer spun to take in Dan's menacing glare.

"Man, you are so dead," the friend hissed.

Using the expanse of his overmuscled chest, Dan backed Spencer and two of his cohorts up to the painted concrete brick wall. "What was that, Spencer?"

The idiots before him stared up at him in wide-eyed terror.

"Uh..." he stammered. "Uh...we were just saying...what a great challenger..."—he stopped to consider before going on—"*Mrs. Vindico* was when she challenged...for the Angels...I mean."

"Funny, that is not at all what I heard you say." Dan stopped short of calling the kid a motherfucker by reminding himself that he could not curse in front of students, yet another thing he hated about this job.

He jerked Spencer's schedule from his stack of binders. "Let's see here." He gave the schedule a cursory glance. "Wow, you're in two of my classes." Spencer's eyes closed in abject defeat. "We're gonna have a lot of fun this year." Glancing at Spencer's last name on the schedule, a broad grin spread across Dan's face. "Coker, huh? I know your father, don't I? Drew's a good friend of my family. You know, since he's an aide to my father...the *governor*. Before I go and phone your father and tell him what I just heard you say, listen up." Dan leaned in as Spencer tried to melt into the concrete wall. "Here's what's going to happen. I'm going to go home in a few hours and tell my incredibly beautiful wife, and the mother of my children, all about your little bet. You know, the one I ruined," he spat at the friend.

"You're going to go home and write me a thousand-word essay on women's rights within the Realm, and how women should be treated with the same respect men afford each other without thought. If I were you, I'd include several paragraphs on how they are not pieces of property to be bet over. Tomorrow, when Fi comes by to have lunch with me, you're going to be invited to join us. While we enjoy our lunch, you're going to entertain us by reading your essay. You want my wife to be your mentor? Perfect. We'll let *her* grade it. I think I'll let it represent at least forty percent of your semester grades for *both* of my classes. A warning to you though—Fi is not a fan of pompous egotistical *children*." Dan dealt the crushing blow to any twenty-year-old male. "I'd study up. She's tough." With that, he shoved the magazine and the schedule into Spencer's chest with a great deal of force. He reveled in the rush of air he pushed from the idiot's lungs. "See you in class."

Dan slammed his office door, making it echo up and down the corridor. "Un-fucking-believable." He slung his briefcase into the cushioned chair in the corner and sank down into his chair behind the desk.

An involuntary smile began to form on his lips. Fionna had designed his office for him, and it reminded him of home. The large canvas painting of flowers in every imaginable color that Aida had created at an event at the Louvre hung on the wall, along with several of her framed crayon drawings.

There were pictures across his large desk of Fionna and him lying in the sands of Kauai after their wedding, one of him and Aida on a log ride in Paris, and another of her beaming ear to ear seated on his shoulders.

The one of Dan knelt down in front of Fionna kissing her belly was on prominent display. There was another of Aida in her grass skirt performing at the recital she'd been in at the end of the summer with her hula class.

He picked up the very smallest of all the photographs. A black-and-white clip of Halia's latest ultrasound. He could see the precious outline of her tiny face and her sweet, rounded belly. He'd been given so much after all he'd taken away. If this job was his penance, bring it on. God knew he'd been through worse.

With a sigh, he downed the last of the coffee and summoned to turn on his laptop. He stared at the names of the four students Portwood, the new Chief of Elite Iodex, wanted Dan to pick from as a paid intern for Iodex. All four kids had outstanding GPAs and extracurriculars. They were all in Dan's first class. It was the only one he was actually interested in teaching. As he reviewed the class list and his lesson plans, a knock sounded on the office door. "In," he ordered, just as he'd always done at Iodex.

Fergus Sherman, a Scholera Predilect mentor's assistant, rushed inside. Dan clenched his jaw to keep from rolling his eyes. He couldn't stand Fergus. He was a useless, driveling, know-it-all.

Right under the nose of his mother, one of the school governors, and the rest of the staff, he'd gone as far as to date a student. She'd graduated in June, and apparently Fergus was hoping to propose. He'd bored every mentor at Venton with this information repeatedly over every meeting they'd been forced to sit through for the last week. It was beyond Dan how no one had called him on the fact that he was proposing to a former student three months after graduation, but he suspected that Governor Sherman had a great deal to do with that fact.

"Just wanted to make certain you knew where your first class was and see if you needed any advice," Sherman offered.

Narrowing his eyes, Dan glared. "As I am the Head of Ioses Order and therefore the lead mentor for all defense classes, I assigned all of the classrooms to my department. I'm well aware of which rooms I'm teaching in."

"Right." Sherman looked concerned as he glanced around. "Well now, I have been doing this longer than you have, so if you need anything at all just let me know. I can show you around, sit with you at lunch, that kind of thing."

"I'm good." Dan wondered if his day had any chance of improving, or if he should just resign now. "I'll probably eat in here. I'm not big on cafeterias."

"You don't want to do that," Fergus panicked.

"Why?"

"Because…you need to understand your reputation."

"My reputation?"

"Yeah, you have this really shielded sort of thing going on. I know you're an Ioses, but you keep everyone at arm's length way more than most Shields. It's like you don't want to be bothered."

"I don't."

"See, that's what I'm talking about. People think you're a hard-ass."

"That assumption is both correct and has never bothered me...*ever.*"

"Several people's feelings were hurt when you and Fionna didn't come to the Venton kickball game."

Dan rubbed his temples. Since Fergus was the mentor that had come up with the kickball game, Dan didn't have to guess whose feelings had been hurt. "Fi had an appointment with the medio, and I don't play kickball as I am no longer in second grade. I'm here to train officers. You can leave me off the invite lists for all of the staff essential oil parties, the lose ten pounds in ten days shit shakes get-togethers, and the Amway pep rallies."

"You used to be Chief of Iodex. You should understand that you have to attend things that promote team building."

Dan slammed his laptop shut and shoved it into his case. "I found that when you and ten of your closest friends are being shot at, and you're trying to get everyone out alive, it tends to really cement the team. No kickballs required."

Opening the door to his office, Dan waited on Fergus to get the message.

"I don't really think anything involving guns would be an appropriate event for Venton, but I'll take it under consideration. I'm in charge of team building for this year."

Not certain if he wanted to laugh or cry Dan made no effort to hide his eye roll. "I need to get to the auditorium."

"Oh right." Fergus checked his watch and rushed from the room. "See you at lunch." Dan slammed the door just for effect, but that was the second time in a ten-minute period. Never a good sign.

Dan grimaced. The corridors were empty. He was late. He hated to be late to anything, even if he saw no point in going in the first place.

His long legs ate up the distance between the Ioses building and the Admin complex. Another memory assaulted his consciousness as he passed the statue of Former Crown Governor Joseph Lawson, the only Ioses Predilect to ever serve as Crown, in the Ioses courtyard. He bristled at his own name on the stone placards under the statue. He'd graduated Head of Ioses Order, an honor he supposed, but he'd never deserve to be anywhere near Crown Governor Lawson. He was a hero. Dan was…a broken Shield, he finally admitted with a heavy sigh.

Dan had recruited Rainer, Joseph's one and only son, to serve on the Elite force the year before. God, how had so much changed in so little time?

As Dan slipped inside the admin building, he stopped short. The hair on the back of his neck stood.

"Those are serious accusations, *Ms. Sherman.*"

Methodically, Dan scanned the empty entrance before him. He noted nothing out of place and couldn't locate the person who'd spoken. Edging along the rounded wall, he could hear the low drone of students in the large meeting hall nearby.

"This is a very serious indiscretion, Chancellor, one the press has apparently gotten wind of. This is the last thing Venton needs now. Just what do you plan to *do* about this?" Governor Sherman demanded.

As soon as he heard the title *chancellor,* Dan eased down a nearby corridor and listened intently. The potential of investigation fed his blood. His heart steadied. His eyes narrowed. His training had been honed for far too many years for him to forget the drive to uncover the truth no matter what the case may be. Intention squared his shoulders. He had no idea what the hell was going on at his alma mater, but he was going to find out.

"Indiscretion," Chancellor Wilshire scoffed a little arrogantly in Dan's opinion. "There was no indiscretion. Nothing needs to be done. If you'll excuse me…."

"Dammit, there are photographs, Dean! You have to deal with this."

Dan heard the whoosh of a door opening and then closing.

Slowly counting to ten, Dan circled to the other entrance of the auditorium and slipped inside. Chancellor Wilshire was greeting the assembled staff seated in folding chairs in front of the students. The Head of Ioses Order's chair was empty, but Dan would have to cross the large room and skirt the chancellor and school governors to access his assigned seat. He decided to take in this ridiculous ceremony from his current locale instead.

His mind automatically sorted, indexed, and recorded what he knew so far. The Iodex seal, the one that resided on all confidential evidence folders of every investigation he'd ever been a part of, formed in his mind. So this investigation wouldn't have a seal. That didn't mean he wasn't interested in taking it on, whatever the hell it was.

Registering Aaron's predictions on Dan being hired to clean up Venton, he studied the chancellor as he took the podium. Chancellor Wilshire was a mountain of a man—solid, able, strong. He'd come to Amelia's funeral twelve years ago. He'd sent Dan and Fionna a wedding gift. He'd written Dan's recommendation to special ops training and then the Elite Iodex Squadron a year before he'd graduated. He'd nurtured Rainer after the death of his father. In Dan's mind, he was a hero.

He had no idea what the chancellor was being accused of, but he couldn't fathom that he'd done anything worthy of trial. Blinking the dust of the past from his eyes, he studied Chancellor Wilshire as he welcomed everyone back for the new school year.

Weary tension weighted his broad physical frame. The wrinkles on his face seemed to have deepened dramatically in the last few months. Illness? Maybe. Dan swallowed down a knot of anxiety. It was difficult to watch the men who'd raised him age. It would always be difficult to see the pillars of your foundation tire.

The odd shift in his chest had him drawing a deep breath. His secondary Predilection eased his shield back. It didn't happen often. Dan's shield was more honed than his Visium Predilection, but he was a Double-Predilect of equal Gift which was almost unheard of. Dan tapped into his Visium Predilection whenever he needed his mind more than his might.

This time his brain and body had forced the issue. Clearly, he needed to stop lamenting the passing of time and get his shit together. Something was going on. He needed to be on top of his own game.

Suddenly, a large group of students seated on three sections of bleachers all stood and responded to the chancellor's prompting of, "Adminis Order."

"To Govern." Their vow was sincere. Ah, to be that young and unjaded.

Dan watched the next group stand as Chancellor Wilshire continued with, "Ioses Order."

"To Protect." Their energy all glowed in varying shades of green. Dan studied the faces he could see and wondered what was to come for all of them.

Next came, "Auxiliary Order."

Dan couldn't help but smile. Fionna and Aida were both Auxiliary Order Receivers. In the past year, he'd come to have a soft spot for the entire order itself.

"To Serve," they vowed readily.

"Valeduto Order."

"To Heal."

Dan scanned the future medios, nurses, and caretakers of the Realm. The energy in that section was more visible due to the large storehouses their Predilections carried for the purposes of healing others.

"Occamy Order," was next.

Wilshire was moving too quickly. Valeduto hadn't taken their seats when the Occamists stood and responded, "To create and provide."

"And my own personal favorite as it is my order," Wilshire chuckled. Dan rolled his eyes. The man had been making that same lame-ass joke for every back-to-school assembly and graduation since Dan had entered as a sub-freshman. "Scholera Order." Wilshire offered the current teaching staff a kind smile instead of the students of Scholera Order.

They dutifully sounded off anyway, "To teach."

"Duco Order," was announced and the relatively small order stood.

"To plan and calculate."

An image of Will Haydenshire, the only Duco Predilect Dan knew well and one of his lifelong friends. Memories of their first day of school at Venton started to play in his head without his permission.

He shook himself and tried to live in the present. What the hell was wrong with him anyway? He'd never had trouble concentrating. The past danced far too closely to his present that day. For a man who wanted no part of his past, damming it back was difficult when he was standing in the halls of his history, being forced through the ceremonies that had shaped and formed him.

With a quick clench of his jaw, he made a methodic study of the staff seated on the other side of the room. Governor Sherman hadn't taken her cold glare off of Wilshire since the assembly had begun. Nothing like bad blood to produce good leads. Maybe he should ask the governor outright what her beef with the chancellor was.

"Vis Virres Order," brought Dan back to the students.

"To will," the Predilects stated succinctly.

"And finally, Visium Order," Wilshire urged.

"To observe, analyze, and understand."

Dan gave a nod to his secondary Predilection and then watched the student body as a whole become bored. They shifted and sighed as Governor Sherman took the podium to explain rules everyone already knew.

Keeping his eyes trained on the assembled crowd, Dan's left shoulder gave another twitch and his shield remained at bay while his Visium Predilection continued to occupy his musculature. He could have forced them to switch. It didn't seem there was anything to protect himself from, however, but something was certainly amiss.

Chancellor Wilshire left the assembly in the middle of Governor Sherman's speech. Dan allowed the chancellor a few seconds to get ahead and then followed him out of the auditorium.

Keeping to the shadows, he watched the chancellor pull his phone from his pocket, type something quickly, and then head to the faculty parking lot. Dan went as far as to step outside to confirm that Chancellor Dean Wilshire was leaving campus on the first day of term of a new school year.

CHAPTER 3

THE PILLARS
GARRETT HAYDENSHIRE

Garrett helped Portwood and Ericcson keep the press away from the governing board as they all made their arrival to work that day. Then he and Will headed to their father's office. As annoying as Garrett found it, his dad always knew what to do in any given situation.

But when Will and Garrett arrived in the office of the Crown Governor of the American Realm, they found him pacing. That was never a good sign. Garrett shared a concerned glance with Will as they entered and closed the door.

"Any idea what you're gonna do?" Will, who'd never seen the point in not getting to the crux of the problem, asked as soon as their father gave them both a weary smile.

"Technically it's not my job to handle anything that goes on at Venton. That falls to Arthur. I don't want to overstep my bounds. I also had no idea that Daniel would ever actually consider teaching as a viable career for him after Iodex. I have a feeling that this wouldn't be getting the attention it has if it weren't for Dan."

Garrett shook his head. "I don't know that it's anything worth everyone birthing live ducks over. Wilshire put his arm around this chick and was rubbing her leg. Context is everything. Fi and I have been friends for years. I've definitely put my arm around her, and I've rubbed her leg. We have nothing going on. Never have, never will. The press still asks me constantly if her baby is mine."

Governor Haydenshire nodded. "I know. And I can all but guarantee you that if I phoned Dean Wilshire and asked him what he was thinking, I'd be assured that it was nothing more than him being friendly with someone on his teaching staff. But you and Fionna have always been very open about your friendship. You've never tried to hide anything because there's never been anything to hide.

"There were complaints about Wilshire's bizarre loss of interest in work last year around amative energies week, and Arthur looked into it. Dean blocked him at every pass. But it wasn't long after a host of other complaints started to come in from academy parents, that I was getting a call that Daniel had cussed out the Russian Governing Board and was fleeing the country. I didn't want to add any more to Arthur's already overburdened plate. A few weeks after that incident, Lindley Vindico was coming before the board with some significant possession charges. Then you know what happened to Fionna. It's been a nonstop assault on Arthur. I'd hoped with Dan and Fionna in Hawaii for a few months the press would lose interest. I should've known better."

A knock on the door pulled everyone from their thoughts. Governor Haydenshire opened the door and forced a smile. Garrett was certain he wasn't the only one who knew it was forced.

"I'm sorry," Arthur Vindico spoke as he stepped into the office. "I have no idea what they want me to say. I just saw the photos this morning. I've phoned Dean four times. He isn't answering."

Will and Garrett both scowled. Will shook his head. "Sir, it's none of my business, I know, but you're the Governor of Gifted Education. If Chancellor Wilshire is refusing to take your calls, that alone is enough to bring him up on charges of insubordination."

Arthur sank down on one of the couches in the office. "I know that, William. I'm trying to give him the benefit of the doubt. It is also the first day of the new term. He should be busy."

"Do you know the woman in the photos with him, Governor?" Garrett asked. He was a detective after all.

"That's Mentor Katherine Bryant. She's been a teacher at Venton for almost a decade. She wasn't there when you two and Dan were there, but she started not long after you graduated. She has outstanding teacher reviews for the most part, and her students typically do well on their finals. She appears to be effective."

Governor Haydenshire nodded. "If memory serves, I think she taught Patrick, Connor, and Emily. I don't think Rainer or Logan ever had her though."

Since there were eleven Haydenshire children in the family, she was bound to end up teaching a few of them.

Governor Vindico nodded. "She typically teaches advanced creative writing and a few Adminis classes. None of those would be required for Shields." He drew a deep breath. "I'm asking your advice, Stephen. I personally don't feel like I can fire the man for putting his arm around someone. I know a picture is worth a thousand words, but Dean has always been an outstanding chancellor. I need something a little more substantial than that. But then this was sitting on my desk when I finally fought my way through the onslaught this morning." He handed a file folder to Governor Haydenshire.

Before he opened it, he nodded. "The pictures might be worth a thousand words, but I think we need to hear the words. And I think we need to hear them from both Dean and Katherine." He flipped open the folder. His brow furrowed.

"What is that?" Garrett reached for the folder and his father handed it over. Garrett gave it a cursory glance. "The drug test reports from Venton. What's weird about this being on your desk?" he asked Governor Vindico.

"Nothing, but read them. Never in all of the time we've required drug tests to be performed on the students of Venton Academy have we ever had *no one* with a positive result. Especially at the beginning of the year. I don't know what to believe anymore, and I'll readily admit that the pictures this morning make me question everything."

Governor Haydenshire sighed. "Because houses don't ever burn down slowly."

∾

Dan Vindico

Dan's first class was a senior level defense class with an accompanying lab where he would be teaching hand-to-hand combat technique and weapons. These were the top students in Ioses Order, the men and women who were hoping for appointments to state Iodex precincts. A half dozen of them might even be good enough for the national team, and the exceptional one, possibly two, could be recruited for the Elite Squadron.

Dan's first job was to select an outstanding student from this class for the one and only paid internship spot with the Elite Squadron for the duration of the school year.

Earning that spot all but guaranteed a job at the national level after graduation. It was a program he should have instituted when he was Chief, but he hadn't. He was far too fucked-up to give a damn about anything but the revenge he sought. Landon Portwood, Dan's replacement, had corrected the oversight.

Whispers hissed around the room as he made the approach, but when he entered, the students fell silent. He moved to the mentor's desk at the front of the classroom and opened his laptop.

"Morning," he offered the class.

"Good morning, sir," most of the class replied dutifully.

He took in the nervous set of the shield energy in the room as he summoned and projected the syllabus onto the white board behind his desk. Dan placed a stack of paper copies on Jeff Strenton's desk on the front row. Jeff was one of the students Portwood was most interested in. He was apparently a tech whiz and one hell of a Shield. He held office within Ioses Order, and had an outstanding GPA. Dan offered the kid a smile. "Mr. Strenton, would you mind passing those back for me?"

"Yes, sir. Uh…you know my name…sir?"

"I know your name. Perhaps more importantly, Chief Portwood knows your name. We're both extremely impressed."

"Thank you." Jeff stumbled out of his desk and handed out the syllabi instead of simply passing them back. He looked like Dan had just thrown him a life preserver in a hurricane.

"Welcome to Senior Defense. This class also has a lab attached to it where we will be learning defense and combat techniques. As I'm sure you're aware, I am the former Chief of Elite Iodex. It is my recommendation alone that Chief Officer Landon Portwood will be looking for when he hires for any available spots in the DC precinct this year." Nervous energy reverberated throughout the room.

"Now." Every eye followed his trek back and forth in front of the white board. He sent an electric pulse from his laptop to the board to project an image of Fionna standing on the beach in a sundress with her hands around her bump. "For any of you who may have been living under a rock, my wife will be delivering my second child sometime in November." No one looked surprised but several people smiled. "What does this mean for you? It means for four weeks after my baby girl is born I will not be here or available to you in any way. The highly esteemed man that held this position before myself, Mentor Glenn Sullivan, has agreed to come back and substitute for all of my classes during my paternity leave.

"Mentor Sullivan will be available for all questions, extra help, and to prepare you for your final exam which will be given December tenth. Any issue related to this class or lab will be handled through Mentor Sullivan. What he says goes. Do not email me with complaints, questions, or really anything at all during those weeks, as I will be hers,"—he pointed to Fionna—"and most definitely not *yours*. Please be aware that if my baby girl decides to run a little late and does not make her arrival until the academy's Christmas break then I will also be gone well into January."

With a quick squeeze of his hand, Dan switched the slide again. "My office hours are Monday through Thursday afternoons during lunch and from two to three. Do not need me on a Friday unless I am your very last option, you have exercised every other possible scenario available to you, and don't even bother unless I really, really like you and your work. Also, do not assume that I like you. There are very few people I even tolerate."

Once the keyboards stopped clicking, Dan continued. "Here is a paper printout of every assignment due to me and when it will be due. Will I add to this?" he asked with a smirk. "Quite possibly, so I wouldn't miss class, and missing more than three of the training labs will result in your failing both classes." He tried not to chuckle as he visibly watched his hard-ass reputation cement firmly in the minds of his students. "Now," he sighed, not really wanting to move on to the next requirement of the lesson plans, but the academy mandated that the mentors offer a brief time during the first day of classes for the students to ask any questions they may have. "Any questions about this class or any of the information we've gone over thus far?"

A girl in the back hesitantly raised her hand. "I was just wondering if there would be any study groups available for your classes?" she managed, though the question appeared to have robbed her of breath momentarily.

"I, myself, will not be offering any study groups, but if any of you would be interested in studying together, then by all means go for it. There are three mentors' aides assigned to Ioses that will be available for extra tutoring. Mentor Jackson will be running an outstanding session twice a week every week. They'll all offer study groups for anyone who may be interested, but you'll have to contact them for dates and times."

A studious looking young man's hand shot up. He was wearing slacks and a tie.

"Cobson?"

"You know my name too, sir?" The kid looked only too pleased.

"I know four of my current students' names. Take that for what you will. Impress me, I'll learn yours too," he informed the rest of the class. "Your question?"

"I was wondering if you could tell us a little bit about running Iodex. You were the youngest Chief of Elite in the history of the American Realm. We'd love to hear more of your story, I guess."

Dan didn't have to guess which parts of the story the class was most interested in hearing. "Long, sordid story, short." He noted the disappointment on his students' faces. "I went into special ops training my last year here at the academy. I graduated Head of Ioses Order with a 4.2 for taking extra classes. I began in the Elite Iodex Squadron the day after I graduated. I worked long days, long weeks, long months. I spent a vast amount of time training and working in

Europe, both in Moscow and Paris extensively. Then I returned to the States." He refused to elaborate on why he'd returned. When he'd buried Amelia he'd had no intention of doing anything at all except killing the man that had killed the love of his life and trying to die while he did it. "I took a little time off." *Because I was perpetually either drunk or high.* "After that, Crown Governor Joseph Lawson made me Chief of Iodex which is a role I served until March of this year."

He was beyond certain that every student staring up at him knew the circumstances of his resignation.

In the middle of the room, a student that was receiving nonverbal encouragement from a friend blushed the approximate shade of her hair.

"Question?" Dan failed in his effort not to glare.

"I was just wondering if we were allowed to ask personal questions?" The way she nervously bit at her lip reminded Dan of Aida. He bit back the retort that was forming in his mind.

"I suppose you're allowed to ask anything you want. Doesn't mean I'll answer."

"We were just sort of wondering if you might tell us a little about your and Fionna Styler's wedding in Waikiki."

Chuckling, Dan tried to remind himself that he was supposed to be forming mentoring relationships with these kids. "*Mrs. Vindico* and I got married on the South Shore of Kauai not Waikiki. Kauai and Oahu are a good hundred miles apart. Don't believe everything you read. It was very small and private, so I think we'll keep it that way."

Another young man's hand shot up. His question poured forth without prompting. "Any chance we might get to meet Fionna?" Dan ground his teeth and fought an oncoming glare. "I'm a huge Angels fan," the kid added hopefully. That was much easier to swallow than yet another one of his students lusting after his wife.

"She'll be up here some. I'm sure she would be happy to sign autographs for any of you that might like one. I would however recommend you refer to my wife as Mrs. Vindico and not by her first name."

"And Aida," another young woman pled without raising her hand. Wondering why they were all so fascinated with his personal life, Dan shrugged. "She's in school so I'm not certain that you'll see her too often, but she might be up here some."

"She's adorable," the redhead gushed.

"I agree, but that opinion will not get you extra credit."

He fielded a few questions about what kinds of things they would be learning in their defensive labs and then handed out the thumb drives all assignments would be handed in on. In an effort to create less waste, Venton had determined that most assignments and all examinations should be turned in via thumb drive.

"I'm supposed to remind you if you need any help with your Venton laptops to see someone in the tech shop off the main dining hall."

"Or Strenton can fix it for ya, for a fee, of course," another young man teased.

"Dude, you had so much porn on that thing I used gloves to work on it." Jeff erupted from the state of slumped dejection he'd quickly returned to. His shield pulsed like he'd been hit, and he was set to retaliate.

"Kidding, man. I was just kidding. Geez." The guy held up his hands in surrender.

"I don't really give a damn who fixes your laptops so long as they work." Dan brought everyone's attention back to him and away from Jeff.

"Jeff really is the best. He used to work at the lab," the kid offered kindly.

"Then by all means seek out Strenton, but do offer to pay for his services. If you have your syllabus and your thumb drives, you can go. First lab class will be next week. Eat well that morning. We're going to be throwing punches."

"You know he only got this job because his dad is the governor of Gifted schools," a female voice carried back as the students drifted out of the room.

Dan rolled his eyes. Nepotism. He'd been accused of that for half of his life. His father being on the national governing board and Dan's penchant for pissing people off always made great fodder for dissenters.

When he was Chief of Iodex, he'd spent years fighting to prove that his father had nothing to do with his appointment. Now, he was old enough to know better. People would believe whatever the hell they chose to believe. Facts rarely mattered.

"Mentor Vindico?" Vivian Lamb, Chancellor Wilshire's long-standing administrative assistant, poked her head into the classroom. "Dean asked me to stop by and tell you that he's assigned you another class. He needs you to cover Katherine Bryant's Sub-Freshman Creative Writing class on Monday and Wednesday afternoons."

"What? Why? I'm already teaching a full load, and I was assured I would only be teaching upperclassmen. I'm not teaching in the prep school."

"Yes, well, disappointment is the theme of the year it seems. Mentor Bryant has…taken a leave of absence…for a little while."

"I have responsibilities outside of this school. Tell Chancellor Wilshire I'm sorry, but I can't take on another class."

"The chancellor wasn't asking, Dan. You're taking the class. I'll let him know you were happy to help out."

Shock and ire roiled in his gut as Dan pulled his cell phone from his pocket. He had the next period off. Third time in one morning, he thought to himself as he slammed his office door yet again.

"Hey, baby doll," he drawled as Fionna answered the phone.

"How was your first class? Wait. What's wrong?" Panic perforated her tone.

"Just found out I'm covering yet another class. Some other mentor decided to take a leave of absence or something. I've survived one class so far and I already want to leave. And who the hell does Wilshire think he is just assigning me more classes. I'm the fucking…"

"Chief of Elite," she filled in for him.

"Only I'm not." Dan sighed.

"If you hate this job, we can…"

"I'm fine. Just needed to hear your voice. How are my girls?"

"I was working on Halia's quilt and crib skirt but I keep getting distracted because I can see her little feet and hands moving across my belly which is pretty much the sweetest thing ever."

Dan grinned. He could do this. It was for his girls. "I can't wait to hold her in my hands. I just need…"

"To know she's real and here and safe and that all of the insanity is really over."

"Yeah. That."

"Just a few more weeks, I guess. How did your first class go?"

"Everyone wants to meet you," he informed her wryly.

"Me? Why?"

Dan shook his head. He found it incredible that his wife still didn't believe she was anything special. "You do recall being a nationally recognized athlete, right? Actually, I need a favor." He explained to her what he needed her to do in terms of Spencer's punishment. She found the entire thing hilarious but agreed to play along.

The hours in his office certainly went by faster than the ones in the classroom. Dan worked until it was time for his Basics of Defense sophomore junior combined class.

This class was much larger than his senior defense class. It was used to begin sorting out Ioses Predilects who would be well-suited for work within Iodex, those that would be better suited for Non-Gifted police precincts, and those that should seek work outside of law enforcement.

Lab classes wouldn't begin meeting until later in the week, so this was Dan's last class of the day. Keeping that thought firmly in his mind, he headed to the front of the lecture hall. The school had been rearranged many times, but this particular classroom made him smile.

This was the very lecture hall where he would sit on the back row and admire Fionna Styler's ass. It had served as a combined creative writing classroom back then. Dan had added it as an easy elective so he could hang out with Will. Fionna would always sit two rows ahead of Dan and Will. Dan had been jealous of Garrett, who'd also been in the class. He was so close with her. He always took the seat beside hers and joked around with her during class. She'd smile at him like he held a very special place in her heart. Dan knew Garrett did, and he owed Garrett his life many times over. Occasionally, he still had to quell the jealousy though.

Fionna had been a serious student, always taking notes and paying attention. Garrett had served to make her laugh and roll her eyes. Dan abhorred creative writing, so his boredom always led him to her backside. He'd felt a tremendous amount of guilt over it then, since he'd been dating Amelia. He would certainly never have acted on his admiring impulses. Other than directing Fionna to the Ioses building her first day at the academy, Dan hadn't even spoken to her much when they were in school together.

He gazed out at the expectant faces staring back at him and went through the same spiel he'd given his first class. He wouldn't be there as soon as Halia was born. There were aides if anyone needed help. When he would be available in his office and when he wouldn't.

"For Thursday's class…" Heads shot up from desks and cellphones that students were beginning to text from. "Read and outline chapter one and be prepared for a quiz over the information as I consider it to be a decent beginning to the reasons we study defense. Any questions?"

Defiance set in the pale-green eyes of the man on the back row as he raised his hand. "Are we going to be studying Wretchkinsides and the Interfeci?"

Clenching his jaw, Dan tried to let the realization that Wretchkinsides was in fact history wash through him. He kept his eyes locked on the student. "Uh…yes. We will be studying the ways that Dominic Wretchkinsides began the Interfeci organization and their impact on the Realms of the world."

"But you're not gonna tell us how you killed him?"

"That is neither in the curriculum nor is it in any way important, so no, I will not. Any less asinine questions?"

Uncomfortable silence drowned the room.

CHAPTER 4

GUILT WITH A SIDE OF GUAC

GARRETT HAYDENSHIRE

Before he even brought his fist up to knock on Dan and Fionna's door, she flung it open and threw her arms around him.

Garrett laughed as he squeezed her. "Are you happy to see me or the food?"

"Can't it be both?" She giggled.

He stepped inside. "You sure you have room for tacos in there?" He gestured to her rather protruded stomach.

She shot him a glare but was still grinning. "Would you shut up and give me my guacamole? I'm starving."

"Yes, ma'am." He set down the bag from Chevy's on the dining room table and pulled out all of her requested food. "How'd Aida do going to school this morning?"

Fionna offered him her sweet smile. "I know you miss her. I can feel it. She misses you too. A lot. Now, I'm going to inhale this taco and you're going to tell me whatever it is that you're trying not to talk about." This was the problem with being best friends with a Receiver. You couldn't freaking hide anything from them. They could detect everything you felt.

"You go first. Was Aida okay this morning?" He was worried about Aida. He'd been worried about her ever since Dan and Fi had taken her to Kauai. It was the longest time Garrett had gone without seeing her since she was four years old. But he wanted them to form a strong family bond, and he hadn't wanted to intrude.

Fionna gave him another grin. "She did…okay, but she really, really misses you. I did too. You have to promise to come to Kauai next summer when we're out there."

"I'm here now, so talk." He knew there was something she wasn't saying.

"My poor sweet baby. She was so nervous. It almost killed me. You don't know what school is like for little Receivers. People sense that we won't be mean because we can feel it if we hurt someone's feelings, and kids are kids. They're all a little insecure and that makes them lash out to establish some kind of foundation. They want a hierarchy. Receivers always end up at the bottom of it."

Devastation tensed in Garrett's shield. A harsh swallow did nothing to remove the longing to go get Aida from school. "I could pick her up." He checked his watch. "She gets out at 2:30, right?"

Fionna's eyes lit. "That would make her entire week!"

"Done. I'm on the pick-up list or whatever, right?"

"Of course. You're the first one on there." She downed another bite of the taco, let her eyes close in the ecstasy of the flavor, and then wiped her mouth. "Now, tell me what's going on at Venton."

"Damn, you're good. I should've kept my mouth shut on the phone this morning."

"Saw it online, remember? Plus, I saw a little of the news this morning. On top of that, Dan just called and said that Wilshire ordered him to take on another class."

Garrett cringed. "Bet Danny loved that."

Fionna's eyes fell. "I wish he hadn't taken this job. I know he hates it, and he's only doing this for me and the girls."

"Hey,"—Garrett lifted her chin—"there is nothing Dan wouldn't do for you and the girls, and doing stuff for you and them makes him happy."

"I know, but still."

～

"If they're not having an affair, why would she suddenly decide to take a leave of absence on the first day of school?" Stephen finally asked Arthur.

"You know everything I know. I should've paid far more attention to the complaints last year. I know that. I clearly relied on Dean more than I should've."

Stephen certainly wasn't trying to make Arthur feel more guilt. But the vise grip of the press was only going to get worse unless something was done. Tired of debating, Stephen used his personal cell to phone Wilshire. He casted the phone so that Arthur could hear the conversation. By the fourth ring, Stephen was grinding his teeth. He ended the unanswered call. "He's either going to talk to one of us, or I'm going out to Venton."

Arthur sighed. "As much as I hate to do this to my son, I think you're right. We need some answers." He laid his cell phone beside Stephen's on the desk.

Daniel answered on the second ring. "Hey Dad, is everything okay?"

"No, it's not, and you're on with me and Stephen."

"Does this have anything to do with whatever the hell is going on with Wilshire?"

Stephen leapt. "What do you know so far?"

Dan rattled off everything that had happened at the academy that morning. His tone went from irritation to fury when he ended with the fact that Dean had ordered him to add on another class. Arthur filled him in on what was in the papers and the press's reaction to it.

Stephen shook his head. "Dean left in the middle of the assembly?"

"I followed him out to the parking lot. To my knowledge he hasn't returned, but I haven't been back to the admin building."

Stephen debated for one quick second. He certainly did not want to throw Daniel right back in the fire that he'd just escaped, but he was their best option and their only one. "Dan, can you go back to the admin building and ask to see Dean? I don't really want him to know we asked you to get involved so if he's there, and if Vivian lets you see him…" Stephen tried to think of a plausible excuse Dan could use.

"This won't be my first time going undercover, Governor Haydenshire. I'm vastly better at that than I appear to be at teaching. I'll figure it out."

"Thank you. Let us know what you find out as soon as you can."

"Yes, sir."

❀

Dan Vindico

Driven by a desperate need to investigate, Dan shoved his phone in his pocket and marched back to the admin building. The knowledge that his father was coming under fire because of him armored in his shield. He would not let his old man fall on the blade because of his actions.

The area surrounding Vivian Lamb's desk was filled with waiting students. They all looked agitated. Every seat in the reception area was full. Most students were clutching their schedules.

Dan stomped up to the admin desk. "I need to speak with Chancellor Wilshire."

Vivian eyed him speculatively. "He isn't here." Her eyes shifted. She definitely knew something she wasn't saying.

Dan feigned shock. "He isn't here on the first day of a new term?"

"Something urgent came up. He had to take care of it."

Dan debated asking what exactly had come up, but he didn't want to overplay his hand. "When will he be back?"

"You can go ahead and let your father know that I don't know when Chancellor Wilshire will be back on campus, Dan."

He narrowed his eyes to avoid smirking. "What does my father have to do with me needing to speak to the chancellor about the extra class that I will not be teaching?"

She attempted to call his bluff. "We all know why you're really here."

"And why is that?"

She rolled her eyes. "I need to see about all of these." She gestured to the lines of students crammed in the room.

As Dan made his way back toward his office, he passed Jeff Strenton in the hall. He didn't know what was up with the kid, but Jeff's shield had set internally. It was locked around his own muscles which meant it had set of its own accord. It was trying to sustain him. Dan had existed inside his own shield that way, and he knew how excruciating it was.

Dan put away his ire for a moment. "Hey, Strenton, are you okay?"

Jeff's jaw visibly clenched. His head fell in a forced nod. "I'm fine, sir."

That might be the biggest lie Dan had ever been told, but he didn't have time to push it. "If you ever need to talk…"

Jeff shook his head. "I swear. I'm fine." His eyes never raised to meet Dan's.

As soon as he returned to his desk, Dan called his father back. "I'm still in here with Stephen. What did you find out?"

"According to Vivian, he's still not here, but that's not all she said." He explained his conversation with Dean's administrative assistant.

CHAPTER 5

DIVERSIONS

CROWN GOVERNOR STEPHEN HAYDENSHIRE

Stephen listened carefully to everything Dan had discovered. He finally spoke. "Ever since the story came out this morning, I've been trying to figure out some way to leave you out of it, but if the administration already assumes you're there as some kind of spy, maybe…"

"Sir," Dan leapt, "I don't want to be left out of this. I'm a damn good detective. I'll figure out what's going on with the drug tests and whether or not Wilshire is having an affair. I'm already here. If I'm the one to uncover whatever the hell is going on, that'll take heat off both of you."

Stephen couldn't disagree. "I just don't want this to take time away from your girls."

"It won't," Dan reassured him just a little too quickly. "In fact, Fi's coming up here to eat lunch with me tomorrow. Assuming Wilshire decides to show up to work, she can tell you if he's having an affair if she gets within ten feet of him."

Arthur had been quiet and thoughtful up until that point. "Even if Fionna can confirm the affair, I am going to need some proof before anything can be done about it. Unfortunately, the board isn't going to take Fionna's word for it."

"But at least then we'd have a better idea what we're looking for. If we know what he's hiding, it's that much easier to find."

As the ramifications of what might happen to Arthur's reputation if it was revealed that the chancellor of the premier Gifted academy—the place where the children of the entire governing board were educated—was involved in an extramarital affair settled in Stephen's mind, he decided to act.

Dan was already in the thick of it, and clearly, the administration already believed he'd been put there to spy. There seemed to be very little to lose. "All right, Daniel, fine. Find out everything you can about whatever is going on at Venton. The rumor mills have been churning since before Logan, Rainer, and Emily graduated last year. We need to figure out what is fact and what is fiction without the press getting too close. I'd like to get Venton cleaned up with as little fanfare as we can manage."

"I'll take care of it." Dan sounded delighted.

⌁

Dan Vindico

Dan decided to see what kind of information he could access via the school laptops. He wanted to know which other classes Katherine Bryant was teaching and who they'd swapped in with her abrupt leave of absence. His Visium Predilection continued to pulse disconcertingly. It made no sense that Wilshire would ask him, an Ioses professor, to take on classes from a teacher who worked in the liberal arts and Adminis departments. Unless…Wilshire was trying to keep Dan busy.

He summoned, turned on the laptop, and then ground his teeth. He drummed his fingers on the desktop waiting on the Wi-Fi to connect. He tried to force the issue, but was met with an error message.

With an aggravated eye roll, he summoned again and amped the signal. Still nothing.

A knock on his office door only further irritated him. "In," he demanded.

Suddenly, Jeff Strenton was standing in front of his desk. Dan tried not to be annoyed as he debated what to say to get the kid talking. An idea formed in his mind. "Hey, you're supposed to be a tech wizard, right?"

Confusion etched Jeff's chiseled features. He shrugged. "I guess."

Dan debated the gamble he was about to take, but his Visium Predilection urged him onward. "Would you mind helping me with something?"

"Sure," the kid suddenly sounded delighted.

Dan stood and reclosed the door. "My laptop won't connect to the school's Wi-Fi, and I need some information about Katherine Bryant's classes. I need to know who all they have covering for her. Any idea where I could find that?"

"Uh…" Jeff studied Dan intently. "I mean…I can get you on the Wi-Fi. The laptops are crap, but that's easy,"—he considered for another breath—"and I can get that information on Mentor Bryant's classes for you, but it wouldn't necessarily be following the rules…exactly."

Dan searched the recesses of his secondary Predilection, and he searched Jeff's strained energy. His shield had released his muscles, but it was still pulsing erratically. Dan found nothing that made him believe he shouldn't ask Jeff to do what he was asking him to do. "I don't want you to do anything you're uncomfortable with, but I could really use some help. Then maybe you could tell me why you look like the end of the world is right after your next class."

A harsh swallow tensed Jeff's throat. He seemed to debate something else. Finally, he shook his head. "It's nothing, sir. Uh…here, do you mind if I cast your computer?"

"Not at all." Dan gestured to the laptop.

Jeff seated himself and casted the machine. "The servers should've been upgraded years ago, and they still haven't done it. That's why it kicks people off so much." He hit a few keys and then casted a secondary pulse and projected it on the laptop. "All right, you should be on now."

Dan nodded. There was no reason that Wilshire shouldn't have put in a request to upgrade Venton's servers. Education was the foundation of everything good. The governing board always set aside vast resources to make certain Gifted academies had the best of everything, and this was Venton. The top of the line. How had an oversight like that even happened?

But Dan's ponderings were quickly washed away by his awe. Jeff did something Dan had never seen anyone do before. His mouth dropped open as he saw binary coding float inside of the shield cast Jeff lifted from the laptop. "Holy shit," he gasped under his breath.

Jeff couldn't quite hide his grin. "I'm going to have to hack into the admin servers. You're sure this is okay?"

Dan managed a nod. "Yeah, my dad asked me to do this. If anybody finds out and says something, I'll tell them I got you to do it. You won't get into any trouble."

"Yeah, but you could get fired for that."

"Let me worry about that."

Jeff shrugged and the coding within his shield spun faster. Dan himself had hired John Ramier as Elite's Technology Specialist. John was a force. There wasn't a hacker he couldn't find anywhere, but this kid worked faster than John did. And Dan had never seen Ramier pull coding into his shield.

Jeff narrowed his eyes in on the screen while managing to keep the code pulsing around him. The kid was a phenom. "It looks like Mentor Bryant was assigned six classes. Four of them were in the prep school. Two Adminis, two creative writing. She has two upper-levels. All creative writing and lit." He leaned in a little closer. His brow furrowed. "It looks like you're supposed to cover all six classes."

"What!?" Dan demanded.

Jeff spun the laptop around and showed Dan what he was seeing. "I take it you didn't agree to teach these."

"I was told I'd be teaching one of them, which I will not be doing, but why the hell would they enter me in as her substitute?"

"It could be an error. I'm sure you've probably already figured this out, but nothing really works right here anymore."

"Explain that," Dan demanded.

Jeff grimaced and glanced at his watch. "I'm sorry, sir. I would, and

I mean I will, but aren't we both supposed to be in your next class?"

"Shit." Dan grimaced. "Yeah, let's go, but what did you need before I rudely asked for your help?"

"Are you kidding me? It was an honor, sir. I'm good. No worries. I'll see you in class." He dropped the cast from the laptop and sprinted out the door.

Dan tried to catch up with him at the end of his History of Defense class, but Strenton slipped out the door before Dan could even gather his laptop bag.

He glanced at his watch and headed straight to the faculty parking lot. There were four young men standing and staring at his car. Chuckling, Dan eased between them.

"Sweet car, Mentor Vindico," one admired.

"Thanks."

"I'm in one of your classes tomorrow. Any chance your students might get a ride?" a tall muscular student wearing an Ioses T-shirt all but begged.

"Doubt that, but anything's possible, I suppose." Dan cupped his hand and pulled his shielding cast off his car. "Told you," he heard one guy hiss. With a chuckle, Dan revved the engine and then headed off campus completely exhausted.

He let the day tumble through his mind as he made his way off campus. An idea suddenly came to him as he noted the time. If he could make both of his girls grin, then he was all in, and Fionna would be delighted. She'd been terrified for Aida to ride the school bus even though Dan's sister Meredith had repeatedly assured her that Aida needed to get used to the bus because once the baby was born, Fionna driving her to school could get tricky.

That was probably true, but there was no reason he couldn't pick up his baby girl after her first day.

Every time Dan pulled into McCarron Elementary, he smiled. When he'd attended there so many years before, he never imagined one day his children would attend the same school. He maneuvered his way around dozens of cars lined up at the entrance. Finally locating a parking space, he lowered the top on the Ferrari before heading inside to pick Aida up from her classroom.

CHAPTER 6

RULES AND RICHES

The school still smelled the way it had twenty-five years ago when Dan had attended there—fresh paint, copy paper, floor polish, and pink Pearl erasers. Some things never changed.

"Halt! Red rule violation! Red rule violation!" rang annoyingly from a woman with extremely frizzy hair, dressed in a long denim skirt, a red turtle neck, and a navy blue sweater vest that had chalkboards and apples displayed on it prominently. She had a nametag on that informed anyone who cared that she was on the school board and her name was Cindy McBeechum.

"Is there a problem?" Dan quipped.

"Visitors are not allowed in the school without first signing in at the office, providing two forms of ID, and wearing a McCarron Elementary 'We are the Caring Caron Bears' school name tag."

Dan nodded. "I was heading to the office. My daughter, Aida Vindico, is in Ms. Powell's class. I'm just here to get her before she gets on the bus."

"Not without a McCarron Elementary 'We are the Caring Caron Bears' school name tag and two forms of ID you're not." She directed him to the front office.

Dan ground his teeth. "Fine."

"Can I help you?" the administrative assistant asked.

The chalkboard-clad woman marched behind the counter that separated the waiting area from the administrative offices. The admin gave her a withering smile.

Dan cleared his throat. "Yeah, I'm just here to pick up my daughter from Ms. Powell's class before she gets on the bus. Here," he pulled his wallet out of his back pocket showing his license and a credit card with his picture.

The administrative assistant glanced at Ms. McBeechum. "The school board sent a representative here today."

McBeechum narrowed her eyes and then puffed up like some kind of aggravated sea creature as she glared at Dan. "Unless your child is registered in the car-rider program, you aren't allowed to take her home with you after two o'clock, and if she is registered in the car-rider program then you'll have to join the waiting parents in the line outside, and her name will be called when you pull up to the drop-off point. If she's in our Big Bears Ride the Bus program, then you won't be able to pick her up after two o'clock either."

Indignation seared through Dan. "Listen up, my child is here in your school, and I need to pick her up before she gets on the bus. I'm her father!" he roared.

"I don't care who you are, Mr. Vindico. School board policy is school board policy. It's our job to keep the children safe, and any child being picked up early has to be picked up before two o'clock."

"School doesn't get out until two thirty."

"The school board makes the rules, and I am here to enforce them."

"It's only ten minutes past two. How do I go about getting my child so that she does not get on the bus as I am here and would like to take her home?"

"If you registered her in our Big Bears Ride the Bus program, then you'll have to fill out additional paperwork to register her as a Caring Bears Car-rider, but she will still have to ride the bus today because we require forty-eight hours' notice to change programs." She was only too delighted to be a pain in the ass. "Here, let me go ahead and get you the Caring Bears packet and perhaps you could fill it out at home and then return it to your child's teacher by the end of the week." McBeechum pulled a thick manila envelope from under the counter and handed it to Dan. Judging by the weight of the envelope, there had to be thirty sheets of paper in it. He debated marching to Aida's classroom and extracting her himself.

The school administrative assistant gave him a discreet eye roll and turned on McBeechum. "Since the child's father is here, perhaps we could make an exception. It is the first day of school."

McBeechum, however, looked like the administrative assistant had just asked her to dip herself in kerosene and set her denim skirt ablaze. "This is precisely why I will be here every day this year. Rules are rules. We do not make exceptions."

Dan bet that the entire school board couldn't keep him from his baby girl, but before he marched down to Aida's classroom and extracted her himself, the administrative assistant caught his eye. She discreetly gestured out the windows in the office out to the large corridor where children were lining up to get on the buses.

"You know what? Fine," Dan snarled for McBusybody's benefit. He stomped from the front office and slammed the door on his way out.

"Garrett!" rang from the sweetest voice in the world.

Dan's brow furrowed, but then he saw Garrett standing in the entryway. Aida raced out of her line and into his waiting arms.

"Hey, Aida Mae!" He squeezed her tight.

Dan joined them, and Garrett laughed. "Great minds, I guess. Wanna go with me and Daddy to get some ice cream?"

"Yes, please!" She wiggled down from his embrace and threw her arms around Dan.

"Hi, Daddy. Thank you for coming to get me."

"Hey, baby girl." The rest of his day washed from his weary soul.

Her teacher joined them a moment later. She gave all of them a broad smile.

"She's an absolute delight." She patted Aida's back.

Dan and Garrett both nodded.

"Would it be all right if I took her with us?" Dan asked.

"Of course."

Aida regaled Garrett with all of the things she'd gotten to do that summer in Kauai while they all devoured cones from Toby's, but she didn't say much about school.

"How was school today?" Garrett finally asked.

"It was a long time. I missed you so much while I was at Tutu's." She crawled out of her chair and back into his lap.

Garrett and Dan shared a concerned expression.

Eventually, Dan and Aida bid Garrett farewell, and they headed home.

Fionna met them at the door. "I saw you pull in."

Aida rushed to give her mother a hug. "I missed you so much!"

"I missed you too, baby." Her brow furrowed and she mouthed, "What's wrong?" to Dan.

"Long, long story," he sighed. Fionna gave him his smile. The one that he knew could light the entire world. Her warmth and her love and her trust flowed through his veins. It restored him.

"I'm just glad you're both home. Halia and I missed you."

Aida beamed. "I missed you, and Daddy, and Halia so much too."

They moved back through the front door, and Dan inhaled deeply. He was home. He let the relief and the contentment fill him.

"You made Aida cookies!" She wiggled out of Dan's arms and raced to the kitchen. Dan had smelled the heavenly scent as well, along with freshly perked coffee and the scent of Fionna. That sweetly seductive scent of coconut and vanilla and the heady scent of her.

"Rough day?" Fionna wrapped her body around him and laid her head tenderly on his shoulder just like Aida had.

"Better now," he vowed. "How's my tiny baby girl?" He rubbed his hand over her bump.

"She missed you talking to her."

"Can I have a cookie too?" he pled.

Fionna chuckled and took his hand. She led him to the kitchen. He joined Aida at the bar where she was gazing at the plate of coconut, chocolate drizzle cookies that were one of Fionna's specialties. Moving as quickly as she was able, Fionna placed two on a small plate for Aida and supplied her with a glass of cold milk. She made Dan a matching plate and poured coffee with cream and honey for herself and her weary husband.

"How was school?" Fionna asked Aida.

"It was a long time, and I wanted to come home," Aida confessed as she ate her cookies, slowly savoring every bite. "I was worried that you might miss me."

"I did miss you, but I want you to have fun in school." Aida took a sip of her milk. "Did you make any new friends?"

Aida nodded again, and Dan saw relief play in his wife's eyes. "Yes, I ate lunch with Sidney, and she says her daddy works with Grandpa."

Dan tried to think of someone who worked at the Senate with his father that had a child named Sidney. Unable to come up with anyone, he continued to listen. "And Haley pushed me on the swings and then I pushed her. She was very sweet, but some of the other kids weren't nice to her." Part of being a Receiver meant that though Aida wouldn't fully be able to access her abilities until she went through puberty, she could already feel the emotions of those around her.

"Why weren't they nice to Haley?" Fionna asked. Tears pricked her eyes as well. She could feel Aida's anguish. "She said her daddy lost his job and they didn't have much money and her jeans weren't new like mine and one of the girls named Jessica made fun of her. And Haley didn't bring a lunch so I split mine with her because I know it makes your tummy hurt if you get too hungry." Tears fell rapidly down Fionna's face.

Dan patted her hand. "How about if Mommy and I make Haley a lunch when we make your lunch?"

Aida's eyes lit. "Can we do that because she was very hungry?"

"Of course, baby."

"Free lunches don't start for another two weeks," Fionna explained how Haley wasn't able to receive the lunch provided by the school.

Dan shook his head. "Richest fucking country in the world, and we can't feed children for free." He spoke through his teeth and made certain only Fionna could hear him.

"What else happened today?" Dan asked Aida.

"I took a reading test on the computer and got put in the Eagle reading group, and Ms. Powell said that I could help the other students with reading, but then a little boy named Felix said that people in the Eagle group were a not nice word."

"Maybe Felix has a little trouble with reading," Fionna suggested.

"It's still not nice to say that word."

"No, it isn't," Dan agreed.

"And I saw Olivia when we were going to the playground," Aida lit excitedly.

Dan was pleased that she was so happy to see his sister Meredith's child.

"Did you get to play with her?" Fionna asked.

"No, because she is in first grade and I'm in second grade, but I waved to her and she waved back. And then a little boy named Stevie said I had to be his girlfriend." Aida grimaced as fury seared through Dan's shield.

Fionna giggled and patted his hand.

"But I said that my daddy said I wasn't old enough to have a boyfriend but that he could be my friend because if I am old enough then I want Alex to be my boyfriend."

Dan fought the urge to whimper.

Alex was Dan's best friend's oldest son. They lived in Paris. Fitzroy was the French Iodex Captain. Dan had taken Fionna and Aida to spend a week with the Fitzroys which had ended up being incredibly stressful as Wretchkinsides's illegitimate son had tried to kill them all on their trip. But Aida and Alex had taken to one another almost instantly, much to Dan's chagrin.

"What is it with Frenchmen?" he huffed under his breath. Fionna choked back laughter.

"Ms. Powell let us pick our take-home folders and I picked purple," Aida announced next. "And we put all of our papers to show you and Daddy in our take-home folders and then one side is the papers you keep at your house and the other side is papers you bring back to school once you show your grownups. Do you want to see?"

"Yeah, baby, is it in your backpack?" Dan asked.

Aida rushed to the entryway to retrieve her purple take-home folder. "Can I watch *Supernova* on the iPad?"

"Sure," Fionna agreed. Aida went to her room to retrieve her baby doll. She settled on the couch, and Dan handed over his iPad after locating the children's show about all kinds of energy.

Fionna began flipping through the folder as Dan wrapped Aida up in one of the quilts that Fionna had created for their home. Dan could tell she was tired as she reclined on the arm of the sofa and settled in.

Fionna returned to the kitchen to locate a pen to fill something out in the folder. "Dan!" she gasped suddenly.

He raced into the kitchen. "What?"

Her hand flew to her mouth in shock. She pointed to a paper she'd laid on the island. Dan moved to her. "All about my Family" was the heading on the worksheet. There were questions about the members of each child's family. Picking it up, he began to read. "My name is…" was the first question. She'd written Aida Santos Hanai Vindico in her best handwriting. Santos had been Aida's last name before she was adopted and Hanai was Hawaiian for precious chosen child.

Dan smiled as he went on reading purple and *The Paperbag Princess* as responses to her favorite color and book. I live with was followed with my mommy and my daddy and my baby sister Halia lives in my mommy's tummy until it's time for her to come out. Dan chuckled as he continued.

My daddy's name is…she'd written Dan Vindico very neatly. The next question had his eyes goggling. After "my daddy's job is…" Aida had written, "To teach at the big school that I can't go to yet, and to play with me, and to give Mommy her baths at night and rub oil on her."

"Oh shit."

"Yeah." Fionna's face glowed crimson. "My mommy's job is…" was followed by, "My mommy takes care of me and daddy, and grows baby Halia in her belly, and makes yummy food, and kisses daddy on the mouth a lot."

Forcing himself to go on, he came to, List three fun things you did over your summer vacation. "Mommy and Daddy and me went to live in our house in Kauai," was listed first. Dan's breath began to return as he continued. "I got to grow my own flowers in my garden with my Papa," was next. "I got to take baths outside on our farm and take hula lessons," filled the third line as Aida clearly couldn't narrow it down to only three.

"Something that made me laugh," was the next prompt. "When Daddy put icing on mommy and ate it at the party for when they got married."

Dan's head fell into his hand. Dan and Fionna hadn't made it a point to anyone at the school that Aida was adopted. They saw no reason. She was just as much theirs as Halia would be. But having your seven-year-old at your wedding reception wasn't a common occurrence. And Dan had in fact put icing on Fionna's face and neckline and then licked it off at the reception.

Grimacing, Dan wondered when the Auxiliary department of the Senate would be showing up to investigate his and Fionna's parenting skills.

"There's a note from the teacher," Fionna whimpered. "I didn't read it. I was too scared."

Dan pulled Fionna into his chest as he switched the papers to the note attached with a paperclip. "Dear Mr. and Mrs. Vindico," it began. Dan swallowed hard. "First let me say that I've been teaching second grade for almost thirty years, and this isn't the worst I've seen. I talked with Aida, and she explained that you and Mrs. Vindico adopted her last spring and that the icing involved a wedding cake. I've attached a blank copy of the worksheet as these will be displayed on my bulletin board for open house at the end of the month. I thought perhaps you could help Aida create a new all about me sheet. Aida is a lovely, caring child that is clearly adored by her parents. I look forward to working with you throughout the year, and please don't worry. It's wonderful to know that Aida comes from a loving family home. Perhaps after Christmas, I could persuade you to bring in Aida's little sister as we'll be doing a unit on how we grow. Thank you, Ms. Powell."

"Thank God someone at that school still has some common sense," Dan sighed his relief.

"Are they taking her away?" Fionna was on the brink of tears.

Dan shook his head and read Ms. Powell's note to Fionna.

"Oh, thank goodness."

Dan grilled the tilapia burgers that Fionna made, which were one of his favorites. Fionna sliced avocado, tomatoes, onions, and pineapple to go with the burgers. After dinner, they helped Aida rework her all about me sheet. They tried to delicately explain that perhaps baths were not the best things to share.

CHAPTER 7

WANTS AND NEEDS

After her bath and story, they tucked her in and retired to their own room. Fionna moved to Dan and wrapped her arms around his neck as he tenderly embraced her.

"How about your bath, Mrs. Vindico?" She nodded against him as he held her closely. "It is one of my jobs after all."

Her sweet giggle eased his day.

She methodically added the oils and salts to their bath. They undressed, and Dan guided her into the tub. He had to help her much more now than when they'd first begun taking nightly baths.

Her grandmother, who made oils, teas, ointments, household products, and remedies of all kinds from the fruits, vegetables, and plants they grew on their farm in Kauai, prescribed taking baths each day with her oils to restore Maylea's energies and her spirit.

Fionna added in heavy doses of lavender and ylang-ylang oils before she relaxed between Dan's outstretched legs. It didn't take long for Dan to begin confessing his worries as he reheated the water with his hands. "I just feel like I owe it to my dad not to let whatever might be going on at Venton fall in his lap. But that and teaching are going to take up a significant amount of time," he explained. "I don't want to take away any time from you or the girls."

"It was just the first day." Dan felt her calming rhythms restore him as she pushed her energy through his skin. "We'll figure this all out. I'll help you. We'll find the balance that works for us."

"You'll tell me if you need me more, right? You're always the most important thing, you and my baby girls."

"I know." She turned on her side and kissed his chest as she tucked her head under his chin. The slosh of the water made her whimper. "I feel like a beached whale."

"You are not and would you stop it," he demanded. "You are beautiful, Maylea. Even my eighteen-year-old students want to bang you." Fury coursed through him again when he thought about Spencer's bet.

She giggled and then promptly shuddered. "That is seriously disturbing." She shook her head but then grew thoughtful. "I'll be able to tell you if Chancellor Wilshire is having an affair." She continued the conversation they'd started in the living room.

"I know, baby, but Dad can't bring him before the board with that," he eased. "The stupid Dinkerton Report." In 1918, a man by the name of Theodore Dinkerton had set out to disprove Receivers' powers. He'd performed rudimentary tests and had concluded that a Receiver's own emotions can affect their reads. The governing board at the time had used the Dinkerton Report to ban Receivers from bringing evidence in trial.

She gave him a weary nod. "I can't figure out why they would've assigned you to all of Katherine Bryant's classes. That's so bizarre."

Suddenly, his Visium Predilection pushed his shield away again, and he knew why. "Because Wilshire wants to know what I know, and he wants to know if Elite is going to help me figure out what's going on."

Fionna sat up. "He wants you to call him on it. He has no idea you have a student with that kind of capability. This is his test to find out what your dad knows and what he's looking for."

Dan nodded. "Vivian was certain enough that I was there as some kind of spy for my old man that she said it to me. They're convinced." He shook his head in an effort to get Venton out of his mind. "So, what did you do today, my stunningly beautiful wife?"

"I finished Halia's crib skirt, and then Garrett brought me

Chevy's." She looked like Garrett had made her entire day, and Dan tried with all of his might not to mind that.

"I baked Aida's cookies and then Halia and I took a nap." She wrinkled her nose adorably.

"Good girl." Dan wished she would rest more often. She also had a praise kink that was several miles wide, and he couldn't help but indulge.

She studied him intently. Her sienna eyes darkened as she stared him down. "I love the way you love me, the way you know me."

Dan's heart picked up pace. "When I look at you swollen full of my baby, at what we made together, it drives me wild." His voice took on the consistency of gravel. Her pulse picked up in her rhythms. She traced her index finger over his strain, making him weak from desire. "That's it, honey. Grab me," he commanded. A breathy moan escaped her as she wrapped her hand around his strain. "You make me so damn hard. You make me ache to fill you full."

"Take me to bed," she ordered.

"Gladly." Dan helped her out of the tub. He sealed heat into the fibers of a large towel and dried her thoroughly. He kissed his way down her belly as he dried her legs.

He pulsed as she led him to their bed. She was his, and he still couldn't understand how something so miraculous could be true. She was perfect, and he wanted her desperately. He needed to bury his day, needed to feel her energy course through him as he filled her full of his love and protection.

"Lie down for me, baby doll. I want to taste you. I want you to fill my mouth."

Dan had rather enjoyed all of the new ways he'd come up with to satisfy his beautiful wife as she expanded. He couldn't quite access her the way he had before they'd conceived his precious little Halia.

Her eyes flashed in desire as the fire he was stirring sparked heatedly. She crawled in the bed. "You are so fucking beautiful," he groaned in reverence. He knew she needed to hear it often, and he longed to fulfill her every need. "Lie back for me."

She reclined as he dropped to his knees beside their bed. A low shuddering moan thundered from his chest as he took in her swollen lips waxed bare for him. He traced his fingers along her slit as she writhed.

Spreading her legs, Dan slowly dragged his tongue over her, listening to her beg for relief. He bathed her lips with his tongue lapping everything her body made for him. The liquid form of her energy was exquisite. "You taste so damn sweet, baby doll. I need more," he commanded as her body bucked.

He pulled her lips in his mouth, sucking and torturing her. He slowly edged to where she desperately wanted him to be. "All mine," he growled as he sucked hard and marked her mound.

She came instantly. He knew she would. He drank everything she gave up for him, let it fill his mouth as he dipped his tongue between her folds. She clawed the sheets below her and writhed from his penetrating tongue.

"More," she begged. The request drove him wild as he marked her inner thighs with his bite. He slipped his fingers inside her, keeping his mouth sucking her sweet lips. Her entire body tensed as her breath washed from her lungs. Her energy spiked hard.

"That's my good girl. I know you have another one for me." With a deep fervent stroke over just the right spot, she came undone again. He loved that he knew all of her secret desires, all of the places to bite and lick and touch to drive her to the brink of ecstasy. Things had changed as she'd expanded. Those spots had moved slightly, and Dan had loved learning her all over again. He reveled in the energy he'd pulled from her. It flooded through him—healing him, mending his weary soul, making him whole because he was wrapped up in her, his own personal saving grace.

"I need you. Please," she begged.

"I know what you need, baby. I'm gonna make you take it rough." He watched the desperate storm swirl rapidly in her eyes. He kept his fingers working her over. Unable to lie on top of her anymore, Dan grasped and lifted her hips as he stood. "You ready for it, baby doll? You ready for me to fill you full?"

"Now," she panted and quaked.

"Take it like a good girl," he ordered as he pulled her over his strain, burying himself inside of her. A shuddering growl echoed from his lungs. The exquisite sensation of making them one was otherworldly perfection.

He began to pump her full. Her hips undulated with his every thrust. The energy began to pass between them from where they were joined. His shield pulled her rhythms in and replaced it with all of him. She met his every thrust.

"I'm gonna…" she gasped.

"Good girl. Come for me." He watched the luscious sight of her coming undone for him. "So fucking gorgeous," he moaned as he throbbed tightly inside of her.

Her body trembled as he built her again. His release gathered fiercely in his groin. Dan slipped his forearm under her backside, supporting her with one arm. He leaned to massage her swollen breasts. She groaned from the sensation as he began to knead the fevered mounds and twist her nipples as they pulsed, begging for his attention.

She liked them to be sucked as he pounded into her, but that would have to wait until after she'd delivered their precious baby girl. Her body clenched tightly as she swelled, and he buried himself inside of her. He spilled his energy deep within her. Their releases mixed as his orgasm drove hers.

Dan fell to the bed beside her, gasping for breath. He pulled her to him and cradled her bump against him as she lay tenderly on his chest. He could feel it instantly. He had her energy inside of him now, and he felt her trepidation and her fears swirl inside of her. "You are so beautiful, baby," he began what had become almost a nightly routine.

She still didn't believe that he could possibly think she was as sexy as when she was twenty pounds lighter and had a waist as she'd phrased it. "I wish you believed me."

"I try," she confessed.

"I'll just keep saying it, and maybe by the time you deliver you'll actually see how phenomenally gorgeous you are inside and out."

Dan pulled the kukui and coconut oils off the bedside table. He'd rubbed her belly, breasts, thighs, and lips down with them every night since she'd first found out she was expecting. It was her grandmother's prescription to keep from getting stretch marks, and so far it had worked. "Lie back for me."

She gave him his smile in the light of the lamp he'd left on. He loved watching her as she lost it all for him. Nothing was more beautiful than that. Lathering his hands, he began to massage the mixture all over her. It was a ritual that he thoroughly enjoyed.

"Are you up for another round, baby doll? You're so fucking gorgeous I'm already hard again." Being a Double-Predilect of equal Gift did come with quite a few perks. His ability to orgasm twice in succession was one of his favorites.

"Yes," she moaned.

He took her again until he was finally sated, and she lay on him in sweet contentment.

"What exactly do you want me to say to Spencer tomorrow?" she quizzed through a yawn.

"He needs to be taken down a few notches and to get his head out of his pants occasionally."

With a wry grin, Fionna giggled. "I think I can handle that."

As Dan had watched her shut down several guys while they were dating but hiding it from the Realm, he knew she was very capable.

He massaged her belly and smiled as Halia responded. "Hey, baby girl," he spoke near Fionna's stomach. Halia's kick delighted her parents.

"I told you she missed you." Fionna beamed.

Dan sent the soothing pulses of his energy through Fionna's stomach and into her womb. Halia responded immediately. Dan was thrilled that she recognized his energy.

This was a practice Adeline, their medio and close friend, had instructed Dan to do from the beginning of Fionna's pregnancy.

"Are Adeline and Logan still coming over Friday?" Dan quizzed as he worked. Dan had handpicked Logan from the academy for Elite Iodex.

"Yeah, I think so." Fionna was still grinning. "Aida's going home with Olivia that afternoon. They're supposed to be here around five."

"After my run-in with the school board representative from hell, we were probably supposed to let them know that Meredith is picking up Aida two years ago."

She sighed. "Hopefully as the school year really gets in full swing, the school board will find something else to do."

Dan pulled the light from the lamp into his hand and cradled Fionna to him tenderly. "I love you," he whispered in the darkness.

"I love you too." She clung to him fiercely.

"I'm right here. There is nowhere else I'll ever be."

CHAPTER 8

CONFESSIONS AND COUNTER INTELLIGENCE

The next morning Dan dropped Aida off at school mostly to annoy what he had dubbed the big bear bus patrol customer service representative from hell. He arrived at Venton a few minutes early and enjoyed a leisurely walk to his office alone. But as soon as he turned down the corridor, he saw Jeff Strenton pacing outside of his office.

"Mentor Vindico…I…I was wondering if I could talk with you for a second…please." Exhaustion weighted his light-green eyes.

"Sure." Dan opened the door. Whatever it was that Strenton had finally decided to confess, it didn't appear that he could handle much more. "Have a seat." Dan held up a protein bar. "Did you have breakfast?"

"No sir, but I'm fine," he managed.

"Is this the same way you were fine yesterday when I asked?"

Jeff grimaced and took the protein bar.

"How about a soda?" Pulling a Dr Pepper from the stack he kept on one of his bookshelves, he chilled the can with his cast and handed it to Jeff.

"Thanks." Jeff downed half the can in one big gulp. Suddenly, the words sprinted from his mouth in rapid-fire, caffeinated succession.

"I just need to know that if I tell you something you won't tell anyone else."

"That depends on what you tell me. If someone is an imminent danger to themselves or others, or I'm concerned for your well-being, I can't promise you that."

"Okay. I guess." His face held no color save the flush that stained his cheeks. His eyes were red and swollen like he'd either been crying or hadn't slept in days. "I just kind of thought you'd understand."

Dan tried to sort through Jeff's energy. He wasn't close enough for Dan to read much other than fear.

"Understand what?"

"I know I'm not supposed to know, but everyone does know because it was all over the papers and the news and stuff."

"What was in the papers?" Dan continued to probe.

"Back in the spring. When you…you know, did what you did, and then the whole Realm found out about Fionna Styler being your girlfriend and that…she was,"—he halted abruptly, unable to say the word pregnant.

Dan suddenly knew where this conversation was heading. His heart sank rapidly into his stomach.

"I thought if anyone might understand, it would be you," Jeff choked out.

"How long have you been dating?"

"Four years, since we were freshmen. I want to marry her. I just can't…yet."

"What's her name?"

"Becca…"

Dan's eyes goggled. Panic clawed at his shield. "Please don't say…"

"Becca Sapman."

"As in Governor Sapman's daughter, Becca?"

Jeff gave a solemn nod.

"How far along is she?" Dan tried to scrub the deep concern from his voice. Governor Sapman was the most conservative man on the governing board by a mile. This was not going to end with a happily ever after.

"I don't know…like a few weeks I guess. I'm not entirely certain how that works."

Dan considered that information and drew another measured breath. He tried to envision himself at twenty and how he would have wanted someone to handle this. After forcing all thoughts from his mind of what he would do to Aida's boyfriend should they find themselves in this situation, he began to plan. "How's Becca feeling? Would you like to go get her so we can talk together?"

"She's not sick or anything. Is that normal?" Jeff panicked as he offered Dan more information. His concern pricked Dan's heart. He clearly loved this girl—the governor's daughter.

"I don't have a tremendous amount of experience, but I don't think everyone gets sick." He tried to think of everything he could tell Jeff to soothe him.

"I don't know what to do, sir."

"Does Becca want to keep the baby?" Dan jumped in with both feet.

"I don't know, sir. She just keeps crying. She won't talk to me. Her dad's gonna kill me." Jeff's eyes closed in defeat. "I tried to get her to just run away with me, but she wouldn't."

"Running away is never the answer. You're going to need support. Your kid is going to need support. Besides, problems are relentless trackers. They don't let us escape. Ever. And I do understand what you're going through. Believe me."

"Yeah, but you were, you know…grown and had a house and paycheck and you lived together or whatever."

Dan sensed that Jeff desperately needed to argue. He needed to scream and rage. He needed to pound something into oblivion.

"Yeah, I had a paycheck and my girlfriend living with me. I also had a mass murderer after me, and my girlfriend was terrified to tell me she was pregnant because the entire Realm thought she was dating my best friend. There was also the fact that had we come out with our relationship and the announcement of her career-ending pregnancy, Wretchkinsides wouldn't have stopped until Fionna and the baby were dead." Shockwaves sizzled through Dan's truth. "So, stress over an unplanned pregnancy is something I more than understand." Jeff managed a slight nod as Dan let him in. "How about we go with I won't tell anyone about Becca yet, and you keep that little tidbit in here as well?"

"Yes sir, of course."

"I don't really know much about you other than what's on your school record and what I saw you do yesterday. Several Elite Iodex officers are very interested in you for the internship, so tell me—best-case scenario, how do you see this working?"

"Best case?" Jeff swallowed. "I've dreamed about working for Iodex here in DC since I threw my first shield. I think I stand a good chance. I'm top of the class and my combat and defense labs last year were top-notch. I've taken a full load every semester and worked in the computer lab part-time. I'm an Ioses Order officer. I've tried to do all of the things the Elite Squadron wants. I...tried to do all of the things you did when you were here."

"I am not someone you should follow in the footsteps of," Dan spoke the first thing that came to mind.

"I just need a real job until I graduate. I want to take care of her and our kid. I'd marry her today, but she's so panicked she won't hear me out."

Since this was precisely what Dan was hoping to hear, he smiled. "How are your core grades?"

"Math and sciences were all above 100 last year. I had a 98 in Histories of the Realm at the end of the year, and I usually have a 94 or 95 in English and Legends of the Realm but those are my worst subjects."

That was fairly typical for Ioses Predilects. "Do you think Becca will want to stay in school once she starts showing if she decides to keep it?"

"I don't know. Like I said, every time I try to get her to talk about it, she just starts crying. It kills me."

A barely audible knock sounded on the door. "Maybe she'll talk now." Dan had a pretty good idea who was at his office door.

"She didn't want me to talk to you. I told her you'd be cool, but she didn't believe me. She...uh...she thinks you're kind of mean." Jeff looked pained.

Dan opened the door and tried to remember the last time he'd seen Becca Sapman.

"Hi, Chief Vindico," she choked.

Not bothering to correct her, as that's what she'd been calling him whenever she'd been to the Senate to visit her father for the last ten years, Dan gave her a nod. "Come on in."

"Jeff," she hissed. "He's gonna tell my dad. His dad plays golf with my dad, like, every week."

"I'm not going to tell your father," Dan vowed. "And this certainly has nothing to do with my father, so have a seat."

"I had to talk to somebody. You won't talk to me," Jeff challenged.

Dan wondered momentarily if every mentor turned themselves into a relationship counselor or if it was only him. "Okay, first, let me say, welcome to adulthood. I can help you if you'd like my help," he allowed. Jeff and Becca gave him pleading stares. "But let me just go ahead and tell both of you that you need to tell your parents. This isn't just going to go away." He went ahead and washed away their secret hopes. He turned to Jeff. "If you really are willing to work then I'll call Chief Portwood and have you appointed as the Iodex intern. You'll train with the Elite Squadron, but that means you put in half a day here, you do all of your assignments for me and any other classes within your Predilect, then you go to the Senate and work from lunch on," Dan laid it all out. "It's a paid position, but it's not going to allow her to live the way she's been living. Her father is well paid for being a Realm governor."

"I don't care." Becca looked disgusted. "I don't want what my parents have no matter how much money my father makes."

"I'll do anything. This is all my fault anyway." Jeff's head weighted with his shame.

"No, it isn't," Becca's voice softened. "I'll get a job too, after school. I just don't want to get rid of it. We made it. Plus, I always wanted to have kids, just not right now so much."

Jeff wrapped his arms around her. Dan was mildly concerned he was going to witness the events that led to their procreation if he let them keep going. "If Fi and I can be of any help, we'd be happy to."

He wasn't certain why, but he was drawn to help Jeff and Becca. He wanted to be there for them.

"Thank you," Becca gushed.

"But you both need to sit down with the governor and Mrs. Sapman and with your parents, Jeff."

"My mom," Jeff corrected. He turned back to Becca. "I'm not gonna do what my dad did. I'm gonna be there for you and the baby. I swear, I really want to do this." With a semblance of a smile, he turned to Dan. "Thank you so much, sir. Really."

"Let me know how it goes with your parents."

"We will." Becca wiped tears from her eyes. Dan offered her a tissue which Jeff took to help her with her task. "I'll give Portwood a call, but he may want you to interview and to see you duel before he makes it official."

"I'll do anything he needs."

"Thank you so much." Becca moved around the desk to hug Dan.

A feeling Dan finally recognized as homesickness cinched his throat as he made the call to the Elite Iodex office.

"This is Haydenshire," Logan answered.

Dan grinned. "Hey Logan, it's Dan. How are you?"

"I'm good, man. How are you? How was Hawaii?"

"It was great. Listen, I have to go in just a minute, but I have a recommendation for the internship."

"Is it Jeff?" Logan suddenly sounded thrilled. "Please say it's Jeff."

"It is actually, but I hope he's got the chops for this. Kid needs the job, that's for damn sure."

Logan laughed. "Have you ever seen him cast a computer?"

"Yeah, just yesterday actually."

"Did he do the code in his shield thing?"

Dan grinned. "Yeah."

"That's not even the half of it. He juiced six Xboxes in Ioses House so we could all play together. He's a freaking tech whisperer. He can hack in his sleep."

"If that's the case, then I might see if I can get him to help me out with a few more things here."

"I'm sure he'd be glad to help you out. Dad told me about Wilshire last night when we were at the farmhouse. That's fucked up."

"I still don't know if it's true. I'm trying not to make assumptions."

"Yeah, I get that. Good luck. Dad's really worried about how this might all fall in your father's lap."

"Yeah, I'm worried about that too. Hey, let me tell Portwood about Jeff, and then I need to go try to teach these yahoos something."

Logan laughed. "Good luck with that as well. Hang on, I'll get Portwood for you."

Landon was chuckling when he finally answered the phone. "I take it I have you to thank for Logan and Rainer bouncing around the office like they summoned from a live wire."

Dan couldn't help but smirk. God, he missed his guys. "Yeah, I'm afraid that all falls in my lap since I picked them for Elite as well."

"You picked well with them, so I have high hopes for the internship too."

"I just hope I picked him for the right reasons. I feel bad for the kid."

"This is Strenton, right?"

"Yeah."

"His scores are phenomenal. Sullivan wrote him a recommendation last spring before you took the job. He holds office in Ioses. Sounds like a great Shield."

"He apparently got Becca Sapman pregnant."

Landon gasped audibly. "Like Governor Sapman's daughter, Becca?"

"The one and only. The Sapmans don't know yet. They're planning to tell them tonight, I think. She's not very far along, and they do seem very committed to each other so there is that."

A long whistle slid between Landon's teeth. "Kind of feel like you and I should train him before he tells the governor."

Dan chuckled. "I thought that myself. I might pull him aside this afternoon for some training if I can."

"Tell him I wish him luck. I'll send Lawson and Haydenshire out there tomorrow to do an official interview, then we'll get him in here and see how well he does with the team. According to Logan, he'll fit right in."

"I appreciate it. I'll talk to you later."

CHAPTER 9
FAULTY FACTS

Dan glared at the folder on his desk that contained the syllabus and lesson plans for Katherine Bryant's English Lit sub-freshman class. Every fiber of his being wanted to march into Wilshire's office and tell the man that he wasn't there to clean up the shit he'd gotten himself into, but something stopped him.

He summoned from the sound energy surrounding him and projected it at the office door. Then he summoned his shield and threw it on top of the sound energy, creating a vacuum. No one needed to hear this conversation. He touched Garrett's name on his phone and brought it back to his ear.

"You're getting a little needy there, Danny Boy. I just saw you yesterday," he drawled derisively.

"Would you can it? I need your opinion on something."

"Yes, I do think Fi gives it up way too easy for you. You should have to work for it much harder."

"I'm hanging up."

"All right, all right, what?"

Dan explained everything he'd figured out about the extra class, and his worries about what was happening at Venton affecting his father. "My options are to march down to Wilshire's office and refuse or to go teach this class that I know nothing about."

Garrett was quiet for a long drawn minute. "My gut says go teach it, but I get that sucks. If Vivian went as far as to say to your face that they think you were hired to spy, then it sounds to me like Wilshire might be looking to fire you. If you need to be the one to figure out if Wilshire's got a side piece, don't give him ammo to get rid of you."

"Fair point."

"Plus, you never know what you might can get out of the kids. Trust me, fifteen-year-olds will say shit twenty-year-olds won't. They're usually impulsive as fuck."

"Another good point. Thank you."

"Anytime. Hey, how was Aida with school this morning?"

"I took her to school mostly to annoy the school board representative."

Garrett chuckled. "Bet Aida liked that though."

"Yeah, I hope she does all right. She's never been in school before. I don't want it to overwhelm her. She did well on the entry tests they gave her."

"Yeah, I was worried about the same thing. If she needs any help, call me."

"I will. Let me go review this bullshit class. I'll talk to you later."

Dan entered the sub-freshman classroom on the other side of campus five minutes late. He was stunned by the difference in fifteen-year-olds and twenty-year-olds.

"Excuse me," Dan snarled. Most of the class had been talking loudly and moving about the room. A few kids were hanging off of his desk.

Two students were in one desk wound around each other, kissing heatedly. "Find a seat that is not in her lap," he demanded of the young lady who was straddled over her make-out partner. "My second grader is better behaved." Flipping open the folder he'd been given, he handed out the syllabus, keeping one for himself to add to his work for the evening.

"All right, I just found out that I'll be teaching this class, so I'll be better prepared next week."

"Did Mentor Bryant really do what they said she did?" a girl near the front demanded.

Intrigued, Dan decided to allow the question. "I'd caution you against believing anything *they* said, but just out of morbid curiosity, what is it you're referencing?"

"That she got caught slapping Wilshire's sausage with her vertical smile," rang crudely from a young man on the back row.

Dan choked back a laugh. "That comment is grossly inappropriate. I have no idea why Mentor Bryant took a leave of absence."

"She wouldn't have taken it if they hadn't gotten caught," the student came right back.

Dan shot him a glare. "Now,"—he glanced over Mentor Bryant's rather detailed class notes and tried not to roll his eyes—"apparently your first assignment is to write a five-paragraph essay on what you did over the summer and how you used your Gifted energies within your Predilect. It's due Monday. You also need to have acquired your copy of *The Awakening* by Kate Chopin at the bookstore before Monday. By next Wednesday, you need to have read the first five chapters and be prepared for a quiz." Dan recalled reading *The Awakening* as a sub-freshman himself. He found the subject of the book to be rather apropos given what everyone believed the chancellor and Mentor Bryant had been doing.

He sighed and went on with, "Does anyone have any questions about the class or myself?" He sincerely hoped they didn't.

Several hands shot up. Dan pointed to a young woman with all but one small section of her purple and black hair shaved shorter than his own. Her eye makeup consisted of shimmery purples and greens and she was wearing black lipstick. Her neck was covered in harsh purple hickies. Dan assumed whoever she was dating hadn't yet learned how to heal the bites. He considered giving her boyfriend a lesson himself but decided against it.

"The Arlington Angels' owners are nothing more than brainless pimps that whore the players out for their good looks. And you are an epic jerk for forcing your wife out of her career so she can stay home barefoot and pregnant for you," she spat furiously.

Dan made no effort to hide his eye roll. "You are certainly entitled to your opinion, but you'll find in life that if you want other people to hear you out, having some evidence to back up your claims would be helpful. So, how about for Friday, you do a research paper for me. Let's say three to five pages on how the Angels were the first all-female Summation team, and before their inception women were not allowed to compete in professional Summation challenges at all.

"I would mention the fact that the Angels worked side by side with the governing board in the twenties for women's suffrage, and then worked directly with Crown Governor Joseph Lawson to make certain women received three months paid maternity leave, equal pay, and bodily autonomy when the new constitution was rewritten. Work your way through the Angels Corporation and how thirty percent of their record-breaking profits are donated by the owners to better the lives of women and girls around the world.

"Be certain to incorporate the Angels' work with the Auxiliary Department and how they were the team that led the charge for Summation teams to be required to do charity work. Also include research done on the fact that all of the Angels' owners, my wife and I included, do service work both with the organization and outside of it. Then you can conclude the paper with several paragraphs dedicated to the fact that women's rights within the Realm should include women who decide that they'd like to work inside the home instead of outside of it. I think we'll let the paper count for three test grades," he quipped before moving back to his desk.

"Now, speaking of the Angels, my own personal Angel is due to deliver our baby in November. I feel certain that Chancellor Wilshire will have found a replacement for Mentor Bryant by then, but if not, you will have a substitute mentor during my absence." He glanced around the room. "Anyone else care to comment?"

Silence drowned the room as every student stared at him in stunned disbelief. "You are welcome to proceed to the library and begin work on your papers or to start reading *The Awakening*." The students filed out quietly.

After Dan's next two periods where he'd repeated his commands about classes and labs and explained his paternity leave, he moved to the freshman sophomore combined Sciences of Defense class.

"Spencer," he drawled as soon as the young man tried to sneak into class hiding behind two of his friends. "Saved you a seat." Dan directed him to the desk in the front center of the classroom. Rolling his eyes, Spencer fell into the appointed seat. "Is your paper ready?"

"Yes, sir."

"Good. Fi's really looking forward to hearing it." He welcomed the class and handed out the syllabus and assignment list. He explained the semester-long project that would be due on the day of finals. A knock sounded on the classroom door near the end of class. Dan smiled. She was right on time.

"Spencer, would you let my wife in, please?" Spencer's eyes goggled as he stood and moved slowly toward the door. "Don't keep her waiting," Dan demanded. Spencer opened the door, and Fionna bit her lips together to keep from laughing.

She moved into the room as Spencer slithered quickly back to his seat, unable to even look her in the eye. Excited whispers moved throughout the room.

"Hey, sweetheart," Dan drawled. Fionna grinned and then offered a wave to the class. She was wearing a black front-tie dress. It dipped low, showing off her heavily swollen cleavage, and then tied above her bump. It was ruffled slightly so she hardly looked pregnant under the gathered layers of fabric.

The dress was relatively short. It hit just below her midthigh and showed off her long legs. The black boots she'd paired with the dress made Dan's mouth water. She'd curled her hair so it hung in loose waves down her back. She was wearing more makeup than usual.

"I had a picture of her for my other classes, but since she's here…" Dan took Fionna's hand and led her to the front of the class, making her laugh. "Obviously, my beautiful wife will be giving birth to our second child,"—he glared at Spencer—"sometime in November." He went through the fact that Mentor Sullivan would be substituting. "Sit down, sweetheart." He gestured to his chair behind the desk at the front of the room. He pulled it out for her and then helped her into it.

"Such a gentleman." Fionna smirked.

"Now,"—he turned back to the class—"if any of you might like an autograph, I'm certain Fi would be happy to do that before we all head to lunch." The class rushed forward to meet Fionna which seemed to thrill her.

Several minutes later, Dan and Fionna headed to his office. Spencer paced several feet behind them. "Go get your lunch then meet me in here," Dan commanded.

"Yes, sir."

"You are just so adorable," Fionna drawled like she was talking to a toddler. Dan had to choke back his laughter as Spencer scowled. He spun to head to the dining hall.

Dan unlocked his office but halted as Chancellor Wilshire approached. "Look who decided to show up," Dan spoke between his teeth.

"Fionna, I didn't know you would be on campus today, sweetheart. How are you?" He leaned in to give Fionna a hug.

She grimaced slightly, and Dan's heart sank. He saw it in her eyes. Whatever she'd picked up in the chancellor's energy, it had her reeling.

"I just came to have lunch with Dan," she managed.

"You're welcome anytime. Some of the Summation teams are practicing this afternoon. You should stop by. The kids would love that."

Giving him a kind smile, Fionna reached for Dan's hand. He supplied it instantly, letting her draw strength and absolution from him.

"I'll have to do that another day. I have to get home before our little girl gets out of school." She ran her other hand protectively over her bump.

"I came by to make certain that you were okay handling that extra class, Dan." Defiance dripped in Wilshire's tone.

"Actually, I'm not. I'm an Ioses mentor. My specialties are in defense and maybe some math and science. I have no idea how to teach English Lit."

"Just follow Katherine's lesson plans."

"It is a disservice to the students to have me teaching that class, *sir*," he begrudged the formality.

"If you can't do the job…"

Dan narrowed his eyes. "I'll figure it out."

As Wilshire disappeared down the corridor, Dan closed his office door and helped Fionna onto the small loveseat. "What did you feel?"

"First panic."

That wasn't what Dan was expecting to hear. "Panic?"

"That I'm here."

"He knew you'd pick up on his guilt."

"Oh, there's lots and lots of guilt and deception and a little excitement about the desire and then desire itself. All of the things people feel when they cheat."

Dan sank into his chair and rubbed his temples.

"How could he do that?" Fionna demanded in a heartbroken whisper. "He's been married for, like, thirty years."

"I don't know," Dan immediately assured her. "I don't know how anyone does that. How does he look his wife in the eye? How does he look at his kids and his grandkids after that?"

"Yeah, and he's the chancellor of the premier Gifted academy on the Eastern Seaboard. This is where all of the governors' kids and grandkids come. This isn't going to be something he can just sweep under the rug. The press is already onto him. What are you going to tell your dad and Governor Haydenshire?"

"The truth, but now I have to have hard evidence, and I've got to figure out if all of the drug test results are accurate. Oh, and that kid I told you about yesterday—the one who hacked in and figured out that I'd been assigned to all of Bryant's classes—he told me this morning that he and his girlfriend are going to have a baby."

Fionna's face fell. "Is she okay?"

"She's Governor Sapman's daughter."

"Oh my gosh. Can I talk to them? I could help. I know what they're going through right now."

Dan gave her what he was certain was a broken smile. He offered her his hand again. "I secured him the internship at Iodex so at least he'll have a decent paycheck, but they've got to tell their parents tonight."

"I'd really like to meet them. I'd like to help them if they need us to."

She rubbed her hands over her belly. Halia was kicking. A

contented smile formed on her face as she caressed their baby girl. "She felt you when I drew from you," Fionna whispered.

Dan longed to rub his hands over her swell to lock on to her energy and then onto Halia's. Desperation coursed through him. He needed to assure Fionna that he would never do something like Wilshire. He longed to make certain that his wife and his girls knew he would always be there for them.

A hesitant knock sounded on the door before Dan could either verbally reassure her or promise that she could meet Jeff and Becca.

"Are you ready?" Dan put his own game face back on.

Fionna nodded and began pulling the lunch she'd packed out of a small cooler she'd left in Dan's office. "I'm ready." Fionna giggled as she arranged their lunches and then returned to her seat.

"In," Dan growled while winking at his wife.

Spencer looked pale as he opened the door slowly.

Fionna grinned at him as she began eating one of the Hawaiian chicken salad sandwiches she'd prepared.

"Have a seat, stud," Dan sneered.

Fionna bit her lips together to keep from laughing. Dan sat down beside her and wrapped his arm over her as Spencer sank down in the other seat in the office while trying to balance his lunch tray in his lap.

"Oh, I do remember your parents now," Fionna drawled. "You look just like your mom."

"Yeah baby, they were at our reception, remember?" Dan played along as Fionna nodded. She laid her hand on Dan's thigh as he kissed the side of her head.

Spencer was visibly uncomfortable, much to Dan's delight.

"Do you have a girlfriend, Spencer?" She delicately placed a slice of pickle in her mouth.

"Uh no, ma'am."

"That would've gotten in the way of his little bet." Dan shook his head.

"Oh right." Fionna chuckled as Spencer turned the color of the apple on his tray. They continued to eat, with Fionna making quite a show of snuggling into Dan. She finished her sandwich, and he cleared away her trash.

"Want anything else, sweetheart?"

"I'm good." Fionna patted the seat beside her and Dan returned. Spencer wasn't eating much as Dan stared him down. "Oh," she moved her hand back to her stomach. "She's kicking." With a chuckle, he slid his hand to Halia. "Do you feel her?"

"Yeah, there's my baby," he lied. He hadn't felt her move, but upon hearing his voice, Halia did respond, much to his delight. A genuine smile cast his face as he rubbed Fionna's swell where Halia was pushing her tiny foot.

Fionna folded her hands on her stomach. "I believe I was supposed to listen to a paper you'd written."

"Yes, ma'am." He drew a long sip of his Dr Pepper and pulled a folded piece of computer paper from his pocket. Dan rolled his eyes.

"Uh," he cleared his throat.

"Go ahead, sweetie," Fionna ordered in a very motherly tone.

Spencer proceeded to read a poorly written essay which listed the dates women in the Realm were given the vote. He added in the formation of the Angels then proceeded on to his feelings that women were confusing and didn't know what they wanted. He wrote the words, "the world has always been run by men and it should stay that way. Women are too emotional."

"Dear God, you not only thought those words, you wrote them?" Dan gasped in shock.

Spencer look confused as he nodded.

His concluding paragraph included the line, "If women don't know what they want, how are we supposed to know?"

Dan fought not to cringe. For a split second, he considered casting a shield over the kid because his wife was about to filet him. But Spencer deserved everything she was about to dish up and then some, and she did not need Dan to fight her battles for her.

Fionna narrowed her eyes and leaned in for the kill. Dan folded his hands in his lap and watched her work.

"Sit down, Spencer," she snarled. "Let's go over just a few things, shall we. Let me tell you just a little bit about what women want."

"You might want to take notes," Dan commanded.

Spencer glanced around, presumably for paper, but Fionna

continued. "Women, who by the way, are the reason that you are here." She pointed to her stomach. Spencer grimaced and offered a hesitant nod. "Women want to be able to do all of the things that you can do without fear. And do you know why we worry about things like walking to our cars at night or going out in public in general?"

Spencer's eyes lit. "Because you need men to protect you."

Dan's eyes goggled, and Fionna erupted from the couch. "Do you know why we need protection!? We need protection because most *men* have absolutely no respect for women's wants or their desires or for them being anything other than a piece of property. What is wrong with you? We could walk to our cars without worry if it weren't for *men*. We could go out in public with no concerns at all if not for *men*. So, do not sit there and tell me that women are too emotional. Men are the ones who can't get their brains to engage anywhere above their waistline and show some damn respect to the very sex that gives *you* life," she roared. Her rhythms vibrated with fury all around them.

"As for your ridiculous, disrespectful little bet, let me assure you that my husband is the love of my life. He is the only person that I would ever share myself with. Because when I looked my husband in the eye and I vowed to love him and only him for the rest of my life, I meant that. He respects me, first and foremost. He also adores me, appreciates me, and takes care of me and our children. Your little essay there showed no respect and no appreciation for women in any way at all. It was nonsensical drivel that you think gives you some kind of lame excuse to treat women like property.

"My husband isn't a real man because he has bulging biceps and can outshoot any man in the Realm. His heart and his mind and his actions make him a real man. I've seen my husband do some terrifying things, stare down the barrels of pistols for one. But the things that he does that mean the most to me," she shrieked, "are when he reads our little girl to sleep each night. When he gets up on Saturday morning and brings me coffee in bed. When I'm sick and he does everything in his power to make me feel better. When he gets up every morning and goes to work and then comes home and helps me make dinner and helps our baby girl with her homework. He does protect me, because despite our best efforts, there are still boys walking around thinking the way you do. He's patient and sweet, giving, thoughtful, and most of all loving. He is a real man, and you are nothing but a cocky egotistical child who needs to learn some respect," she sneered.

"He keeps his vows to me, to his children, to his family, and to the Realm. That essay proves that you not only have no idea how to behave like anything other than a neanderthal, but that you have no idea how to even begin to treat women. Women can do everything men can do, other than peeing standing up, a million times better than you can. But men who know that women are at the very least their equal, don't want them to have to. They want to help. They want to make her world a better place because when you do that," she vowed. "When you give a woman your very best, then you'll get the very best out of her and that, Spencer, is better than anything you've ever imagined. So why don't you try thinking with the head above your waist and see if you can't rewrite that paper? Show a little appreciation and a great deal more respect for women in general. And if you don't think you can come up with something better than this," —she held up the paper—"then forty percent of your grade for this semester will be failing.

"I for one am thrilled that Dan is going to be your mentor because you clearly need to learn more than the energy of defense. You need to learn to be a human being."

Dan raised his eyebrows and awaited Spencer's response.

He nodded morosely.

Dan stared him down. "Put some thought in it this time. Women deserve your respect and your time. You need to listen to her mind and her heart and you need to understand that the things they want are just as important as what you want. Do all of that before you try to unzip her jeans."

"Yes, sir. I'm sorry, Mrs. Vindico," he offered quite sincerely.

"You should be."

He slunk out of the office with his tail between his legs.

Dan grinned. "That's my girl."

"Ugh, what a little prick."

Fionna tossed the original essay in the trash can.

"Oh, now wait." Dan retrieved it. "I want to keep this in case I do end up calling his father."

He added it to a file in his desk with Spencer's name on it.

"Can I meet Jeff and Becca before I head home?" Fionna asked hopefully.

"I don't know where they are right now."

"They're probably in the cafeteria," she insisted.

"Okay, just remember that I don't think anyone else knows about the pregnancy."

"I just want to let them know if they need any help, we'll help them. That's...the only way for us to really heal."

Dan's brow furrowed. "What do you mean, baby?"

"I've been struggling the past few days. I'm worried that if I'm too excited about Halia, something bad might happen or it might mean that I didn't mourn our first enough. But helping people who are going through something we went through, that's the whole point, don't you think? If we can help them, we'll also heal a little of our trauma."

Dan forced another smile. "Come on."

CHAPTER 10

WORDS

As they stepped out in the hallway, they heard a somewhat disconcerting squeal. They turned around and saw two students whose hands were firmly clasped with one another.

"Oh, holy discontinued Balenciaga Black City Giant 21 work bag with the original hardware." A girl with long black hair and pale skin grabbed Fionna's handbag. She looked up the next second and let out an even louder squeal. "You're Fionna Styler! Like, *the* Fionna Styler. Do you know who you are? You like challenged for the Angels for like a really long time and you won Top Receiver of Summation last year and then you were dating Garrett Haydenshire who is like totally, totally a manwhore, and I totally did not think that was gonna work out because…you know, once a cheater. I told all of my friends that it wouldn't work out even though you were like a super cute couple together 'cause he is so freaking hot and there was that picture of you two the one where you were carrying a Valentino Garavani tote and he was like not dressed up enough to be with you…but then like everyone found out you were actually dating Chief Vindico who has like a broody kinda bad boy but like good guy vibe. Is he like that IRL?

"I heard he was like working here or something." She turned to the guy with her without even a pause. "Didn't you tell me that?" She turned back to Fionna. "Did you get the Valentino at Bergdorf's or at Neiman Marcus. It was Neiman Marcus, wasn't it. That's like a kind of better store for some things but it isn't the better store for other things so then you end up having to like go to more than one or both. One time, I was there and I was gonna get Chancey some cologne and there was supposed to be a sale only they didn't have Clive Christian on sale and like what is the point of a sale if you're not gonna also have all the cologne on sale?" She said all of that without so much as taking a breath.

Fionna and Dan both stared at the child in abject bewilderment. Fionna cleared her throat. "Hi there." She grinned. "What's your name?"

"I'm Ariel Marshall and this is my boyfriend Chancey Winters. We're like *together* together."

Fionna nodded. "It is very nice to meet both of you. Oh, I was never dating Garrett. He's my best friend."

Ariel looked thrilled with that little bit of information. "Do you like just tell yourself that because he cheated on you because I don't think it's the person being cheated on's fault if someone cheats you know? My friend Christen was dating this really good-looking guy from Hans Beathe and then she found out he was cheating, and I was like well I told you that was going to happen because he doesn't go to school with us so he could get away with it so he did because that's just what he did."

"We need to go," Dan interjected. He pulled Fionna down the hall and away from Chance and Ariel. Fionna was covering her mouth as if that would keep the hysterical laughter at bay.

"Wow," she finally spoke.

"Yeah, she definitely needs to switch to decaf. She could fly from here to Neiman Marcus on her own wind."

Fionna was still trying to quell laughter. "Her poor boyfriend. Does he ever get to talk?"

Dan rolled his eyes. "I have a Chance Winters in one of my senior defense classes. I'm assuming that's him and that his name is not Chancey. I guess we'll see."

They entered the lunch room, but Jeff and Becca weren't in there.

"Maybe he took her out for lunch." Dan shrugged. "I might stay a little later today and see if I can talk him through what to say to the governor tonight." He left out that he might also give him a little practice in how to take and throw a punch. Becca had two older brothers who were as mean as they were worthless. All of Iodex had collectively named them the Sap-Asses, and they lived up to the name.

"Yes. Do that!"

He walked Fionna to her car and returned to his office. He debated which governor to call. There was a decent chance they were together, so he touched his father's name on his phone.

"We just got off the phone with Dean," was his father's greeting. "You're on with me and Stephen."

"Oh yeah, what did he say?" Dan asked.

Governor Haydenshire sighed audibly. "Insisted that there was nothing inappropriate going on and reminded me, a little too vehemently, about what the press did to Rainer and Emily on their honeymoon."

"What did you find out?" his father asked.

"That he just lied through his teeth to you. Fi says he is definitely having an affair, but I don't have you any hard evidence yet. I'll figure something out. I haven't had time to dig in on the drug tests either. I need a better understanding of normal procedure around the tests, which means I'm going to have to access the administrative office at the very least. I'm likely going to need to get into the digital files for both the affair and the drug tests."

"I hate to open this up as an Iodex investigation, but if you need Ramier's help..." Governor Haydenshire offered.

"No sir, I think I might have a workaround. I'll find out this afternoon."

"Let us know, and thank you, son," Governor Vindico vowed.

"No problem."

Loathing what he was doing with every fiber of his being, Dan closed and locked his office door. In his vast experience, if you wanted to find something out, places like teachers' lounges or anywhere that people felt relaxed and like they had a limited amount of time were the places to go.

Dan despised gossip in all of its many forms. That came from growing up with a mother who drank it up like her life's blood and from enduring the endless rumors the press loved to create about him and Fionna.

After he'd accepted the job at Venton, he'd had every intention of being an excellent mentor, of training up Ioses Predilects to defend the Realm. He never imagined that he'd be stalking around the mentors' lounge hoping to hear gossip on the chancellor's extramarital affair. With a sigh, he opened the door.

He moved quickly to the vending machines. He met no one's eyes. He needed to blend in with the environment so people would talk, and clearly at least some of the staff believed he was there to spy.

He pressed the button for Dr Pepper, though he had several in his office, and sat down at a small table with only one chair in the back corner. He clicked on several files on his laptop and pretended to look them over. Dan didn't know even half of the dozen or so people in the large, well-equipped room. He'd had no intention of ever setting foot in a room designed for taking a break from the job.

Dan let his eyes study his new surroundings. Work drove him. It always had. When and if he relaxed, he preferred to be lying on the couch with his wife and his girls, on a beach on Kauai watching Aida play in the water, or building sandcastles with her after he rubbed Fionna down with sunscreen.

When he was at work, he wanted to work, but he knew not everyone functioned the way he did. Working the farm in Kauai had been the most cathartic thing he'd done thus far in his life. He couldn't wait to get back as soon as school let out for the summer. But he supposed Scholera Predilects found teaching fulfilling.

There was a table in the center of the room where snack trays had been laid out for the taking. Several mentors were working on laptops quietly. There were three women Dan didn't know hovering around the snack table discussing the caloric intake of each of the offered dishes.

While fighting the urge to inform them that none of the prepared foods were particularly healthy options, Dan continued to listen. They each picked up a small plate and loaded it down with deviled eggs and a salad that had been deemed a healthy choice based on the fact that it contained almonds.

Dan's ears perked up as he heard, "I had coffee with Katherine yesterday."

"Really?" One of the others looked thrilled. Dan recognized the knowing grin coming from the mentor who'd participated in the coffee outing. They were like prey being baited for the kill.

"Is she okay?" the other asked concernedly, and Dan amended his original stance. She appeared genuinely concerned.

"Not really," the informant sounded only too pleased that the ladies were interested.

"What did she say exactly, Debbie?"

"Here, let's sit down." Debbie guided the women to a gathering of cushioned chairs and couches near Dan. He slid farther down in his chair and stared at his laptop screen.

"Did she say anything about Dean?" the woman who was eager for information pressed.

"Not really. She just said she was having a rough few weeks. She's moved into an apartment," the woman vowed with a gotcha grin.

"Who's paying for the apartment?" the other woman continued her inquisition.

"I'm not certain, but I can tell you that Katherine offered to pay for my coffee, which just goes to confirm my suspicion that she's still being paid. I suppose I might let him in my bed too if it meant I got a whole year off with a paycheck."

"Or it means that she needed someone to talk to," the quieter woman pointed out.

"Has her husband filed for divorce?" The other woman sounded like that would serve everyone right.

"Now see, this is how to improve your reputation," a nasally voice drawled near Dan.

His head shot up. "Sherman." He ground his teeth.

Fergus pulled a chair from another table and joined Dan. "How have your first few days been? Don't be upset if the kids don't respond to you at first. Not all of us are as popular with the kids as I am."

Dan continued to glare. "I was just working on my lesson plans," he lied, hoping to get Sherman to leave him alone as the women were still talking.

"We're having a bonfire and hayride this Friday night up near the Summation Stadium. You're coming, right?"

Dan narrowed his eyes. "Mentor Sherman, my wife is almost seven months pregnant with my daughter. I'm certain you've never thought of this, but she's not particularly comfortable most of the time. So, I'm not going to bring Fionna and put her on a wooden flatbed to be bounced around by a tractor, any more than she would ever agree to inhaling the copious amounts of smoke from a bonfire into her lungs."

"Dude, you are, like, way too hung up on your kid. People have kids all the time. Tell her to get over herself."

Trying to forcefully remove the fantasies from his mind of his choking Fergus Sherman, Dan drew a deep breath. "We have friends coming over Friday night."

"Bring them along. The Venton family is an open relationship kind of deal."

"No."

Fergus leaned in. "Hey, did you hear about Wilshire and Mentor Bryant? I didn't even know what I was taking pictures of, but I'm the guy who broke the story."

"What pictures?"

"The ones from the conference this summer."

"How did the press get photos from a teaching conference?" Dan glared at the idiot responsible for making his father's life more difficult.

"I put them on the school website."

Dan rubbed his temples.

"It seems that they might've been doing the 'deed,'" Sherman finger quoted the word deed. "You know, like in the biblical sense."

"Yeah, I got it."

"I heard Wilshire's wife is talking to Jack Stariff," he lied.

Dan could tell he was exaggerating the story trying to sound impressive. Jack Stariff was the top lawyer for the Senate.

"Stariff is a criminal lawyer. He doesn't do divorce cases."

"Oh well, I just overheard that." He shrugged. "I mean, I get it. It's tempting. You're a married man. I'll be getting married here in five years."

Dan's brow knitted tightly. "I thought you just got engaged."

"Yeah, but my parents won't let me get married until I'm twenty-seven," Fergus stated as if Dan should have known that. "All I'm saying is that we're here surrounded by beautiful women. We're good-looking guys. I understand the temptation."

Dan's mouth hung open in shock. "There is no temptation," he snarled. "I am madly in love with my wife. I vowed to love my wife, and only my wife, for the rest of my life, and that's precisely what I will do. No one else ever. That's not how this works. I don't give a damn who I'm surrounded by, but just for the record, have you ever seen my wife?"

Fergus hemmed. "I don't really see what everyone's going on about with Fionna Styler. I guess if you like that tall, tanning-booth skin, brown-eyed, long hair, big-boob type then she's okay, but she doesn't do much for me. She's really putting on weight."

Swallowing back the bile that flooded his throat, Dan leapt across the table. "Do not ever, ever talk about my wife's chest ever again. Do you understand me? Ever," he commanded. "She doesn't go to a tanning booth. She is Hawaiian!"

Fergus shrank back. "You have a real temper problem."

Dan's biceps pulsed in desire to sink his fists deeply into Fergus Sherman, but he sank back in his chair instead. "What does your mother think about the rumors about Wilshire?" If he was going to have to endure this, then he was going to get something out of it.

Sherman seemed too frightened not to answer. "Wilshire was pretty insistent that it was just a rumor when he talked to the school governors. He said that Mentor Bryant was leaving because it wasn't true, and she was embarrassed. They don't really have any proof." Fergus shrugged.

Dan stood and packed his laptop. "I have to get to my next class." He stomped out of the lounge.

His head ached as he let the past few minutes work through his brain. Wilshire lying to not only the governing board but the Venton board as well was going to blow up in his face in a big way. What the hell was he thinking?

Dan managed his way through his last class trying not to take his fury with Mentor Sherman out on the Energy of Defensive Maneuvers class. After assigning his first paper, Dan let the class out five minutes early. He stopped Jeff before he left.

"Want to talk a little about what to say to Governor Sapman and maybe do a little training before you meet Portwood?"

Worry had consumed Jeff's features for most of class, but suddenly he looked thrilled.

"Thank you. That'd be great, sir." He offered Dan an abashed grin. "Worried the Sap-Asses will try to work me over?"

Dan chuckled. "The thought did cross my mind."

"I'll be okay."

"Do you know what you're going to say to her parents?" Dan led Jeff back to his office.

"I think mostly just how much I love her, and that we've been planning to get married since we first started dating. Promise them that I'll take care of Becca and the baby always. That they're my top priorities. Her family already hates me. I figure it can't really get worse."

Dan was impressed with his deep sincerity, but he forced a nod and didn't point out that it could get much, much worse.

"Hey Strenton, could I make a deal with you?"

"Sure." Jeff nodded.

"I need some help with some stuff my father asked me to look into, and you've got the skills I need. If you wouldn't mind finding some stuff out for me, then I'll help you with your training for Iodex and with all of your Ioses classes."

"I mean, yeah…of course. I'll help you out. You don't have to do anything for me though."

"I'd like to if you're willing. I can get you trained so you'd be able to jump in at Iodex faster. That would stead you in a good position to get hired on at the end of the year."

"This is probably not what I should say now, but I can't think of anything else and I haven't slept in days. I was really bummed when you resigned. I wanted to be trained by you. You're the best of the best."

Dan shook his head, but Jeff continued. "You really are."

"Thank you, but I'm sure Portwood will do an excellent job training you. I just want to help in exchange for you finding out a few things for me up here."

"About Wilshire and Mentor Bryant?"

"Yeah, and this doesn't leave this office, but there's some concern over the most recent drug test reports."

"Yeah, I know a bunch of kids are using now. I don't get it. It's definitely not my thing. Plus, they're going to get caught."

CHAPTER 11

WOUNDS

The next morning, as Dan neared his office door he spotted a middle-aged woman dressed in a waitressing uniform with a well-worn cardigan awaiting him. Smiling kindly, Dan tried to figure out whom she might be and why she was at his office. She was rubbing her hands together nervously, and her face was drawn in deep concern.

"Can I help you, ma'am?"

"Are you Mr. Vindico?"

"So they tell me." Dan unlocked the door.

She forced a smile that never got anywhere near her eyes. She continued to wring her hands. "I'm Grace Harrickson,"—she stepped into the office with an appreciative nod—"Jeff Strenton's mother."

"It's nice to meet you." He offered her a kind smile.

"I don't mean to take up your time."

"It's fine. Jeff's a good kid."

Relief played in her weary eyes as she nodded. "He really is. He's always looked up to you. He followed your career through, uh," she fumbled.

"Iodex."

"Yes. I'm sorry. I'm not Gifted," she explained what Dan already knew. He hadn't picked up on any energy from Ms. Harrickson. Jeff's father must have been Gifted. "I just wanted to thank you for talking with him and offering to train him. He was so excited. I've been trying to get him to talk to me for weeks. I knew something was wrong.

"They told me last night that Becca's pregnant. I just feel like this is all my fault. I wasn't there as much as I wanted to be. I usually work two jobs. Jeff's father left the day I found out I was expecting," she whispered. Shame etched her face.

"Ms. Harrickson, Jeff didn't do anything wrong. He's an excellent student, a great kid, and he loves Becca. Trust me, he and Becca are not the only couple doing that. They just happen to have gotten a little ahead of themselves, and now they're going to have a little catching up to do. But it can be done, and my wife and I would like to help any way we can."

She managed a haggard nod. "I, uh…I was worried that perhaps with Mr. Sapman's power, he might try to have Jeff removed from the academy."

Dan shook his head. "He doesn't have that kind of power, and my own father is the Governor of Gifted Education. He would never allow that to happen."

Ms. Harrickson continued to rub her hands together with worry but she managed a nod. "Jeff just idolizes you. He always has."

Dan bristled. No one should idolize him.

"I always felt like I was letting him down. He could do all of these things that I didn't understand."

"I don't think you let him down at all. He's a tremendous kid." As he thought over just a few of the conversations he'd had with Jeff the afternoon before and how quickly he'd picked up the things Dan was teaching him, he added, "I wouldn't have secured him the internship if I didn't believe that."

She appeared to choke down emotion. "Could I ask you one other favor?"

"Of course."

"Well, uh…he really didn't want me to tell you, but I'm so worried. The Sapmans didn't take the news all that well. Becca's older brothers and a bunch of their friends were waiting on Jeff by his truck last night." Tears sheened her eyes and then cascaded down her kind face.

Dan's heart sank. "Where is he?"

"In my car. He didn't want to go to the hospital, but I think he probably should've. I didn't know what to do."

"Come on." Dan sprinted out of the office.

"Can you heal him?"

"I'm going to try." Fury coursed through him. Greg and Brent Sapman were just a few years older than Becca. They were entitled assholes who'd always been perfectly happy to lie around living on the governor's prestigious salary.

Dan arrived at Ms. Harrickson's old Buick. He yanked open the passenger side door and grimaced. Jeff was sporting two black eyes and a broken nose. As Jeff stood, Dan realized that he had several cracked ribs as well.

"Becca doesn't know," he managed to gasp through his pain.

"Greg and Brent are…" Dan halted as he remembered that Jeff's mother was standing beside them crying.

"Yeah, but I deserved it."

"No, you didn't. Try to relax for me, okay? I'm gonna do your ribs first."

Jeff tried valiantly to relax, but he was in a tremendous amount of pain. His shield blocked Dan out.

"Come on. You're going to have to let me in. Think about Becca, a good memory."

Closing his eyes, Jeff tried again, but his shield kept Dan from casting him.

"Gonna have to be a better memory than that. Come on. It doesn't have to be one you'd tell Mom about, okay?"

Jeff managed a slight grin and nodded. A moment later, he relaxed and allowed Dan to harness his energy.

Working with a great deal of finesse, Dan guided Jeff's energy and added in heavy doses of his own as he forced his body to heal. When Jeff could draw full breaths without any pain, Dan dropped the cast. "Let's go in my office so I can do your face."

"Thank you." Jeff arched his back and allowed his lungs to fully expand.

"You go on to work. I'll take care of him, and I can drop him at home after my last class," Dan offered Jeff's mother.

"You don't have to do that, Mentor Vindico. I can just take the bus."

"If you'd rather take the bus than my Ferrari, I guess I can't stop you."

Jeff gave him another slight grin.

"Come on, let's get you healed up before Becca gets here." He guided Jeff in after Ms. Harrickson thanked him profusely.

"All right. You're good as new," Dan assured as he finally got Jeff's eyes to heal.

"They had, like, eight of their thug friends with them."

Dan shook his head. "There's no winning that. I don't care how strong your shield is. Plus, you're untrained." He grabbed two water bottles from his shelf and handed one to Jeff.

"Still, could you maybe not mention this to Chief Portwood?"

"Done," Dan agreed. "What did the governor say?" He eased into his chair, exhausted after healing Jeff. He wasn't a medio, and though he'd healed plenty of his officers in the field, he wasn't equipped with all of the additional energy that Valeduto Predilects had. He pulled two power bars from his desk and instructed Jeff to eat as he inhaled the other.

"They told Bec that she could stay at home if she dumped me and got rid of the baby." Jeff's eyes narrowed spitefully. "I love how he ran his campaign on an anti-abortion ticket, and then his daughter is pregnant and that's fine for her. Hypocritical much?"

Dan nodded. "I know you're just starting out, but most of us learn quick that it's easy to apply rules to nameless masses. It's all well and good not to extend anyone empathy because it's easier to see them as a group instead of individual people who are hurting. You'll be a better officer if you can remember that every group is made up of real live people with real problems and sometimes no options."

"Yes, sir." Jeff downed another sip of water. "Mom said we could stay with her, but it's a one-bedroom apartment. I sleep on the couch." Shame tensed in his weary shield.

"Your new job should get you a decent apartment, and I can front you some cash if you need it."

"Mentor Vindico, I can't take your money. You've done so much for me already."

"I really am happy to make certain that you and Becca are taken care of."

"Thank you."

"You know the Haydenshires own a few rental houses out near their farm. If you don't mind me telling them, I feel certain that you and Becca could rent one."

"Really?" Jeff sounded intrigued.

"Really, and you'd be close to school."

"I was kind of afraid Governor Sapman would get Governor Haydenshire to kick me out of Venton or keep me out of Iodex or both. He was so pissed."

"Governor Haydenshire wouldn't do that. I don't care what Becca's dad asked for, and neither would Portwood."

"Why are you being so nice to me? You don't even really know me, sir."

"I can tell you're a good kid, and I think you deserve a break. You know you screwed up, but instead of denying it or running away, you want to work through it. I admire that. And...my wife."

"Your wife?"

Dan nodded. "According to her, and trust me she is always right, helping people who've been through something we've been through is a way for us to heal. I've done a lot of things I regret. I took this job because I want to give back, so it would be mutually beneficial."

Jeff gave him an uncomfortable nod.

"Go find Becca. She's probably a mess." Dan gestured his head to his office door. "I'll call the Crown Governor and see if we can't get this show on the road."

"Hey, uh, I know this is probably kind of weird, but Bec and I thought maybe we'd see if Governor Haydenshire would marry us one afternoon after school or something." His face flushed in his embarrassment. "And if you and Mrs. Vindico would come, that would really mean a lot to me."

"Let me know when, and we'll be there. I can even offer you a flower girl if you want."

"Bec deserves that. She deserves a big deal Senate wedding, and I ruined it for her. Her parents will never agree to that now."

"Nothing is ruined, and it's not the wedding. It's the marriage. Trust me."

"Thanks, sir. For everything." He rushed out of Dan's office.

Governor Haydenshire answered on the first ring. "I worry when you call me this early."

"I'm sorry, sir. I have a student who could really use some help. He's also the one I'm going to get to help me with the cases here, so I was hoping he might could move into one of your rental houses if you have any available. His name is Jeff Strenton. Great kid."

"I know Mr. Strenton. He's good friends with Logan and Rainer. I think he's even been out to the farm a few times, and I agree with your assessment. He is a great kid. However, George Sapman just left my office. Unfortunately, he doesn't agree with us." The governor sighed.

Dan bit his tongue to keep from informing the Crown what Governor Sapman's idiot sons had done to Jeff.

Governor Haydenshire filled in the silence. "I informed George that if Becca was going to marry Jeff and bear his children that it would be best if he graduated with a degree and had a job, so either removing him from Venton or from the internship serves no one but his ego. George and I rarely see eye to eye on things, but I don't think I've ever been so disgusted.

"I phoned Lillian to tell her what he'd had the audacity to ask me to do. She was quick to remind me how I acted about the belly shot and when Emily got her tattoo, so I'm trying to remember what it's like when your one and only daughter grows up rather suddenly."

Dan chuckled. "You might have to remind me of that same thing in a few years."

"It's good you recognize that now. I'll give Patrick a call. He handles all of our rentals now. To my knowledge, we have two available. There might be more. They'd both be a suitable place from which to dig yourself out of a hole."

"Thank you. They do both seem willing to sling the shovel. I've been really impressed with Strenton every time I've interacted with him. "

"Then that's all it will take."

"Jeff was wondering if you'd perform a marriage ceremony for them. I think they want to get settled. They seem more than willing to give up the last year of their childhood."

"It seems like Jeff's really taken with you. Be careful, son. You may have just become his role model, father, and big brother all in one day's time, but it sounds like this kid could really use your and Fionna's help if you're willing to be there for them."

"I really do want to be there for them. I have a lot to make up for, and this seems like a great way to start," Dan explained his desperation to help Jeff and Becca.

"I can't think of a finer role model," the governor complimented though Dan disagreed. "Why don't you and Fionna bring Aida and Jeff and Becca by the house tomorrow night for dinner? It might be nice for them to get away from the Realm for a little while. I know Lillian would love to see Aida and Fionna. Keaton too for that matter." He chuckled.

Three-year-old Keaton Haydenshire had quite a crush on Fionna.

"The kid has great taste," Dan teased as the governor continued his hearty laughter.

"After we eat, you and I can take Jeff and Becca out to a few of the houses. If they want to get married tomorrow night, we can do it out by the lake. That seems a more peaceful place than my office."

"Fi and I would love to see all of you, so that'd be great. I'll let Jeff and Becca know."

"Great, we'll see you then."

Dan phoned his wife next. He explained everything that he'd been doing since he'd arrived that morning. "The Haydenshires want us to bring Aida and Jeff and Becca over tomorrow night for dinner. They're going to let the kids rent one of their rental houses. The

Sapmans are kicking Becca out if she stays with Jeff and keeps the baby."

"That's awful." She sounded as devastated as Dan felt.

Dan couldn't fathom his children doing anything that would have him demanding that they move out of their home, but he supposed not everyone felt that way. He also suspected that Jeff had never been deemed worthy of the governor's daughter, and that the Sapmans saw this as a way to get rid of him.

"Wait," Fionna gasped. "Where are they staying tonight?"

"I...don't really know. I guess with his mom."

"No. They're not sleeping on the floor of a one-bedroom apartment. I'm coming up there. We're talking with them, and they're staying here tonight."

"Fi, baby, I don't know about having students stay with us."

"I'll be up there as soon as I get ready." She ended the call.

Dan's eyes closed in defeat, but his phone rang a second later. He answered Portwood's call.

"Hey Dan, we just got a call from Portsmouth. Norfolk Iodex found a massive weapons shipment hidden in loads of soccer balls. All of Elite is heading to Norfolk. Tell Strenton I'm sorry, but I'll have to send Rainer and Logan out there tomorrow. He can still start Monday, though, as long as it all works out."

"I'll tell him, but listen. The steel isn't just going to be in the containers. Check the funnel and especially anchor. Look for remnants of drugs there because they use the anchor to dump the evidence when they know they're caught, and it might not just be weapons. The vents too, and it's not always a deal the captain's got going, but it will almost always be one of his subordinates. " A longing to go with them ate at Dan.

"I know, Dan," Portwood reminded him.

"Yeah...just be careful."

"This isn't my first goods seizure."

CHAPTER 12

OVERDOSE OF HOSPITALITY

Dan stopped by Jeff's desk as he entered his senior defense class. "I need to talk to you after class for a few minutes."

Jeff gave him a hesitant nod. "Yes, sir."

Dan moved to the front of the room. "All right, today we're going to start with the reasons why people break the laws. Since most of you are looking to work in Iodex offices whose primary goal is to enforce laws set by the Senteon, it will make all of you better officers if we consider the reasons why people do the things they do."

He watched fingers fly across keyboards and heads nod.

"When I was in school, we were readily taught that people break laws for six reasons—greed, revenge, lust, excitement, anger, and ego. I can assure you, as the guy who headed up Iodex for the past decade, that those are not the reasons. What I was taught was incorrect. Now, I'm not saying that those are not resulting factors, but they are rarely the underlying cause.

"In my vast experience, people break laws because of poverty, position, pity, privilege, peace of mind, and power—either their own or power someone holds over them. Preventing crime is vastly easier than prosecuting it. If we understand where it comes from, we can try to stop what's causing it before the crime is committed."

Ben Cobson's hand shot up, and Dan nodded to him. "How would someone break the law because of pity?"

"You're a Shield. Ever gotten into a fight because someone was hurting someone you care about or someone who you didn't think was capable of defending themselves?"

"Yeah, a few times," he admitted.

"So, you have committed assault in defense of someone else because on some level you felt sorry for them."

Cobson looked impressed and went back to his typing.

Raya Patel's hand went up next. Dan nodded to her.

"What about Dominic Wretchkinsides, sir? He did seem to be driven by greed, ego, excitement, lust, and definitely revenge, wouldn't you say?"

Dan took a moment to force the image of Wretchkinsides's drained body from his mind. He nodded. "I would absolutely agree with all of those things, but that doesn't change the fact that none of those were the foundation for his heinous crimes. Nic's father, Hadrian, was a Russian oligarch. He was no better than his son ended up being, trust me. When Nic neared the age where he could begin to claim some of his inheritance, it pissed Hadrian off. He kicked him out and left him with nothing. So, right there we've got poverty, position, privilege, and power. His father held both power and position over him, and Nic set out to reclaim what he'd lost.

"He'd grown up the son of a ridiculously wealthy man. He believed he was entitled to whatever he wanted and that he was above the law just like his father had always believed. Their belief in their privilege and position ultimately led to their downfall."

Another hand went up, and Dan nodded to the young woman on the back row.

"What about things like religious wars?"

Dan smiled. "These are outstanding questions by the way. I'm very impressed. What is the aggressor in a religious war ultimately trying to assert? It's the very same thing that someone who attacks someone at a protest and claims they commit crimes motivated by their beliefs is really trying to gain themselves."

She considered for a moment and then nodded. "Power and usually to make certain that their privilege remains intact."

No one else raised their hands, so Dan continued. "Let me remind all of you that it's not only criminals who are subject to reacting to any of the reasons I gave you as to why people ultimately break the law. Before you ever set foot inside any Iodex precinct anywhere, you need to make certain you've checked your power, position, and your obvious privilege at the door. If you cannot do that, you have no right to be an officer."

He assigned a paper where the students were allowed to pick any one of the six reasons originally taught and draw the parallels to the actual reasons people break laws. "Make certain the papers are turned in next Friday via the thumb drives the school issued all of you," he concluded as the bell rang and the students began gathering their things.

Dan headed out in the corridor with Jeff. "I talked to Governor Haydenshire…" Dan began explaining but was stopped by someone shouting his name.

"Mentor Vindico!"

Dan spun around. His eyes goggled as he watched two students try to keep another guy of about the same age from collapsing on the floor.

Dan raced to them. "Here." He took the guy's weight and laid him gently on the floor. His pupils were drawn into tight pinpoints. His fingertips were purple. His Adminis rhythms were erratic and broken as his body temp crashed. "Shit! He overdosed. Jeff," he shouted. Strenton rushed to him. "There's Narcan in my top desk drawer." He thrust the keys to his desk into Jeff's hands. "Hurry!"

Jeff sprinted down the corridor. Dan cast his shield around the child and tried desperately to both regulate his faltering rhythms and to raise his body temperature back to something sustainable.

Jeff returned in less than sixty seconds. Dan dropped his shield and took the packet. He had it unwrapped and in the kid's nose as fast as he was able.

When the kid drew breath, Dan finally did the same. "Call an ambulance," Dan ordered one of the friends. "What did he take?"

The child who hadn't grabbed his cell phone shrugged. "I don't know, sir. He's been messing around with a bunch of stuff for a while." Dan's Visium Predilection once again forced his shield back. So, the kid had been using for a while and yet every drug test performed just one week ago was clear.

Dan's eyes narrowed. "Why wasn't he worried about the drug testing?"

"I don't know. Why are you asking me?"

Eventually Dan helped load the student onto an ambulance and returned wearily to his office.

Fionna was standing outside of his door with Jeff and Becca. "Will he be okay?" Devastation drowned her rhythms.

"I don't know. The medio said they're going to have to keep him in an induced coma. He could definitely have brain damage. He's lucky it didn't kill him."

She shook her head, and they all moved into Dan's office. "You've probably already made introductions, but this is Jeff Strenton and Becca Sapman." Dan smiled kindly. "Jeff, Becca, this is my wife, Fionna."

"Hi." Fionna offered Jeff and Becca her hand.

"Uh, hi." Jeff and Becca both appeared to be in awe of Fionna.

Dan closed the door, offering them both seats. "Like I was saying, I spoke with Governor Haydenshire. He has two relatively small houses that are both available. He wanted to know if perhaps you'd like to have dinner out on the farm with the two of us tomorrow night.

"He also mentioned that if you'd like him to do a small ceremony, that he could do it out by their lake before we go take a look at the houses." He wondered what Becca would think of all that Jeff had done. She appeared stunned. Her eyes were still bloodshot, and defeat had settled on her features.

"Thank you so much for all of this," Becca managed though she started crying again immediately.

Fionna was heartbroken. She handed her a tissue and wrapped her arm over her shoulders. In what Dan assumed was a show of female solidarity, Becca let Fionna comfort her.

She turned her head and began sobbing into Fionna's shoulder.

"It's going to be okay," Fionna began whispering, and Dan saw her powerful soothing cast move over Becca.

"Daddy's just being awful, and I know he's not telling me something." She gestured to Jeff. "I know Greg and Brent did something, but he won't tell me what."

"He doesn't want you to worry."

"Daddy wants me to get rid of it, but I just can't," she gasped through her shuddering tears.

"I know. I promise you it's going to be all right. You two are going to stay with us until we get you settled in your new house."

"Mrs. Vindico, we can't put you out like that," Jeff argued.

"You're not putting us out. We have a guest bedroom, and I love to cook. That way we can all get to know each other better."

"Daddy won't even let me back in to get my stuff unless I break up with Jeff." She shuddered against Fionna.

"Your father will come around when he sees that you're going to stick to your guns," Dan promised her and then immediately decided that he was going to have a little chat with Governor Sapman.

After Fionna repeatedly insisted that Jeff and Becca were staying with the Vindicos, they left to get ready for their next class. "Fi, baby, that's really kind of you, but are you sure about letting them stay over?"

"They are sweet and he adores her. And she adores him. I could feel that from both of them. He was going to let her sleep on the couch, and he was going to sleep on the floor because he's a good guy, but he can't go to school all day, then go work at Iodex, then go home and do all of his homework over and over until the end of the year sleeping on the floor. They can just stay with us. He's still exhausted from what those horrible Sapman boys did to him."

"They cracked his ribs, so I'm certain he didn't sleep all night. He didn't tell his mom how bad he was hurting."

Fionna shook her head. She was on the verge of tears. "You know Spencer could learn a great deal from Jeff." She narrowed her eyes in disdain but then shook her head. "If you can't fix the wrongs of the world, create love in it," she spoke almost to herself. Dan's brow furrowed. "We can help them and make their lives a little easier. We can love them and accept them, and they both desperately need that, so that's what we're going to do. I'll pick up a few things for dinner and then I think I'll go by and get Aida. If they tell me I can't have her, then I'll cry." She giggled.

"Let me know if that works, and if they try to do a body scan or they come at you with some sort of probe, I'm going to make them cry," he informed her.

"Aida will be thrilled. She loves to take care of people."

"She gets that from her incredible mother." Dan pulled Fionna close to him, allowing himself just a moment to cast his shield around her and hold her inside of his protective embrace. He needed the world to exist for the two of them alone, even if only for a moment.

"All right, if you're sure you want to do this."

"I really do. This is the right thing to do. I can feel it."

"Yeah." Dan smiled. "I feel it too." He surprised himself. Ioses Predilects didn't feel much of anything. They were driven to protect with every ounce of their energy. But being intertwined with a Receiver had made Dan a better person. She'd taught him to feel not just to think.

"Do you know what Jeff might like to eat?"

"He's a twenty-year-old guy. He'll eat pretty much anything as long as it's supplied in mass quantity."

She chuckled. "Got it."

"I have the next period off if you want to stay." Dan hadn't intended to sound as pleading as he did.

Fionna gave him his smile. "I need to go get everything ready."

"I guess I should probably see what I can find out about Chancellor Wilshire, and I need to call my dad about what just happened. Something's not right with the drug tests."

Fionna looked crestfallen once again. "I don't know what's going on with the drug tests, but Chancellor Wilshire did it. He's having an affair."

"Oh honey, I know," Dan assured her. "I knew as soon as he got within ten feet of you, but they have to have more evidence if they're going to suspend him."

"Well, good luck, I guess. It really shouldn't take more than a Receiver telling them something."

"I know, baby doll. I just don't know how to change it." He squeezed her tight again. "I love you…so much. I would never ever do something like that." He sensed the plaguing murmurs in her mind.

"I know. I'm the luckiest woman in the world. I have a real man."

CHAPTER 13

ADMIRATION AND ACCOLADES

Jeff met him outside of his office. "Mentor Vindico, really, you don't have to put us up. I can't thank you enough for all you've already done."

"If I go home without you and Becca, my wife will be thoroughly disappointed, and here's a piece of advice if I may—if it is at all within your power not to disappoint your wife, don't."

Jeff offered a chuckle. "Are you kidding me? I'll take your advice all day long. Keep it coming, please."

Offering him a half grin, Dan tried not to be flattered. "Just let me grab my stuff. Do we need to go by your mom's and get your things?"

"Yeah, if you don't mind. I told Bec she could just wear my T-shirts. Her parents won't even let her come get her clothes. She only has the stuff she snuck out with this morning."

"I plan to have a little chat with the governor."

"Do you think you could get through to him?"

"If I can't, I'd be willing to bet the Haydenshires could."

"I hate that I'm doing this to her." Jeff sounded utterly heartbroken.

Dan offered him a kind smile. "You aren't the one that won't let her back in her house. If you want to make something better, then fight for it."

Determination set in Jeff's eyes as he gave a single nod, but he also looked overwhelmed and exhausted. Becca appeared, glowing crimson and biting her lip nervously. Jeff immediately relieved her of her backpack. "We'll just follow you. I can get my stuff later. I don't want you to have to go out of your way."

Becca shook her head. "I'll go by your mom's and get your stuff. Riding in his Ferrari is the only thing that's actually made you smile in, like, two weeks," she whispered.

"Where's your mom's apartment?" Dan asked.

"It's way out."

Dan wondered if Jeff didn't want him seeing where he lived.

"In Triangle," he explained uncomfortably.

"If you don't mind my taking you, it's only a half hour," Dan pointed out. "Fi and I live in Arlington."

"You're sure?"

"Becca, if you want, I can give you directions to the house and you can go on, or you can follow us." Dan led the kids toward his car.

"I'll follow you," Becca assured him.

Dan didn't point out that it was a waste of gas, and he was beyond certain that she had a gas card that her daddy paid the bill on. If the governor was determined to break Jeff and Becca up and to get rid of the baby, he'd probably canceled all of her credit cards. Dan decided to keep his mouth shut. They didn't need any more stress at the moment.

He unlocked the doors and withdrew his shield cast. Jeff walked Becca to her car in the student parking lot and then returned. He couldn't quite hide his grin as he eased into the passenger seat.

Chuckling, Dan backed out and waited on Becca. Uncomfortable silence drowned the car momentarily.

"Uh...so...how'd you meet Fionna Styler?"

Figuring that was as good a place as any to jump off, Dan smiled. "She attended Venton with me, so we knew each other. But I officially got together with her at an Angels' after-party at Anglington's Bar the last challenge of the season."

"Cool," Jeff offered distractedly.

"Yeah, it was that." Dan smiled. "Can I ask you something?"

"Sure."

"What do you think of Mentor Sherman?"

"Honestly?"

"I won't say anything. Just tell me the truth."

"My God, he is such a loser."

Dan cracked up. "I knew I liked you."

"He's the mentor's aide in my Energies of Physics class, but he has no freaking clue what he's doing. Half the time I teach the class for him. And he's always like, 'I'm best friends with Rainer Lawson and Logan Haydenshire,'" Jeff continued. Dan had struck upon something. "And I'm like, dude, I was friends with Rainer and Logan before they graduated. They were friends with you because Logan's, like, a *really*, really nice guy. They are cool. You are not."

Still laughing, Dan could hardly believe that it had only been a year since Logan and Rainer had graduated. "I'm sorry they couldn't come out today."

"It's okay. We hung out a lot when they were in school. Rainer was the Head of Ioses, so I worked with him a bunch. He was always with Emily though."

"Yeah, well, they've sort of been attached at the hip since they were toddlers."

"Yeah, I know. I was supposed to go to their wedding with Bec, but I took a subcontracting job on the weekends, so I had to miss it. You and Mrs. Vindico were in the wedding though, right?"

"Yeah." Dan got onto the interstate and made certain Becca's car was behind him. "And my daughter was their flower girl."

"Aida, right?" Jeff quizzed. Dan nodded. "Oh and hey, you don't have to worry. I'll just sleep on your couch or whatever. I'm used to it. We won't do anything at your house." Jeff's cheeks blazed red.

Assuming that Aida was Jeff's concern, Dan shook his head. "You're not sleeping on my couch. We have a guest bed in the guest bedroom. You desperately need a good night's sleep. You're marrying her tomorrow, right?"

"Yes, sir," Jeff pledged. "Becca's actually really excited despite everything."

"This might not be how she had it in her head, but women tend to like knowing that you're going to be there no matter what, just like we like knowing that."

"I'm going to be there. My dad never wanted to have anything to do with me. He stopped even paying child support when I was, like, four. I'm not doing that. I'm not making Becca go through this alone, and I'm gonna be there for my kid. I love her." He sounded almost shocked by his own determination.

"Then you're already ten times the guy your father is. And I really don't care what you and Becca do. I'm pretty sure she can't get more pregnant," he joked. "I mean, I'd rather not hear it," he offered wryly, making Jeff glow purple.

Dan pulled into the ancient apartment complex and drove to Jeff's mother's apartment in the very back.

"I'll hurry," Jeff assured.

"I'm good."

True to his word, Jeff returned less than three minutes later carrying two duffle bags. He offered three times to drive Becca's car for her, but she insisted that he ride with Dan.

"He's like your biggest hero. Ride with him. You've been the best guy ever with all of this. You were so brave to talk to him and to my parents, and they were so mean to you, and then my stupid brothers. I love you. I want you to smile again. You were so bummed when he resigned, and now you get to hang out with him."

They hadn't realized that Dan had lowered the windows. He wasn't supposed to have heard that.

"Hey, you said you'd marry me, so I'm the happiest guy around."

Dan stared down at his phone. Watching them made his heart ache.

"Let's go," Becca urged. "Maybe I can help Mrs. Vindico do something. I want to help however we can."

Jeff walked her back to her car before returning to the Ferrari. He was silent for a minute, and Dan debated asking him about Chancellor Wilshire.

"I read online about you taking down Wretchkinsides's son in Paris." His energy was frantic and nervous as he broached the subject.

"Yeah." Dan nodded. "That was pretty much the worst vacation ever."

The tension in Jeff's energy strains eased. "What an idiot. I mean, messing with Mrs. Vindico and your little girl. He had to have a death wish or something."

"I assured him when we arrested him that if he ever tried something like that again, he'd get his wish."

Jeff looked deeply impressed. "It's okay if my mom comes to the wedding thing tomorrow, right?" His thoughts appeared to come in confusing bursts.

"I'm sure."

"I need to get Becca a ring."

"Do you have any money?" Dan hoped he wasn't being nosy.

"A little. I've been saving for a ring for a while. But I also tried to help my mom pay the bills so... I hate to get her something from a pawn shop, but that's really all I can afford."

"My ring came from a little open-air market in Kauai. I think we paid around seventy-five dollars for it, but I've never taken it off. And Fi has her mom's wedding band. Just like the wedding, it's what it means to you not how much you paid for it."

Jeff studied Dan for a long moment. "Yeah, I know, but that engagement ring you gave her had to cost you a bundle."

Dan couldn't deny that. "Okay, so life's a little easier if you get your girlfriend pregnant in your thirties than in your twenties, but doesn't mean this can't be done."

"I couldn't have done any of this without you. I really can't thank you enough for the appointment."

"I really am happy to help. Fi and I would like to be there for you and Becca. This is going to be a long, hard year," Dan explained though he knew that Jeff was aware of that. "Can I ask you something and you keep it between you and me?"

"Of course."

"I know you heard the rumor about Chancellor Wilshire."

"Becca was in one of Mentor Bryant's classes last year. Trust me, it isn't just a rumor."

Stunned disbelief rocked through Dan. "They were messing around at the school?!"

"Not really, but I knew. He was always coming in at the end of Bryant's classes. She was always up in the admin office. They were just a little too close, you know. I could tell something was up."

Dan offered Jeff a smile. "You're gonna make a great detective and an excellent Iodex officer."

"That's what I've wanted to be forever."

Dan understood that. It was all he'd ever wanted to do right up until he'd walked out of Anglington's Bar with Fionna Styler.

"Thanks, but that stuff with Wilshire, that's not cool. I know I'm only twenty or whatever, but when you marry someone, it seems like that should be forever."

"Good man."

Jeff visibly hemmed for a moment. "Hey sir, could I ask you something about the lecture this morning? By the way, that was awesome. I learned more today than I have in the last five years at school. But this has to do with Chancellor Wilshire."

"Ask." Dan already knew what was coming.

"Why do you think the chancellor decided to have an affair? It's against the law in the Realm even though it's not prosecuted much, but for him it could lose him his job."

"What you just said is along the lines of what I was really hoping someone would ask. Not about Wilshire necessarily, but about why the consequences aren't a deterrent. It could and most likely *will* lose him his job, but consequences very rarely outweigh the underlying reason that someone does something wrong. The knowledge that someone could end up serving time rarely makes them stop and think."

Intrigue lit in Jeff's shield. "Okay, so why did Chancellor Wilshire and Mentor Bryant do what they did? Power?" he guessed.

Dan nodded. "And privilege and a whole lot of position. Anyone involved in an affair quickly decides that it is within their power to indulge their lust, and in doing so, they feel more powerful. That can quickly become an addiction. Then they tell themselves that they are powerful enough to keep other people from finding out, so what's the real harm." Dan shook his head in disgust. "But in this case, their positions played a big part. He is in authority over her. That can be very compelling from both parties, and again with position, if you've indulged once, it's very easy to keep going because you've already broken all of the barriers. There's always fear that if you're the one who calls it quits, your partner in crime, quite literally, will then have power over you. They could always tell people. You've enslaved yourself to the lie."

Jeff shook his head. "The whole thing is sick."

"That it is." Dan pulled into the garage and Aida appeared. Becca pulled into the driveway.

"Daddy!" She raced into his arms.

"Hey, baby girl." Dan scooped her up in an exuberant embrace. Jeff carried his duffle bags along with the few items Becca had snuck out of her house that morning. Aida smiled at them. "Aida, this is Jeff and Becca. They're students of mine and friends of mine and Mommy's."

Jeff looked thrilled, and Becca grinned over his exuberance.

"Hi, I'm Aida."

"Hi there." Becca beamed at her. They entered the house through the garage. Jeff looked deeply impressed with his surroundings. Becca seemed much more comfortable.

"Mommy said you're going to spend the night, and that I get to help," Aida explained.

"Oh, we can help," Becca leapt. Fionna appeared in one of her many aprons. She loved creating aprons from vintage fabrics with her own design flare, and she was wearing one of her favorites.

"Hey, sweetheart." Dan relaxed as soon as he saw her.

"Hey." She brushed a kiss on his cheek. "Well, come on in. Aida, why don't you show them the guest bedroom so they can put their things away?"

"Okay." Aida wiggled out of Dan's arms. "It's this way." She pointed up the stairs. Jeff and Becca shared an uncomfortable glance but followed Aida. "This is baby Halia's room," she gave them a guided tour. "But mommy's sewing machine won't still be in here when Daddy takes baby Halia out of her tummy," she explained, making Dan and Fionna chuckle. "And this is the guest room."

Jeff deposited the bags but Aida kept going. "This is the bathroom, and this is my room."

"It's a really pretty room," Becca assured her. "I love your unicorn pillows."

"Thank you! This is Sophie. She's my baby doll that Emily gave me. You can hold her."

Dan eased up the stairs to investigate.

"Oh, thank you." Becca was cradling the doll when Dan approached. Aida appeared to have picked up on something in Becca's energy as she held the doll.

She moved to Dan and cupped her hand around her mouth. He leaned down so she could whisper in his ear. Feeling his heart prick, he smiled. "Aida wants to know if she can give you a hug."

Becca began to cry in earnest as Aida embraced her.

"It's okay," Aida soothed. "When I lived in the orphanage, sometimes I cried at night because I was so scared and I missed my mamãe and pai, but then I got to come live here. And I have a mommy and a daddy and a baby sister, and if I get scared and miss mamãe and pai here then Mommy says it's okay to miss them, and we talk about them, and then Daddy makes me feel better so they'll make you feel better too."

Jeff closed his eyes momentarily as Dan slapped him on the back. "For about the first week she lived here, every time she spoke I was in tears," Dan assured him.

"No joke, man." Jeff swallowed back the emotion that was coursing so closely to the surface in his exhaustion.

Fionna moved up the stairs. She took in Aida and Becca embracing and grinned.

"Do you want to see Mommy and Daddy's room?"

"We better not do that." Jeff shook his head as Dan and Fionna guided everyone back down the steps.

Dan turned on *Supernova* for Aida and joined Fionna, Jeff, and Becca in the kitchen.

"Dr Pepper, or water, or anything," Fionna was concluding her drink offer.

"Am I allowed to have Dr Pepper?" Becca asked.

"I have maybe two or three a week, but the rest of the time I drink water."

"Except for her coffee," Dan teased.

"Halia likes coffee too." Fionna laughed.

"I don't know anything about what I'm supposed to do, so I've just been drinking water," Becca explained.

"If you have any questions, I'll do my best to answer them. I have a little experience." She rubbed her hands over her bump. "And if I don't know, Mrs. Haydenshire will."

"I'm sure," Jeff vowed.

"You don't mind me asking you questions?" Becca sounded both thrilled and terrified.

Fionna gave her a sweet smile. "Of course not. Here, why don't we make the boys go play, and you and I will have some girl talk."

Chuckling, Dan nodded. "I believe we're being kicked out."

"Sweetly," Fionna assured him. "Dinner will be ready in about an hour. Why don't you see if our little girl wants to go to the park?"

Dan understood that she wanted Becca to feel comfortable asking anything and that she wanted Dan, Jeff, and Aida farther away than the living room.

"Do you need to do your homework or anything," Dan asked Jeff.

"Oh no, sir. I usually do it in my off periods and at lunch."

Dan was impressed. "You mind hanging out with me and Aida at the park?"

"No, I'm good with anything you want me to do."

A few minutes later, Dan walked hand in hand with Aida out their backyard to the adjoining park behind the house. It was one of the reasons he'd purchased the home after Amelia had been killed. There were dozens of running trails, and Dan had run them all repeatedly. Now, he ran in the mornings and then walked them with Fionna and Aida after dinner.

Aida was telling Dan about her day as they walked along, with Jeff trying not to intrude. "And Haley says thank you so much for her lunch. I told her my mommy makes the best sandwiches, and when she took a bite she smiled and said yum," Aida explained. "I would like Haley to come to my house to play."

"Sure, baby, just ask mommy, okay?"

They reached the large swing set a few blocks from the house. Aida spied a little girl from her class and ran off to play while Jeff and Dan seated themselves on a bench.

"I wonder what Bec wants to know?" Jeff glanced back the direction they'd walked.

"Probably the same stuff you want to know but aren't asking me," Dan allowed wryly. Jeff joined in his laughter.

Aida waved from the top of the slide. Dan blew her a kiss, making her beam.

"You're a great dad. She feels so safe with you. I could tell."

Dan smiled. Making someone safe was always the top priority to a Shield, so that would've been what Jeff noticed. What he was actually saying was—she feels so loved.

"I'm sure we'll screw a bunch of stuff up, but she knows I love her and that I'll keep her safe. I kind of think that's about eighty percent of the game. The rest is just doing whatever my wife says."

"I just wish I knew what to do for her." Jeff finally seemed to prick the surface of all of the strain and worry he'd been carrying for the last few weeks. "I never really had a dad, but I want to be a really good one. And I want to be a good husband, but I don't really know how." Defeat threatened to drown his tone. "Mrs. Vindico looks so happy. You must do everything right."

Dan shook his head. "No one does everything right, but I think at the end of the day, if you're there with her no matter what the day held—if you keep talking and telling her and showing her you love her—then in the end, it will work out. You just have to be determined not to let her parents, or the baby, or school, or work—or hell, the world—tear you apart. Think about her first in everything you do. You don't have to be perfect. You just have to be there."

"If I'd done that, she wouldn't be pregnant and kicked out of the Sapmans' mansion," Jeff sighed dejectedly.

"Right, because she didn't want to do that. It was all you, right?"

This brought on another blush, but Dan seemed to be getting through. "I just feel so freaking stupid. How could I have forgotten to cast her?" Jeff let his head fall into his hands.

"Been there," Dan agreed with a sigh.

Jeff seemed to let more of his guard down. "You really don't care if I ask you stuff?"

"How many times do I have to tell you that Fi and I want to be there for you two?"

"No one's ever wanted to be there for me, except for maybe Becca and my mom," he amended.

"Add me to the list, and ask me what you want to know." Jeff grew thoughtful. "You can ask anytime."

Realization tensed in both of Dan's strains.

"What's wrong?" Jeff asked.

"I kind of think you and Becca might should stay with us until you get a paycheck. How are you going to buy food?"

"I don't know. I don't know how we're going to buy anything. Furniture, food, clothes, stuff for the baby," he listed himself further into depression.

"One day at a time. The baby won't be here for a long while. And Fi and I have a storage unit full of furniture from when we combined our houses. Her bed's in there, couches, tables, tons of stuff. If you and Becca could use it, you'd be saving me a hundred bucks a month." Dan tried not to make Jeff feel like a charity case.

"I'm such a loser."

"Hey, stop. You're not a loser. You know Rainer and Logan lived rent free in the Haydenshires' guesthouse for a year, and they used furniture from storage. I'm certain you know what kind of money Rainer has," Dan reminded him. Jeff gave a hesitant nod.

"You put in the time and the hard work now, save every penny you can, eat at school and at the Senate when you can, and by the end of the school year, you can step into the National Iodex office with a year of training under your belt. That's a pretty substantial paycheck for a guy right out of the academy."

"Yeah, plenty enough to take care of Bec and the baby. She wouldn't even have to work if she doesn't want to, but I can't buy her a mansion."

"I didn't get the impression that she wants what her parents have. She seems to want to be married to you and to have a family with you.

Believe me, I grew up in Governor Vindico's manor house, and I don't want what my parents have. I want Fi and my girls, doesn't matter where we live so long as they're with me. In fact, the cottage we live in when we're in Kauai—our favorite place in the world—you could fit that entire cottage in my living room and part of my kitchen."

"I can't let you feed me and Bec for a week and give me furniture and stuff," he finally managed in a heartbroken whisper. Dan considered momentarily. "I just don't think my mom can afford groceries for me and Becca."

"Tell you what, you and Becca agree to stay with us until Senate payday next week, and I'll let you help me out with some stuff around the house. We weren't here all summer, and I'm a little behind with the yard. Fi wants the nursery painted and the dining room wainscoted," he began listing off chores that needed to be done.

"I'll do it. I'll do anything you need. I'm good with stuff like that. I usually do manual labor all summer because it pays quick and a lot of money."

"I appreciate your help. And in answer to the question you desperately want to ask, but just can't seem to, no, you won't hurt Becca or the baby if you sleep with her. It's actually really good for the baby to feel your energy, not just Becca's."

"That obvious?" He grimaced.

Dan laughed and shook his head. "Not obvious at all, but that was my first question too, both times I found out she was pregnant."

Jeff seemed to fully relax as he nodded. "I know it's none of my business, but I am really sorry about what happened the first time. That was rough."

"It was that." Dan found it oddly cathartic to discuss it with one of his students of all people. "But you know, we took a horrible situation and turned it around. Doesn't change the pain or the heartbreak over what happened, but we have to go on. If I'd decided to let it end me, then I wouldn't be sitting here talking to you watching my baby girl pick wildflowers and feeling my other one kick when she hears my voice."

"She knows your voice?" Jeff sounded impressed.

"Yeah." Dan smiled. "I've been locking onto her, talking to Fionna's stomach since we first found out she was pregnant again. So now, she knows my energy, and she recognizes my voice. It's pretty cool."

"Do you, uh…do you think you could teach me how to do that?"

"Sure." Dan was pleased that he wanted it badly enough to have asked. Jeff gazed out at Aida and the little girl from her class. They were to the side of the slide picking the last of the wildflowers before the first freeze.

"Is that why you decided to adopt? Because of what happened the first time?" Jeff sounded truly heartbroken for Dan.

Dan shook his head. "We didn't really decide to adopt. Some people would say it was all a big coincidence, but I don't believe that. She was brought to us by way of Garrett Haydenshire, but there were definitely heavenly angels involved. Fi and the Angels went to Brazil last year to work in the orphanage there. Emily and Fionna fell in love with Aida, of course," he explained.

"So, Rainer arranged for Aida to come live on Haydenshire Farm for the summer and be in their wedding. Anyway, while we were all there getting ready for the wedding, Aida arrives and we found out that the guy who shot Fi and killed the baby,"—Dan choked back a sudden onslaught of emotion—"also killed her parents and her older brothers." He gestured his head to Aida. "But she doesn't know that."

Jeff nodded his understanding.

"We didn't even talk about it." Dan chuckled to cover his emotion. "Fionna looked up at me with those beautiful brown eyes full of tears, and Aida smiled, and I was sold—no going back. One of the best damn decisions I ever made."

Jeff grinned. "You do look a lot happier now than you did when I'd watch you do press reports when you were Chief of Elite."

Dan laughed. "I'm glad someone noticed."

Aida rushed toward them, smiling and effectively ending their conversation.

"You ready to go, baby girl?" Dan asked as she crawled up in his lap. Jeff watched them intently.

"Yes, and I picked Mommy some flowers and Becca some." She divided the large bouquet she'd created. "You can give them to her. She really likes you, and she doesn't want you to be sad anymore."

"So now, I'm surrounded by incredibly strong Receivers." Dan chuckled.

Jeff accepted the flowers. "Thank you. I'll give them to her when we get back."

They worked their way back to the house. The ladies were both smiling and looking thick as thieves.

"I made my pulled pork tacos." Fionna seemed worried that Jeff and Becca wouldn't like them.

"Anything is fine, and it smells amazing," Jeff assured her.

"They are amazing." Dan kissed the side of Fionna's head.

"Daddy made me some tortillas. I just picked them up after I got Aida, so they should be fresh." As Fionna had prepared a huge pot full of tender pulled pork marinated with peppers—a recipe from her stepmom, Gretta—there was plenty to go around.

Jeff ate four helpings at Fionna and Dan's urging. He didn't look like he'd ever eaten something so delicious or that he'd ever really eaten until he was filled.

Fionna had sliced mangoes, onions, lettuce, and corn for the tacos, and Jeff and Becca seemed to finally relax and settle in after they ate. They cleaned the kitchen thoroughly.

Dan fixed the tea Fionna had been drinking at nights since she first found out she was pregnant for both of the ladies.

Fionna grinned at Becca. "My mom drank this tea every night when she was pregnant with me. It'll help your hormones stay balanced and help you relax. I'll order you the Scholera tea Tutu makes so you can have that as well."

After Aida was in bed, Dan retold the story of him trying to pick Aida up from the first day of school. Everyone laughed heartily.

"I went in, I cried, I came out with my baby girl," Fionna explained wryly.

"I'll try that next time," Dan teased.

CHAPTER 14

ENERGY OF INTENTION

"I think Jeff and Becca might like a little instruction on how Jeff can lock on to the baby's rhythms," Dan eased. Becca looked intrigued.

Fionna smiled. "I don't have to do this anymore since Halia is so big now, but at first I had to try and suppress as much of my energy as I could."

Dan tried to recall everything he remembered from the first time he felt Halia. "Put your hands on her lower abdomen. The baby starts out a lot lower than I'd thought." Jeff nodded. "Work your way through Becca's rhythms and then the baby's are much faster with much smaller arcs."

"I'll give you the stuff to put on your belly so you don't get stretch marks too," Fionna reminded Becca.

"You don't have to do that. I can't even pay you for that or the tea."

"You don't have to pay me for it. I want you to have it. I have tons and my grandmother will send me more whenever I need it. That's when Dan started out locking on to her at first. After he rubbed me down at night, I was relaxed so it was easier to feel her."

Becca had been yawning since dinner. "I'm so sorry," she apologized after another deep yawn. "I don't know why I'm so tired."

Everyone gave her quizzical gazes and tried not to chuckle. "But it's so little. How is it making me so sleepy?"

"I do remember thinking that," Fionna agreed. Then she headed up the stairs. She returned with a new brown screw-top jar of kukui and coconut oils and handed them to Becca.

"Take her on to bed. We're heading up in a little while," Dan urged Jeff.

"Are you sure you don't mind?" Jeff pointed up the stairs. He looked bewildered and terrified.

"It's that or the crib, but you're not sleeping on the couch."

"Thank you so much for everything." Becca threw her arms around Fionna's neck. "I just don't know what we would do without you."

"You'll be fine as long as you stick together," Fionna vowed. "But let us make it a little easier."

"Thank you, and really, I'll do anything you need," Jeff reminded Dan.

"Just take care of her. That's the most important thing."

Jeff took Becca's hand and seemed to will courage from the air around him. He led her up the stairs after several more thank yous and good nights.

Dan heard the door close and he smiled. "They've never spent the night together," he explained as Fionna tucked herself onto his chest.

"I figured." Fionna sighed. "He's so terrified, and she just doesn't know what to do."

"They'll figure it out, and we'll help them," Dan promised. "You were right. This helps us too."

"I told you." She whispered a kiss on his jaw.

~

Jeff Strenton

Unable to determine why his heart was racing, Jeff eased the door to the guest room closed. Becca reached for his hand. He supplied it, and she instantly drew from him.

The sensation had him panting. It was heavenly. It was everything he so desperately wanted to be for her—her Shield, her protector. His energy held everything he wanted to give to her—his love and his adoration, though he knew he'd never deserve Becca Sapman.

"Are you okay?" he whispered

"The Vindicos are so nice. I feel bad I thought he was mean for so long."

"They are really nice." He was just as overwhelmed by their generosity as she was. She blinked back another round of tears. They seemed to come with no provocation at all.

He couldn't stand to watch her cry. She'd been in tears off and on for the last several weeks, and it was all his fault. Becca turned and buried her head on his shoulder. He embraced her immediately.

"I'm so sorry," he pled for the thousandth time though it didn't change anything.

"Please stop saying that. I know this isn't how we planned it, but I want to make this work. Just please stop saying you're sorry and start saying that we're not gonna end up divorced and hating each other. Because if I have you, then I know I'll be fine. That's all I need."

"Hey." Jeff pulled away to look her in the eye. "I'm not going anywhere. I want to be married to you. I've wanted to marry you since I asked you to the freshman formal, and you actually said yes." He was still unable to believe his luck. "You're just so sweet and good and perfect." He tenderly pushed a strand of her long blonde hair behind her ear. She let her eyes close from the touch. "I don't deserve you. I feel like now I've ruined everything for you."

"You haven't ruined anything," Becca pled. "That's what I keep telling you. We can make this work. It's just like Mrs. Vindico said— we'll be okay as long as we're in this together."

Jeff pulled her back to him, desperate to feel her wrapped up in the safety of his embrace. "I'm right here, and I'm not going anywhere. Just you and me, okay?"

She nodded and then she gave him her sweet smile. "And the baby," she whispered.

"Of course." Jeff certainly hadn't meant to leave out their child. He hesitated but then forced himself to go on. Delicately and with precise gentleness, he let his hand caress her abdomen. She swallowed. Her heart raced as his touch joined their rhythms.

"Do you want to try and feel it?"

Jeff nodded and tried to will away his fear. He wanted to be the man she needed and the dad he'd never had. Becca stepped back slightly and unsnapped her jeans. Jeff's heart raced as he began lambasting himself. He didn't deserve to be with her, not after all of this, but God, he wanted her so badly he hurt.

He was desperate to feel her around him again. It was the most exquisite thing he'd ever experienced. That tight, wet, perfect heat of her—he'd take on armies to feel that.

They used to lie in her bed up in her room in the Sapmans' gargantuan house. They would start out studying, but it always ended up with their books shoved on the floor and him slipping her jeans off and then slipping deeply inside of her. He would hold her close and whisper how much he loved her until just before her parents came home from work.

Then they would redress and finish their homework. The past summer had been perfection. She would bring him lunch wherever he was working. Then when he finished for the afternoon, he'd take her home. She'd meet him in the shower and they'd finish in the bed unbeknownst to anyone else. They would talk about after graduation, dream about Jeff having a job at Iodex and her teaching at the private preschool where she desperately wanted to work, but her parents wouldn't allow it yet. The Sapman children weren't to work until after graduation. They would talk about buying a house after he somehow convinced her father to let Becca marry him.

Jeff knew the governor didn't think he was good enough for Becca. Jeff also knew he was right. They just disagreed on whether or not Jeff could *become* good enough for her.

Becca hoisted her jeans off and carefully pulled the decorative pillows off the bed. She pulled her sweater over her head and a slight moan escaped Jeff. He couldn't seem to help it.

She moved to her duffle bags and pulled one of his Ioses T-shirts out. Jeff moved to her and brushed a tender kiss on her lips. He needed to taste her, needed to feel her energy just for a moment.

His hands caressed her sides. Her skin felt was satin to his callused fingers, rough from the work he tried to pick up on the weekends. She shuddered. Her breath came in the familiar pants that drove him wild.

Unable to stop himself, Jeff slipped his right hand down her back, kneading her backside in the soft lace panties she was wearing. She shuddered against him, and the war in his mind waged on.

"Come here." Becca took his hand and led him to the bed. She left the T-shirt on top of her bag. She reclined and edged the panties past her mound. Jeff's mouth went dry and then began watering so fiercely he could hardly speak. He watched her eyes close as she tried to suppress her own energy. Trying to remember everything Mentor Vindico had instructed him to do, Jeff concentrated.

"Where do I put my hands?" he whispered, trying not to break her concentration.

"I'm not sure. He said low, so try here." She took his hands and laid them on her abdomen just over her mound. Swallowing down his desperate yearning, Jeff let his eyes close. He felt Becca's energy first. He concentrated as he let it permeate him. She was worried and fettered, but there, beneath the worry, was desire and love and contentment.

Elation filled him as he realized that she wanted to be right where they were. He seated himself on the side of the bed and continued to concentrate. He gasped as he thought he felt something.

Sliding his hands just slightly to the left, he caught it again. Becca's eyes flew open as tears fell from them. "Do you feel it?"

Jeff nodded, unable to believe that he'd had a part in something so miraculous. He felt his baby's tiny developing rhythms. With stunning realization, he understood that they were smaller, faster versions of his own.

"Fionna said that she knew they were having a girl because she's a Receiver, but I can't tell yet."

"I don't care what we're having as long as it's healthy and you're okay." Jeff lost the rhythms as he spoke.

"Jeff," Becca whispered. She gazed up at him with all of the love he felt for her.

"Yeah, baby?" He hadn't called her that since she'd told him, terrified he'd bring on more tears, but it seemed to bring her peace instead. "Will you please just hold me?"

"Of course." He kicked off his boots and undressed. He moved around the bed and climbed in beside her, still unable to believe that he was getting to sleep all night with Becca in Dan Vindico's house.

It was like a very bizarre dream come true. She popped the clasp on her bra as she rolled and laid her head on his chest. He tried desperately not to stare at her breasts and to be there for her.

His breath caught and his cock strained as she clung to him wearing nothing but a pair of panties. Her breasts were swollen larger than he'd ever seen them. They were fevered. He knew that had to hurt. They moved against him as she drew breath.

"I love you so much." He was desperate for her to know.

"I love you too," she whispered. Her energy rolled in languid waves. She was finally happy and content. It seemed like a lifetime since he'd felt her rhythms ease and spin around him without stress or fear making them tense.

"I'm always gonna be there, okay, baby. Always," he vowed.

"Promise?" she choked.

He kissed the top of her head sweetly as he held her to his bare chest. "I promise," Jeff vowed.

Becca moved suddenly. She leaned up and studied him. "Please, just for a little while. Just be with me. Make it all go away for a while. I don't want to think about it anymore. I just want to feel you. I want to get lost in you."

She moved her mouth to his, and he cradled her head with his hand and guided her luscious lips to his. He began devouring her mouth. It had been too long. He knew it was wrong. He knew he should never have done it in the first place, but he wasn't strong enough to tell her no. She just felt too damn good, like a drug he never wanted to stop taking. He turned her so she was under him as she began panting for breath.

"Becca, baby, mmm," he grunted as her hand wrapped around his strain timidly.

"I want to feel it," she begged. She grasped him with more force, and he gasped for breath. His eyes rolled back in his head. "I want to feel it deep inside me. I want our baby to feel your energy inside of mine."

A shuddering groan echoed from his lungs. He gave up the fruitless fight knowing that it was a futile endeavor. He'd never been able to turn her down, and he was going to make her his wife the next day. He slipped his hands to her breasts but immediately felt their tenderness.

He forced his hands away by sheer strength of will. "Does it hurt if I touch them?" He couldn't stand for her to be in pain. The afternoon he'd taken her virginity two years before had threatened to make him violently ill. He shut that thought down quickly as Becca shook her head.

"It feels better when you lift them and rub them. It feels amazing, actually," she confessed. His cock pulsed against her. She moaned as she felt it as well.

Working timidly, he gauged her energy and her responses. Jeff eased her breasts upward and lifted their weight. She cried out for him, and he added to the pressure driving her wild. Her back arched as she pushed them toward his mouth, and he almost lost it all. He dipped his head to her and swirled his tongue over her nipples as they pulsated in his mouth, begging for more.

"Yes," Becca urged. "Please."

With a furtive moan, Jeff gave himself over to the ecstasy of her desire. He sucked her and reveled in her erotic energy as it flowed through his mouth. She writhed between him and the mattress.

He longed to shut out the world to be with her and her alone. To let everything that had gone so wrong go and to cling to the only thing in his life that was right. He slid his hand from her breast to her mound. He pulled his mouth away just long enough to pull the panties from her.

Air hissed from his lungs. He fought a voracious growl as he felt the tender wet heat that had gathered in the lace. Gently, he brushed his fingertips over the sweet soft curls just slightly darker than her hair that covered what Jeff was certain was a portion of heaven between her legs.

Her breath caught deliciously as she bucked under his touch. He slipped his fingers hesitantly inside her, terrified he might somehow disturb the baby or hurt her. But she wanted more. Her eyes flashed in a hungry plea as she ground her body against his hand.

"God, I missed touching you." He crawled back up her, coaxing the spots that made her the wettest with his plying fingers. The way her body moved against his, the way she melded into his soul, set him on fire. He inhaled the sweet scent of her mixed with the heady scent of sex as it permeated the air around them. His shield lit in craving delight.

He loved the way he could always smell her scent on his skin whenever he had the extraordinary honor of being with her. He dipped his fingers in farther and gave her more friction.

"Are you ready for me?" he pled, unable to wait any longer. She nodded, her breath coming in stuttered pants.

"Please, now," she begged, sounding terrified to make the request.

"Spread your legs for me," he soothed, watching as she opened herself up for him. He separated her lips gently, feeling them swell under his prodding. He pushed in slowly, taking her inch by delicious inch, easing himself inside of her perfection.

Letting the heavenly sensation wash through him, mend and heal his weary mind, he gasped as she took him all. Her sweet moans grew louder and more frantic. He kissed her quickly, letting her bury her need in his mouth as he buried himself inside of her. He pulled away, gasping for breath as he began slowly thrusting into her. She was tight and swollen. She felt like heaven, but he didn't want her to hurt the next day.

"You feel so damn good," he gasped, unable not to tell her as he forced his shield out of his pores until he surrounded her in it. "Your sweet pussy is so wet for me."

She went wild as she inhaled the essence of him in her panting breaths and felt him pull all of the terror and fear and all of the rejection from her soul and soothe it with his love and his tender care.

Her breath washed from her body as she writhed underneath his thrusts. He ground against her, and she spilled out for him in trembling waves that shook through her body. He lost it all.

He was unable to bring her again. It was a skill he'd been working on, but it had been too long. There had been too much tension and too much need buried in the harrowing fear. He filled her full, and she clenched tightly around him, pulling the energy from him as he took hers.

Jeff fell to the bed beside her, trying not to squeak the mattress as he was finally able to remember where they were. He cradled her to his chest.

"I love you so much," he began his customary reassurances though he was exhausted. It seemed so much more important this night that she know of his undying love and devotion. He was certain the next year would be the hardest of their lives, but he would fight every single day for her.

"Do you want one of my T-shirts to sleep in?" He wished that she would just stay the way she was. Having her caught up in his arms with nothing between them was perfection. Becca hemmed. He could feel nervous energy move in where satisfaction had been moments before.

"Mrs. Vindico told me that she always sleeps naked. That the baby kind of lies against Mentor Vindico when he holds her. She loves that," Becca whispered hesitantly.

Finding that information uncomfortable and somewhat shocking, Jeff laughed. "She told you that?"

"I'd never tell anyone but you, but she answered all of my questions—even the ones she probably thought were stupid." Becca shuddered slightly beside him. "Why?"

"Because every heterosexual male at school would probably give their right arm just to know that," he tried to explain. They laughed together. It was a sensation Jeff had missed almost as much as being with her.

"Do you want me to put that stuff on you?" Jeff recalled Mrs. Vindico giving Becca a jar of what looked like ointment.

"I almost forgot. Oh my gosh, I'm gonna be a horrible mother," she panicked.

"Bec, this is all kind of new." He recalled Mentor Vindico telling him to take everything one step at a time. "And you're gonna be a great mom."

The thought of her swollen full of his baby had him reeling. He tried to envision her giving birth or him feeling the baby move, but it was just too hard to imagine.

~

Dan Vindico

Inhaling deeply before he opened his eyes, a smile spread across his face. Fionna was naked and intertwined in him. She smelled of the coconut and kukui oil he'd rubbed her down with the evening before after their bath. His brow furrowed as he caught the heavier scent. "How am I lying in our bed holding you and still smelling bacon and eggs?"

Fionna stirred against him. "I don't know, but whatever it is, I like it." She yawned deeply. "Yum, and coffee." She lifted her head and blinked as she tried to read the clock. "How early did they get up?!" She crawled on her hands and knees and arched her back to stretch it out.

Dan gave her a sexy half grin. "Yum, stay just like that."

She shook her head at him. "It's barely six. They need to sleep."

"They want to do something for us to show that they appreciate all that we're doing for them," he pointed out. Shaking her head, Fionna pulled on her robe but then halted. "I don't mind if Aida gets a peek of you, but my students are another story," Dan commanded.

Fionna was his natural beauty. She was very comfortable with being naked. It was something that drove Dan wild. She'd always slept naked, and she'd spent a large portion of their summer tucked away on her family's farm topless.

She started pulling clothes out of her dresser drawers. When Fitzroy had stayed overnight, she'd worn sweats, but that was months before she was pregnant. She dug deeper and emerged with a pair of maternity yoga pants and a black tank top that stretched over her swollen bump.

Dan pulled on a pair of workout shorts and an Iodex T-shirt. He followed her down the stairs.

Aida was sitting on the counter, still in her princess nightgown, with her hair in a tangled mass on her shoulders. "We made you breakfast," she announced.

"You did?" Fionna kissed her cheek.

"And Jeff let me crack the eggs."

"I worked as a short order cook last summer for a while when we had all that rain and construction kind of dried up, so…"

"Okay, you can stay forever," Fionna gushed as Jeff supplied her with a plate heaping with bacon, eggs, and pancakes. Becca handed her a large mug of coffee. They'd set the table neatly and added syrup, cream, and sugar near her place. Dan discreetly snuck her the honey which was her preference for coffee.

Dan gestured to the meal. "This was really nice, but you didn't have to get up and do all of this."

"I know, sir, but I really want to help out while we're here."

Dan tried not to notice how much more relaxed and serene both Jeff and Becca were that morning. He had a very good idea how they'd gone about soothing their harrowing week.

CHAPTER 15

CONSEQUENCES, CONFIRMATION, AND CHEESEBURGERS

Dan was greeted by a scowling senior standing outside his office door. "Can I talk to you?" the student demanded.

"I've got five minutes. Can you talk fast?" Dan wasn't going to be ordered around by his students.

"Yes, sir," the young man simmered down slightly. Dan opened the door and allowed him in. "What's on your mind?" Dan recalled that his name was Brent. He was in Dan's History of Defense class.

"Well," Brent seemed to lose momentum under Dan's glare. "I guess," he stammered. Drawing a deep breath and adjusting his shirt, he clenched his jaw defiantly. "I guess if I knocked up one of the governor's daughters then I'd have a guaranteed spot at Iodex as well," he finally managed to sneer. Terror cast his face as soon as the words exited his mouth. Dan calmly opened his laptop and pulled up Brent's record.

"Actually,"—he narrowed his eyes—"you wouldn't have a spot at Iodex because you have three complaints from different mentors about your disrespectful attitude and language. Now, we'll make that four, and because you have a D in Creative Writing, an F in Energy of Emotions, and a C in Humanities."

"Those aren't my defense classes. My Ioses classes are all As," Brent retorted.

"I fail to see your point. Iodex officers graduate in the top ten percent of their class. You won't be doing that with those grades nor will you be holding a position in the order with mentor complaints."

"Jeff Strenton has a B in Literature."

"I am not discussing Mr. Strenton's grades with you, but I will remind you that Mr. Strenton is in fact in the top ten percent of the graduating class and the top two percent of Ioses Order. He held office in the order last year and was unanimously reelected this year. And all of his defensive classes aren't just As, they're perfect scores. Anything else you have to say?"

Scowling, Brent began to pout. "No, sir." He spun and stomped his way out of Dan's office.

Dan drew a deep breath and wondered how many other students heard about Becca and about Jeff's appointment as he headed toward his first class. He knew better than to hope it wasn't going to get ugly.

Jeff was on the front row with his head in his hands. No one was seated near him, and the frantic whispers drowned out as Dan entered. Dan worked through the class notes. As class ended, Jeff hung back.

"What happened?" Dan saw tension move through Jeff's rhythms as he neared. Glancing around the empty classroom, Jeff shut the door.

"Bec got sick when we got here. Maybe the bacon was too much for her. She ran in the bathroom, and there were tons of other girls in there, I guess. Anyway, Paula Dickson was in there. She hates Becca. I don't know why she hates her so much, but she's a bitch."

"I would go with because Paula Dickson's father ran against Governor Sapman when he ran for office. Governor Sapman wiped the floor with him." Dan put the puzzle together for Jeff.

"She never told me that."

"She was young when he took office. She might not have known."

Jeff went on. "Anyway, Paula asked her rather loudly if she was pregnant. Becca's pretty much the worst liar ever, and then some other girl that's friends with Paula heard Becca ask me if I thought her being sick would hurt the baby. She was kind of freaking out." He concluded his account of what he clearly considered a tragedy.

"It's not an easy thing to hide," Dan reminded him.

"I know. I just didn't want it to be any harder on her."

"Just be there for her. That's all you can do."

Another round of determination armored itself in Jeff's shield. He thanked Dan and raced out of the room to walk Becca to her next class.

A broad grin spread across Dan's face as he made his way back to his office for lunch.

"Mentor Vindico, I like it." Logan Haydenshire offered Dan his hand. "But dude, I'm pretty sure you have to wear, like, sweater vests, and be carrying around some stale coffee, and losing your hair to work here," he continued to tease.

"You caffeinate him again or something, Lawson?" Dan shook Rainer and Logan's hands. He unlocked the office door, allowing two of his favorite people inside.

"Adeline's working nights. He's been like this for days," Rainer harassed. "That's why Portwood sent us out here. We can't take him anymore."

"Shut it, man. You know if it hadn't been for my little sister you would have married me," Logan quipped.

"Every day I thank God for Emily." Rainer cracked up as Dan shook his head.

Feeling nostalgia and raw regret wash through him, Dan fought the desire to beg Governor Haydenshire for his old job back. He'd been so focused on taking down Wretchkinsides, especially the last few months of his post as Chief, he hadn't had any fun with his team. He'd almost forgotten how hilarious Logan could be when he wasn't being worked to death and shouted at constantly.

"How's Jeff?" Rainer asked, losing all sense of playful banter.

"Poor kid. He's had it rough."

"Dad said the Sap-asses worked him over." Logan grimaced.

"You know we need some new punching bags in the Iodex gym," Rainer snarled.

"Hey, how'd your dad find that out?" Dan asked.

"Dad finds everything out, but I'd assume Governor Sapman let it slip."

"He really doesn't want Portwood to know."

Logan and Rainer both nodded.

"How long will he be staying with you?" Rainer asked.

"At least until payday."

"Hey, if he needs some money, I'm happy to help him out."

"You can ask him, but I can't even get him to agree to stay with us without him wanting to overhaul my house. He was up at five this morning making us breakfast."

"He's a good guy," Rainer vowed.

With that, a knock sounded on the door.

"May I?" Logan begged with a smirk.

Laughing, Dan gestured Logan to the door.

"Rainer, look!" Logan clutched his chest, batted his eyelashes, and moved beside Rainer. He laid his head on Rainer's shoulder. "It's our little Jeff-y. He's grown so much, big senior now, knocking up governor's daughters and shit."

The entire office exploded in uproarious laughter as Jeff blushed the shade of an overripe strawberry.

"Geez, Logan, would you can it?" Rainer shook his head and reached to shake Jeff's hand and slap him on the back.

"I missed you too, Logan." Jeff was still laughing, much to everyone's delight.

"Are you going to interview him or haze him?" Dan quipped.

"I'd go with both." Logan shrugged.

"Great." Jeff seemed to revel in the fact that Rainer and Logan weren't upset or disappointed in him. Logan proceeded to try and pace in the three feet of space between Dan's desk and Jeff.

"Seriously, you are never drinking Red Bull again," Rainer demanded, keeping the laughter going.

"All right, all right, let's hear it. Life right now A. Kind of sucks B. Is a shit storm, or C. Is looking up because you're getting to marry your sweet Becca-boo tonight?" Logan continued to tease Jeff.

"Is that an interview question, because I need to call Portwood if that's the shit he sent you over here with." Dan feigned concern.

"Becca-boo?" Rainer shook his head at his best friend.

"I'd go with all three or whichever choice gets me the internship," Jeff joined in the teasing, making everyone smile.

"Dude, you got it. We're just here to make sure you haven't gone nuts since we left." Logan checked his watch. "Hey, let's go get a quick lunch."

"My treat," Rainer immediately offered. Jeff looked intrigued but then shook his head. "I can't leave Bec here. Everyone's treating her like crap."

"Bring her along," Rainer scoffed. "And remember food is the only way to effectively shut him up." He pointed back to Logan.

A little while later, Dan was seated between Rainer and Logan at Big Buns, one of Dan's favorite burger joints. Rainer and Logan did settle down and explain to Jeff what some of his responsibilities would be at Iodex. They asked him the questions Portwood sent them with. Dan was both impressed with the questions and with Jeff's answers.

Jeff kept his arm draped over Becca's shoulders. She was quiet but seemed happy to be off campus for a while. Occasionally, Jeff would get a dreamy look in his eyes when she would draw from him. Rainer and Dan shared a quick chuckle but said nothing. "Hey, could you both come to your folks' tonight for everything?" Jeff asked as the burgers disappeared from their plates.

Becca looked excited for the first time. "Can Emily come?" she begged Rainer.

"Sure, we'll be there."

"I live there so sure." Logan shrugged. "Ad has to work though."

"She's the obstetrics medio, right?" Becca asked.

"She is, and because I am pretty much the very embodiment of awesome, my wife is going to see if you'd like a checkup while we're at Dan and Fi-ooo-na's Friday night."

Logan's drawing out Fionna's name coupled with his declaration of his own awesomeness elicited a giggle from Becca, which Dan knew had been his goal.

As they stood to leave, Rainer pulled Jeff to the side and walked him several paces behind everyone else. Dan saw Jeff shake his head, but Rainer was persistent.

Dan stopped at the counter to purchase Fionna some Big Buns chipotle pesto sauce which was her favorite. Logan joined Dan. He bought an, "I like Big Buns" T-shirt.

Dan continued to glance Jeff's direction. He hoped he'd let Rainer help him. But Dan saw Jeff's eyes goggle and his mouth drop open. Dan followed his gaze to the back of the restaurant. Seated in the very back booth was Chancellor Wilshire. There was a woman seated across from him. She had long, brown hair. Dan couldn't see more than the back of a hunter-green blouse she was wearing, but he knew that Mrs. Wilshire had distinctly grey hair just like the chancellor's.

"Ah geez, are you freaking kidding me?" Logan spat under his breath. "As if Dad isn't getting enough phone calls, he's gonna parade it out at restaurants five miles from campus."

Dan urged everyone out of Big Buns. Becca took Jeff back by his mother's apartment to pick up his truck. They were also going to pick up wedding bands. According to her, Jeff's truck only ran about half of the time. After deciding that he would take Jeff and his truck to visit Sam, Dan drove home with his mind full of the debacle with the chancellor.

CHAPTER 16

HOSTILE NEGOTIATIONS

An hour later, Dan drove his girls out to Haydenshire farm. They were greeted heartily by Mrs. Haydenshire who seemed thrilled to see them all.

"George, I promise you that you will regret this ridiculous decision for the rest of your life," spat from Governor Haydenshire as he stepped out of his office holding his phone to his ear.

Mrs. Haydenshire shook her head and shared a heartbroken glance with her husband as he ended the call.

"Aida, how did you get so tall in one summer?" The governor beamed at her.

"I don't know," Aida replied thoughtfully.

"Ni-on-na!" Keaton rushed into the kitchen and flew to Fionna.

"Keaton!" She leaned to pick him up.

"Uh." Dan shook his head in concern.

"Keaton, let Fionna sit down and then she can hold you, son," the governor commanded. Fionna settled in the rocking chair in the kitchen, and Dan lifted Keaton into what was left of her lap.

"I take it that was Governor Sapman." Dan gestured to the governor's phone on the counter.

Governor Haydenshire nodded. "No one is more protective of

their girls than I am, and I would have gone to the wedding if this had happened to Rainer and Emily."

Aida moved into the living room to sit beside baby Abigail who was on a blanket under a specialized baby gym for children with developmental delays. Dan joined her and watched her with the baby.

Rainer and Emily arrived with Logan coming in a moment later. Becca and Jeff arrived several minutes after that.

"Oh, sweetheart." Mrs. Haydenshire pulled Becca in to her all-encompassing embrace. "I have been right where you are, and you will get through this together."

"You have?" Becca seemed stunned.

"She has," the governor sighed. Emily and Becca hugged next.

"Did you want us to hug you, 'cause I'm not really into that?" Logan teased Jeff.

"I'm good, thanks," Jeff assured him just before he laughed.

"Mom and Dad won't let me have any of my clothes or anything," Becca was explaining to Emily. "Or my hope chest which has stuff I've been saving for when I get married and have a baby." Frustration rolled off her in waves.

Dan saw determination etch Mrs. Haydenshire's face.

"Stephen honey, I have a real craving for drive-thru," she informed the Crown Governor. He beamed at his wife and shrugged into his jacket before grabbing his keys and phone from the counter.

She turned to Dan, Fionna, and her children. "You all watch the little ones while we make a little run out to Idylwood."

Idylwood was the community in Falls Church where the Sapmans' mansion stood.

"The chicken is in the oven and everything else is on the counter. I casted them to stay warm. We'll be back in a little while. Logan, here are the addresses and keys of the houses. If you finish eating before we're back, you can take Jeff and Becca out there."

"No problem, Mom."

"Thank you, Mrs. Haydenshire." Becca threw her arms around her.

She wiped away Becca's tears. "Sometimes it's just so hard to understand that we can't live our children's lives for them or make them do things just the way we'd like them to, but that our children can choose to live their lives without us if we push them away. I think your parents need a little perspective."

They pulled away in Mrs. Haydenshire's Suburban. Abigail began crying, and Fionna scooped her up. Rainer, Jeff, and Logan took the twins and Aida out to play on the swing set.

Emily prepared the food while Dan heated Abigail's bottle following Fionna's instructions. When he finished the job, he was given little Abigail and told to feed her.

Dan cradled the precious Abigail with all of her abundant abilities despite her chromosomal anomalies. He sank down in one of the recliners and fed her the bottle, trying to envision doing the same thing with his own little girl.

It comforted him endlessly that Abigail seemed happy in his arms. Part of her phenomenal abilities was that even as an infant, she could read people's energies. The fact that she wasn't wary of Dan despite the fact that he'd summoned the very life force out of Dominic Wretchkinsides proved to Dan that he wasn't evil—that he'd been fighting evil and instead of being consumed by it, he'd let the vengeance die with the man who'd taken so much away.

Fionna and Emily set the table and loaded the food in the center. Dan laid a very sleepy Abigail in her crib upstairs and returned to help wash the twins' and Aida's hands. Everyone sat down to eat, all hopeful that the Haydenshires might get through to the Sapmans.

Jeff's mother arrived after her last shift, tearful but very proud of her son's decisions. Dan and Logan decided to take Jeff and Becca along with his mother out to the rental houses after dinner. Everyone else stayed to watch the little ones and do the dishes.

Logan directed Dan to one that was less than a mile down the same road that the farm was on. It was back toward the highway and in a small older neighborhood.

"This looks nice," Dan commented.

Logan smiled. "Yeah, Will and Brooke lived here when they first got married, and Levi's rented it a few times when he gets sick of the city."

Dan was impressed with Becca's resolve. He knew the home was nothing like what she was accustomed to. At barely eight hundred square feet, Dan ventured a guess that it was much closer to the size of Jeff's mother's apartment. But Becca drew a deep breath and held tightly to Jeff's hand.

Logan unlocked the front door and flipped on the lights. "Dad'll have to tell you the rent and utility prices and stuff. I don't really know. Patrick usually handles the rental properties, and he and Lucy stayed for the week after we all left the beach house. They're baby-mooning down there."

Jeff glanced around. The home was built in the early eighties. It was small and formed in a wide rectangle except for the concrete patio off the breakfast area in the kitchen. They entered through the living room. There was no entryway, but small built-in bookshelves surrounded the fireplace.

"Based on Levi's stories that I won't repeat now since your mama's here, I know the fireplace works," Logan informed them, making Jeff grin again.

They moved through the kitchen which had a decent amount of counter space, a small pantry, and a refrigerator. There was no dishwasher Dan noted but decided against commenting.

"This is nice, Jeff," Ms. Harrickson choked. Sadness clung to every feature of her face.

Dan's heart ached as he realized that Jeff had really been the one taking care of his mother and not the other way around.

"I know, and I can do whatever Bec wants done if it's okay with Governor Haydenshire."

"And this is a nice, safe part of town."

Dan watched as Jeff's burdens increased tenfold in a matter of moments. His shoulders tensed and he swallowed harshly. His mother didn't live in a particularly safe part of town, and he'd been her security and quite literally her Shield.

There were two equal-sized bedrooms with a bathroom between, but Dan doubted it would be great for a new marriage with a newborn to have his mother living with them.

"It has a big tub," Becca pointed out hopefully. There was a decent-sized jetted tub in the bath.

"Oh, you'll like that," Jeff started out strong but clammed up by the end of his statement as he realized that he shouldn't know that. No one commented.

"There's a laundry closet here off the kitchen." Logan led everyone out of the single bathroom. "No garage in this one," Logan lamented. "The other one has a garage, but it's smaller. I'm sure it would run you a couple hundred less each month," he offered hopefully.

This visibly intrigued Jeff, but Becca's face fell slightly with the word smaller.

"Why don't we go see it and then get back. We need to get these two married," Dan urged Logan on.

"Yeah, and I have an Energies of Early Childhood test tomorrow morning," Becca tried for a joke but the realization of how hard merging married life with a baby and still being students was going to be had Dan and Logan only offering forced chuckles.

Dan tossed Logan the keys to Fionna's Mercedes SUV and took the passenger seat. Everyone loaded in, and Logan drove toward Oakton which would put Jeff and Becca farther away from both the academy and the Senate.

He pulled into a cottage with a large three-car garage that was the floor level of the home. To say it was small was an understatement. Dan grimaced slightly as he followed Logan up a set of stairs through the garage and into a small hallway. Directly in front of them was a linen closet.

"The washer dryer hookups are in the garage," Logan pointed out.

Garages were particularly cold in Virginia in the dead of winter, and a new baby was certain to bring on vast amounts of laundry. They moved through the hallway and came to a bedroom on the left.

"This would be a palace for the baby," Logan drawled. The tiny room did have a decent-sized closet, Dan pointed out. "Then you have your living room, dining room, kitchen combo thing in here." Logan led everyone into the largest part of the house.

"Nice deck…" He pointed out the French doors off the living room near the fireplace. On the other side of the single kitchen wall was another hallway that contained the only bathroom, and then the master bedroom was attached. The bathroom did have a tub, Dan noted as he watched Jeff and Becca.

Shutting out the plaguing buzzing in his head that this was the kind of home where the walls could begin to feel like they were closing in all around you, Dan started to point out the two closets in the master bedroom. He thought better of it when he recalled that neither Jeff nor Becca currently had enough clothing to fill even half of one.

"Do you think we'd be able to hear the baby, you know, at night?" Becca pointed to what would become the nursery on one side of the house and the master on the other.

"Oh, sweetheart, you'll hear your baby. It's just part of being a mother," Ms. Harrickson assured Becca.

Dan's cell buzzed in his pocket. "Governor Haydenshire says they'll be heading back in a few minutes. He sent over the rental prices."

"What are they?" Becca asked.

Dan smiled. Governor Haydenshire was a saint. "He says for this one it'll be $500 a month and the other is $675 and then your utilities."

"They're both paid for," Logan whispered.

Dan knew that the Crown Governor had taken what would be twenty percent of Jeff's salary as an intern at Iodex for the smaller of the two houses and set that as his rental price. There wasn't anywhere else in the entire commonwealth they could've rented for less.

"Could we have just a second?" Jeff asked.

"Of course." Logan joined Dan and Jeff's mother on the other side of the house. There wasn't really anywhere they could escape as the house was so small. Everyone tried very hard not to listen.

"We should take this one, right?" Becca stammered.

"But you like the other one more."

"No, this is fine," Becca lied outright. Logan grimaced as he shared a sorrowful gaze with Dan. "It's all we need really."

"We can get something bigger and nicer as soon as I get hired on at Iodex. I just…I'm not sure with everything that we're going to have to buy for the baby and for us that we can really afford the other one." Defeat perforated his tone.

"No, I mean…it's so nice of Governor Haydenshire to let us stay here. He really cut the price a lot. They're such great people."

"They really are."

"So, let's make this home, and get married, and have a baby, because,"—she paused thoughtfully—"I'm gonna have a baby."

This elicited a slight chuckle from Jeff. "*We're* gonna have a baby," he corrected her, making Dan smile and his mother cry.

They emerged from the bedroom holding hands with Becca wiping away tears. Logan offered Jeff a kind smile.

"Portwood says you can start Monday afternoon, and Dad's gonna let you have the first month free so you can move in anytime."

Becca broke down again. "Your family is so nice. I don't know why everyone's being so sweet to us."

Logan and Jeff both panicked.

Chuckling at their eyes goggling over her tears, Dan smiled. "Crying's not that unusual right about now," he whispered.

Jeff wrapped his arms around Becca and patted her awkwardly with so many witnesses. He got Becca relatively calm by finally just letting his cast surround her until she eased.

Dan drove everyone back to the farm with a fervent prayer that Jeff and Becca could get through the end of the school year.

He smiled as he pulled up. Fionna and Aida were outside picking flowers from Mrs. Haydenshire's flower beds. Fionna was cradling Abigail sweetly and kissing the top of her head. Abigail adored Fionna, and she was cooing happily when Dan reached them.

Fionna smiled. "Did you find something?"

"Yes, ma'am," Jeff said.

"Aida wanted to make you a bouquet," she explained to Becca sweetly.

"Thank you." Becca grinned.

"Little overwhelmed," Dan explained under his breath.

"Look at you feeling and all," Fionna giggled as she shifted Abigail to her other hip.

"Comes from being surrounded by beautiful Receivers." He kissed Abigail's cheek, making her grin.

The sun was giving off its last vestiges of light as the Haydenshires' Suburban crested the slight hill on the gravel drive.

"Dan." Fionna pointed to another car following the Suburban. Dan recognized the Lexus belonging to Governor Sapman driving slowly behind the Haydenshires.

Glancing at Jeff, Dan's heart ached. He looked terrified. All of the blood slithered quickly from his face as he swallowed down his fear.

"All right, while we still have a little daylight," Mrs. Haydenshire tried to soothe over the tension that hung thick in the air as she exited the Suburban. Governor Sapman nodded to Dan who returned the gesture. It was readily apparent that Mrs. Sapman had been crying.

"Daddy." Becca wrapped her arms around her father. His chilling disposition melted in the light of his daughter's embrace.

"Sweetheart," he choked as he held her tenderly.

"I love him so much," she vowed.

Governor Haydenshire shot Governor Sapman an expectant glare.

"You're certain?" the governor asked.

"I've never been more certain of anything. He's amazing and he loves me and he works so hard. He's everything I've ever wanted, and I know he'll take care of me just like you did."

As this was not at all what the governor wanted to hear, he drew a deep, steadying breath.

"Actions make the man, George, not the last name and certainly not the bank account," Governor Haydenshire vowed.

Governor Sapman released Becca. "Fine." He swallowed down his indignation and his prejudices. Turning to Jeff, he nodded. "You understand that no one would have been good enough for her, and that I do not appreciate what you were doing with my daughter in my home."

"Yes, sir." Jeff nodded. "But I swear to you, I will take care of her always. I'm not running away from this. I want to be with her for everything. I really love her, sir, so much. Just please give me a chance." Becca laid her head on his shoulder. In a moment of spite-driven determination, Jeff wrapped Becca up in his arms. He kissed her forehead, cradled her head in his hand, and shot a cold glare at her father.

Dan fought the urge to shake his hand. He needed that fire in his gut if he was going to get through Iodex and school and a new baby all in the same year.

"Let's get this show on the road." Governor Haydenshire stepped in as everyone headed toward the lake with the governor summoning and lighting the outdoor lights on the back deck and on the dock.

Dan wrapped his arm around Fionna as she laid her head to the side on Dan's shoulder, still holding Abigail. Aida stood with them, watching intently.

Mrs. Sapman broke down and offered Ms. Harrickson a slightly begrudged hug as they stood with Mrs. Haydenshire and Rainer. Logan stepped in as the best man, and Emily served as the maid of honor. The twins ran around the swing set, chasing each other and squealing out their glee.

Governor Haydenshire stood under the vast oak tree that just obscured the dock from the house. He smiled wryly at Jeff and Becca. "All right, George, who gives this woman to be married?"

"Woman?" Governor Sapman asked in a terror-filled whisper.

"Woman." Governor Haydenshire offered Governor Sapman a sympathetic smile.

With a deep breath, Governor Sapman squeezed his eyes shut for the length of one heartbeat. Then, with a defeated nod he rubbed the tears from his eyes. "Her mother and I," he managed in a begrudged choke.

Becca beamed as tears began pouring down her face. She kissed her father's cheek. With a great deal of determination, the governor offered Jeff his hand. Shock tensed in Jeff's rhythms. He released his grip on Becca just long enough to shake her father's hand.

Governor Sapman stepped back in what appeared to be the most difficult walk he'd ever taken as he joined his wife. Governor Haydenshire led Jeff and Becca in the customary vows, with Logan and Emily providing the pawn shop rings at the appropriate time.

"Mr. Strenton, you've gotten yourself a beautiful wife and a baby on the way, so what you make of this is entirely up to you, son," Governor Haydenshire urged.

"Yes, sir." Jeff nodded.

"Then you may kiss your bride."

With that, Jeff turned and wiped away the tears flowing steadily down Becca's face. "I love you so much."

"I love you too," she managed between sniffles. He leaned and kissed her sweetly and then with more force as she threw her arms and the small bouquet behind Jeff's neck and pulled him closer.

They broke apart with Rainer and Logan both wolf whistling and clapping.

"Let's go in. I made a little cake." Mrs. Haydenshire guided everyone into the kitchen.

"Your father and I packed some of your things for you, and maybe this weekend we could help you move into your new home," Mrs. Sapman eased.

"Thank you," Becca accepted.

"I know you both need to be at school in the morning, but how about if I put you up in a suite at the Ritz for the night," Governor Sapman begrudged.

"Wow, Daddy. Thank you."

"Yes, sir, thank you." Jeff looked stunned. "You don't have to do that."

"I know I don't."

"Sir,"—Jeff paused but then went on with—"we're going to make this work. I'll do anything for her. I swear to you."

CHAPTER 17
HOME

Everyone entered the soothing Haydenshire kitchen. Emily and Rainer volunteered to put the twins to bed as Fionna settled in the rocking chair with Abigail. Mrs. Haydenshire revealed a white chocolate and raspberry layer cake that smelled heavenly.

"Dad, I think they're gonna take the house out near Oakton," Logan said.

"Had a feeling." The governor smiled.

"It's bigger than the apartment your father had when we got married." Mrs. Haydenshire grinned.

The governor nodded. "I had a studio downtown. Will's crib took up most of the living room." He offered Jeff and Becca a wry grin.

"We never had hot water in the showers," Mrs. Haydenshire recalled.

Governor Haydenshire grinned at his wife. "You didn't seem to mind me heating the water for you though."

"Ugh, okay, stop." Logan grimaced.

"Is that how we got Garrett?" Fionna giggled.

The governor kissed his wife's cheek sweetly. "Only one eye on the stove worked unless she casted them."

"Well, honey, we only needed the one burner to make Top Ramen," Mrs. Haydenshire teased.

Everyone laughed as Dan winked at Fionna. "Fi was still eating that occasionally when we started dating. You know my Arlington Angel," he pointed out.

Fionna feigned offense. "The creamy chicken kind is good every now and then. But only use a little bit of the seasoning packet because it's too salty." She wrinkled her nose.

"Oh, I'm sure I'll get it down to an art." Becca didn't seem to mind.

"You seemed to have worked it all out," Dan reminded the governor and Mrs. Haydenshire as he gestured around the expansive eight-bedroom, six-bath farmhouse. He wanted to make certain Jeff and Becca understood the perspective they were being given.

Mrs. Sapman smiled suddenly. "Honey, remember that little place in Ellicott City that we rented right after we got married?"

Dan and Governor Haydenshire shared a wry grin.

"Oh God, that place was horrible." Governor Sapman shuddered as Mrs. Haydenshire supplied him with a large piece of cake.

Jeff was immediately intrigued. He hadn't taken his hand out of Becca's even to eat. Holding on to her seemed to be his lifeline. Dan knew that feeling all too well.

"It wasn't horrible," Mrs. Sapman fussed. "It was sweet and it was ours."

Everyone in the kitchen watched her mind travel the well-worn passages of time to a place where she wasn't the governor's wife and life wasn't quite so charmed.

"The walls were painted Day-Glo orange when we moved in, and they were so thin we could hear the neighbors arguing constantly," Governor Sapman reminded her. "Lillian, this cake is outstanding," he added.

"Thank you, George." Mrs. Haydenshire smirked.

"You went on to become governor, so I'd say the orange paint and the shouting must've done you all right," Governor Haydenshire pointed out.

Governor Sapman narrowed his eyes. "Yes, well, I didn't bring my children home from the hospital to that."

Mrs. Haydenshire rolled her eyes. "Will seems to have managed even though he survived on my homemade mushed carrot baby food and applesauce. I remember one of the things I was so overjoyed about when Joseph, Regis, and Stephen took office—oh, and your dad as well, Dan—was that I could buy baby food from the grocery store. If I hadn't have been eight months pregnant with Garrett, I would have done cartwheels in the Safeway." Everyone joined in her laughter.

The Crown Governor smirked. "Yeah, Joe went out and bought Maggie a brand-new Camaro. All Lillian wanted was liquified squash and disposable diapers for Will." He gazed at his wife like he was quite certain she was a celestial being sent to save him from himself.

She'd stuck by him when times weren't so good. They'd buried a child together, suffered three miscarriages, and brought the only known Gifted child with Down Syndrome into the Realm. Dan knew they were just as in love as they'd been back in the studio apartment in DC.

Talk of Governor Lawson and his wife, Maggie, clammed up as Rainer and Emily returned. No one wanted to make Rainer uncomfortable with memories of his parents.

"Oh Becca, I wanted to ask you." Mrs. Haydenshire turned the attention back on the newlyweds. "I don't know if you know this or if you've ever heard it from most of the Realm that loved to talk about me behind my back or right to my face depending on their mood, but several of our children were born kind of close together," she quipped. Everyone laughed, having to agree with her wry humor.

"Yes, ma'am." Becca bit her lip. She'd been staring affectionately at the tiny diamond ring on her left hand and then giving Jeff longing gazes. It didn't appear that she cared where they spent their wedding night just so long as she got to go to bed with her husband and stay tucked up in his tender embrace.

"Well," Mrs. Haydenshire continued, "we have four cribs in the back barn. If you might be in need of one, you are welcome to any of them. As soon as the pregnancy test showed the second line, Stephen went out and bought a new one." She shook her head at her husband who was beaming.

"Abby Hope likes her crib, don't you, baby girl." He scooped

Abigail out of Fionna's arms and cradled her sweetly. "'Cause you're Daddy's girl," he cooed.

Dan tried not to crack up at the Crown Governor of the American Realm speaking baby talk to his seven-month-old daughter.

"I thought I was Daddy's girl," Emily feigned offense making everyone laugh.

"You're Rainer's girl." Rainer winked at her.

"Yeah, Abby doesn't make me share her. You started telling me that you were Rainer's when you were four."

"Thank you so much, Mrs. Haydenshire, for everything." Becca kissed Jeff's cheek.

"How about if we all pitch in this weekend and see if we can't get the Strentons moved in their new place?" Dan urged the assembled crowd. "We've got tons of stuff in our storage unit."

The Sapmans nodded hesitantly.

"Becca, I have that heirloom china dish set that belonged to Nana that I was saving for when you got married, but I suppose you just got married." Mrs. Sapman still seemed unable to believe that her little girl was now a married woman.

Becca embraced her. "Thank you, Mom," she whispered.

Mrs. Sapman swallowed harshly as she clung to Becca. After a moment, Becca pulled away, and in a gesture that spoke several thousand words, she moved back to the table and sat beside Jeff. He wrapped his arm around her and fed her bites of cake, unable to take his eyes off his wife.

"Okay, say your new name. I said Emily Haydenshire Lawson like a hundred times on the way to the Keys. It was so fun," Emily commanded Becca.

Becca laughed. "Okay, Sarah Rebecca Sapman Strenton. That's a lot of S's. "I like Becca Strenton better." Her eyes danced in delight as she grinned at Jeff.

Dan watched Jeff's eyes close and him grin in sheer bliss as he let the sound of her new name wash over him. Governor Sapman, however, looked like she'd just backhanded him.

Governor Haydenshire offered him a discreet slap on the back.

"That's the way it works." He held Abigail on his shoulder. She was sound asleep with her tiny fist clutching the governor's tie.

Governor Sapman's jaw clenched as he glared at Jeff. Mrs. Haydenshire cleared her throat rather loudly, and the governor buried his fury the best that he was able.

Aida moved to Dan. She laid her head against his stomach. He lifted her up to his chest, and she nestled her face against his neck with a deep yawn.

"I think it's time for us to head on." Dan motioned to his wife.

"Did you want us to take anything with us? We can just put it in your room until Saturday and then we can get you moved," Fionna asked Becca.

"Oh, uh," she stammered uncomfortably. Terror etched Jeff's face as he glanced between her and Governor Sapman. He didn't want to stay at the Sapmans' mansion before they moved.

"Oh, hey yeah, Em, do you have the card," Rainer recalled.

Emily pulled a card out of her purse and handed it to Jeff. "We wanted to get you something," she explained.

Jeff grimaced. "Does this have what I think it has in it?" he asked Rainer.

Rainer shrugged. "Why not wait until you're at the Ritz tonight to open it?"

"You didn't have to do this," Jeff choked uncomfortably. With that, Fionna, Mrs. Haydenshire, and Ms. Harrickson all produced cards from their purses. Visible shock rocked through Jeff and Becca.

"Ms. Harrickson, no," Becca demanded.

"Oh honey, I wanted to get you something. He's my little boy even if he is all grown up. I wish I could do more."

"Takes a good bit to set up a household, sweetheart," Mrs. Haydenshire guided. "None of us did anything more than what we wanted to do. Let people help you, and then when you're in a position to help someone, repay the kindness."

"If you'd had the full Senate affair wedding, we would have gotten you a gift," Governor Haydenshire reminded them. Becca nodded though tears loomed on the horizon yet again.

"I have to work the breakfast shift Saturday morning, but I'll be right over to help after that," Ms. Harrickson explained.

"Thanks, Mom." Jeff wrapped his mother up in his arms.

"Patrick will be back Friday. I'll have him draw up the rental agreement and you two can sign it Saturday morning." Governor Haydenshire seemed to decide business might help Jeff over the emotional moment.

"Yes, sir. Thank you."

"Why don't we go put baby girl in her pink flower seat and help Jeff load Becca's things into our car?" Fionna soothed. Aida lifted her head, her eyes barely at half-mast.

"Thank you for letting me come play with Keaton and Henry and baby Abigail. I had a very nice time," she managed before her head fell back on Dan's shoulder.

Dan offered Governor Haydenshire his hand. The governor grinned as he shook it. "Have any plans for lunch tomorrow, Mentor Vindico?"

"No sir, I'm free."

"Mind coming into DC?"

"What time?" he asked.

"Around noon. A little farther off campus."

Dan immediately understood what the topic of lunch would be. "I'll see you tomorrow."

The Sapmans had packed Becca's hope chest. Mrs. Haydenshire had seen to that. They'd also haphazardly loaded a few suitcases with her clothes and shoes. Dan and Jeff loaded everything into the back of the Mercedes while Fionna covered Aida in a quilt she kept in the car for just such occasions.

"You can get the rest Saturday." Mrs. Sapman sounded lost somewhere between fearful loss and cutting anger.

"Thanks." Becca hugged her mother again.

Governor Sapman phoned a personal contact at the Ritz DC and booked a club-level suite for Jeff and Becca though he looked anguished to fulfill his promise.

"Thank you," Becca offered again as she hugged her father.

"You're welcome, sweetheart." The governor kissed her cheek. She pulled away as Jeff extended his hand.

"Sir," he urged.

The governor begrudgingly shook Jeff's hand. "You better take care of her, son, or so help me."

"George,"—Governor Haydenshire shook his head as Dan narrowed his eyes—"you are not going to bully him, at least not on my farm."

"I will, sir. I promise." Jeff didn't seem as offended by the threat as Dan felt. Logan and Rainer joined in Dan's glare.

"He's a great guy, Governor Sapman," Rainer vowed.

"She chose well." Logan nodded his adamant agreement.

"We'll see you Saturday," Rainer and Logan both volunteered.

"Thanks for everything." Jeff shook their hands.

With a quick agreement that Jeff and Becca would swing by the Vindicos' to pick up their things for the next day, everyone departed.

CHAPTER 18

COMPLICATIONS

JEFF STRENTON

After closing Becca safely in the passenger side of her Volvo, Jeff moved into the driver's seat. As he drove off Haydenshire Farm, he offered her a sweet smile.

"Are you okay, Mrs. Strenton?" His heart raced as he called his wife by her new name like it was giving some kind of standing ovation.

Becca's energy rolled in placid waves of elation as she nodded. It made Jeff able to breathe and think clearer than he'd been able in the past several weeks.

"So, your dad really hates me." He rolled his eyes. He was impressed with his own tone. Every time he'd spoken in the last two weeks, he'd sounded distant and frightened even to himself.

"No, he doesn't," Becca lied and then blushed just like she always did when she told a fib.

The effect had Jeff reeling as he tried to remember that he was driving and needed to keep the car on the road.

"Have you ever stayed at the Ritz?" she asked. He assumed she didn't want to discuss her father.

While making a concerted effort not to laugh outright at his wife, Jeff shook his head. "I helped fix their air conditioning systems last summer, remember? But I've never stayed anywhere like that. I've never stayed in a hotel at all."

Becca laced her fingers through his. "I've never stayed at the one here, but I've stayed at them in other places." She grimaced. "But this will be new for both of us."

Jeff knew that the other places were probably European vacation locales where her parents often took her.

If I work really, really hard and I climb the ranks at Iodex, I can afford to do stuff like that for her.

Fire ignited deep within his gut—the same flame that had him working tirelessly to be the top of his class and to have just a little money to take her out for burgers or pizza and to a movie after he helped his mom with rent and groceries.

When they'd first started dating exclusively, she would offer to pay. But she could tell that it hurt his feelings when she offered, so after the first few weeks she'd stopped.

"They're really nice," she offered humbly.

"Good, because you deserve really nice. You deserve the best."

"I have the best." She stared up at him with determination set in her eyes as well.

Certain that wasn't true, Jeff lifted her hand and kissed it before taking the Arlington exit to the Vindicos' home.

Discomfort filled Jeff's energy as he helped Becca grab the things they'd need for their wedding night. It was distinctly odd to be packing from someone else's home while everyone knew what they were going to be doing or at least what he fervently hoped they were going to be doing. *Becca's pregnant. She may be tired or not feeling well, and she has a test in the morning.*

Jeff began listing all of the reasons why she might not be in the mood for him to join them together as one, for him to try desperately to wash away the wounds he'd inflicted as he made her his wife.

Mentor Vindico seemed uncomfortable as well. He'd carried Aida to bed and then stopped back by the guest room.

"Do you need anything before you head out?" he offered kindly though he seemed unsure of himself. It wasn't something Jeff ever thought Dan Vindico felt. It was somehow reassuring that his hero wasn't always as self-assured as he came off.

"No, sir, thank you." Jeff smiled.

"Hey, don't be late for class tomorrow," he teased. His brow furrowed slightly from the oddity of the statement.

"Yeah," Jeff lamented the fact that his honeymoon was going to consist of a few brief hours before school.

"Hey, I'm having lunch with Governor Haydenshire tomorrow. After that, I thought I'd see if Portwood might be amenable to letting me work out with a few of the Elite guys at the Iodex gym. You're welcome to come with. Leave Becca the Volvo, and you can ride with me."

Thrill lit through Jeff, but as he recalled just a few of the names Becca had been called at school after she'd been sick, he forced down the desire.

"I'll be fine. You go." Becca seemed to read his thoughts. There were no classes after one o'clock on Fridays. As Jeff had set up his schedule with the desperate prayer that he would be chosen for the Iodex internship, he would be finished well before noon the next day.

"Fi was actually hoping Becca might want to hang out with her and Chloe and Emily," Mentor Vindico continued to bait.

"You mean like Chloe Sawyer?" Becca gasped.

"Yeah, I think they want to take you shopping. Truthfully, you never really know which Angels might make an appearance." He gave Becca a wry grin as pure delight formed in her eyes. "Then Logan and Adeline are coming over, remember?"

"I remembered," Becca assured him. "Jeff, really, I mean working out with Rainer and Logan and Mentor Vindico," she whispered though Jeff was certain Dan had heard her.

"That's like a dream come true. You should go."

Jeff wished she'd been a little more discreet.

"You're sure it's okay?" he asked Mentor Vindico.

"Yeah, Portwood wants to meet you along with the rest of the team."

"That'd be great." Jeff prayed he didn't sound like some kind of kid who'd just been given a new Xbox or something.

Mentor Vindico seemed to study Jeff intently. "Would you come here a minute?" he finally asked as he headed down the steps.

Jeff's heart took off in a sprint as he tried to figure out what he'd done wrong. *Maybe he's upset we're going to the Ritz.* Jeff raced down the stairs as quietly as he was able. Mrs. Vindico was curled up on the couch sipping tea. She beamed at Jeff.

Mentor Vindico gestured to the table and drew a deep breath. Jeff's stomach churned uncomfortably.

"Do you want a beer or something?" he asked.

Jeff was certain he wouldn't have offered if he'd been thinking clearly. "I'm about to drive downtown, sir, and I know I'm old enough to drink in the Realm, but I'm not to the Non-Gifted cops. Plus, I would never drink even just a beer, and then drive Becca somewhere." He explained his own personal set of rules.

"Right, sorry." Mentor Vindico looked deeply impressed. "I forget how old you are, I guess." Jeff was secretly delighted. "Here," he handed him a Dr Pepper that he chilled with his hands. He lowered the temperature until ice crystals just began forming in the drink.

"Thank you." Jeff was still nervous over what Mentor Vindico wanted to discuss with him.

"Sit down for just a second." They took seats at the bar. He considered as Jeff took a sip of his drink. "Listen, I know you've had kind of a hell of a week or two. I don't know why I'm being so formal," he seemed to chastise himself.

"Did I do something wrong?"

"No," Mentor Vindico vowed instantly.

With a deep breath, Jeff was able to concentrate again.

"I just wanted to say to try to loosen up and have a little fun tonight. You've got quite a year ahead of you, and Governor Sapman gave you hell. But," he hemmed, seeming uncomfortable again, "your wedding night's a big deal."

"I know, sir."

"You don't know yet," Mentor Vindico huffed cryptically under his breath. "I just wanted to say to try and relax. Enjoy this because what you're about to do, none of it's going to be easy. Iodex wants you, but you have to keep your grades up and perform well when you're at work. You and Becca have never lived together and that's going to take some adjustment.

"I moved in with my first fiancée when I was your age," he explained in a choked whisper. Jeff knew the story of Amelia but didn't think he should interrupt.

"She wasn't pregnant, but it was tough. We fought a lot," he admitted in a regret-filled whisper. "It gets tense, and you have even more to deal with than we did."

"I know it'll be hard, sir. I'm going to make this work, you'll see."

He nodded. "Just promise me if you need my help, you'll ask," he commanded.

Wondering how anyone ever told the man no, Jeff nodded again. "If you want, for the next few months until my little one makes her arrival, I'll meet you at the academy early and train with you. You need to make Elite in June, and I think I can make that happen if you're willing to put in the extra time."

"Really?!" Jeff gasped. Making the Elite Iodex Squadron would not only be his dream come true, but it would be substantially more money each year. And to be trained by Dan Vindico was more than he could ever have hoped for.

When the story had broken after the takedown at the gentlemen's club by the airport, that Vindico had killed Dominic Wretchkinsides and that his girlfriend, Fionna Styler, had been shot and subsequently lost his baby, no one in the Realm could have been more stunned than Jeff.

But the next day, when the papers began reporting that Dan Vindico, youngest and most esteemed Chief of Iodex, had resigned, Jeff had been crushed. He refused to allow himself to believe the reports that Vindico had summoned black to kill Wretchkinsides. He'd wanted to be trained by the best, and Dan Vindico was the best.

"That sound like something you'd be interested in?"

"Are you kidding me? That would be great," Jeff gushed.

"Then we'll start tomorrow afternoon. But tonight, just try to let it all go. The baby, Iodex, the house, everything." Pain etched Vindico's features though he tried to hide it. "Try to just take tonight, because you may need to hold on to it when times get tougher."

"Yes, sir."

"Give yourself a break. This isn't all your fault, and I believe in you and that you can make this work, if you and Becca do it together."

The fact that Dan Vindico believed in him did more for Jeff's psyche than anything ever had.

"Just have a little fun. Don't take it all so seriously all the time."

This had Jeff chuckling as he nodded. He recalled a press conference Vindico had given right after Christmas that Jeff had watched intently. He'd just taken down Adderand, a top-level brutal hit man for the Interfeci. Jeff recalled wondering if Dan Vindico ever smiled, and here he was seated in the man's kitchen being told not to take it all so seriously. "You didn't go to Vegas because you knew Adderand was going to be there," he gasped as he recalled the circumstances of the arrest. "You went with her." He pointed back into the living room.

Mentor Vindico laughed heartily as he nodded. "Not sure where that came from, but yeah, I did."

Mrs. Vindico appeared. She didn't look like she felt well.

All traces of laughter instantly left her husband's face. "What's wrong, sweetheart?" He gave her his hands so she could draw from him.

"I'm okay." Jeff wondered if he should leave, but they were blocking the entry to the kitchen. "I'm just having those Braxton-Hicks contraction things again," she explained, but Jeff knew if he saw the fear in her eyes then her husband certainly did.

"Maybe we should call Adeline," Mentor Vindico ordered.

"If you want Bec and me to stay with Aida, we can. We don't have to go tonight if you need to take her to the hospital." Jeff joined in his mentor's obvious panic.

Mrs. Vindico smiled but shook her head. "No, I'm okay. I was just wondering if you'd…" She gestured her head to the living room. She wanted to be casted, Jeff realized instantly.

"We'll get out of your hair," he stammered, still trying to locate an escape.

"It just kind of scares me to think about how badly the real ones must hurt if these are just practice."

Jeff had no idea what she was talking about, but he tried to blend in to the kitchen counter.

"Fi," Mentor Vindico pled.

"I promise I'm fine."

"Yeah." Mentor Vindico seemed to decide that she was okay for the moment. Jeff wondered if he'd locked on to her energy long enough to read the baby's. "Go lie down."

"You and Becca have fun tonight." She moved back to the couch.

"Yes, ma'am. We will. Thank you." Jeff watched her tense and then try to ease herself onto the couch. "You sure you don't want us…?" Jeff began pointing up the stairs toward Aida's room.

"No, you go on. If she needs to go to the hospital, I'll take care of everything."

"If you change your mind, we can come right back." Jeff climbed slowly up the stairs.

"Thank you." He situated himself on the couch and wrapped his arms around his wife.

"You ready, Bec?" Jeff thought that they needed to get out of the Vindicos' home so that Mentor Vindico could take care of his wife. If she wanted to be casted beyond holding his hands or him shielding her, then clothes would be coming off. He knew they were waiting on them to leave.

"Oh yeah." Becca leapt up nervously like she'd been doing something wrong. She threw a book and binder in her backpack and grabbed her makeup bag. Wondering what she was up to, Jeff studied her.

He relieved her of the backpack and grabbed the duffle bag they'd thrown clothes in for the next day. Escorting her down the stairs quickly, Jeff offered a hesitant smile to the Vindicos.

"Thanks again for everything. We'll see you tomorrow."

Mrs. Vindico was lying in her husband's lap under a large quilt. Mentor Vindico's hands weren't visible. Jeff assumed they were on her stomach as her eyes were closed, and she was clearly drawing from him deeply.

"No problem." He sounded just as uncomfortable as Jeff felt.

"Have fun." Mrs. Vindico sounded very relaxed.

"We will." Becca followed Jeff out the front door frantically.

They climbed in the Volvo.

"What's wrong with Fionna?" Becca asked.

Jeff's brow furrowed. "She said something about practice contractions or something. I can't remember what she said they were called."

"Oh." Becca looked relieved.

"Is that normal?"

Becca nodded though fear tensed her rhythms. "Yeah, I learned about them in my Gifted fetal development class. It's sort of like your body gets ready to give birth. They can be painful, but not like the real kind, I guess."

Jeff squeezed her hand, feeling heat wash over his body followed by his blood running ice cold from thoughts of her being in pain. "It looked like once he casted her she felt better."

"Yeah, that's what my book said. He can sort of drown the pain in his energy."

"I'll do that," Jeff promised.

"I know you will." She drew from him suddenly, making Jeff pant and long to get her inside their suite. He wanted so badly to be with her. To let it all go just like Mentor Vindico had urged him to.

He wanted to wrap himself up in her and pretend that the night would go on forever. That the sun would leave them in quiet darkness in the peaceful serenity of the bed where he longed to make Becca Sapman his wife.

Needing to change the subject lest he start pulling her clothes off before they even checked in, Jeff drew a deep breath. "Who's giving you a test the first week of school? I thought Vindico was going to be the toughest senior teacher this year."

Becca chuckled uncomfortably. Her cheeks flushed.

Furrowing his brow, Jeff noted the tension in her energy. "What's going on? We just got married and this isn't going to work if you keep things from me. We have to do everything together, remember?"

"I wasn't trying to keep things from you. I just didn't want to worry you anymore. You've kind of been really stressed out since I just blurted out that I thought I was pregnant while you were playing Valorant," she stated wryly.

This brought a genuine laugh from Jeff. "Little taken off guard."

She brought her thumbnail to her mouth and began chewing. She always chewed her nails when she was nervous or worried. According to her mom, she always had.

"I'm, uh…" she began but halted just as quickly.

"What, baby?"

"I just sort of thought if I could test out of a few classes then I could work more hours," she began.

"You don't have to do that."

She rolled her eyes. "We're doing this together. You just said that. So anyway, I asked Mentor Hannon if I could test out, but she was kind of mean about it. She said I could, but I have to take the semester exam tomorrow," she confessed in a terrified choke. "And whatever I make tomorrow counts as my final semester exam grade. If I don't pass, I have to stay in the class all year and try to bring the grade up. I don't get a chance to retake the final."

"Is she even allowed to do that?"

"Yeah, and she asked me why I wanted out of her class. I told her we were getting married and that I wanted to get a job. She seemed to know why we were getting married now, though, and she's kind of…" Becca hemmed but Jeff knew.

Mentor Hannon was well known for her staunchly conservative stance on premarital sex. She wrote articles about it for the Venton Views newspaper, held rallies at the school denouncing amative energies week, protesting the girls learning to set the cast, and had bumper stickers on her car informing everyone that if you had sex before you were married that you would burn in hell.

Jeff had always chalked her stances up to drivel. People were going to have sex. It was inevitable. It seemed the more people that had the means to keep a woman from getting pregnant the better. He'd found out how to cast Becca months before they actually started sleeping together. He wanted to share the responsibility of birth control with her. But he did wonder if Mentor Hannon's message had been wrapped in a modicum of tolerance or understanding if it wouldn't be better received on campus.

Everyone Jeff knew was having sex. It seemed to him that posters reminding the students to set the cast before they were intimate would go a lot further than telling them they were bad for being human.

"I'm helping you study all night," he immediately vowed.

"We are not studying all night."

"You need that class to graduate with a Scholera degree."

"I know, but this is our wedding night."

"Bec, come on."

"We can study a little. I really think I'll be okay. I just have to pass. Whatever I get will be my final grade unless I fail, then I'll work all year trying to bring it up with all my other assignments."

"Why didn't you tell me this?" Jeff tried not to yell at her, but he was blindsided.

"I didn't want to make you even more worried."

"What time do you have to take the test?" He negotiated the DC traffic near the Ritz and tried not to remember that he had very little cash on him and wouldn't be able to tip anyone.

"At ten, and she did say she'd grade it as soon as I'm done," Becca offered hopefully.

"I'll skip my first class, and we can study right up until you have to take the exam."

"Absolutely not. You have to graduate in the top ten percent. I just need to graduate with a Scholera degree. You're not skipping class ever."

Unable to argue with her reasoning, Jeff nodded his defeat. "Fine, but I'm helping you study tonight, and we're not doing anything else until you're ready for that exam."

Becca pushed her soothing love through his hand, and he drank it in like life's blood. "It's our wedding night, and I know I have to study some. But we are doing other things," she explained calmly but fervently. "I want to be your wife. Really Mrs. Jeff Strenton. That means more to me than anything else."

Mrs. Jeff Strenton. Her name still made his heart stutter and swell.

How did I ever get lucky enough to have Becca wanting me to make love to her over anything else?

"Okay," he soothed. "I love you so much, and I swear I will get you through this. All of it. But no more not telling me stuff so I won't worry. I worry when you don't tell me things."

"I promise."

Jeff parked in the lot. He couldn't afford to valet. He was certain Becca had never stayed in a hotel and carried her own luggage, so he grabbed her backpack, laptop case, and their duffle bag along with their toiletries. She wouldn't start doing stuff like that because of him.

"I can carry some of that," she offered.

"I've got it." He guided her into the vast hotel entrance. The cherrywood-paneled walls along with the cream marble floors complete with a solid marble counter for checking in had him reeling momentarily. People like him didn't stay places like this. Clenching his jaw in defiant ambition, Jeff stepped up to the marble counter.

"Uh, Governor Sapman made our reservation." He was impressed with his forced but confident tone.

"Yes, sir." The woman checked her computer. "I have a club-level suite for the Sapmans."

Jeff rolled his eyes and fought the urge to correct the woman. "I'm certain that's it."

Becca shook her head. "Why does he have to be like that?"

"It's fine." Jeff willed away his irritation in order to soothe her.

"I'll just call the bellman for your bags." The attendant offered them a smile.

"No, ma'am, I've got it."

With a confused nod, the woman handed Jeff two keycards and one card she informed him was for the elevator. "You look so familiar. I never forget a face. Do I know you from somewhere?"

"I worked here a few weeks last summer," he choked uncomfortably.

"Right." The woman smiled and nodded. "A bellman, right?"

Jeff shook his head. "No, ma'am. I was a sub on an HVAC job when your air conditioners weren't working."

"Well, you did a great job. It hasn't broken since." She studied him a little more intently.

"Good." Holding up the keycards, he smiled.

"Your room is ready."

"Thanks." Jeff led Becca toward the elevators.

"I'm sorry my dad's being such an ass," Becca apologized as soon as the fogged glass doors closed in front of them. Jeff chuckled over her assessment of her father. He certainly would never have said that, but he wouldn't deny it either. He grinned at her, but she was blinking back angry tears.

Not wanting anything to make her cry on this night of all nights, Jeff shook his head. "He has every right to be upset, but I'm gonna prove him wrong. I'm gonna be everything you need."

She brushed a tender kiss along his jawline that had him panting instantly. "You already are everything I need. I keep telling you that."

Suddenly desperate to get her inside their suite and away from the invading, corrosive world, Jeff summoned and forced the elevator to the upper floors in a moment's notice. They located the room, and Jeff slid a magnetic pulse through his hand over the lock and then opened the door.

His eyes landed on a hotel suite three times bigger than his mother's apartment. Becca beamed as she moved into the sitting area. "When you stay up here on the club levels, there's a twenty-four-hour buffet."

"Are you hungry, baby?" He wondered if that was why she'd explained the club-level room. She nodded hesitantly. "Why didn't you say something? I would've stopped somewhere on the way." She was eating for two after all, he reminded himself.

"I just got hungry. We can just go make me a plate and bring it back here."

"We'll do whatever you want," Jeff assured her and guided her back out to the corridor.

They returned several minutes later with Jeff carrying a tray of food. He set it on the glass top table in their suite. Suddenly, Becca threw her arms around his neck. He embraced her tenderly. *I don't care what her father thinks. This is right where she belongs, safe in my arms.*

"Will you kiss me?" she whispered. "You know, since I'm your wife and all."

Giving her the groan she was clearly after, Jeff let it all go for just a minute. He caressed her beautiful face and then as she angled her head up eager for his lips, he kissed her tenderly. God, those lips. He'd known from the first time he'd ever brushed his lips across hers that if all he got to do in this life was kiss Becca, he'd die a happy man. They were full and lush, the precise shade of pink as her nipples, and full of her delicious energy that his shield craved constantly.

The electricity of their need lit in arcs all around them. Their energy was eager to be joined.

She leaned her head the other way, and he began devouring her mouth. She was so sweet. Her energy filled him and soothed the plaguing restless murmurs of his heart. If he was beside her, everything would work out. A needy moan spilled from her mouth into his along with copious amounts of her energy. It drove him wild as he slipped his hands to her breasts, lifting their heavy weight.

He shuddered. She was his, and he wanted so badly to own her, to show her that he'd fulfill not only every need but every desire of her heart. Kneading the swollen, fevered flesh with his right hand, he slipped his left up her skirt. She panted as he began to work his way up her thigh to the heart of her.

"Yes," she gasped as he groaned in desperation. His eyes closed in covetous need as he felt the slick wet heat forming rapidly between her legs. He pulled the crotch of her panties to the side. "Touch me," she whispered, spreading her legs farther. He traced her lips as she trembled. But he pulled his hand away and forced himself to think with the head above his waist.

Shooting him a mutinous glare, Becca huffed.

"No." Jeff shook his head and closed his eyes. He couldn't look at her dark, hungry eyes and her kiss-swollen lips, knowing that she was fevered, hot, and dripping wet for him, and tell her no. "We have to study for your test," he forced the words from his mouth. "And this is our wedding night. This should be amazing for you. I want to do everything that lets you know how much I love you and how bad I want you, so let's eat and study. Then later, I want to give you a bath in that pool-sized tub," he tried for a joke and got a half smile. "I want this to be more than me reaching up your skirt." She smiled sweetly as she nodded though disappointment was her primary expression. "Okay, but I don't want to wait too much longer," she confessed in a lust-filled whisper. "I want to be your wife."

"Baby, if you don't stop saying that, I'm gonna lean you over this table. You have to study." He tried to keep the thought of her not graduating in the forefront of his mind.

But the idea of being taken on the table seemed to thrill Becca.

"For a little while," she negotiated.

"Until I know you're gonna ace that witch's exam." He tried to sound like Vindico when he was ordering someone he cared about to do something, but he fell very short.

"We should open those cards first though. I want to get thank you cards tomorrow while I'm out." She headed to her purse.

Jeff had forgotten about the cards in light of helping her study. They sat on the bed as she opened the card from Rainer and Emily.

"Oh my gosh," she gasped.

A disconcerting mix of humiliation and regret washed through Jeff.

"How much?" He was certain he didn't want to know. She held up a check that Emily had signed out of what Jeff was certain was one of her and Rainer's many, many accounts written for a thousand dollars. His eyes goggled as his mouth fell open. "We cannot accept that."

Becca nodded. "I know, but Mom says you should never say that to someone. That it's rude and that's what they wanted you to have."

Not certain what to do, Jeff handed her the card from the Vindicos. It revealed a check for two hundred and fifty dollars with a note written from Fionna telling them to accept gifts now and then use them to help others later.

"She's really amazing. I mean, all the stuff she just knows from being around you just for a little while."

"She's the strongest Receiver of our generation," he reminded her.

The card from the Haydenshires held another two-hundred-fifty-dollar check and several recipe cards from Mrs. Haydenshire. Jeff

180

realized they would be very cost-effective meals along with her recipes for all kinds of homemade baby food.

Drowning in embarrassed confusion, neither of them spoke.

Becca laced her hand in his and pushed soothing energy into his body. It helped to soak up the embarrassment and chagrin. "We have to use what we have to get through having the baby. I'm not going to be able to work more than a few hours in the afternoons, and go to school, and be pregnant if I can even get hired pregnant," she pointed out with a sigh. "We aren't going to be able to work for several years and save up and then have kids like we always planned. So, now we have to fix it, and we do need some help." She gestured to the cards.

"We're gonna fix it," Jeff vowed adamantly.

"I know." She gave him her sweet smile as she leaned and brushed a tender kiss along his cheek.

"Let's study. We have to get you through that exam first and foremost." Drawing from his resolve, Becca stood and put the checks back in her purse.

Jeff watched his wife slip into a pair of her Scholera Order short knit shorts and one of his Ioses T-shirts. He tried to hide the effect her breasts swollen over the top of her bra and her damp satin panties had on him.

Shaking himself, he opened her laptop, turning it on. He knew most guys gave their girlfriends all of their Order shirts. He usually gave Becca the ones from the year before along with one or two of their current year. As the academy provided numerous Order shirts for each student free of charge, if he wore them then his mom didn't have to buy him anything but jeans.

As Becca was a full head shorter than Jeff, she always insisted that she liked the smaller ones better anyway, but Jeff knew she just didn't want him to be embarrassed by his lack of money. He pulled off his tie and dress shirt, wearing his undershirt and the only pair of khaki pants he owned.

He switched quickly into a pair of jeans and returned to the computer. Summoning and working quickly, Jeff tapped into the hotel's main line. Leaving the free Wi-Fi for other guests, he hooked Becca's computer up to the connection used by the hotel.

It offered her vastly better download speeds, and the faster he got her ready for her exam, the faster he could get on with making her his wife. He fought the threatening groan from the thought alone.

He wanted her more than he wanted to draw his next breath. Wanted to claim her, wanted to make each and every inch of her belong to him. No one else had ever existed in the tight slick heavenly space that he'd opened all for himself, and no one ever would.

Becca opened her book and binder. As it was only the first week of school, she didn't have much in the way of notes. This was her sixth Energies of Early Childhood class, Jeff reasoned. He immediately moved to the Gifted Internet sites that were best for what he needed. A few minutes later, a broad grin formed on his face.

"Okay, baby, here."

Becca looked up from her textbook. "What?"

"Here are all of her senior exams from the last few years. They aren't that different. She doesn't change them that much."

"Oh my gosh! You are the best." Becca sprang up on her knees and wrapped her arms around his neck, effectively landing his face in her swollen cleavage. *She has to study, she has to study, she has to study.* He repeated the mantra in his mind over and over.

"Okay, I'll ask you the questions, and if you don't know then we'll look it up and go over that."

"Okay." Becca returned to the bed beside him with the tray of food. Jeff began reading over the exams in between bites of the massive sandwiches and fruit they'd gotten off of the buffet.

CHAPTER 19

SUITES AND SWEETS

DAN VINDICO

"I wonder what Jeff and Becca are doing right about now," Fionna teased.

Laughing, Dan shook his head. "I'm sure they're eating or sleeping or studying or some other activity the governor would approve of."

"I'm sure." She laughed. "I just hope they make it through this year." All of their laughter abated. She was still exhausted from being in pain.

"He's determined. I'll give him that."

"So is Becca, but it's not going to be easy. I want to help them all we can."

"We will, baby. He'll be in my classes all year, and I'm going to train him. I'll know if something's going wrong."

Fionna shifted slightly in the bed. Dan wondered if she was hurting again. "Are you okay, honey?" He moved his hands back to her bump.

Fionna grinned. "Halia's playing." Dan knew she wanted to go to sleep, but as he placed his hands on her swollen stomach, he felt his baby girl kicking and squirming. Dan let his eyes close as he flooded Fionna's womb with soothing energy. "You have to let Mommy sleep, baby girl."

Halia kicked near Dan's lips where she'd heard his voice. Unable to believe the miracle of that, Dan kept talking and soothing his wife and his precious baby girl.

~

Jeff Strenton

"Okay," Becca sighed. "Gifted children suffering from malnutrition are most likely actually missing protein-based energies. This can affect their Gifted development by robbing them of their developing burgeoning energies, and the full effects might not become apparent until later in their life after they've gone through the energy changes at puberty. The most common symptoms are lethargy, weight either too high or too low, and erratic weaknesses in their rhythms," she concluded with a deep yawn.

"Right. Good." Jeff nodded. "Just a few more."

"No." Becca slammed the laptop shut and then her book.

"Come on, I cannot let you fail because of me."

"I'm not going to fail. I haven't missed a question in over an hour. No more studying. I want you."

With his heart and his mind at war with one another, Jeff willed himself to argue with her, but he wanted her so badly he could taste it. His every breath held the need of his body to be one with hers. His shield was craving and desperate for her rhythms.

Before he could formulate another argument, Becca grabbed her duffle bag and moved into the bathroom. She closed and locked the door.

With a sigh, Jeff moved the laptop off the bed. He stacked her book and binder on the desk in the room. Wondering what she was up to, Jeff glanced at the locked bathroom door. His mind went over everything that had happened in the long day.

Recalling her being sick that morning, Jeff raced toward the bathroom. "Are you okay, Bec?"

She giggled. It was one of his favorite sounds in the world. He smiled automatically as soon as he heard her.

"Yeah, I'll be out in a sec. Just a little nervous," she admitted.

He wondered why on earth she was nervous. He began dispensing with throw pillows that seemed to multiply as he threw them off the gargantuan bed.

Finally locating sheets, Jeff swallowed as he began going over everything he wanted her to feel on this night. He cupped his hand, summoning heat from the air around him, and heated the sheets and blankets. He tried to think of anything that would make her comfortable.

She had nothing to be nervous about. Clearly, they'd done this before. But on this night of all nights, he wanted it to be everything she'd ever dreamed of, even if this wasn't exactly the honeymoon he knew she'd wished for.

It should be really romantic. He tried to think of everything he would have done had they been engaged for the time required for her parents to throw them a huge Senate wedding.

He would have worked tirelessly for Iodex, saving every penny to buy her a nice house and take her on the kind of honeymoon she deserved. He summoned and casted the lamps on the dresser, lowering the light to a soft glow.

The bathroom door opened slowly. Becca appeared, and Jeff felt his heart stop and then pound back to life in a thundering jolt. His eyes goggled as his mouth watered, and he had to consciously remember to draw breath.

"Wow," he gasped but his voice held no tone. "You are so beautiful." He was unable to take his eyes off the delicate white lace gown she'd put on. It had straps so small they were barely string and two loosely gathered lace cups holding up her breasts. She hadn't been pregnant when she'd purchased it, clearly, as they were spilling deliciously over the top of the gown.

It partially obscured her waist, and the hem scalloped around her backside. It was entirely made of delicate, gauzy lace so Jeff could still see her nipples drawn in dark puckered beads and the bottom of the curves of her backside. He'd never seen something so enticing in all of his life.

"So, you like it?" Unable to believe she had to ask, Jeff moved to her.

"My god, baby, you are gorgeous. Is this what you were nervous about? Wearing this for me?"

"A little, I guess." She nodded.

"You are the sexiest thing I've ever seen. You took my breath away." He wrapped his arms around her. She'd never worn lingerie for him before. He'd never even really thought of it.

He was perfectly happy to lower the zipper on her jeans and skirts she wore to school, but this was exquisite.

"I saw it at the store at the beginning of the summer, and thought, someday I want to wear something like that for Jeff on our wedding night." Her energy spiked in nervous, jagged twists. "So, I put it in my hope chest. That's part of why I was so mad Mom wouldn't let me have it." The pain of her parents' harsh rejection was still evident in her tone.

"I love you so much." He was desperate for her to know what she meant to him. Her ocean-blue eyes were dark and timid. Hunger swirled in their depths.

"I love you too." Her pulse raced in her rhythms. Her long blonde hair hung tenderly on her shoulders, and her lips were already swollen in desire. Jeff was certain he couldn't possibly deserve something so astoundingly beautiful or so damn sweet.

"God, Bec, I want you. I need you. Right now." He could think of nothing but burying himself deeply inside her. "I want to make you my wife. You're mine, and I want to show you that." His words had her energy quaking and pulsing in heated need.

"Now." She tugged his shirt over his head. He helped her as she moved to his belt.

"I've got it." He caught her hand. He didn't want her to do a thing. He wanted to take care of each and every thing she needed and wanted. "Go get in the bed, baby. I heated it for you."

Giving him a sweet grin, she nodded. He watched her glide slowly to the biggest bed he'd ever seen. Her curves swayed as she walked, and his cock strained, desperate for her attention. Swallowing down his ardent desire, he reminded himself all that he wanted to give her.

Stripping quickly, Jeff watched her chest rise and fall in fevered pants. Suddenly, she arranged herself on her knees on the side of the bed, giving him a mischievous smirk. He groaned as she ran her hand up his strain. She lowered her head to him, and he pulsed hot and heavy in her face. A thundering growl echoed from his lungs. His baby dressed in a deliciously innocent white lace gown with her tongue running up his length and her eyes locked on his was pure unadulterated perfection. Unable to help himself, he laced his fingers in her hair and guided her to his length.

"Suck me, baby. Please."

She moaned against him, the reverberations shuddering through his soul. His neck went slack as his head fell back. He was overwhelmed from the heavenly sensations she brought him as she sucked and licked. She set him on fire, and she held the only antidote to his exquisite pain.

He cupped her cheek. There were so many things he wanted to do to her. He needed her to stop. She pulled away with a heady grin, swirling her tongue over his head once more just to listen to him groan.

"Lie back for me." He tenderly lifted the gown from her, revealing all of her to him. She trembled as he gazed at her luscious body. "You are so fucking beautiful," he groaned.

She was his. Jeff still couldn't believe that. He vowed to always keep her safe as he traced his hands up her thighs and then eased her legs apart.

Frantic moans spilled from her. She would only ever be vulnerable to him. He would safeguard every single secret of her heart, her desires. Everything they shared would be for the two of them alone.

He lowered his head and kissed his way down her inner thigh as her breath hitched in her outcries. Unable to wait, desperate to taste the liquid form of her energy, Jeff licked up her slit. A loud shuddering moan let him know he was driving her wild. He wanted more. He *needed* more. He began to suck, desperate to drink her.

She gasped for breath and spread her legs farther for him. She wanted more as well. Her hunger nearly broke him. She was so wet he ached to bury himself in her depths, but not yet.

"You taste so sweet, baby," he groaned as he went back for more. She spilled out suddenly in his mouth. He devoured the liquid form of her energy as it flowed throughout his body. It mended his wounds and filled him with her love. Her body convulsed and shook as he released all of the tension, all of the doubt the day had brought. He replaced it with his adoring love and tender care. Jeff crawled up her body and covered her with all of him.

He leaned and swirled his tongue over her left nipple. It tightened against his tongue as he began to suckle. He drew the energy from there as well. She gasped out his name, and he moaned against her breast. The sound drove him wild. He moved to her right and granted it equal attention.

Her scent, like ripe strawberries and the first day of summer, mixed with her own heady musk, filled his starving lungs. If they'd bottle that scent of her, he'd become a lush.

"Please, please," she begged in ardent desperation. Jeff dipped his fingers inside her with force. He teased at her clit with his thumb. Her body contorted as he moved them over all of her most delicious spots. "Oh yes," she gasped as he brought her again. Smiling, Jeff slowed his strokes and let it wash through her. "Please," she began again as soon as she regained the ability to beg. He lay tenderly on top of her but kept his weight on the mattress.

"What are you begging for, baby? Tell me."

"You," she pled.

The gravity of what it meant this night settled firmly in his mind. She was his and he was tired of waiting. He lowered himself slightly and pushed inside her. It was different. He paused, momentarily taken aback. How could it feel so different? Becca's eyes flashed. She pulled him closer. She felt it as well.

Forcing himself to concentrate, Jeff began thrusting gently and grinding his body against hers. He would never have believed that anything could feel better than being with her already had. But it did. It was a pleasure like he could never even fathom. Her back arched. Her pussy tugged and milked his cock. Her body contorted in pleasure.

It was exquisite. He'd never felt anything so amazing. All the times he'd had her underneath him before had never felt so perfect and so complete. Their energy combined readily. The pulsing waves of them together reverberated from the bed. He pushed her open to his hilt, claiming every inch of her for himself.

She fit around him so perfectly. The tight, wet space that felt like heaven was made only for him. He formed her to his strain, satiating their needs as he made them one.

"That feels so good." She clung to him like she was somehow afraid he might move away from her.

"Do you like that, baby?"

"Yes. More." Her voice caught suddenly and then she broke. With the first tender tremble of her climax, Jeff came undone. It was too perfect, felt too astoundingly good. He buried himself inside her, pumping her full of him, as she quivered and shook from the force of their combined releases.

Working from habit alone, Jeff fell to the bed beside her and cradled Becca tenderly on his chest.

"Uh, wow." She was still shaking from the last of her orgasms.

"That was incredible," he agreed when he could draw a full breath.

"You felt it too?"

"Yeah, baby, I felt it."

"It was amazing."

He wished he could take credit. He brushed a kiss on her forehead. "You're incredible."

"Do you promise you'll hold me all night every night for the rest of my life?" she begged suddenly. She sounded terrified.

"That's all I've ever wanted to do. I used to lie on the couch at home, and every night all I wanted was to come back to your house and climb in your window and hold you all night long."

"You could've," she whispered.

"Little afraid your dad might catch me," he pointed out. She nodded against him. He tried to soothe her energy. She was frantic from all that had just happened between them. "Go to sleep, baby. I've got you. You're all mine, my wife," he whispered. "And I will always be there to hold you and to take care of you. I'll always be your Shield."

He held her tenderly. Kissing the top of her head, he set his shield out over her until she was sound asleep in the serenity of his arms. He let his mind recall in slow, perfect detail the heavenly way it felt to be with her now. His heart picked up pace once again.

He thought about her nervousness to wear lingerie for him, though he'd seen her naked numerous times over their four-year dating relationship. *It should always have been more.* It should always have been more than kicking textbooks off her bed and crawling over her body in the very same move.

He'd gladly work extra shifts just to fund her lingerie. He smiled and brushed another sweet kiss over her forehead as she slept. He knew it couldn't and probably shouldn't always involve candles and lingerie and any other distinctly romantic things, but she deserved for it to be more than him pulling her panties aside in her car in the driveway of her parents' home after going to see a movie.

All right, Mr. Strenton. You've gotten yourself a beautiful wife and a baby on the way, so what you make of this is entirely up to you, son. The Crown Governor's challenge rang in Jeff's mind. A wife and a baby. He let that settle on him harshly. He was only twenty years old. How could that be possible? *Probably should've thought of that before you lay down with her in the bed to do homework knowing perfectly well what was going to happen.*

Jeff lambasted himself, but it had been his eighteenth birthday. He knew what she was going to offer, and he'd been unable to think at all. His cheeks burned as he recalled his rabidity. *So it was several years before I thought I'd be married and having kids, but we did this and we're going to make it work.*

He'd never been more determined in his life. He let his mind move over all of the marriages he admired. His parents were never married, so he started with the Vindicos. His whole face lights when she comes in the room. He recalled sitting in the kitchen of the Vindicos' home watching Mentor Vindico stare at his wife.

He thought about the rumors going around school, that Mentor Vindico had overheard that punk Spencer Coker make a lewd comment about Mrs. Vindico and that he'd pinned him up to one of the concrete walls and threatened him. There was talk that he was going to get in trouble with the chancellor for threatening a student and assigning him a paper that would be counted as a test grade, but he'd defended his wife even at risk of reprimand. Jeff pulled the lesson from the tale.

He moved on to Logan and Adeline. He didn't know Adeline that well. She never seemed to talk at the academy. She always seemed to be reading, but Logan was crazy about her. He and Rainer and his brothers had ended up in more than one scuffle on Adeline's account. People always said awful things to her because she didn't have a Gifted last name or a crest. Logan never seemed to care what people thought about her. He loved her and that was all that mattered to him.

Rainer and Emily came back into his mind. They seemed to exist as one at all times. He rarely saw one without the other. Though Emily never asked for the things Rainer gave her, he did spoil her. Guilt coursed through Jeff. He pacified himself with the thought that in just a few months and after the baby was born, he could spoil them both.

The Haydenshires were a classic entity. The Crown Governor and his wife had lived through the rough times and seemed to have made it out relatively unscathed. He recalled Logan talking about Cal's death. He certainly remembered all the press when Abigail was born. They just always clung to one another.

These lessons set firmly in Jeff's mind as he cradled his wife on his chest.

CHAPTER 20

THE REFRAIN AND THE BRIDGE

DAN VINDICO

After his first class, Dan sauntered back toward his office. He was trying not to think about what he was going to have to tell Governor Haydenshire at lunch. Jeff was pacing outside a classroom. He looked terrified.

"What's going on?" Dan demanded. He'd expected to find Jeff in a state of bliss-filled euphoria after his wedding night at the Ritz. Jeff grimaced and tried to offer Dan a kind smile.

"It's Bec." He pointed to the door of the classroom. Furrowing his brow, Dan tried to see in the narrow window.

"Is she sick again?" Holing up in an empty classroom was an odd place to try and recover.

Jeff shook his head. "No, well, I mean she is kind of not feeling so well, but she asked her Energies of Early Childhood mentor if she could test out of her class early. She was thinking, like, around Christmas or whatever, but her mentor got mad and is making her take the final today, right now. And whatever she gets is her grade. If she fails, she can stay in the class and try to bring it up with her other assignments, but the failing grade stays as the grade for her final."

Dan cringed as he peeked back in the window. "Let me guess…"

"Hannon."

"She's been beating that drum since I was going here." Dan rolled his eyes. "I'm certain I'm a great disappointment to her."

This elicited a genuine smile from Jeff. "I'll consider myself in good company then."

Dan forced a chuckle, but he was still uncomfortable with Jeff's admiration.

"She has to be done in, like, fifteen minutes." He began pacing again.

"You went to class this morning, right?"

"Yes, sir. I studied with her for hours last night. I just hope it was enough."

Dan shook his head and tried not to laugh. "You used hours of your wedding night at a suite in the Ritz to help her study?"

"Was that bad?"

"No," Dan immediately assured him. "No, I was just gonna say you're a hell of a guy and a lot stronger than I've ever been."

"Right." Jeff rolled his eyes and gestured to Dan's large biceps.

"Anybody can build muscle. You'll be bulking up plenty once Portwood starts putting you through it. I was talking about strength of character."

Dan returned to his office. The next week, he would be teaching a defensive maneuvers lab during the next hour, but labs didn't start until the second week of school, so he was finished for the day. Looking forward to being finished with work for the week, Dan grabbed everything he wanted to take home with him and two Dr Peppers. He returned to Jeff's post and handed him one.

"Thanks," Jeff offered uncomfortably. "But, Mentor Vindico, you kind of need to stop being so nice to me." He stared steadfastly at the ground. "Kids are talking and complaining and stuff. I don't want you to get in trouble."

Dan smirked. "I've had a habit of pissing people off most of my life. It seems to be the way I exist. Honestly, I kind of enjoy it. As long as Fi's happy and my baby girls are good, then I really don't give a damn what anyone else thinks or says. Let me worry about what people think of me, and I happen to think you're a tremendous guy."

A minute later, Becca burst from the classroom. Joy lit her face as she bounced up and down. "I got an eighty-seven!" she squealed.

Jeff slumped in abject relief. He wrapped his arms around her. "I'm so proud of you!"

Dan backed away, trying to give them a moment. He grinned over their exuberance. Mentor Hannon appeared, carrying her briefcase and scowling.

"Mentor Vindico," she sneered.

Smiling broadly, Dan gave her a polite nod. "Mentor Hannon."

"Well, Mrs. *Strenton*," she sneered Becca's new name, "I do wish you the best of luck with everything." She gave Jeff a haughty glare. Everything about her demeanor said that she thought Becca would be sorry she'd attached herself to someone like Jeff Strenton. Becca's eyes narrowed hatefully as she clung to Jeff's hand.

"Thank you," she spat in disdain. Hannon rolled her eyes as she marched away. "Ugh, she is such a self-righteous bitch," Becca huffed under her breath.

Dan and Jeff cracked up.

"Sorry." Becca shuddered as she realized what she'd said in front of Dan. He shook his head.

"We were all thinking it."

"Okay, I have to go to one more class and then I'm actually going to hang out with Fionna Styler and Chloe Sawyer, and Emily." Becca was euphoric as they walked toward her last class of the day.

"Vindico," Dan corrected.

"Right." Becca grimaced again. "Clearly, I should just stop talking."

Jeff Strenton

"Thank you for helping me study. I couldn't have done nearly that well if you hadn't found me those tests online. Oh, get this,"—Becca leaned in—"one of them was an exact copy of the test I just took. I guess she uses the same ones year after year."

Jeff's brow furrowed. The mentors weren't allowed to do that.

He'd heard several mentors complaining about having to recreate tests each semester, but leave it to Hannon to spend all of her time protesting sex instead of actually doing her job.

"I'm so proud of you," Jeff continued to tell her.

She beamed at him. "You go work out with everyone. I love you." She kissed his jaw.

"Hey, come here to me." He pulled her back in and gave her a long drawn kiss. That is until Mentor Sherman cleared his throat right beside their faces. Jeff jerked back and glared.

"Public displays of affection aren't allowed," he chirped annoyingly.

Jeff ground his teeth. He'd had enough of everyone's bullshit. "Yeah, well, neither is dating a student when you're a mentor." He spun and marched out of the building.

CHAPTER 21

PORTWOOD AND PROPOSALS

DAN VINDICO

Dan drew a deep, reassuring breath as he cranked the Ferrari, thrilled to be leaving the week behind him.

Jeff chuckled. "That bad?"

"Been a long week."

"You're telling me."

When they entered the Iodex parking deck, security waved Dan through, though he no longer held any credentials or a badge.

"Look what the cat dragged in." Ramier beamed at Dan as he waltzed into the Iodex office.

Chuckling, Dan worked his way around the office. Homesickness threatened to pull him under as his body absorbed the sights and sounds of Iodex.

Tuttle had a lascivious grin on his face as he stared at his phone. Rolling his eyes, Dan's entire body cringed.

As soon as he saw Dan, Tuttle slammed the phone face down on his desk. "I didn't know you were coming by."

Rainer and Logan chuckled from Tuttle's discomfort.

Scowling, Dan lifted the phone off the desk. Tuttle shuddered as Dan turned the screen back on.

"What the fuck is wrong with you?" he snarled. Dan swallowed back the vomit that flooded his mouth. The picture of Dan's youngest sister, Lindley, had him gagging. She was posed like a cheap print porn star. Legs bent and spread. Her hair a mix of its natural blonde with purple highlights. She was wearing nothing at all and sucking her own index finger. Dan's eyes shut tightly as he took in the placement of her other hand. Her eye makeup was dark and covered her entire eyelid.

"Hey, I didn't tell you to look at my phone."

"That is my sister."

"I know, and I'm thinking very, very soon, I'm gonna be your brother."

Ryan Tuttle was an outstanding officer. He was also a disgusting pervert that Dan could hardly stand to be around. He and Lindley had met a few years back when he'd been her arresting officer for a drunk and disorderly. Somehow, they'd started hooking up after she'd completed her lengthy stint in rehab.

"What?!"

Tension weighted the energy of everyone in the room as they watched.

"She's so damn hot and wild. She's amazing."

"You think Lindley will actually marry you?" Dan rolled his eyes.

Lindley typically messed around with drugged-out losers for a few weeks before moving on. She had, however, been dating Tuttle for almost four months. It was by far the longest relationship either of them had ever maintained.

"She brought it up," Tuttle challenged. Gripping the side of Tuttle's desk, Dan felt like he'd been sucker punched.

"And you're actually going to settle down and stop chasing everything that breathes and will spread their legs for you?" Ramier, Tuttle's partner, quizzed in abject disbelief.

"I'm not settling down, man. With Lind, you don't have to. She is wild like the wind, trust me. And the stuff she does…damn." He got a faraway look in his eyes.

Dan was certain he was going to vomit. Jeff looked extremely uncomfortable and tried to blend in behind Rainer and Logan. Backing away from Tuttle lest he sink his fist in his face, Dan focused on Jeff.

Portwood appeared with a smile.

"Mentor Vindico." He chuckled and shook Dan's hand.

Dan appreciated the escape he'd been offered. "Landon, this is Jeff Strenton," he introduced. Portwood gave Jeff a kind smile. Jeff shook his hand, staring at him like he was a celebrity.

"How's Fi doing?" Landon asked.

"Good."

"Are you ready to be a daddy again?" He looked thrilled for Dan and Fionna.

"Definitely." Dan let that fact further ease him. "Is Julie doing well?"

"Yeah, she's great." Portwood's smile spread rapidly across his face. "We decided this morning that we'd start telling people, so sometime around next Valentine's Day, I'll be joining the daddy ranks myself." His rhythms lit in sheer joy.

"Congratulations." Dan shook his hand again. Everyone in Elite Iodex joined in the congratulations.

Portwood was elated, and everyone knew it.

"So, Strenton, I'm in a really good mood. Why don't we go get you a badge and officially make you Officer Strenton, and then I'll let Lawson and Haydenshire teach you to shoot. If you beat Rainer's shots by three o'clock, I'll let you keep the badge," he joked.

"Are you serious, sir?"

Portwood laughed. "Actually, you have to have a badge to work here, but since you're still a student, you can't arrest people yet or flash it around to anyone but your friends. "

"I won't. I promise, sir."

"Hey, loosen up. If Dan says you're the man, then you're the man." Portwood tried to get Jeff to relax. "I know you're married now, but I'm still going to have to have an underage allowance form signed by your mom, just so you can occasionally go out with the Elite Squadron."

Glancing at his watch, Dan slapped Portwood on the back. "I'm going to eat with Governor Haydenshire. Don't beat him up too badly until I get back."

Landon chuckled. "I do want Logan and Rainer to work you out on the gun course. Then we'll see what you're made of once Dan's back. Go make him official, gentlemen," he directed Rainer and Logan.

Jeff nodded nervously though he looked up for anything Portwood wanted to subject him to.

Rainer teased, "Don't worry. Logan still holds his badge when he sleeps at night."

Logan rolled his eyes as Jeff laughed. He looked relieved to be with Rainer and Logan.

"Don't go too rough on him. He's kind of had a hell of a week," Dan whispered to Portwood.

"I do need him to work, so I can't go too easy on him. I'm aware he probably didn't sleep much on his wedding night."

"No, he didn't. Apparently he stayed up for hours helping Becca study for an exam she was forced to take this morning." That statement alone should tell anyone just what kind of man Jeff Strenton really was.

Stunned disbelief etched Portwood's face. "Are you kidding me?"

"I could not be more serious. They not only studied, but she got herself an eighty-seven on a year-end final."

A low whistle slid between Portwood's teeth. "The kid has standards. I'll give him that."

"He's a great kid."

"I thought I'd find you here." The Crown Governor chuckled as he moved through the doors from the governor's wing of the Senate into Iodex.

"I'm sorry," Dan apologized.

Governor Haydenshire shook his head. "You're not late. I just needed to get out of my office. I'm seriously considering having the phone removed altogether."

"Calls about Venton?"

"It's like there's nothing else this Realm has to talk about."

～

Feeling another round of wistful longing wash through him, Dan pulled his cell from his pocket as he slid into the booth at Frye's across from Governor Haydenshire.

Chuckling, he shook his head as he read Fionna's text. "Fi apparently wants to know if I would mind bringing her home cream cheese sushi rolls with extra wasabi and sour gummy worms," he informed the governor. "And I quote,"—he held up the phone—"They sound so incredibly delicious right now."

Governor Haydenshire laughed as his customary drink order, a tall glass of sweet tea with lemon, was supplied to him without him even having to order. "When Lillian was pregnant with the twins, I came home one day to find her inhaling her mother's peanut brittle." Dan didn't think that was a particularly odd craving. Nana Anderson's peanut brittle was outstanding. He'd had it numerous times when he'd been out to Haydenshire Farm with Will and Garrett. The governor chuckled. "She was dipping it in ranch dressing." He shook his head. "The kids and I had to just sit by and watch her eat Nana Anderson's fantastic brittle like that." He sighed over the loss, which made Dan laugh.

Dan assured Fionna that he would gladly bring home anything she'd like and then returned his attention to the Crown.

"I invited your dad to come along. He'll be by as soon as he's off the phone," Governor Haydenshire seemed to suddenly remember.

Dan grinned. He found it mildly odd that he was looking forward to seeing his father.

"Tell me about Kauai. Your dad said he'd never seen you so happy and that Fionna and Aida seemed to be in heaven."

Dan grinned as he ordered a Dr Pepper, and the governor placed an order for a large platter of appetizers to be split. This apparently wasn't going to be a quick lunch.

"It was great. We really needed that time. Last year was hell."

"It was that," the governor agreed.

"Fi and I talk about moving out there all the time, but we can't seem to decide."

"You have to do what's right for you and all of your girls, but we would sorely miss you and your lovely family."

"Thanks." Dan picked up a tortilla chip, dipped it in the provided salsa, and noted that the food appeared rapidly when one dined with the Crown Governor.

Governor Vindico appeared and Dan grinned. "Hey, Dad." He scooted over to allow his father to sit beside him.

"How are my girls?" he asked with a broad grin. Governor Vindico's water was supplied immediately as well.

"Aida's over the moon because she's spending the night with Olivia tonight, and Fi wants sushi and sour gummy worms," Dan explained as his father laughed. "So, I'd say just the way they're supposed to be."

"And the little one's good?" Governor Haydenshire quizzed.

"Yeah, she's moving all the time. Adeline and Logan are having dinner with us tonight, and she's going to check Fi. So far, everything has been perfect though."

"Don't forget the worms," Governor Haydenshire commanded with a grin. "I promised to get Lillian pumpkin seeds with one of the boys and then forgot. Good grief." He shook his head. "You know, I adore my wife and that when she is not eight and a half months pregnant with one of my sons, she has the patience of Job, but that night,"—he shuddered slightly—"I went right back out and got them, only I was unaware that there was a certain kind of pumpkin seed she wanted that they only sell at a shop near the Senate. It was a long night on my farm, trust me."

The appetizers disappeared, and everyone ordered. Governor Haydenshire leaned in with a sigh. "All right, let's have it. You give me your bad news, and we'll give your ours." He gestured to Governor Vindico who nodded morosely.

"I don't really have much other than what I've already told you. He did it, and the students knew about it while it was happening."

"I was afraid you were going to say that." Governor Haydenshire rubbed his temples. "Why do people do that? He's been married longer than Lill and I."

"Yeah, and she's half his age."

"And there you have your reason." Governor Vindico shook his head.

"Are you going to fire him?" Dan bit into one of Frye's delectable Philly cheesesteaks.

"I don't know yet. There's a bit more to it that I'd like to figure out before I do that."

Dan wondered what he didn't know that the governors were so hesitant to tell him. "Fi had him figured out when he was within ten feet of her."

"I just don't understand it. If something is wrong in your marriage then you go home and you talk and you work until you fix it or you end it. You don't find yourself a woman on the side," Governor Haydenshire growled furiously.

The Realm had chosen well when they'd elected him Crown Governor. Even the Haydenshire crest, the lion, stood for strength of family. Dan was certain a more honest man couldn't be found in the entire Realm.

Governor Vindico raised his glass to the sentiment which Dan joined. "According to the staff I've gotten to talk to me, it's apparently been going on for years."

Dan choked on his soda. "What?" He'd been under the impression it had been a summer fling.

Governor Vindico waved the waiter back and ordered beers for everyone. "I'm certainly not used to knowing more about a case than my son, but I suppose I've been hearing about this one longer since you were working a farm in Kauai for the past four and half months.

"One of the accountants told me that based on the rumors flying around the academy, Dean pursued her, but that she was up in his office constantly." He convulsed slightly. Dan's cheesesteak threatened to make a rapid return.

"He was out with someone at Big Buns yesterday. I didn't see her face, but she looked like Mentor Bryant from the back," Dan explained.

Governor Haydenshire shook his head. "That was his daughter apparently. At least, I was assured that it was Amber when I spoke to Dean this morning. He's still denying everything though." He took another bite of his club sandwich.

"What was your bad news, sir?" Dan asked.

Governor Vindico tossed down his napkin. "I spoke with the hospital about the young man you revived. They managed to restore most of his Gifted energies. He'll make a recovery, but doesn't it strike you as odd that there wasn't a single positive drug test result and then two days later someone overdosed?"

"Did you ask the medios to question him?"

"I did, and the kid swears that was the first time he'd ever used. However, Medio Khatri, who is an outstanding internist, says he doesn't believe that's true. We've got to figure out if someone is fabricating drug test results before someone gets killed. Not only that but *how* they would manage such a thing."

"And,"—Governor Haydenshire drew a deep steadying breath—"Dean Wilshire isn't the only person I've gotten complaints about."

Immediately understanding where this was going, Dan nodded. "I take it the complaints about me have made it to your office as well."

"My personal opinion is that most people who complain about whatever they're complaining about should take a close, objective look at themselves and fix whatever they're blaming on others. But," he sighed, "you apparently ticked off a few parents with your demands and your assignment load. There were parents that just knew that their kids were going to get a free pass their senior year and now they're going to have to actually work.

"Your policy on out-of-classroom help didn't make a lot of people happy, but the mentor aides has long been Venton's policy so I've tried to explain that. You taking up with Mr. Strenton upset a lot of people as well.

"They feel that you took pity on the kid because of what happened with you and Fionna last year, and that's how he got the coveted spot in Iodex despite the fact that he really is a tremendous student and a tremendous Shield. We are also going to have to talk about your assigning extra papers and then allowing your wife to grade them."

"There's a lot more to that story," Dan assured the governor.

"I had a feeling."

"As long as we're laying everything on the table,"—Governor Vindico sighed—"twice last year, I asked Dean to turn over the Venton chart of accounts and yearly budget. I never got either. But..."

he continued with a grimace, "between Nic Wretchkinsides trying to buy his way onto the governing board, my daughter needing to go to rehab, and my daughter-in-law being shot, I let it slide. However, I asked him for them again when this all broke Monday, and I still haven't received them. Lies never ride alone. They can't. My gut tells me there's something in the books Dean doesn't want me to see. I'm betting it has to do with his extramarital affair."

Governor Haydenshire nodded. "I'd say that's a very safe bet. I got a call just before I headed home last night from a mother who was deeply concerned. She wasn't after my head, which is unusual. She was really worried. She says she caught her son looking at test answers online for one of your classes."

Dan's brow furrowed. "How would my tests be online? I just started teaching. I haven't even given any of them yet."

"Excellent question. Logan and Adeline came up to the house for breakfast this morning. I was telling Lillian about the test, and Logan informed me that last year when you sent him and Rainer to Venton to keep tabs on Clarence Pendergrath, that they caught him trying to break into the test vault. Now, he didn't get very far, obviously, but according to Logan, Clarence told him that some kids had already broken into the vault and managed to get some test copies and answers out. Rainer and Logan both figured he was trying to get out of what they'd just caught him doing. But I wonder if he was telling the truth."

"I doubt anyone with the last name Pendergrath is capable of telling the truth," Dan informed him.

He nodded. "Let's remember that Clarence had no choice but to be what his father created him to become. That's why he's in a prison work camp. But if your tests are online, it means someone knows how to get in that vault. It does give credence to what Clarence said."

Governor Vindico's brow furrowed. "Not only does it give credence to what he said, it means someone has been in that vault since you turned your tests in to Wilshire, Daniel."

Dan rubbed his temples. "That was just last week when we got back from Kauai."

Governor Haydenshire's eyes closed. "Then we have quite a few more problems at Venton than the chancellor having an affair. I'd dare say it's not just your tests that are online. I'd bet it's every subject, every Predilect."

"The only answer I can come up with is that I should clearly resign." Governor Vindico threw up his hands. "I cannot believe this all happened on my watch."

"What?!" Dan gasped. "Dad, no. You are not giving up a job you love, that you've given your life to, that you were elected to do thirty years ago because Wilshire can't keep his dick in his pants long enough to do his own work. I'll figure everything out, and I'll do it before this gets any worse in the press. I am a pretty damn good detective."

"You are the best, Dan, and we both know that," Governor Haydenshire vowed.

Governor Vindico nodded. "But, you're right, I have been governor for thirty some odd years now. Maybe it's time for me to retire. All of my kids are having kids. I hardly ever get to see any of my grandkids. I'm sure Halia won't be any different. I want to spend time with them. And I'm still not certain what I think about this, but yesterday, Ryan asked me if he could propose to Lindley."

"Ryan Tuttle?" Governor Haydenshire stared at Governor Vindico like he was afraid he might be having a stroke.

"The one and only."

"What did you tell him?" Dan demanded.

"What was I supposed to say? I can't tell them they can't get married any more than I could have stopped you and Fionna when you called me an hour before your ceremony," he reminded Dan. "Not that I would ever put that sweet, sweet, wonderful woman who saved my son's life and that has given me not one, but soon to be two, precious granddaughters in the same boat with Ryan Tuttle, mind you."

This had Dan and Governor Haydenshire chuckling as they nodded their understanding.

Dan's cell chirped again, and he grinned. He didn't even have to read the text to know perfectly well what it said. He pulled his phone from his pocket and chuckled.

"Fi wants to know if I'm okay." She knew. She always knew. They were so distinctly intimate, so perfectly paired, she could read him from miles away.

Governor Haydenshire smirked as he watched Dan type a quick response that he missed her and that he'd explain everything when he got home.

"I'll just say that I know you'd never cheat on her or break your vows, Daniel, and that's a good thing, because I think she'd have you figured out if you even entertained the thought," the Crown Governor vowed.

"I'd never even entertain the thought, so she has nothing to worry about. I keep my word, and I sure as hell keep my vows." Dan was infuriated with the chancellor and Katherine Bryant and all that their amorousness had caused.

A pride-filled smile formed on his father's face. "Every now and then your kids do or say something that makes you think you just might've done something right when they were coming up." He slapped Dan on the back.

Governor Haydenshire chuckled and nodded to Governor Vindico. "You and Marion did a whole lot right, Arthur. Whenever one of my kids makes me feel that way, I like to think it makes up for all of those nights when I wanted to beat my head against a brick wall because yet another teacher had phoned me, or two of them had attempted to kill one another.

"I still shudder when I think about the time I was called out to McCarron because Garrett had informed his third-grade teacher that she was a hottie."

Governor Vindico guffawed as Dan nodded. "Sounds like Garrett."

"I know." Governor Haydenshire rolled his eyes.

"How's he liking it back at the precinct?" Dan asked.

"He likes that routine and having a little time off when he's not on call. Garrett likes to play just as hard as he works," the governor allowed. "Now, before we leave, I'd love to hear the story of Mr.

Coker's son. Mind you, Coker hasn't complained to me about the extra assignment, but a mother of one of his friends called."

"Mr. Coker announced rather loudly in the corridor while holding up a large photograph of my wife that he'd bet his friends a hundred dollars that he'd get Fionna to sleep with him by the end of the year."

"My word." Governor Vindico choked on his water as Governor Haydenshire's eyes goggled.

"The assignment and the grade stand," he decreed.

As lunch had been consumed, Dan followed his father and Governor Haydenshire back to the Senate. Everything he'd been informed of weighed heavily on his mind.

Governor Haydenshire stopped him just outside the Iodex entrance doors. "Are you sure you can figure everything out that's going on at Venton? You have a baby on the way."

"I can do it, sir. I won't have this all falling in Dad's lap."

"That's my biggest fear in all of this, and you heard him. He's already taking responsibility when you and I both know this falls on Dean's shoulders. I need this taken care of quickly and quietly, but I don't want to pull you back in when I'm the one who effectively forced you out."

"I'll be fine. I'll take care of everything. I don't need a badge to get this done."

CHAPTER 22

GUNSHOTS

J eff was trying very hard not to grin as Dan made his way back into Iodex.

"Not bad." Portwood looked extremely impressed. He was holding up a practice shooting target.

"Wow." Dan nodded to Jeff. He'd shot well for a new trainee.

"I didn't outshoot Rainer," he lamented though everyone knew he was pleased with his scores.

Rainer scoffed, "Yeah, but Dan Vindico trained me so…"

"All right, let's see you work out," Portwood commanded as the Elite team headed to the locker room to change.

"Who taught you to shoot?" Dan asked as he followed the team.

"My grandfather. I mean, my mom's dad. He used to take me hunting in the summers when I was younger. He passed a couple of years ago."

"I'm sorry. My grandfather was my hero too." He offered Jeff a grin. "Looks like he was a great teacher."

"Yeah, he was a great guy."

Dan let his mind work as hard as his body as he executed one of his favorite workouts from his own Iodex days. He released the world in a sea of endorphins.

When he finished and leapt off the treadmill after completing his two-mile cooldown, he scanned the gym for Jeff. Portwood was handing him a towel and chuckling. Jeff was red-faced and soaked in sweat. He was gasping for breath.

Wiping off his own face, Dan shook his head. "What'd you do to him?"

"We did your 'I'm pissed at all of you losers' workout that you used to make us do when we screwed something up," Portwood explained.

"That is a good one." Dan laughed. He recalled the first time he'd worked out Rainer and Logan the year before. They'd grown up working Haydenshire Farm. Dan had been mildly disappointed that his original workouts didn't wear them out.

It appeared that Portwood had discovered the same problem with Jeff. He worked manual labor most any chance he got, so Portwood must've decided to up the ante.

Logan mopped his own face with a clean towel. "If you're not passing out or hurling after that workout, then you're golden." The rest of the team nodded their agreement.

"When I got up here from Vegas,"—Trenton McCoy chuckled—"I'd been in Vegas Iodex for four years, so I thought it wouldn't be that different. Then Vindico worked us out, and I thought I'd died and gone to hell." Everyone laughed as Dan shook his head.

Jeff, though visibly exhausted, look thrilled to be chatting with the Elite Iodex Squadron as they hit the showers.

Logan asked Jeff if he'd like to ride to Dan and Fionna's with him which Jeff accepted. Dan assured him that it was fine and checked with Fionna to determine if she still wanted cream cheese rolls and sour gummy worms.

He stopped by the store near their home, picking up the largest bag of sour gummy worms he could find along with turkey pepperoni which had replaced the desire for sushi. He rushed in the door and let the soothing smells and sounds of his house flood him with relief.

"Hey there." Fionna gave Dan his smile, the one that made him feel like everything would really be okay as long as she just kept smiling. Unable to help himself, Dan set the grocery bag on a nearby table and pulled the very reason for his existence to him. He wrapped his arms around her.

"Hey," he whispered. He just wanted to hold her close. Her cast moved through his forearms and hands. She reached her hands up the back of his polo and pushed more of her soothing energy inside of him.

"Rough day?"

Chuckling and inhaling the scent of her, Dan nodded.

"You could say that."

"Come here, and bring my gummy worms." She took his hand and led him to the couch.

Dan handed her the bag and then attempted to pull her into his lap.

"I am too big to sit in your lap," she fussed.

"Fionna Kalani Halia Styler Vindico," he huffed. "You are not. You are carrying our child, and I want both of you to sit in my lap. Now stop arguing with me. I've had a rough day."

Rolling her eyes, she pulled open the bag of gummy worms.

"Neon sour, right?"

"Yum." She wiggled in her excitement.

"I love you so much."

"I love you too." She kissed his cheek before devouring the gummy worms.

"Did you have fun with Becca today?"

"I hope Chloe and Sasha didn't freak her out," she lamented. "Garrett came and had lunch with us. He asked me just how exactly you were accessing, as he put it, my candy land," she giggled. "I kind of forgot that Becca isn't used to hanging out with all of us, so I proceeded to tell him that you hadn't had any trouble and that I was thoroughly enjoying playing candy land with you. I, uh, might've gotten a little too detailed.

"Becca choked on her lunch and then turned the shade of Emily's hair. She was red all afternoon." Fionna wrinkled her nose. "I felt bad. Emily explained that her big brother was just teasing and that we'd been best friends since the academy, but I kind of think we horrified her."

"Garrett can take a little getting used to."

She laughed. "I know, but you know Becca's kind of young, and

Emily grew up with him." She tried to make sense of the differences in Emily and Becca even though they were the same age.

"Emily did a lot of growing up graduating a year early, and when everything happened when Rainer's dad was killed and again when Cal was killed. She's not like any of my seniors this year. She seems way older than all of them."

"Tell me about lunch with Governor Haydenshire," she changed the subject abruptly.

Dan began the long tale of everything from Chancellor Wilshire and the worries over the books, the complaints about his teaching style and work load requirements, along with the leaked tests. He was exhausted by the time he finished. "I promised Governor Haydenshire I'd figure everything out before the Realm is calling for my dad's head on a platter. At least that's something I'm good at."

"Explain that."

"I don't even know if I like being a mentor,"—he shrugged—"but I know I'm a good detective."

"I already knew you didn't like it," she eased. "I was just waiting on you to want to talk about it."

"I guess I hadn't really acknowledged it or allowed myself to acknowledge it."

"I knew that too."

Dan could feel the heat from her cheeks against his shoulder. Fionna was often embarrassed by her incredible abilities. She never wanted to make anyone uncomfortable with the fact that she could read their emotions so readily.

"You could have told me, baby doll. I mean, I'm a little slow." He tried to earn a chuckle he didn't receive.

"Dan, I don't want you to do something you hate."

"I know, but I want to figure out what the hell is going on at Venton, and I need to be there for that. Being a mentor is the perfect cover."

"Okay, but even after our newest little princess makes her arrival," —she rubbed her hands over her swollen midsection—"I still want us to keep talking about this."

"Of course," Dan agreed. There had been a period of time not so long ago when Fionna was pregnant the first time. She'd been terrified to tell him, and she'd shut him out. He'd stupidly allowed it. They hadn't talked at all.

He'd watched her sink into the depths of depression. He'd been unable to find a way to access her. One of the things they'd agreed to after they married was that they would never let that happen again. They would keep talking until they'd worked through whatever the problem might be.

"I was going to order some pizzas for everyone. I'm really tired," Fionna admitted hesitantly.

Concern pulsed through Dan's shield. "I'll take care of the pizzas. Why don't you go upstairs and lie down before everyone gets here?" He was aware it sounded like a command.

She raised her eyebrow letting him know that he needed to cool it.

"I'm just worried about you. I love you, and I need to know that you're okay. I'm your Shield. I don't know any other way to be."

Nodding, she reached for Dan's hand and let him help her off the couch. "Just for a little while," she negotiated. While fighting the deep concern that was washing through him, he forced a nod.

The fact that she'd been willing to go and lie down when they had friends coming over wasn't like Fionna. Dan tried to shut down the nervous terror that coursed rapidly through his veins.

Knowing that both Jeff and Logan could put away a tremendous amount of food and that they'd worked out hard, Dan placed an order for numerous pizzas. He straightened up the den, then carried a book of Aida's and a few of her tiny doll sets back to her room. He pulled his cell from his pocket and phoned his sister Meredith.

After making certain that Aida was fine and having fun with Olivia, he checked on Fionna. She'd pulled on a loose maternity top over a pair of stretch pants. He joined her on the bed and smiled as she crawled on his chest. Dan locked on to her energy by placing his hands on her back. Her rhythms were exhausted and tensed.

"Fi, baby, what's wrong?"

"I don't know," she confessed. "I kind of have a bad feeling about the stuff you're going to be doing at the academy, and I really miss having you and Aida with me during the days. I'm just really tired. I've been spotting some." She was blinking back tears all of a sudden. "I'm struggling."

Her energy was fraught with fear. Dan lambasted himself for going to Iodex that day. He'd had no business going to hang out with his old buddies and showing Jeff around. She'd needed him, and he'd let her down. He'd taken the job at Venton so he would have time to be at home with Fionna and the girls.

"I'm telling Wilshire Monday morning that he can find someone else to teach Mentor Bryant's class. He made his bed. He can lie in it."

"Dan, no," Fionna fussed, but he was extremely adept at reading her rhythms as well, especially when she was lying right beside him. He felt relief flow through her as soon as he'd made his vow.

"I need the extra time to investigate whatever is going on out there, and I'm not taking time away from you so I can clean up somebody else's mess." He felt stupid for agreeing to teach it in the first place.

Fionna sighed against him. "I'm just a little off today, and I'm really worried about you doing all of this investigative work for your dad and Governor Haydenshire. It just seems like you're going to be in danger again."

In the nearly four-month span that they'd dated before they'd married, his job had made her a nervous wreck on many occasions. She wasn't really made to be an Iodex officer's wife, and Dan had known that fairly early on in their relationship. All he'd wanted was Wretchkinsides, and he'd resigned happily when he'd taken down the Interfeci.

"I'm not certain yet what we may be dealing with at Venton, but I promise you that I am by far the best-trained person at the entire school. If I feel like I'm putting myself, or you, or my baby girls at risk in any way, I'll quit. I'll turn the cases over to Iodex.

"Let me do this so my dad doesn't feel like and look like he really dropped the ball last year, but I won't put myself or anyone I love at risk."

Fionna nodded and smiled as her abdomen protruded slightly. "Halia hears you." She rubbed the spot where Halia's tiny foot had just nudged her.

"Halia knows her mommy is upset and tired," Dan corrected her. "And Halia's mommy needs to stay up here and rest and let me send Adeline up to check on you. I'll get Jeff and Becca squared away and then I'll come back and give you your bath and put you to bed."

"I'm not staying up here while we have guests," she balked.

"Why don't we see what Adeline says," he offered, though everything in him wanted to argue.

"Fine." Fionna acquiesced just a little too quickly.

Someone knocked on the door. Fionna started to stand, but he halted her. "I'm sure it's the pizza. Just relax."

She reclined against the pillows and stared at her belly. She ran her hands over it almost quizzically.

Terror pulsed through his shield as Dan moved down the stairs and prayed that it was Logan and Adeline arriving and not the pizza. A relieved breath left his lungs as they entered followed by Becca and Jeff.

Becca had gone home with Emily, and Logan had picked her up on the way.

"Come in." Dan gestured into the living room. "I ordered pizzas. They should be here soon. Make yourselves at home. There's beer and Dr Pepper in the fridge."

"Where's Fionna?" Adeline seemed to have picked up on Dan's nerves.

"She's lying down upstairs," he choked, and Logan joined his wife's concerned stare. "Would you mind doing her exam before dinner, please?"

"Of course." Adeline followed Dan into the master bedroom.

"Dan," Fionna huffed, "you were supposed to come get me when they got here."

"Why don't I just check you out before we eat and then I can examine Becca after." Adeline tried to soothe Fionna's obvious tension.

"Fine." Fionna shot Dan a look that said she wasn't pleased.

"He's just trying to take care of you," Adeline gently reminded.

Fionna gave a begrudged nod. Having the routine down by now, she pulled her shirt up and her stretch pants down below her belly.

Adeline scrubbed her hands in Dan and Fionna's bathroom and then summoned a light heat cast before touching Fionna. She pressed several places on Fionna's abdomen and stomach. She measured Fionna's stomach, a process she abhorred but allowed. "She's measuring right on schedule."

Adeline plugged in her laptop and casted Fionna's womb to send the sound waves onto the monitor until Dan and Fionna could see their baby girl on the screen in a black-and-white shot.

Adeline smiled. "She's sucking her fingers."

Fionna swooned and Dan was unable to halt his broad grin. Adeline moved slightly and then made a slight grimace.

"What? What's wrong?" Fionna demanded. Dan moved beside her. He took her hand. His heart thundered in his throat.

"Your previous wound looks agitated."

"I had Braxton-Hicks contractions kind of badly last night."

"Halia is perfectly fine. Everything looks healthy, but I think your body is reacting to everything changing. Your rhythms are reading erratically. I'd say you're under more stress than you need to be, and you aren't resting enough. Your hormones are changing rapidly because you're nearing the end of your pregnancy. She's growing very quickly. It's too early for you to be experiencing contractions bad enough to need to be casted."

"I casted her last night," Dan informed Adeline. She nodded again.

"I'm sorry, Fionna, but you had a near fatal gunshot wound just a few weeks before you and Dan conceived again. You're going to have to take it easy. Let your body relax and complete the pregnancy fully.

"I expected this," Adeline confirmed as Dan and Fionna furrowed their brows. "You didn't leave yourself much time to extract yourself and Halia from Kauai, which regulated both of your rhythms easily because that's where both of you were conceived. I'm sure you already know this, but the volcanic energy of the Hawaiian islands affects Gifted people immensely. It's very healing, especially for people who were born there and carry the island rhythms."

"She is kama'aina," Dan repeated just a fraction of what he'd learned from spending time on Kauai with Fionna.

Adeline smiled and nodded. "A child of the land," she confirmed.

"Right. But you arrived back here and jumped into Dan's new job and Aida's going to a new school and you only have eight to ten weeks of your pregnancy left. You're going to have to take it easy. I'd really like your little girl to stay inside of you for as long as she's able. Give your body and Halia time to adjust to being away from the Kauaian rhythm strains. Stress will cause contractions, and your rhythms are extremely stressed."

"I know." Fionna nodded her defeat. "What do I need to do?"

"Do we need to go back to Kauai?" Dan asked. He'd put them on a plane that night. He'd break his contract at Venton and have Aida in school in Kauai by the next week.

"No," Adeline soothed. "But I don't think you need to be throwing us a dinner party. Let's go with no more yoga for a week, lots of rest, naps, early bed, everything. I'll check you at Georgetown next Friday. If the scarring from the gunshot wound is better, then we'll ease up. If it isn't, you're going to have to go on bed rest."

Drawing a deep breath, Fionna nodded. "Okay. I just want her healthy." Tears began to leak out the sides of her eyes.

Feeling his heart fissure and break, Dan squeezed her hand and tried to will calm into her, but he wasn't able to access much himself.

"She is," Adeline assured them again. "Let's just let her rest for a little while. I really think taking time off will be the cure."

"We're supposed to help Jeff and Becca move tomorrow," Fionna reminded them.

"You will not be helping anyone move. You will be here relaxing. I'll go unlock the storage unit for them and tell them to take anything they need or want. Then I'm coming back here, and we're lying on the couch all day." Dan dared anyone to argue with him.

Adeline chuckled as she lifted Fionna's stretch pants back over her belly. "This is always so hard on Shields. How about a compromise? You can help us move Jeff and Becca in tomorrow, but no lifting and lots of sitting. After lunch, Dan should bring you home and let you rest and relax," she explained the slight changes Fionna would need to make for Halia. "Be patient with him,"—she gestured her head to Dan. "He adores you and he takes excellent care of you, so whatever he says goes."

"Don't tell him that." Fionna laughed.

"Can I get that in writing?" Dan was only partially kidding.

"Lots and lots of casting, Dad. Your rhythms soothe Halia's. Remember that. This isn't an entirely normal pregnancy, Fionna, as much as you'd like for it to be. The timing between the gunshot, your miscarriage, and your conception changes it. You're going to have to give your body time to work through all you're asking it to do."

Drowning grief and guilt threatened to choke Dan yet again. It was his fault. He tried not to let Fionna feel his horrifying sorrow as he held her.

"Can I at least come downstairs and see everyone? I feel worse lying up here."

"That's fine," Adeline soothed. "But for tonight, no getting up to make people more drinks or to fix more food. We can do that."

"We're supposed to have Dan's family over Sunday night."

Rolling his eyes, Dan clenched his jaw before he could inform his wife that his family would get over the fact that she was doing nothing Sunday other than lying around in sweats and letting him cast her and take care of anything she or Aida might need.

"That's fine too, but you cannot stand all day and cook. How about this? You sit or lie down at least six of the twelve hours during the day, preferably one hour off for every one hour on, which means no more extended shopping trips either. So, if you're having people over, maybe Dan should cook. Drink lots of water. If your rhythms are calm and smooth according to your husband—not you—then you can keep going. If you feel your rhythms tense, sit down and relax."

Fionna nodded her defeat. Adeline smiled as she closed up her laptop and bag. She moved out of the room.

"Fi, baby," Dan soothed as soon as Adeline made her exit.

"I didn't mean to hurt her." Fionna began to cry in earnest. Her moods changed rapidly. She did her best to curl herself up in her customary ball as Dan tried to move his body around her to encase her in his love. She couldn't quite maneuver her ball anymore as her stomach prevented it now.

"Hey," he soothed, "Halia is fine. You're the one that taught me that we have to find a balance that works for us, and it has to work for

Halia as well. I think everything that we've done this week—Jeff and Becca, Aida's new school, along with all of the shit at Venton—it's been a little too much.

"We're not too far away from me holding my baby girl in my arms instead of in your stomach," he reminded her gently. Her rhythms tensed with fear and anxiety, but he felt the excitement beneath the fear. "And I will be right here for each and every single thing, but I think we need to settle in and find a better balance. We overdid it this week. I'm sorry. I know this is mostly my fault."

"No, it's not."

He shook his head. "Let me take care of you. You and my baby girls are all that really matter. We will make this work, but I need you to promise me that even when I'm at work, you'll rest for me. No more whirlwind days. A little at a time and a lot of rest."

"I promise. I think I…" She shrugged. "I don't know."

"What, baby?"

A harsh swallow tensed her beautiful neck. "Maybe I've been trying to stay really busy so I don't have to…think about other things."

Realization tensed in Dan's shield. He nodded. "Maybe we should talk more about the miscarriage instead of you avoiding feeling the emotions around it by surrounding yourself with other people's emotions."

She gave him a slight nod. "Okay, but not right now."

"Whenever you want to."

CHAPTER 23

HIS FATHER'S SON

D an kept his hands on his wife as she moved down the stairs. Logan's eyes held grave concern as he watched Dan seat her on the couch. Jeff and Becca halted their whispering. "I got the pizza." Logan pointed to the dining table where numerous pizza boxes were stacked.

"Let's eat." Dan tried to save Fionna from the urge to do anything at all. He fixed her a plate of pizza and a large glass of water.

Quickly deciding they would all eat in the living room so Fionna could stay curled up on the couch, everyone immediately caught on to the fact that she wasn't to lift a finger. After they ate, Becca cleaned up, including storing the leftover pizza in the refrigerator and wiping down the kitchen.

"Are you ready?" Adeline asked her when she finished.

Nervous tension swam in Becca's rhythms as she nodded.

"If you'd like to know the sex today, I can try to tell you, or Fionna can cast you after I examine you. She'll be able to read the energy and tell you if they're male or female, if they aren't strong enough for me to discern yet."

"Oh…well…I mean," Becca stammered. "Do you feel up to that?"

"I'm fine," Fionna assured her. Dan didn't argue though he didn't necessarily agree. Adeline scrubbed her hands and donned gloves before following Becca into the guest bedroom.

"Uh, Jeff." Dan gestured his head up the stairs.

"Oh." Jeff leapt off the couch. "I'm supposed to go too?" Logan and Dan both nodded. "Right." He took the stairs two at a time.

"Poor guy," Logan whispered after Jeff closed the door. "He's kind of a mess."

"He'll figure it all out. Hey, can you and Rainer help get them moved tomorrow? Fi needs to take it easy."

"I'm fine," Fionna sighed as Dan shared a look with Logan letting him know that she wasn't fine. Logan nodded his understanding.

"Sure, it's no problem."

"I told him I'd take him up to Sam's tomorrow evening," Dan recalled.

"Dan, really. I'll be fine. Go with Jeff to see Sam. You were going to see why that airbag light keeps coming on in my car, remember? I promise I'll lie on the couch and watch *Supernova* with Aida the whole time you're gone."

"I could cart Em over here. Make her sit on Fi for you," Logan teased.

"I may take you up on that."

~

Jeff Strenton

Letting the all too familiar feeling of overwhelming helplessness wash through him again, Jeff offered Becca a sheepish glance. "Sorry, I didn't know I was supposed to be up here."

"It's okay. This is all kind of new."

Supplying her his hand, Jeff eased as much calming energy as he could manage into her. He was still exhausted after working out at Iodex that afternoon though he would never admit that to anyone but her.

Adeline gave Jeff a kind smile. "Becca, if you'll just pull your shirt up, lower your jeans a little, and lie down for me."

It was distinctly odd to have Becca undressing in a bedroom with another person beside her. Jeff tried to focus on the baby though that did nothing to soothe his nerves.

Becca lay on the bed and unbuttoned her jeans. She slid them down slightly. She lifted her shirt to her bra line and gnawed her lip.

"I'm right here," he assured her.

Adeline gazed at them sweetly but then wrinkled her nose. "I'm sorry, Jeff, but I need you to wait over there." She pointed to the other side of the room.

"Oh...okay." Jeff nodded. Trying to think of what Mentor Vindico would do for Fionna, he leaned and kissed Becca's cheek.

"I have to work through all of Becca's energy and read the baby's, which isn't easy this early on. It's really just a tiny sack of cells."

Jeff moved to the other side of the room. He had no idea what he was supposed to feel. Nervous confusion was all he could access at the moment.

"Don't be nervous," Adeline guided both of them. "I looked over your chart from the last time Medio Metzger did your exam, and everything looked perfectly healthy."

Becca nodded but Jeff knew she wished Adeline would get on with whatever she was going to do.

Adeline reached and hoisted Becca's jeans down farther until Jeff could see everything that only he'd ever seen. "Just relax for me," Adeline soothed. Becca nodded and then let her eyes close. Jeff fought the urge to pace.

Adeline smiled as she locked on to the baby. "There we go."

"You can feel it?" Becca pled.

"I'd say you're about eight weeks along."

"And it feels like it's supposed to?"

"Perfectly healthy," Adeline assured her.

"I'd say he's about the size of a raspberry, in what we call the tadpole stage."

"Wait. He?" Becca gasped, tears beginning to fall rapidly. Jeff couldn't stand it. He rushed to her.

"He," Adeline confirmed. "Sometimes, I can't tell so early on. That's why I was going to get Fionna to tell you, but you're definitely having a little boy. His rhythms are very similar to Jeff's."

Stunned disbelief rocked through Jeff as he fell to his knees beside the bed to be closer to Becca. She was beaming and sobbing all at once.

"Is that what you wanted?" she asked him.

"I just wanted you both to be healthy. That's all that matters to me."

"Good dad," Adeline complimented. "All right, Jeff, if you'll give me your hands, I'll let you lock on to your son. I can show you right where he's implanted."

Dad. Jeff let the word bounce around in his mind as he held his hands over Becca's abdomen. It took him a few moments to calm enough to feel his son's rapid rhythms. They were tiny, quick versions of his own.

"If you want me to be your medio, we can wait until you're around twelve weeks for your first appointment as long as all goes well. Then it'll be once a month for the second trimester and more often in the third. My office is at Georgetown. Medio Metzger was actually my mentoring medio. As long as everything goes according to plan, you'll be delivering around the middle of April," she concluded with a kind smile.

The middle of April—Jeff swallowed harshly. He tried not to think of what the last six weeks of their senior year would hold. Exit exams, finals, graduation practices all tallied in his mind. None of it even mattered anymore.

"Do you have any questions for me?" Adeline offered.

Becca's brow furrowed. "Is there anything I should or shouldn't do?"

"Limit your caffeine, absolutely no alcohol or nicotine, limit your ocean fish intake to less than once a week, and my own personal recommendation is to have sex often."

Jeff blushed violently.

"That's what Fionna said," Becca admitted.

"There's a reason that little Halia responds so rapidly to Dan's voice. Babies that feel the mother's partner's energy throughout their development are generally happier, healthier, and better adjusted. Their Gifted rhythms tend to be stronger and more fluid. Although that isn't the only factor," she assured them.

Jeff assumed Logan had informed Adeline that his father had abandoned his mother before he'd ever been any bigger than a tadpole.

"If you have any questions, feel free to call my office. If a nurse can't help you, I'll call you back between my appointments."

"Okay, thank you. We won't be annoying," Becca promised.

~

Dan Vindico

Jeff and Becca headed back down the stairs. They both looked excited and overwhelmed.

Logan grinned as Adeline slid beside him on the love seat.

"Can I tell them?" Becca asked Jeff.

"Sure, baby."

"It's a boy!" She sounded overjoyed.

"Congratulations," were immediately supplied from all around the room. Jeff turned to Dan. He seemed to be trying to gauge him.

"Hey, Mentor Vindico, I was thinking, if it'd be okay with you, I could go ahead and paint the nursery now. It's still really early, and I have to start working next week."

Fionna's energy trilled, and Dan didn't know how to respond.

"You don't have to do that tonight," Fionna insisted though Dan knew the idea excited her.

"I'd really like to. I'm used to working in the evenings."

"He would work around people's houses doing odd jobs after they got home from work." Becca looked immensely proud of her husband and his astounding work ethic.

"Here,"—Logan stepped in—"why don't we let Mama and Daddy Vindico relax a little, and I'll help you."

. . .

An idea had been pulsing in Dan's mind for most of the afternoon, and he decided to go on with it. His little girl was going to be making her arrival sooner than later. Things like getting the nursery painted and arranged needed his attention.

He felt his drive begin to set in. Not in any way convinced that he wanted to continue his career at the academy after this school year, Dan locked his plan into place in his mind.

"Actually,"—he kissed Fionna's cheek as he stood—"why don't we let the ladies chill out and we'll all work on the nursery. It's not a huge room. We could finish it in a few hours, and I'd like to ask both of you for a little help with a few things."

Logan nodded. "Hell yeah, man. I missed you this summer. I'd love to hang out for a while if it's okay with my phenomenally beautiful wife who's been working hard all day, delivering kids, and you know…sticking her hands up things I don't want to think about."

Everyone cracked up.

Rolling her eyes, Adeline shook her head at him. "I don't mind. Fionna has the full box set of *Sex in the City*, and I'm about to recommend, as her medio, that she let me watch them while you paint."

Pure delight lit in Fionna's eyes. "Yes, definitely! I'll get them." She tried to get off the couch, but Dan halted her.

"I'll get them. You'll sit, and I'll make you popcorn before we head to the hardware store." Jeff watched him intently. He seemed to be taking mental notes.

"My mom did say I could watch them when I got married, and I did that," Becca announced. She cracked everyone up again.

"You've never seen it?" Fionna gasped. "Oh my gosh!"

"I'm going, I'm going." Dan took the stairs two at a time and returned with Fionna's beloved set of all six seasons of *Sex in the City* in their pink faux leather case. Fionna applauded as she bounced on the sofa.

"You know we could just get these digitally," he reminded her yet again.

"Then I wouldn't get to experience the joy of the pink suede case."

Chuckling, he loaded up the first season in their player and handed Jeff and Logan bags of microwave popcorn. They all summoned and popped the bags in their hands and added them to the gargantuan bowl the Vindicos used to hold popcorn for movie nights. The ladies settled in as Dan led Logan and Jeff out to Fionna's SUV.

CHAPTER 24
ROSES / OIL ON GYPSUM

"You get to sit in the pink flower seat." Logan directed Jeff to the middle row of seats in the SUV.

Rolling his eyes, Jeff took the seat beside Aida's car seat while Logan climbed in beside Dan.

"What'd you need help with, sir?" Jeff asked.

"There's a lot of stuff going on at Venton besides Wilshire and Mentor Bryant."

"The drug tests," Jeff assumed.

"Yeah, the kid I revived swears it was his first time using, but that isn't what his friends said, and the internist who's attending him says that isn't true. My dad asked me to look into all of it."

"And my dad," Logan said. Dan nodded his agreement. "Ha!" Logan exalted. "I just got information out of the man."

Dan laughed. "As I was just about to inform you of that, I wouldn't break your arm patting yourself on the back, Officer Haydenshire."

"I was having a moment." He mocked heartbreak.

Dan went on to explain that he needed to figure out if and how Mentor Bryant was still being paid, if Chancellor Wilshire ever used Venton money to fund their rendezvous, and what else he may be lying about.

Jeff seemed utterly thrilled to be working his first case with Dan and Logan. "Seriously, this is awesome," he gushed as Dan parked in the hardware store parking lot.

"Okay, there's more I need to tell you, but the first rule of being an Iodex officer is that you zip it up whenever you're out in public. You never know who might be one aisle over or who they might know," Dan commanded.

"Got it." Jeff was still beaming with pride.

Logan chuckled as Dan carried in the floral print fabric that Fionna had created Halia's bedding from. She'd already sewn the quilt of soft greens, creamy yellows, with touches of varying pinks, blues, and whites. "Dude, you look super manly carrying in flower fabric. Don't let anyone tell you different."

Rather enjoying the harassment, Dan rolled his eyes. "First of all, Haydenshire, you can kiss my ass. Second, I am incredibly manly *because* I am here carrying this lovely fabric for my wife who is pregnant with my baby. You know, the one I put in there with all of my manliness." Jeff lost his battle against his own laughter. "And if you don't shut it, I'll get my gorgeous wife to tell you just how manly I am."

"I was kidding." Logan gagged. Dan chuckled as they headed to the paint counter. He pointed to the portion of fabric that was a creamy yellow and ordered a gallon of paint in that color. As the attendant began mixing the paint, Dan moved to the brushes and rollers. He reached for a package of rolls of tape.

"Oh, you don't need that." Jeff shook his head. Dan shuddered to think of what Fionna would say if paint ended up all over the baseboards and closet doors. "I can show you how to cut it in so it looks really good. Tape just pulls off the paint. Use this." He lifted a wide metal spatula type item. "It's a taping knife. Just trust me. It's way easier and looks way better. And if we get the nicer brushes and rollers, it'll look totally professional."

Assuming that Jeff would know far better than he did, Dan followed his suggestions for painting supplies. He picked up the paint after it had been mixed, and they headed back to the Vindicos' home.

As soon as the car doors were closed, Dan leapt back into the cases at Venton. "There's also been some kind of security breach of the exam vault. One of my tests is apparently online. I have no idea how it would have gotten there. Governor Haydenshire is fairly convinced that there might be a lot of exams available online too."

Jeff went pale. "Are we not supposed to use those to study?" He sounded terrified that he'd somehow cheated. Logan and Dan shared a quick glance. Dan had a pretty good idea how Becca had gotten a high B on an exam that should have been given at the end of the year.

"I thought they were from the years before. I didn't know they were this year's."

"It's fine," Dan allowed. "The problem is who is stealing them and how they're being stolen?"

"I thought the mentors were putting their old exams up there to help us study. Governor Haydenshire is right. There are a bunch of them online."

"He always is," Logan sighed.

"Can you show me the websites hosting them?"

"Yes, sir," Jeff agreed though he looked bereaved. "But could you not ever let anyone know that I told you because I'm pretty sure I wouldn't survive long enough to see my kid be born."

"Actually, let's put the tests on the back burner for now," Dan negotiated. "The mentors can come up with new exams. My first concern is the money and Wilshire."

"The affair was officially outed on Instagram, if you want to go back to the beginning," Jeff explained.

"Really?"

"Yeah, and if you need to see the books without Wilshire knowing, I'm pretty good at cloning laptops and phones and stuff. That way we can figure out everything your dad needs to know without confirming to the press that you're helping him."

Logan rolled his eyes. "He's *pretty good* at cloning laptops like Hendrix was pretty good on a guitar."

Dan chuckled. "I take it what you showed me Tuesday was just the beginning."

Jeff shrugged. "I've been casting electronics since I was twelve. They've just always made sense to my shield. We could never afford game systems or anything, so I would take the broken ones that gaming stores were getting rid of and make them work so I could play them. I knew I needed a laptop for school. I didn't want to tell my mom or ask for one of the free ones from the computer lab because they suck. Before I started at Venton, I spent a whole summer working with a contracting crew, bought a secondhand laptop and all of the programs I was supposed to have for the school year, and then I casted it until it did everything I needed it to do.

"Bec gave me one of Brent's old cell phones that he was getting rid of. I couldn't afford the contract so I just keep it casted." He seemed to want to confess anything he'd ever done that might not have been completely honest. Deeply impressed, Dan nodded his understanding.

"If you're both sure you want to help me, I'll never let it get out. My dad's name is on the line for all of this. He didn't do anything wrong, but that's not how the Realm will see it."

"I'm in," Logan assured him. "It kills me all of this is going down at Venton. Kind of makes me sick. I want to figure it out before both of our fathers come under fire for it."

Jeff's rhythms lit with excitement. "Are you kidding me? This is huge. I can be your inside man because I know all the kids and hear all of their shit and stuff in the cafeteria."

Dan and Logan tried not to chuckle at his exuberance. He sounded like a little boy playing police detective.

They entered the house.

"Do you feel okay, baby doll?" Dan instinctively moved toward Fionna. She was cuddled up under one of her quilts, inhaling popcorn. Becca and Adeline were in identical positions, all staring at the large television.

"Ah, Mr. Big." Logan smirked as Chris Noth made his original debut on the show. "I have so much in common with that guy." Adeline rolled her eyes as Fionna laughed at him outright. Becca, however, glowed crimson.

"You sound just like Garrett," Fionna informed him. She gave Dan a grin. "I'm fine…Mr. Big." She waggled her eyebrows at Dan as Logan groaned.

Dan shot him a cocky smirk. "See, Haydenshire, what'd I tell you?"

Jeff and Logan headed up the stairs. The ladies on the screen began discussing anal sex, and Jeff nearly fainted as Samantha declared that a hole was a hole.

They entered Halia's nursery, and he set to work though he looked extremely uncomfortable. "Maybe Bec shouldn't be watching that. Her parents were super strict, and she's really, really naïve."

Logan stepped in with an understanding smile. "You're letting your Ioses flag fly a little high there, my friend. Might want to tuck that back in."

"Yeah, but she's probably never even heard of that before." Jeff gestured back down the stairs. "I don't want her to be embarrassed."

"She'll be fine," Dan assured him. "She's grown, and married, and we're not saying you have to participate in that."

Dan began spreading the drop cloths around the floor in an effort to get Jeff's mind off *Sex in the City*. After Jeff instructed Logan and Dan on how to load their brushes and to keep them moving, he began cutting in.

Dan considered Logan's quip to Jeff. He was an Ioses Predilect through and through. He would protect Becca with his very life if need be. Dan also considered the fact that according to Jeff, Becca had been overly sheltered by her parents. Yet, she was eight weeks pregnant. Letting that filter through his brain, Dan made a vow to himself not to keep his girls from knowing things and to answer questions they had.

CHAPTER 25

PANDORA'S BOX

Following all of Jeff's instructions, they completed the nursery in three hours. It did look professionally done. Pride etched his face as they closed the door, leaving the lights on to let the paint dry after they'd heat casted the walls.

Logan moved to Adeline and with a teasing grin. He lifted her off the couch and then fell to the spot she'd previously occupied and cradled her in his lap.

"Logan," she squealed. "We should go. I told her she was supposed to be resting, and I'm sitting here watching her television at ten o'clock," Adeline admonished herself.

"Yeah and we're getting the Strentons all moved in early tomorrow, so we should head out."

Dan had a feeling he was more interested in getting Adeline into bed after hours of watching *Sex in the City* than he was getting himself to sleep.

Adeline stood and tugged Logan up though she was much too light to have really helped pull his tall muscular frame off the couch.

"Here, you can borrow the first few seasons." Fionna eased herself up off the couch.

"Are you sure?" Adeline sounded thrilled.

"Of course." Fionna moved to the DVD player and extracted the first two seasons and handed them to Adeline.

"I won't keep them long."

"It's fine. We don't get to watch them all that often. Aida's still a little young for Carrie and Samantha."

As the Haydenshires made their exit, Jeff pointed to Dan's laptop on the coffee table. "I can show you that stuff on Instagram before we hit the sack."

Dan was intrigued but shook his head. "Nah, I need to get my wife in the bed."

Fionna and Becca cracked up immediately.

Dan cocked his eyebrow and chuckled at his wife. "And where is your mind, honey?" he chastised.

Fionna blushed a deep crimson as she continued her mischievous giggling. "Right where you like it," she sassed.

"Okay, you've embarrassed poor Jeff enough for one night."

"Oh, sorry." Fionna wrinkled her nose, her cheeks still overly pink. Unable to help himself, Dan leaned and kissed one.

"S'ok," Jeff managed though he stared steadfastly at the carpet.

"Wait. What stuff on Instagram?" Fionna asked. "You hate Instagram."

"That is very, very true," Dan agreed. "But apparently Wilshire and Mentor Bryant were outed there." He rolled his eyes out of habit. He abhorred every kind of digital social network. Dan couldn't fathom why anyone would care what other people ate for lunch, were cooking for dinner, or to see the pictures from their drunken weekend intermixed with people you didn't know telling you how to live your life. Dan was also well aware that once you posted something on social media, it was out there forever.

Once it hit, it was gone and could never be recaptured. If you made a poor decision then announced it, even if you decided to take it off your feed at a later date, it was already screen-shotted and being discussed liberally. Whether or not it was still digitally available, people cannot un-see or un-read something.

The genie could never be returned to the lamp. Pandora's box was opened. It was nothing more than a lethal combination of monetized narcissism, dopamine surges, and people who profited off of pain. Dan couldn't recall the sheer number of times that the Senate would ask Iodex to check up on a potential personnel hire. In a matter of moments, Ramier would have Instagram, Facebook, and TikTok wide open, and more times than not, the candidate never received a call back.

"Chancellor Wilshire has an IG account?" Fionna was simultaneously intrigued and shocked.

"No, ma'am, not a personal one," Becca assured her. "It got posted on the Venton account. We all saw it."

"I want to see it."

Dan watched her rhythms closely. She didn't seem to want to see the confirmation of what she already knew. There was something else that appeared to deeply concern her.

"Please." She turned the full power of her pleading sienna eyes on her husband. "I'll lie here on the couch."

"All right." He handed Jeff his laptop and settled beside Fionna. He kept his hands on her legs. She seemed to need reassurance. Something was scaring her. Her bands pulsed with nervous tension.

Dan kissed her cheek again. "I love you and I would never ever do something like this," he whispered. She nodded but then wrapped her arms around his bicep and clung to him. Dan was much more concerned about his wife than what Jeff was doing with his laptop.

"Venton's first idiotic mistake was making Sherman their social media guy." Jeff rolled his eyes and Becca giggled. "He posted these on Venton's page from some teacher conference over the summer. The Venton page has tens of thousands of followers. It's not just current students. Alumni follow it and a ton of other people because Venton's the premier academy."

Spinning Dan's laptop toward Dan and Fionna, he showed a post from the week before. Directly in front of his own camera lens, in the six available photos from the event, was Sherman mugging stupidly in the conference room of some no-name hotel in Boise.

Other accounts of mentors who had attended the event had been tagged in the post. In the background of several photographs from what appeared to be a hotel conference room dinner, the chancellor and Mentor Bryant were seated beside one another.

"There." Jeff looked thoroughly disgusted as he pointed to the photo. Everyone seated in the dining area was staring up at a man on stage with a microphone, but there in the photo, Chancellor Dean Wilshire—the highest paid head of the most esteemed Gifted academy anywhere in the United States—was massaging Katherine Bryant's inner thigh. It was extremely well hidden under the cheap polyester white tablecloths that covered each table. Fergus had been photographing the man on stage whom he'd labeled as his hero. He'd had no idea what else he'd captured on film.

"Does Mentor Bryant have a personal page that you can show me?" Dan asked.

"Yes, sir, of course." He opened another tab and displayed what Dan had requested a moment later. Her page displayed numerous photos of her son and daughter, both of whom appeared to be in middle school. She'd posted a picture of her daughter's recent sleepover with several of her preteen friends.

Dan shuddered. If she knew half of the cases Iodex had worked beyond Wretchkinsides and the Interfeci, she never would have put something like that on social media.

Dan read her profile. *Happily married to my hubby of twenty-eight years, love my kiddos at home and at school, love biking and reading, love to laugh, love my life.* Glancing at her birthday, Dan was surprised to realize that she was forty-eight—much older than he'd originally guessed only ever having seen her at a faculty meeting that he'd paid very little attention in.

Wilshire was sixty-two, just three years from retiring. He was several years older than Dan's father and Governor Haydenshire.

"Didn't Chancellor Wilshire tell you to set up an account?" Fionna asked Dan.

"He said it was a great way to connect with my students. I politely informed him that on seven different occasions Elite had arrested high school teachers and admins who were also child molesters, and they all used Instagram to look at pictures of their students. I told him it was incredibly dangerous to the kids to encourage mentors to have accounts, and that my students could connect with me in my classes or in my office, but that I didn't do social media."

Jeff and Becca both scowled.

"Are you serious?" Becca sounded horrified. She instinctively rubbed her hands over her nonexistent bump.

Dan nodded.

"Our little boy is never having social media," she decreed.

"Yet another reason I don't have any." Jeff shuddered.

"Most Shields don't do social media. We sense how dangerous it is," Dan agreed.

Jeff opened two additional tabs. "Wilshire has a Facebook account, and Venton has a page. He also set up a group for Venton teachers, only he joined the group from his private page. The password for both is his initials and birthday." He rolled his eyes. "Everyone can see everything. A bunch of kids went in and made themselves admins in the group." His eyes lit. "One time, Ben Cobson went in and spoofed Wilshire's account. He announced in the group that it was Shield Appreciation Week, and all of the Ioses Preds got free lunch and no homework." He and Dan both cracked up. "It was hilarious how many mentors thought it was real."

On the public board were the dates of upcoming formals, order meetings, Summation Challenges, and an advertisement for a sale going on at the school bookstore.

Jeff switched to the chancellor's more personal page. The most recent posting was of his birthday party that had been a few weeks before school began. There was one of him and Ellen, his wife of forty years, both smiling at the backyard barbecue. There was another of him kissing her cheek.

"She knows," Fionna choked.

Dan turned to her. "What, baby?"

"Look at her in the photo. Can't you feel it?" Fionna was on the verge of tears as she pointed to the picture of the birthday kiss. "Look at her eyes. She knows."

Dan studied the picture. He was certain his wife was right though he had no capacity to feel the energy in a photo, but Ellen Wilshire's eyes held the pain and the betrayal, the rejection of all that her husband was doing to her.

Jeff moved farther down the page to the happy birthday wishes from all of the chancellor's friends. He'd responded to one that appeared to be from his brother. *You know you're old when you offer to get a prescription for the little blue pills and your wife tells you not to bother...ha!* Numerous people had liked the status. Dan wondered just how much truth was in the joke.

"What does that mean?" Becca asked Jeff quietly. "What are little blue pills?"

"I'll tell you later, okay?" Becca nodded and almost instinctively scooted closer to Jeff on the couch. Dan understood his earlier concern about *Sex in the City*.

He'd been her Shield in most every way for the last four years. Most of their academy careers, he'd guided her into adulthood. He'd kept her safe and explained things to her that her parents never would've. He'd been her first, but in exchange, he'd tried desperately to keep her innocence relatively intact for everyone but himself.

"But their Facebook pages aren't going to prove whether or not the school funded their affair." Disgust perforated Fionna's tone as they stared at photographic evidence of a person they'd respected falling rapidly from their pedestal.

"Uh...well, they might actually." Jeff seemed to consider for a moment. "Wilshire has a WhatsApp account connected to his personal profile. They share data."

"What is WhatsApp?" Fionna asked.

"It's big in pretty much every other country. Primary form of digital communication all over the world, but in this case, I'm betting..."

Dan gave a morose nod. "He had it so he could chat up Katherine Bryant without either of their spouses seeing the messages on their phones."

Jeff nodded. "Yeah, and that account's password is also his birthday. If you have a casted thumb drive available, I can copy all of the messages off for you."

"I only need the ones between him and Bryant."

"Yes, sir. And if you happen to have an external hard drive anywhere, I can clone Wilshire's laptop for you. That should give you access to his school email account."

"You can do that from here without having to have his computer nearby?" Dan was stunned.

"He's amazing," Becca assured Dan though that was woefully unnecessary. Dan had seen Ramier clone laptops dozens of times, but he was always in the presence of the laptop being cloned.

"I can do his phone as well, but I *would* have to be near his phone, and he'd have to be talking on it. I'd also need a spare phone to put the data on."

"We have all of those old cell phones we let Aida play with," Fionna reminded Dan.

"I'll get you several, and Monday at school I'll arrange to be on the phone with the chancellor while you're near him. Thank you for all of this."

"No problem. This is the case, right?"

Dan dug in his computer bag until he located an external hard drive that only contained a few pictures he'd transferred off his phone. He moved them to Fionna's laptop and handed over the drive.

Jeff casted the hard drive and then spun the laptop back. Focusing intently, he summoned, casted Dan's computer, typed rapidly for several long minutes, and worked until he had what he was looking for.

"Okay, here you go. I pulled his email accounts into a separate area so you can get to those without having to be in his entire hard drive, but it's all on there."

"You just...did that...that fast?" Fionna was equally impressed it seemed.

"Yes, ma'am, but I would never do that normally. I mean, we have to figure this out, right? This is what your dad wants you to find out," he reminded Dan.

"Yeah, and I definitely picked the right person for the internship. No one else could even come close."

Jeff's cheeks now blazed with the heat of his embarrassment. "There's more stuff on Mentor Sherman's page as well." He seemed to want to move the attention back to the case. "They must've gone to, like, a dozen conferences over the summer."

Dan was immensely thankful that he'd informed the school governors that every summer he would be spending in Kauai with his family, and therefore unable to attend any such conferences. Dan didn't have to guess why Wilshire would have wanted to attend so many out of state.

"Here." Jeff pulled up another photograph from Mentor Sherman's conference event pages. "I swear that guy is such a moron."

The photograph was of Chancellor Wilshire and Mentor Bryant standing side by side, smiling broadly with their arms slung over one another. *Venton Love* was the title Sherman had given the photo.

Becca nodded and a mischievous light cast her eyes. "Remember last year when he taught your amative energies class." She giggled hysterically.

Jeff brushed a kiss on her cheek. He didn't seem to be able to help himself. "It was so bad," he admitted. "Sherman somehow ended up assigned to the Ioses, Vis Virres, and Valeduto juniors." He choked back laughter. "We're in there about two seconds before everyone realizes that he's teaching amative energies, but he's never done it.

"All of the Valeduto guys start correcting his vocabulary. They're all going into medicine, and he couldn't seem to call anything the scientific term. So, they kept asking him to explain it more. Eventually, he starts putting slides up, and he's taking notes off of the slides." Jeff laughed over the memory. "Trust me, every guy in that classroom had way more experience than Sherman. He eventually started asking us questions.

"Two guys from Vis Virres summoned really quick and flipped the slides of the female parts where the erotic energy storehouses are. Those were the ones he was taking notes off. I don't know if he and Tilly McIntyre have consummated their engagement or whatever, but trust me, she was very, very confused the first time they did it."

That did it. Dan and Fionna guffawed. Everyone seemed eager to leave Wilshire and Bryant behind for the evening. Laughter held much more appeal than deception and lies.

"Tell them what that guy Michael from Valeduto said," Becca urged.

"Bec." Jeff shook his head. "I can't say that in front of her." He gestured to Fionna. The statement in and of itself had Fionna laughing even harder.

"Okay, I'll tell them. This guy Michael Bowers was in the class with Jeff, and he's Head of Valeduto Order. Mentor Sherman keeps asking all of these weird embarrassing questions. So, Michael tells him that he can make his, you know, thing longer." She gestured to her own crotch. "Wait, what was it?" she quizzed Jeff.

"If he eats bananas and drinks tomato juice," Jeff supplied immediately though he was shaking his head.

"Right." Becca jumped back in. "To this day, we still see him with V8 and eating bananas all the time." She cracked up as Dan and Fionna shook their heads.

"All right, before I start to feel genuinely sorry for Sherman, I think I'd like to put this very long day to bed." Dan stood and helped Fionna off the couch.

"Okay," Fionna agreed as she forced a smile. Dan could still feel the grief and the fear that were choking her energy. "I want to see the nursery first."

This seemed to greatly please Jeff as Dan began drawing the light from the lamps and checking to make certain the doors were locked.

"I really appreciate everything you did and your willingness to help me," he assured Jeff.

"I'm happy to help. You've done so much for us."

"Just please be careful. I shouldn't really have asked for your help. Portwood might not like that you took a case on the side."

"I really want to help. I won't get caught. It'll be like part of my training."

"Just watch your back and don't talk about this to anyone but Becca."

"Yes, sir."

CHAPTER 26

CATWOMAN, CONFUSION, AND COURSE CORRECTION

Fionna seemed thrilled over the nursery, but something was still amiss. Dan's heart ached as he followed her into their bedroom and closed the door quietly behind him. He wanted to lock the world out. Infidelity, heartache, sorrow, and the caustic corrosive world had no place in their sanctuary.

They would stay away from his baby. He would see to it. He would demand it. She was too perfect, too sweet. He loved her too much to allow her to ever feel that kind of pain and doubt. But he couldn't keep it locked away because she'd stepped into their refuge desperate for relief from what she was carrying in her heart.

"Come here, baby." He pulled his wife into his muscled embrace. "Talk to me."

Fionna's neck tensed as she swallowed down emotion. "Thank you," she fussed and effectively broke Dan's heart.

He slipped the stretch pants she'd donned from her legs. He pulled the T-shirt over her head and fell to his knees. He kissed her swollen belly and watched tears fall from her beautiful eyes. Leaving on her bra and panties, Dan stood.

He kept one of her hands in his as he moved to their bed. Pulling the throw pillows off, he heated the sheets and quilts and then guided her in. She remained seated as he pulled off his jeans and T-shirt and then moved beside her. He sat in front of her, both cross-legged with their knees touching. This seemed to elicit a small smile.

Dan brushed her cheek with his thumb and kissed her forehead. "I'm right here, sweetheart. I will always be right here." He pointed to his current position right beside her. "What's wrong?"

"It's all confusing in my head," she admitted.

"You start talking, and we'll make it make sense together."

"Please don't say no," she began in a heartbroken whisper. Confusion perforated Dan's thoughts. That wasn't at all what he'd expected his wife to say.

"To what?" He wiped away her tears. Fionna grasped his hands in her own and drew from him deeply. Concentrating, Dan supplied her with soothing calm and strength, careful not to push too much through her at once. He calmed her, and she caught her escaping breath.

"I don't want you to work on Chancellor Wilshire's affair without me. I want to be there for all the investigating part. Please, please let me. I need you to let me," she begged as her tears returned with vengeance. "I have a really bad feeling about this."

Dan tried to figure out how that might work. "Baby, you need to be here. You're supposed to be resting, and honestly, as selfish as this is…" he hemmed.

"What?"

"This week hasn't been anything at all like I expected. I never even fathomed that stuff like this was going to get dumped in my lap, but no matter what crap has come up at work, or with life in general, when I walk in that door and I see you and I hear Aida say daddy, and jump up in my arms, when you kiss me, when you let me hold you, that means more to me than you'll ever know. Those are the moments that I've lived for. Those quick moments have made everything bearable.

"I'm sorry that I let the world get to you. That's not my job. I'm supposed to protect you from all of the shit that's out there. That's all I've ever wanted to do. I guess I just want to keep you tucked up here, where you're safe and happy and my girls are safe and with their mommy. I love to walk in and see you smiling, and eat the things you make for us because they don't just feed Aida and me and Halia nourishment. They somehow feed my soul. I love that you do that for us and that it somehow makes you happy...at least I hope it does.

"I know that's probably incredibly chauvinistic, and you can yell at me if you want. But that's the truth, and I don't ever want to lie to you."

Fionna broke down in sobs, and Dan held her tightly, not certain what might be coming next. But suddenly he felt it—whatever he'd said had brought her a modicum of contentment. She nodded against him.

"It's not chauvinistic *because* I love to do that. Being here and creating things centers me. It lets me heal a little from what happened to me. And now I need to stay here and rest so Halia will be healthy, and I can carry her full term, but I need you to let me help you with this part of the investigation, please." She grasped Dan's biceps fiercely. He fought not to wince from her fervor. "I know I can't be up at Venton much. I have to take care of my girls, but all of the stuff Jeff just found for you, I want to go through it with you. You don't understand. You don't know what I know."

Whatever was ricocheting violently in her mind and in her rhythms, Dan had to rescue her. It was who he was. When she leapt out into the cold, cruel world, he would always catch her.

"Okay." He rubbed her back and cradled her head on his shoulder. "It's okay. You can be my partner for this," he soothed. "I'll find out what I can at the academy, and then I'll come home and we'll work on it together. If that's what you need, then that's what we'll do. But tell me what you know that I don't. I'd like to understand. If you're gonna be my crime fighting partner, you have to tell me everything you know." He'd hoped for a smile. She delighted him by giving him a slight chuckle.

"Okay." She wiped away her tears. "But I get to be Batman cause when I'm not pregnant I look damn good in black leather." She seemed lost somewhere between her sweet, teasing sense of humor and the terror she was feeling. Constantly telling himself that there was no danger in her helping him, that with her phenomenal abilities she would probably have the case solved in a matter of days, Dan laughed as he kissed her wet cheek.

"How about you play Catwoman to my Batman? Her black leather suit will show off all of your best assets, and I'd love to see you with a whip."

"Meow." Fionna waggled her eyebrows, her moods still shifting rapidly.

Dan was pleased that she was feeling more herself, but he wasn't fool enough to believe that her terrorizing fears had disappeared. She'd just pushed them farther under the surface.

"Tell me, baby doll. What is it about all of this that scared you so badly? I would never, ever cheat on you."

"That's what you say now." Devastation suddenly had her entire body trembling in terror.

"Fionna!" Dan tried to remember that she was extremely hormonal, that she was terrified, but truthfully, she'd cut him deep and fury pulsed in his veins. She shook her head as she felt his anger. "Please just say whatever it is you're thinking. We'll figure it out, but I would never cheat on you."

"Okay," she choked as he handed her tissues and helped her dry her eyes for the moment. "It's different from other emotions."

"What's different?"

"All of the emotions tied up in an affair. They're different from what I feel from everyone else."

"Different how?" He was still hurt over her disbelief in him, but he was desperate to know where this was coming from.

"You know I can feel emotional energy even from Non-Gifted people," she whispered.

"I know."

"Men and women that aren't Gifted but that are thinking about cheating or are cheating, I pick up on that much easier than any other emotion from anyone else. Those energies are so palpable, they run in such a constant continual wave, that a lot of times I can read those easier from a Non-Gifted person than I can read the normal everyday emotions of Gifted people."

Confusion cast her sweet face as she tried to explain what being

Fionna Styler Vindico, the most powerful Receiver of their time, meant. "It consumes them. They can't think of anything else. They don't feel anything else. It's an addiction.

"It starts out with nothing at all. A look, a glance, an innocent flirtation, but it fills something that's missing in that person's spirit, and they become instantly addicted to the feeling. Then the deception takes over. The desperation to feel whatever they felt from that person dominates every single thing they do.

"That's why it never matters what the other person looks like. It has nothing to do with the fact that a woman is married to a hunk but cheats with the guy that's decades older than her that's losing his hair and has a beer gut. It's that feeling they're after.

"Whether Chancellor Wilshire made her feel safe, or taken care of, or like she was sexy and beautiful, or just complimented her lesson plans, she was desperate for something, and he filled it. It may have been completely innocent at first, but one of them let the feeling overtake them and then they do everything in their power to have that drug again and again, until it's too late." She shook her head. Devastation continued to tense in her rhythms.

"Most women I know that have cheated on their husbands can't even tell you what the other guy looks like. It isn't him she's consumed with. It's the desperation to feel the way the lover makes her feel, the passion that she feels from him because it's new and it's exciting. I wish I could explain to you how much of the person it occupies. They can't think of anything else.

"They get careless and stupid because they're so desperate. It's like they don't care if they get caught because they need the next hit—the next email, the next text message, whatever. But there's a reason that so many women cheat in their late forties and early fifties, and there's a reason that marriages fall apart when you go from being just a couple to having kids. It's like Papa always says,"—she shuddered as she reached the pinnacle of her terror—"it's a balance. If your energy is off or your soul is out of sorts, the balance of your spirit is broken. If it isn't restored, it will ultimately ruin your life.

"Your chemical balance can drive you to do things you never thought possible. No one walks down the aisle with the intention of cheating. Things get off, and they're off for a while. No one bothers to try and steady the tipping balance, or to swim against the dangerous tides. All of a sudden you're choking and drowning in the drug."

Letting everything she'd said wash over him, Dan held on to his wife forcefully. "I know you're scared, and that on top of everything else that comes with us having Halia, you're terrified that something will tip out of balance between us. But baby, please hear me say this, I will not let that happen. It will be different and things will change, but not for the worse—for the better. I know that it might take us a few weeks to find the balance and that it will continue to change. But Fi, I'm not going to let us get out of sync.

"If something's wrong, we'll fix it together. I will swim any tidal wave. I will fight with everything that I am. I will never let you go, and I will never, ever let you drown.

"And I don't just mean now in our thirties," he went on. She had to hear him, and he would talk until she knew beyond a shadow of a doubt that they would take the leap of faith together and that he would never let her go.

"I mean forever. When you're having hot flashes, and I'm using little blue pills. And a few decades after that when we're sitting in rocking chairs somewhere watching our great grandkids, I will still be chasing you in my wheelchair because when I said I do, that's what I meant, for now and forever."

A smile formed between her tears as she nodded. "Okay, but Dan..." She looked pained to tell him more.

"What, sweetheart?"

"You're just..." She shook her head. Drawing from him again, she forced herself to go on. "I'm sorry, but you're not so good at not getting consumed by something, and sometimes it scares me, because what happens if I don't hold your attention anymore. If something else prettier or more interesting comes along."

He knew that a small part of what she'd said was true. His single-minded ferocity had been his downfall on many occasions. His dogmatic drive to hunt down and end Wretchkinsides had consumed his very being for ten long years until she'd rescued him on her angel wings and pulled him from the suffocating depths of hell.

"I used to be terrible at it," he agreed. Her brow furrowed. Apparently, she thought he would argue. "But once I met my own personal guardian angel, she changed everything. She taught me how to live again, taught me how important balance was. She gave me her sexy smile and offered me her hand, and I was done for—hook, line, and sinker.

"I grabbed her hand, let her lift my head up off my desk, and followed her out of my office, out of my own hell, out of the nightmares I lived day in and day out. I followed her right into her bed, and then I was woefully unable to deny her access to any part of me. I let her resuscitate me. She wound her way into my heart and made me realize that I actually had a soul because she *is* my soul, and it had been gone for so long.

"Then she went and found us our own amazing little angel that looks up at me with those innocent brown eyes. I will never forget lying down with both of you in the Haydenshires' living room the night before Rainer and Emily's wedding and her telling me that she loved me. You have no idea what that did to me, and it was all because of you.

"And now." He moved his hands tenderly over her bump. Halia was moving rapidly. She was frightened from Fionna's harrowing emotions. Dan let his eyes close as he filled Fionna's womb with his own soothing energy. He leaned centimeters from Fionna's belly. "It's okay, baby. Daddy's right here." Halia's energies soothed almost instantly. He lifted his head to stare Fionna in the eye. "I'm never, ever going anywhere," he vowed yet again.

"I hear what you're saying to me. I really do," Dan assured her. "Whatever Wilshire made her feel or she made him feel, no matter how consuming it was, they both had the chance to stop it a thousand times over. I certainly don't know the emotional side of cheating on your spouse, and I never will, but I can promise you that it is a series of terrible decisions and of choosing to give in to the weakness instead of fighting for what is right and making what you have the best it could possibly be.

"You can always turn around from where you are and decide to change course. Neither of them did and that makes me madder than anything else," he spat. "You know, an incredibly beautiful, brilliant woman said to one of my punk-ass students just a few days ago that if you give a woman your best, then she'll give you more than you can even fathom. Fi, baby, you deserve my best, and I'll never give you anything less than that."

"You promise?" Fionna begged.

Dan smiled as he nodded. "Do you remember when Papa put your hand in mine at our wedding? Do you remember what he said to me?"

Fionna's brow furrowed as she shook her head. "He said, 'my Maylea,'" Dan whispered. "Take care of her for you hold her spirit, and she holds your fire. That's it for me. If I somehow get to be lucky enough to be the man that gets to hold and protect your spirit, then at the end of the day, that's all that matters to me. That's all that I will ever allow to drive me. I let Wretchkinsides drive me for long enough and that led straight to hell. You take me to heaven, and no one else gets to take me anywhere but you."

"Will you just cast me?" She let him recline her in the bed. Wrapping her up in the sheets and quilts, Dan let the melding of their skin, of their spirits, soothe him as he pushed his shield out over the only thing that would ever truly matter.

"Dan?" she finally managed to speak with any volume at all.

"Maylea," he whispered. Feeling her smile against his chest eased his own spirit.

"I miss you calling me that."

"I love to call you that. It's who you are, and I love each and every part of my beautiful wildflower."

"I want to go home." She finally broke down and said the words that Dan had felt tensing in her energy for the past week.

"I know." He didn't want her to feel guilty for anything she felt. "If you want me to quit, I will, but I really feel like I need to stay at Venton long enough to figure out what's going on. I'd like to help out my dad. I think we should ask Adeline tomorrow about us going back for the week of fall break. But how about if we work on finding a balance here for the next few weeks and then I'll take you home. We'll spend the week forgetting everything going on here."

Relief drowned her erratic rhythms. She soothed in his embrace and in his shield. "That sounds perfect, and you promise you won't do anything about the affair without me."

"You're my partner for this. I think I'll call you Officer Hot Lips or maybe Sexy Ass," he teased as her rhythms continued to calm as he casted her. She giggled sweetly. The sound soothed his soul.

"I kind of like Officer Hot Lips."

"Sexiest damn partner I've ever had, Fitzroy included." He cracked her up, which had been his goal. As Dan soothed her to sleep, he thought over her desperation that he not investigate Wilshire's affair without her.

Clearly, she believed somewhere in her soul that Dan could somehow become as caught up in the affair as those actually participating in it. He hadn't ever shown her that he could have a real life separate from his work. He'd worked the farm all summer, but he'd worked it with her by his side.

She'd found solace in their togetherness, and Kauai regulated her rhythms for her. She'd spent the summer surrounded by the calming serenity and healing sanctuary the farm provided them. Halia magnified her already overwhelming abilities. On Kauai, the people she was with certainly weren't involved in affairs or any kind of scandalous acts of any kind. Family was everything to the Hawaiian people.

She'd been able to relax.

In DC, she was bombarded at every turn with disturbing emotions from those around her, and Fionna had to pretend for the most part that she didn't know what was going on in the mind of the seducer, the mind of the mistress, the deceptive lies that people thought they could keep hidden away. The most terrifying of all were the ones they told themselves, but his beautiful Maylea felt them all. She was happiest at home because it was exhausting to expose herself and Halia to the things she felt outside of the nest she'd created for their family.

CHAPTER 27

LIFE CAN BE LEAKY

Dan grabbed his phone to turn off the alarm. He still deeply regretted setting it the evening before. Running his hands over his face, he reminded himself that he needed to get Jeff and Becca moved into their new home. They needed a nest of their own, and he and Fionna needed theirs back.

The fact hit him that their baby girl had spent the night away from home, and instead of him and Fionna engaging in an evening of more carnal pleasures that lasted for hours, they'd read Facebook pages and cloned laptops to investigate other people's affairs. A desperate need to rebalance their lives coursed through him.

In one week's time, he'd let the world invade his home, his family's safe harbor, and that was going to stop. Fionna groaned and whimpered, still exhausted from her emotional night.

"Just stay in bed. I'll take them out to the storage unit and then I'll pick us up some breakfast and bring it back. We'll stay in here until Meredith drops Aida off."

Fionna grinned against her pillow. She was in her customary position, arranged on several pillows so that she could sleep half on her stomach and half on her side despite her declaration that it was like trying to sleep on a watermelon.

She shifted slightly and then her eyes flew open in horrified shock.

Dan had been gazing at her sweetly and rubbing her back, hoping to coax her into staying in bed.

"What?" he panicked.

"Oh my gosh," she groaned.

"What's wrong?"

"This did not happen!"

"What?"

"You go away. You can't see this."

"Tell me what is wrong. I am not going anywhere," Dan ordered.

"I am stuck to the sheets," she whimpered.

"What? How?"

"My boobs are stuck to the sheets because I've been leaking all night long," she finally managed though she was glowing crimson.

Dan bit his lips together trying not to laugh.

"I am just a huge mom blob, and I will never be sexy again." She buried her face in her pillow in abject defeat.

Dan eased her off the circular wet marks on their sheets and onto his chest. "You have never stopped being sexy. You are gorgeous, and I know there are a lot of things going on in that beautiful body, sweetheart, but I still want you just as badly as I did that night I followed you home from Anglington's."

"I don't even want to nurse. Why am I leaking?"

Trying to fortify himself to combat her raging hormones, he brushed a kiss on her head. "I don't think your body knows that yet. You're getting ready to nurse her even if you don't plan to." He knew that somewhere under all of the confusing emotions and wavering rhythms brought on by her hormones, she knew that.

"Now my nipples hurt," she fussed with a precious pout.

"Want me to see what I can do about that?"

"You aren't afraid you might get more than my energy?"

Determined to prove to her that he thought she was phenomenally gorgeous and that he loved her, leaky breasts and all, Dan turned and slid down her body.

"Not even a little." He delicately swirled his index finger around her right nipple. It was throbbing red and raw. "Can't let my baby hurt."

He massaged her right breast, and she began to give in. Her eyes closed as she let him have the worry and the fear she was experiencing. She was going to let him wash them all away.

Moving slowly, reminding himself that they were tender and fevered, Dan lapped his tongue in slow vacillations over her throbbing nipples.

"Oh god, yes." She arched her back, desperate for more. Smiling, Dan continued his slow delicious moves on his wife. He sucked her fiercely and pulled the erotic energy from her. Switching sides, he spun his tongue over her left nipple and then proceeded to pull it deeply in his mouth. She laced her fingers in his hair, urging him on.

"Don't stop, please," she begged.

Moaning against her, Dan realized what the added nerves and changes in her breasts might afford her if she'd let him own her. He pulled with more ferocity, massaging them in his hands, groping and tugging until he pushed her further toward the depths of ecstasy.

"Oh my god." Her eyes flashed open. Her body began to writhe. Dan dragged his teeth over the fevered flesh before suckling her again. "I'm gonna…"

"I know, baby doll. Relax for me. Just feel it. Let me have you."

"Yes." Her eyes rolled back in her head as she gave in to the overwhelming sensations. Dan nipped her and sucked. He marked her breasts all for himself. She went wild. Her nails dug into his scalp as she pushed her tits deeper into his mouth.

"More," she pled.

Dan set to work. He left his purple markings of ownership along her breastbone and neck just like she preferred. "Yes," she gasped suddenly as her eyes flew open.

It took hold of her forcefully. The climax consumed her as she thrust against him. Her breath tangled in her throat. She clung to him as her lungs begged for air.

Trying to hide his cocky smirk, Dan held her tightly to his chest. "See," he soothed as she regained the ability to breathe, and her scowl was replaced with a replete smile of satisfaction. "Never quite got you there that way before you were pregnant with my baby girl."

Fionna laughed. Her energy now rolled in waves of satisfied pleasure.

"Maybe June and Bonnie being overly sensitive does have its advantages."

"You know, I don't think I know which is which."

"Bonnie is just a little bigger." Fionna pointed to her left breast and blushed again.

"Gotcha." He kissed her temple and cradled her in his protective embrace, before he began healing the purple markings from her chest and neck.

He found it adorable that his wife loved to name things. She named everything from her cars, and her aprons, to her vibrators, and her breasts. According to her, she'd named June and Bonnie when she was eleven. She'd woken up one day with buds that had deeply concerned her. She was worried she would have a more difficult time surfing which she did on a daily basis growing up in Kauai.

Her best friend, Malani, had developed around the same time and had announced that they had finally gotten Pointer sisters, and they'd named them thus.

Dan eventually eased to the kitchen to make Fionna coffee, after having convinced her to drink it with him in bed.

Still smirking as he replayed Fionna coming undone for him with his mouth on her luscious tits, he was startled to find Jeff with Becca backed up to the large center island. His hands were up her T-shirt, and he was consuming her mouth rather heatedly.

Clearing his throat, he tried not to chuckle as Jeff jerked away from her, and Becca gasped for breath.

"Morning," Dan drawled as he began working on Fionna's coffee.

"Sorry, sir," Jeff choked out as Becca nodded her agreement.

"Probably good we're getting you your own place today." Dan wasn't offended at what he'd found. They were newlyweds after all.

CHAPTER 28
COFFEE WITH CREAM AND WISDOM

An hour later, Dan and Fionna were driving toward their storage unit with Jeff and Becca behind them. Dan and Jeff were going to take his truck to Sam's that evening, and Dan sincerely hoped Sam could fix whatever might be wrong with it. Having another car would make their lives much easier.

Logan and Rainer had already arrived with Emily, Adeline, the Crown Governor, and Mrs. Haydenshire along with Connor, Garrett, and Patrick.

Dan unlocked the lift door on the storage unit.

Fionna cornered Adeline and Mrs. Haydenshire to plead her case for returning to Kauai for a week and to discuss her latest pregnancy symptom.

Jeff and Becca thanked Dan and Fionna without end for allowing them to use the furniture, though they constantly assured them that they preferred it to be used instead of stored.

The trucks were loaded and everyone was greeted by the Sapmans and Jeff's mother at the rental home.

"Where are the boys?" Governor Haydenshire asked Governor Sapman rather pointedly as he and Dan unloaded Fionna's old mattress.

"They were out late last night, and this isn't their mess." Governor Sapman rolled his eyes as he took in the home Jeff and Becca had chosen.

Governor Haydenshire gestured his hand to all of his sons that were perfectly willing to help though they had nothing to do with Jeff and Becca or their current situation. "If we only try to help improve the problems we feel we're personally responsible for, we end up in a very sad state of affairs."

Fionna and Mrs. Haydenshire set to work in the tiny kitchen. Dan all but demanded that Fionna sit for a little while once her old sofa was carried in. It took up a large portion of the living room.

"Becca, would you like Emily and me to put your dishes on the hutch or in the cabinets?" Mrs. Haydenshire asked.

"I don't know. I don't know how to do any of this." Panic tensed in her rhythms.

Fionna and Mrs. Haydenshire shared a knowing glance.

"How about a little advice?" Mrs. Haydenshire offered.

"Please." Becca nodded.

"It takes very little to make a happy life," Mrs. Haydenshire began.

Fionna nodded. "My hunky husband, my baby girls, my best friends,"—she kissed Garrett's cheek—"and coffee. That's all I need."

"Coffee and Garrett are at the top of my list too." Mrs. Haydenshire chuckled as Garrett put his arm around his mom. "Anywhere can be a castle if you and Jeff choose love over irritation. Try to be patient even when you want to strangle him. Try to assume the best from him, and trust me, if your home doesn't make sense, nothing else will either."

Becca drank in the advice like she was being given oxygen after drowning.

"Clutter is stressful even if you tell yourself it doesn't bother you. It's nothing more than indecisions, so figure out where you want to keep things and put them there. If it doesn't have a place to live, you probably don't really need it. And if it'll take you less than ten minutes to do something, just get it over with. You'll be so glad you did."

Emily held up the heirloom dish set that the Sapmans had saved for Becca. "I think these dishes would be really pretty on the hutch."

"And then you can save your cabinets for cookware and food," Fionna concluded.

Becca began helping Emily arrange the dishes on Fionna's hutch that partially covered a window since there wasn't a tremendous amount of wall space.

Dan moved to Fionna as their conversation lulled. Grinning at him and well aware that he was approaching to read her rhythms to make certain that she didn't need another break, Fionna rolled her eyes.

"Try to remember that when he drives you crazy it's mostly because he loves you so much and he's trying to take care of you."

Dan chuckled. "When you remember that, call Fi and remind her."

"I don't know how to cook much beyond scrambled eggs and toast," Becca continued to confess her concerns. "I've never even done laundry." She seemed to realize all that she was going to have to learn now that she was married with a baby on the way.

"Jeff's done laundry, sweetheart, and he's a great cook. He can teach you, and I can come over and help whenever I'm not working," Ms. Harrickson immediately vowed.

"Thank you so much!" Becca threw her arms around her mother-in-law.

"You and Jeff take just a little of the money you have and pick out a basic cookbook," Mrs. Haydenshire guided. "Work your way through it. You'll pick things up quickly."

"Oh, and I take Aida to the central library and they have tons of cookbooks. I keep checking them out while she listens to the story and gets her books, and that's all free," Fionna pointed out.

Becca looked excited to begin her adult life as long as Jeff was nearby. She reached for him and drew from him frequently throughout the day.

Dan and Garrett hoisted Fionna's old television over the mantel while Logan guided them as to the placement. Jeff screwed in the brackets.

"Are you sure you don't mind us using this?" He gestured to the TV.

"It's been in storage for almost a year now."

"Jeff told me it was a boy," Dan overheard Ms. Harrickson whisper as Becca nodded excitedly. "Little boys really love their mamas." Jeff chuckled as he hugged his mother fiercely.

"Yes, they do," Mrs. Haydenshire agreed as she found herself surrounded by Logan, Garrett, Rainer, Connor, and Patrick all forcing her into an awkward five-man hug. The Crown Governor shook his head but grinned at his sons.

Mrs. Haydenshire continued to offer wisdom which everyone, not just Jeff and Becca, was keen to listen to. "There are very few things that either a cup of tea, a deep breath, or a long nap won't make better. If you come to a place where you want to pull your hair out, ask for help."

"Have a seat, Mrs. Vindico, and I'll bet Jeff and Becca will let me use your old coffee maker to make you a cup of coffee," Dan commanded.

"Of course." Becca nodded. "Uh…do we have coffee?"

"I packed you a little box of a few things from the supermarket. You know, until you can get your first groceries," Ms. Harrickson explained.

"Mom." Jeff shook his head, clearly thinking the same thing Dan was. He hoped Ms. Harrickson hadn't taken her own grocery money to buy food for Jeff and Becca.

"Don't worry," she assured him with a knowing smile. "I wasn't going to tell you this…" She cradled Jeff's face in her hand sweetly. "But I don't guess I realized quite how much food I used to buy for you. I hardly spent anything on groceries this week since I eat two meals a day at the diner."

To save Jeff further embarrassment, Garrett leaned and hoisted Fionna up in his arms. "Oh my God, baby, *what* have you been eating?" He groaned for effect as he laid her gently on the sofa.

Fionna scowled as Dan popped Garrett on the back of the head rather hard. Everyone laughed as Dan began a pot of coffee.

"Now I know why you're not married." The governor shook his head at Garrett who was still laughing.

Logan and Rainer helped Jeff attach his enhanced Xbox and PlayStation to the television along. Then they set up his gaming computer. As the house really only consisted of three basic room divisions, it didn't take long to have everything squared away.

"Are you sure you don't mind taking me out to see Sam this afternoon?" Jeff asked Dan for the third time.

"Not at all. Fi's airbag light keeps coming on. I need him to check that anyway," Dan explained.

"That just means she wants her airbags squeezed, man. You married her. How do you not know that?" Garrett sneered before cracking himself up. Rainer, Logan, and Patrick guffawed. The Crown Governor closed his eyes in defeat, and the Sapmans looked utterly horrified.

"Garrett, do you think you could behave, son?" Mrs. Haydenshire commanded.

"It's been thirty years. I'm not holding my breath." Governor Haydenshire elicited more laughter.

An hour later, Dan and Fionna were lounging on their couch with Dan's hands on her belly.

"Did you tell Sam about Jeff and Becca?" Fionna relaxed and let Dan cast and soothe her and Halia.

"Yeah, he's going to see what he can do to the truck as a wedding present. I told him if it was too much, I'd pay him later."

Fionna kissed his cheek.

A knock sounded on the front door that had them both grinning. Dan opened it and caught Aida in her sprint into his arms.

"Daddy!" she trilled.

"Hey, baby girl." He hugged her tight.

Meredith laughed as she carried in Aida's duffle bag and her school bags. "How are you feeling?" she asked Fionna.

"Oh, I'm all right. Adeline says I have to rest more."

"We don't all have to come over tomorrow. My mother's ridiculous grandparents' day thing." Meredith rolled her eyes. "If you are a grandparent, then theoretically you are also a mother or father. Why can't we celebrate them on Mother and Father's day?"

Fionna giggled. "I want you to come over. Dan will help. It'll be fine."

"Can I bring something then?"

"Sure. Why don't you bring dessert?"

Aida and Olivia hugged goodbye, after professing their undying love and best, best, best friendships before Meredith dragged Olivia away.

"Bye, sis." Dan waved from the door.

"Is Halia tired?" Aida placed her hands on Fionna's stomach. "Is that why you need to rest more?"

"Mommy and Halia are tired so Mommy has to rest, but they're both going to be just fine," Dan assured her.

"I'll bring you water, and I can pat Halia like this." She tenderly patted Fionna's stomach.

"How about while Daddy takes Jeff to see Mr. Sam, you lie with me on the couch and we watch *Supernova*?" Fionna asked.

Aida's eyes lit as she nodded. "And I can read to you if you want because I got to go to the library yesterday at school. And I told Ms. Powell that you and Daddy take me to the library too and that there's one near Tutu and Papa's. I never knew there were so many libraries."

"Go get your books and show me," Fionna urged.

Aida whirled to her backpack. She pulled out a piece of paper and two books. "Ms. Kinder the librarian got angry at Mrs. McBeechum because she said I had to get you to sign this or that I wouldn't be able to check out books from the panda section again." She handed Dan the sheet of paper.

"Look!" She held up a well-worn copy of a book called *The Ordinary Princess* to show Fionna. "Aunt Meredith let me read it to Olivia for a little while last night, and it's wonderful!"

Fionna pulled her in for a hug. "I missed you," she informed their little girl.

"I missed you too, so much, and I wanted Daddy to hug me, but you were here. I want to not go away for a while."

"Come here, baby girl." Dan pulled Aida up in his lap as he read the note from the school board pain in the ass.

Dear Mrs. Vindico,

I have allowed your daughter Aida to check out a copy of The Ordinary Princess even though it is considered a fourth and fifth grade reader and is in the Panda section.

Mrs. Powell insisted that it would be a fine choice for Aida, but I thought I should take it upon myself to inform you that Aida's reading level is well above her age and therefore is difficult for her teachers and the other faculty to negotiate. I will need this note signed by you and any of Aida's additional guardians if you intend to allow her to read above her grade level.

This will serve to mitigate the school board of any responsibility if Aida should read a book with subject matter that you do not approve of. Please also be aware that children do not need to be exposed to inappropriate themes that the school board does not agree with. Otherwise please explain to Aida and to Mrs. Powell that she will need to stick to the koala reading shelf.

Mrs. McBeechum

Dan rubbed his temples and tried not to say the string of exasperated expletives that threatened to spew forth from his mouth. He handed the note to Fionna as Aida carried her bags up to her room and began putting her laundry in her hamper per Fionna's request.

Rolling her eyes, Fionna shook her head. "It's an elementary school library. Do they have some kind of adult erotic section I'm unaware of?"

"It would appear." Dan wondered what had happened to the school he'd attended growing up. It used to be that if you had a book in your hand, reading beyond what you were instructed to read, someone slapped you on the back and called you a good kid. He highly suspected the school board was the entirety of the problem.

Aida returned and joined Fionna on the couch. "Wanna watch *Mary Poppins?*" Fionna asked.

"Can we have popcorn?"

"Sure." Dan fixed his girls popcorn as Fionna turned on *Mary Poppins*. "I'm gonna go." He kissed Fionna, then her belly, then Aida, making them laugh as he made his exit.

CHAPTER 29
SAM

Dan followed Jeff's Ford Ranger onto the gravel lot. A smile formed automatically on his features as he turned off the Mercedes. His boots hit the gravel, and his soul lightened its burdensome load as he inhaled deeply of the gasoline, oil, and the scent of Old Spice aftershave.

"Well, if it isn't Big Man Vindico and a new sidekick." Sam approached, wiping his hands on an old shop rag. He was sporting his customary coveralls.

"Sam, this is a good friend of mine, Jeff Strenton," Dan introduced.

"Mr. Strenton." Sam offered his hand. "I'm Sam and you can call me Sam."

Jeff chuckled as he shook his hand. "It's nice to meet you, sir. Rainer told me you helped him build his Mustang and you got him his Porsche."

"Rain Man knows an outstanding mechanic when he sees one." He pretended to dust off his coveralls. "And how is Miss Amazing Wife and Miss Amazing Aida?" he asked Dan.

"They're good. Fi's at home, hopefully resting."

"She's about to pop isn't she? You're gonna have a house full of little Vindicos."

"She's got a few more months. I can't wait honestly." His emotions always seemed to flow easier from his mouth when he was in Sam's presence.

"Uh-huh. I'm sure, but you might get to thinking that baby girl number two was a whole lot quieter inside of Miss Fi-on-na than she will be once you get her out here."

"I'm sure." Dan was still eager to hold Halia in his own hands, kiss her head, and tell her how much he loved her in her ear instead of through Fionna's stomach.

"Mr. Strenton, you need yourself some spark plugs and you need to clean your fuel injectors. I do believe you need little work on that torque converter but not much, and as it is Saturday and Big Man called and told me that you've got yourself a new wife and a little Strenton in the oven, then I am happy to announce that spark plugs and fuel injector cleaning is my standard wedding present."

Jeff's mouth fell open as Dan chuckled quietly. "Sir, you don't have to do that. How did you know all of that already? You haven't even lifted the hood."

"Big Man," Sam called back to Dan.

"Yes, sir," Dan supplied, moving toward the truck as Sam popped the hood. "Did you not just hear me say that I'm Sam?"

"I did hear you say that."

Sam turned back to Jeff. "Then that's how I know."

Dan grinned. "You know how good you are at computers?" he asked Jeff.

"Yes, sir."

"That's how he is with cars. There's nothing he can't fix. He's like that with life too."

"I need to come out here more often, I take it."

"You'll never regret it."

Jeff smiled at Sam. "Mentor Vindico needs his car worked on first. That way he can leave."

"I'm fine." Dan waved him off. "Fi's airbag light keeps coming on."

"Mm-hmm, sometimes when Sam enhances the safety features the non-enhanced parts get a little jealous, and I have to rub them just the right way. Just like a woman. Rub them until they're smiling again."

"All right, Mr. Strenton,"—he lowered the hood on the truck—"go ahead and pull her in the shop. I'll get her fixed up." Sam gestured to an empty bay beside his own GTO.

After a few minutes, Jeff got the truck started again and drove it forward.

"Can I ask you something, Sam?" Dan pled.

Sam was, in Dan's opinion, the smartest man in the entire Realm. The Crown Governor often said that if the Realm really wanted the wisest man running it, they would elect Sam.

"I will be charging you extra of course," Sam teased.

"I'll pay."

Sam shook his head. "You bring my Aida out here soon and maybe that new little one when she gets here, and we'll call it even."

Sam and Aida had formed a bond from the moment they'd met. They were both able to recognize a kindred spirit when they saw one.

Sam began working on Jeff's spark plugs as Jeff and Dan looked on.

"Why do you think guys cheat?" Dan posed his question.

Sam lifted his head out from under the hood and narrowed his eyes. "You hurt Miss Amazing wife and you hurt my sweet little Aida, I'll come after you with a tire iron, boy. Don't think I won't."

Dan shook his head. He was disgusted by the thought. "Never ever. I'd never hurt my girls. I keep my vows. I don't understand making them if you're going to break them. But my dad asked me to look into a rather high-profile infidelity case. The whole thing makes me sick. If it weren't for my dad, I wouldn't be doing this. I hate that Fi even has to think about it. I just want to figure out what happened quickly. I want it out of my house."

Jeff studied Dan. He looked rather impressed.

Sam nodded. He began replacing spark plugs. "Yeah, I seen in the paper that the big deal chancellor got himself into trouble. Marriage is a lot like this truck," he explained. Jeff and Dan moved closer to listen intently. "You've got yourself a bad set of plugs, and you need a little maintenance. But people would rather sell the whole damn truck instead of fixing the plugs or putting a new battery in.

"If you run it hot for too long, the engine will give on you. Then you find yourself on the side of the road with smoke pouring out from under the hood, scratching your head wondering what happened. People want to make everything so much harder than it needs to be."

Dan watched as he casted the electrodes on the plugs. "Love isn't a feeling as much as the television might like you to believe it is. You wake up in the morning and you decide before your feet ever hit the floor that you're gonna love her and you're gonna take care of her. You tell her good morning. Give her a kiss. If you're lucky, you might get a little more than a kiss.

"Then you do whatever it is God put you here to do and you go home. No stopping in between unless she asks you to get some milk and bread on your way. Then you kiss her, tell her she's gorgeous, listen to what she wants to tell you. Tell her about your day. Kiss those youngins you made together, and then you get up the next day, do the same thing. And listen to me, boys, if you do that, you'll have a life you wouldn't trade for anything."

Dan's heart ached. Sam's wife of fifty-two years had died suddenly in her sleep a few years before.

"You hear that?" Dan commanded Jeff.

"Yes, sir." Jeff looked up to the task Sam had assigned.

"I'll tell you this too." Sam went back to his cabinets and pulled a bottle of injection cleaner that he added to Jeff's gas tank. "People cheat in their minds for a right long time before they cheat in the bedroom. You've gotta stop it before it ever gets to that. You've gotta decide that there aren't any other options. My sweet Dolores used to say if you're angry, good for you. Now you go out on the front porch and calm yourself down because then we gonna talk and we gonna fix it. I may come after ya with my frying skillet, but we aren't getting divorced."

"Sounds like she was quite a woman." Dan raised the glass bottle of Coke Sam had provided them from his old Coke machine in the shop.

"Pretty too," Sam agreed with a faraway look in his eye. He sighed as he began working on Jeff's converter. "Tell you this though, I know what the good governor really wants to know. Once you're standing on the side of the road covered in smoke, people begin to ask what else you let slide. It's always a little different from the inside looking out than it is from the outside looking in. And I'll tell you the truth of it, if my opinion is worth the nickel in your pocket."

"Worth a hell of a lot more than a nickel," Dan vowed.

"The governor knows that if you gonna break your vows, you gonna break her heart and yours too, you're gonna give up something real good for something you decide you just can't live without, then there isn't a whole lot that you won't break.

"Once a man breaks his word, he's worthless. Not worth a damn thing because once you're lying you got to keep right on lying. That's the only way to cover it up. People want to get caught up on the specifics instead of looking at the whole deal. Trust me, bad's bad and wrong's wrong. No matter which way you want to slice that cake, you had a choice. One bad choice is always followed by a whole host of others, and that's what your daddy wants to know. Just how many bad choices did the big-time chancellor make when he built himself a web of lies?"

Dan felt his soul soothe. "It doesn't matter why they did it," he restated. "It was wrong. End of story." He'd wanted to get caught up in the details, wanted to come up with some plausible digestible reason why a man would hurt people he loved.

"See, I told Miss Amazing Wife you weren't even half as dumb as you look," Sam goaded, making Dan and Jeff laugh heartily.

It took Sam less than five minutes to fix Fionna's air bag light. Dan shook his hand as Jeff thanked him profusely.

"Tell me what Mrs. Strenton's name is," Sam asked.

Jeff beamed. "Becca." His energy lilted in happy waves suddenly.

"Tell Becca I said hello, and that I'd be happy to take care of anything else you might need."

"Thank you so much, sir. You're a life saver."

"Been called worse I s'pose." He turned to Dan. "You tell Miss Fionna I said to keep you straight and tell my sweet Aida that I love her."

"You got it," Dan agreed.

Returning home, Dan let everything Sam said work through his mind. He wondered what Jeff had heard at twenty years old with barely two days of marriage under his belt.

Climbing the stairs to the door in from the garage, Dan paused and listened to the sounds of his precious girls' laughter. Smiling, he eased in the door.

They were curled up on the couch snuggling and giggling.

"Can I get in there somewhere?" Dan gazed at Fionna with more love than he ever thought his body could contain.

"I want to be an Aida sandwich," Aida gasped.

"You do?" Dan scooped her up and squeezed her between him and Fionna.

CHAPTER 30

FIX THE FOUNDATION

After dinner, Fionna gave Aida her bath and rubbed her down with kukui oil. Dan read to her from her new book as Aida lay on his chest.

"Daddy," she whispered.

"Yeah, baby?"

Aida wiggled closer into Dan's embrace. She needed to feel safe, he realized. Setting the book down, he turned and held her in his arms. He kissed the top of her sweet head.

"I love you."

Feeling his heart beat disjointedly, Dan swallowed down the emotion that had come on so suddenly. "I love you too, baby, so much."

"And I love Mommy, and baby Halia, and Garrett," she explained. Smiling, Dan nodded and wondered where all of this was coming from.

"And Mommy loves you and Halia loves her big sister and Garrett loves you so much," he promised her.

"And you love Mommy."

"Very much. I love you and Mommy and Halia more than anything else in the whole world."

Fionna appeared. She must've picked up on Aida's tension from the floor below.

"Hi, Mommy." Aida beamed.

"Hey, baby girl. Are you okay?"

Aida nodded as she played with the button on Dan's polo. "Does Uncle Tim love Aunt Meredith the same way you love Mommy?" she asked Dan pointedly.

Dan and Fionna shared a nervous glance. "I think so," Dan answered as honestly as he could.

Truthfully, he couldn't stand his younger sister's husband. He was a slug. He had a new and more involved fake illness with each passing week. He slept at most family gatherings, and Meredith did most of the work that went on in their household. Tim and Meredith were both accountants in the Senate finance office for the Auxiliary Department.

Meredith had been promoted numerous times over Tim, so Dan had always assumed that he didn't accomplish much at work either.

"Uncle Tim yelled at me," Aida admitted fretfully.

"What?!" Dan's blood began to boil.

"Dan." Fionna shook her head.

"I didn't mean to be loud," she managed before her chin trembled and tears welled in her eyes. Dan clenched his jaw so tightly it ached as Fionna's eyes closed.

"Maybe Uncle Tim had a bad day at work and he was tired. He shouldn't have taken his bad mood out on you, but maybe we can give him a chance to realize that." Fionna tried to soothe Aida.

"I didn't know he had gotten home. Aunt Meredith said he wasn't going to be home until late because he went out to eat dinner and have some milk."

Dan's brow furrowed as he continued to listen. "He went out to have milk?"

"Olivia said her daddy doesn't like pizza 'cause it makes his tummy hurt, and that's what Aunt Meredith got for us, so he went out for dinner and something to drink. I always drink milk with my dinner."

Fionna nodded. Her soothing cast moved through Aida's hand. She relaxed instantly.

"When did Uncle Tim yell at you, baby?" Dan needed to know just how loudly he was going to shout when he got his brother-in-law on the phone after Aida fell asleep.

"After Aunt Meredith gave Oliver his bath, he got water all over the bathroom, so I told Aunt Meredith that I would clean it up because she felt very, very tired."

Dan noted that Aida hadn't said that Meredith looked tired. She'd *felt* tired. His sister was so exhausted Aida had read it in her energy. Dan tried not to envision his hands in a chokehold around Tim's neck.

"I didn't mean to say it loud, but Uncle Tim was in their bedroom watching TV and Olivia and I both said we would clean it up. He yelled at us because he couldn't hear the show," she lamented dejectedly. "But then Aunt Meredith yelled at Uncle Tim, and she said he never helps. And then they both said not nice things and then Uncle Tim slammed the bedroom door.

"It hurt my ears, and I got scared, and I said I want my daddy. I wanted you to come get me, but I didn't want to hurt Olivia's feelings," the tale finally bled from Aida's heart out of her mouth.

Dan cradled his baby girl in his arms and let his shield move over her.

"Thank you," she whispered as she drank in his love and his protection. She buried her face in his neck. Her fists knotted his shirt. She trembled in his arms, and Dan amended his plan. He was driving over to Meredith and Tim's and letting his brother-in-law know precisely what he thought of him and what would happen to him if he ever yelled at Aida for offering to help again. "And Garrett always tells me that if I want him, he'll come. But I was scared to ask Aunt Meredith for her phone to call him because she was crying."

"If you are ever anywhere and you want Mommy or Daddy or Garrett to come and get you, we will. You won't hurt Olivia's feelings or anyone else's. Even if someone is upset, if you need any of us, it's okay to tell them that. And even if it does upset them, it's okay. What you want is important," Fionna explained.

Aida nodded against Dan. "I don't want you to tell Daddy that you hate him." She began crying again. Fionna looked horrified as Dan's mouth fell open.

"I would never, ever say that," Fionna vowed. If Meredith was screeching that she hated Tim to his face in front of her children, things were much worse than Dan had ever dreamed.

"If you and Olivia want to have another spend-the-night party, then Olivia can come over here, okay, sweetheart?" Dan decreed.

"Yes," Aida agreed instantly. "When I'm at home, there's sunshine in my tummy, but last night I couldn't find it anywhere, and you weren't there to make it come back."

Fionna blinked back tears as she lay on the other side of Aida. Dan extended his shield to cover all three of his girls. They lay there together until Aida was fast asleep. Fionna extracted herself, and Dan heard her in the kitchen. He kept Aida inside of his shield until he was certain he'd allayed each and every fear from the night before.

"Give these to Meredith." Fionna handed Dan a small wooden crate that had come from her grandmother's store in Kauai.

Dan pulled on his riding jacket. He noted all of the bottles of oils and supplements that Tutu prescribed for balancing hormones and dealing with depression along with the papaya enzyme facial scrubs that Fionna adored.

She'd added a jar of 'Ōhi'a lehua, the natural lubricant that Tutu sold out of on a regular basis. Dan and Fionna used it often. It carried the energy of your partner to you readily and made what was already a heavenly experience that much more intense.

"I'll be back quick."

Fionna leaned on her tiptoes to kiss his cheek. "These are the little things that turn into huge things that I was talking about last night. No one wants to fight them until it's too late."

"I know, and I plan on telling him that. He's not doing this to my baby girl or to my sister or my niece and nephew."

Fionna nodded. "You're my hero."

Dan kissed her forehead. "Save my spot. I'll be back in a little while." He gestured his head to the couch.

"I will." Fionna grinned as he headed to the garage.

276

Stowing the oils and tinctures in the bike saddle bags, Dan kicked his Agusta to life. He was at his sister's home, just a few neighborhoods over, in a matter of minutes.

He rang the doorbell with fury still coursing through his veins every time he thought of Aida's trembling tears in his arms. Meredith answered the door quickly. Her eyes were red and swollen. Dan drew a deep, steadying breath.

"I had a feeling you'd be by." She tried and failed to blink back more tears.

"Where's Tim?" he demanded.

Meredith swallowed and then forced a smile. "He's upstairs. I just put the kids to bed."

Dan reminded himself that he needed to remain in control if he wanted Tim to listen.

"Here." Dan handed Meredith the crate Fionna had packed for her. "What's this?"

"A few of Fi's grandmother's remedies. Make yourself a cup of that tea. Tim and I are going out for a while. Why don't you relax and take a bath? It'll help—trust me."

Meredith looked shocked. "I never really thought of that."

"Fi wrote down what everything does and how to use it," Dan continued his orders.

Meredith nodded, and Dan saw a hint of relief in her eyes. She was counting on her big brother to help her find herself again and possibly to save her crumbling marriage. Dan was determined to do his best.

He stomped up the stairs and flung the master bedroom door open. Tim was lying on the bed in a stained T-shirt, flipping through the channels on the TV.

"Get up," Dan spat in disgust.

"Why are you here?"

"I said get up. Put some fucking pants on, and for God's sake start acting like a man. Your wife is downstairs. Your kids are asleep. What the hell are you up here alone for?"

Tim, not being manly enough to argue, slithered from the bed with a huff.

"We're gonna go have a little chat, and when I get back, I'm taking that out of your bedroom." He pointed to the television.

"What? Why? Meredith never wants to watch anything but those stupid bachelor shows."

"Then watch them with her." Dan pointed down the stairs.

CHAPTER 31
EFFORT AND ERRORS

"Are you cheating on my sister?" Dan demanded as he shoved Tim into a booth in the back of a bar a few miles from their homes.

"What? No!" Tim sounded genuinely offended. "I would never do that."

"You'd never do it and live," Dan assured him.

"What are you so pissed off about?" Tim finally demanded. A waiter approached hesitantly.

"Beer?" Dan offered.

"I guess."

"He'll have whatever you have on tap. I want a Talisker 10, and don't mess with it," Dan demanded.

"You don't want it on the rocks?" The waiter sounded confused.

"No, I don't." Dan tried to remember that it was Tim he was furious with not the waiter that barely looked old enough to be serving alcohol.

As the waiter scurried away, Dan turned his glare back on his brother-in-law. "Did you yell at Aida last night?"

"Are you seriously upset because I got onto Aida?"

"If Aida does something wrong, then by all means, get onto her. I won't say a word. But she wanted to help because my sister is exhausted and then you yelled at her and at my niece and then you yelled at my sister, so yeah, I'm pissed the fuck off. And don't get it in your head that I won't whip your ass just because you married my sister."

"I don't really think what goes on between Meredith and me is any of your business," Tim spat with more vengeance than Dan thought he had in him.

"When I got to your house a few minutes ago, Meredith was in tears, and you were locked up in the bedroom alone watching television. I don't think I have to go too far out on a limb to say something is wrong. You don't have to take my advice, but you're going to sit there and listen."

Scowling, Tim rolled his eyes as he sipped the beer he'd just been supplied.

"Do you like having sex?" Dan knew how to get any guy's attention.

"Don't know. I don't have it anymore."

"But you're good, and I just need to stay out of it." Dan effectively trapped his brother-in-law.

"You know, you don't have this all figured out. Just wait until you get home from work and Fionna's covered in drool, hasn't showered or changed clothes in three days, has the baby hanging off of her, and falls asleep in the recliner every night."

"Or," Dan snarled, "you could come home, take the baby off of your wife, make dinner, let her go take a shower, you put the kids to bed, and let her sleep."

"I'm tired when I get home from work," Tim whined.

"But she's not?"

Tim scowled and began to pout. Trying to remember that part of what Meredith liked about Tim was that he generally let her run the show, Dan supposed she couldn't be too upset when he became more of himself as the years went by.

"Look, I love my little sister. I don't want to see you two end up in front of the governing board miserable and divorced."

"We're not miserable."

"She is miserable, Tim," Dan assured him.

Not seeming to have a rebuttal for that, Tim drew a deep breath. "All right, fine. Why don't you sit there and tell me how I'm making your sister miserable."

"I'm not saying it's all you." Dan surprised him again. "But if she's miserable then you are too." Tim shrugged and refused to meet Dan's gaze. "When was the last time you took her out to dinner just the two of you, or gave her a bath, or let her know that you care, or even think about her occasionally? When is the last time you did anything at all to treat her like your wife instead of your mother?"

"She doesn't even talk to me at home. Why would she want to go to dinner? And she's not three. Why would I give her a bath? She can't even stand to be in the same room with me much less in a bathtub. She sleeps on the couch every night," he admitted with his face flushing.

Dan's heart sank. "Bring the kids over Friday night. Fi and I will watch them. I don't care where you take her, but it had better be nice."

Pulling his cell from his pocket, he called his parents' home. "Hey, Dad." Tim stared at him in confusion. "No, not yet. I have a bunch of stuff to go through, but I haven't really started yet," he responded to the question whether or not he'd determined anything about Wilshire. "I'm helping Tim with a surprise for Meredith. He wants to take her out of town the week of fall break. Fi and I are going to Kauai, so I was wondering if you and Mom would mind watching Olivia and Oliver for him." He narrowed his eyes at Tim who seemed completely bewildered.

"Great. Thanks. We'll see you tomorrow night." Dan ended the call.

"Where am I supposed to take her? She hates everything I do."

"You put forth the effort and really try to come up with somewhere that would mean something to the two of you. She won't hate it," Dan vowed. "And Mom and Dad are thrilled. Dad said he'd get you tickets on a Senate jet if you wanted."

Tim looked intrigued as Dan watched the defeat begin to ebb from his features. "Maybe she'd like to go back to New York. We haven't been since I proposed."

Smiling, Dan nodded. "Perfect."

"Do you really think she'll want to go?" Tim sounded almost frightened that there would be more rejection from his wife.

"I'll talk to her."

"No, I want to tell her," Tim argued.

"Okay. Between now and then, maybe you could come out of the bedroom and interact with your wife and your kids. They aren't just hers."

"Yeah, I know, but everything I do with them isn't the way she wants it done."

"One of you is going to have to change, or this isn't going to last." Dan laid it all out on the line. "But I guarantee you this, if you really try, really try to help her out—get the kids out of her hair for a little while, bring her coffee in the morning, take her out occasionally, ask her to go to bed with you instead of hiding up in your room with the TV blaring while she cries herself to sleep on the couch—you can fix this before you're on the side of the road with a smoking engine that can't be fixed," he explained, though he knew the analogy might be lost on his brother-in-law.

"Maybe," Tim allowed.

"Put some effort in. Live your life," Dan demanded. "In fact, get up tomorrow morning and jog to my house. Be there by six. I'll jog back with you and then run back home. We'll keep doing it every morning until you feel better or until you get enough oxygen in your body to realize everything you're missing out on."

"That's like three miles both ways," Tim whined.

"Humor me. Give it two weeks. If you don't feel any better, you can stop. And if you feel like you need to see a medio or an Auxiliary counselor, then do that. You work for the Auxiliary Department. Surely, you can think of a counselor who could talk you through whatever is happening."

Dan walked Tim back in his house a few minutes later to check on his sister.

"Oh, they're back." Meredith was on the phone. She was smiling and looked genuinely relaxed. She had a notepad in her lap and was taking notes. "Yeah, I'm sure Dan will be home in a few minutes," she assured Fionna, Dan assumed. "Okay, love you too."

"Hey, uh, I was just thinking maybe I'd…put that TV in our room in the kids' playroom," Tim choked out.

"Really?" Meredith sounded stunned.

"Yeah." Tim looked morose.

"Okay." She nodded. Tim disappeared up the stairs, and Meredith threw her arms around Dan. "Thank you!" Tears began to fall again.

"Hey." Dan rubbed her back. "Give him a break. If all you ever tell him is that everything he does is wrong, he'll stop doing anything at all. Nothing is ever perfect, sis. It doesn't matter who does what as long as you're both happy."

"Yeah, I know. That's what Fionna said. I've just been so angry and hurt and furious with him."

"I know." Dan hugged her tighter. "But you can change all of that before it's too late."

She nodded as she pulled away. "So, this stuff really works?" She held up the jar of lubricant.

Dan chuckled. "Why don't you give it a try and see?"

"That tea and the bath made me feel a million times better," she admitted.

Dan glanced at the large notepad on the sofa full of the notes Meredith had been taking on Fionna's advice. He pressed his lips together as he saw the name brand of Fionna's favorite clitoral vibrator written in the center of the page with circles drawn around it prominently. Shaking his head, Dan waved to his sister and headed back home.

He pulled the heart-shaped note off the door. As he stepped inside, he opened it. *Mentor Vindico, I was really hoping I might get a little extra credit. If you come upstairs, I'll show you where I need to be kissed and where I need to be bitten. You can tell me what I can do to raise my A to an O. Love, Your Maylea*

Biting back the fervent growl that threatened to thunder from him, Dan kicked the door closed and took the stairs two at a time.

CHAPTER 32

FINGO-NUBBY FINGER FOODS

The next evening, Dan helped Aida set the table. He was still scowling from the text he'd received from Lindley informing him that Tuttle would be coming with her.

Aida scampered off after completing the job, and Fionna wrapped her arms around Dan the best that she could.

"Lindley has stayed clean since she got out of rehab, and she's held down a steady job," she reminded Dan.

"I know."

"And, I think it's been an even longer time since I last saw your sister's vajayjay than when I last saw my own, and trust me that's been a while."

Dan gagged and shuddered. "Trust me, yours looks sexy as hell. Hers I don't even want to think about."

Fionna laughed and nodded as they both recalled the see-through outfits that Lindley would don for shock value alone.

"And that was so thoughtful of her to purchase Kara and Meredith and me matching 'Spank Me' T-shirts when the sex boutique where she's currently employed put them on summer clearance." Fionna cracked up at her own joke as Dan squeezed his eyes shut in horror.

"You know, he asked Dad if he could ask her to marry him."

"Since that is the seventh time you've mentioned that, I was aware."

The doorbell had Dan's stomach churning again as he moved to answer. Relieved to find Kara and Zach, who was sporting baby Aiden in a carrier on his stomach, Dan gestured them inside.

"Oh, he's getting so big!" Fionna moved in front of Aiden's face. He offered her a drooly smile.

"Did Daddy tell you about Ryan?" Kara demanded.

"Yes," Dan spat.

Zach chuckled as he headed to the appetizer tray on the coffee table.

"I can't believe Lindley is going to get married. I mean, are they gonna have kids?" Kara shuddered. "Just try to imagine that...Lindley with children."

"Just because he asks, doesn't mean she'll say yes."

"Hey, I heard you took Tim jogging this morning." Zach laughed as he began inhaling the pineapple and mango salsa Fionna had prepared.

Dan rolled his eyes. "I jogged. He whined, and then told me he was certain he was developing some kind of lung exhaustion that comes from exertion."

Fionna patted Dan's arm. "But he went, and he wants to go again tomorrow, so that's good."

Fishing his cell phone from his pocket, Dan's brow furrowed as he read Tuttle's name on the screen. "What?" he spat. Fionna elbowed him.

"Hey, what did Fionna say when you asked her to marry you?" Tuttle demanded.

"Since we are married and she is currently seven months pregnant with my child, it seems fairly obvious that she said yes."

"Right, right. Where'd you ask her?"

Dan didn't really want to think about that. "A trauma room at Georgetown Hospital."

He tried to push away the memories. Fionna soothed him instantly.

"Georgetown just let you use a room for that?"

"No!" Dan thundered. "She'd just been shot. You were there when she was injured. My God."

"That's when you asked her?"

Letting his eyes close in defeat, Dan listened to his wife and sister crack up. Zach shook his head and slapped Dan on the back. "Yes, that's when I asked her."

"Okay," Tuttle agreed, though to what Dan wasn't certain. "I'm picking up Lind from work. We'll be there in a few."

"Great."

Dan's parents arrived next.

"There's my boy." Governor Vindico hoisted Aiden out of Zach's arms. "And my girl." He laughed as Aida threw her arms around his waist.

"Fionna, dear, I made the salad." Mrs. Vindico held up a large can of what appeared to be a peeled and cored whole pineapple, a bag of wet, wilted lettuce wrapped in a paper towel, and a small container of mayonnaise. Fionna tried to hide her confusion as she nodded and let Dan help her up off the couch. He followed them into the kitchen.

"I just need to heat this a little and then I need a platter for it," she continued her demands.

"Oh…uh…okay." Fionna and Dan shared a quizzical glance as Fionna grabbed the rounded glass dish that she put sliced pineapple in when she served it.

Watching his mother in horror, Dan's eyes goggled as she laid the wilted lettuce on the platter and then held the can in her hands. She summoned a heat cast over it. She opened the can. Fionna covered her mouth in horror as Mrs. Vindico slid a cored pineapple covered in a green gelatinous glue onto the lettuce.

"What is that?" Dan demanded.

"I used to make this for your father when we first married. He loves it," she announced proudly. "Kara suggested I just cut a few pineapple rings, but I thought this was more festive for the holiday we're celebrating." Dan rolled his eyes. "You take a number two can of pineapple, pour out half of the juice, and fill it with a lime Jell-o packet and then let it set up," she explained as Fionna shuddered. "Then you just slather it in mayonnaise." She went about her mayonnaise slathering.

Dan scowled as the chips and salsa he'd already consumed threatened to make a rapid reappearance. As she finished the odd frosting ritual, she proceeded to slice the horrendous concoction with one of Fionna's expensive knives that was intended for meat cutting.

The doorbell rang once again, and Dan and Fionna immediately fled the terrifying scene in their kitchen to let Tim, Meredith, Olivia, and Oliver in. Dan smirked as he noted his sister's smile and the fact that Tim was carrying the dessert plate in one hand and had his other arm around Meredith.

"Olivia," Aida cried in delight as the girls raced up to Aida's room to play.

"I too." Oliver poked his lip out.

"Aida, can Oliver play too, please?" Fionna called.

"Yes, ma'am," Aida replied with a frustrated sigh as she reappeared and helped Oliver up the stairs.

"Tim went and got a pound cake from the store, so I just sliced a few strawberries." Meredith sounded confused.

Fionna giggled. "That's perfect and that means that you didn't have to bake anything," she reminded her.

"It was a really nice, relaxing afternoon." Meredith kissed Tim's cheek. It seemed to shock him.

He nodded. "We talked." He put his arm back around Meredith.

Dan offered up a fervent prayer that at no point in his life would it be awkward for him to put his arm around his wife.

The doorbell rang again. Governor Vindico was closest. He was walking with little Aiden. He was discussing the football season with his infant grandson. He opened the door to reveal Tuttle and Lindley making out heatedly. "Excuse me," he demanded.

"Oh, sorry, sir." Tuttle wiped the back of his hand over his mouth, only serving to smear the remnants of Lindley's black lipstick over his chin.

Lindley swaggered into the room with a smirk. "Mere," she drawled. "Brought the vibe you requested from the store, and you spent enough to get a free glow-in-the-dark fingo nubby. I got you purple." She dropped a shopping bag from the sex shop into Meredith's lap.

"You weren't supposed to bring them here!" Meredith cringed as she turned violet in her horror.

Fionna cringed. "I'm thinking she just turned the color of the fingo nubby," she whispered to Dan.

Tim looked confused as Dan covered his mouth with his hand, trying not to guffaw.

"Why don't you just stick that in our room until you leave?" Fionna guided Meredith to the stairs.

Covering her face with her hands, Meredith rushed out of the room.

"What?" Tim pointed after Meredith. He stared confusedly at Dan.

"Later. Much, much later."

Eventually, Fionna rushed upstairs to coax Meredith into coming down for dinner. Dan placed the platters of food on the table. He'd grilled steaks and made baked potatoes with all of the toppings. He begrudgingly added his mother's strange pineapple experimentation to the table as everyone began seating themselves.

"Before we eat, can I just do something?" Tuttle looked thrilled.

As one could never be certain what Tuttle and Lindley might do, Dan considered. "That depends on what it is."

"Okay." He turned to Lindley who looked equally thrilled. "You know you're, like, the girl out of my wildest wet dreams."

"Yeah." Lindley waggled her eyebrows.

All of the blood in Dan's body slithered to his feet.

Kara's eyes goggled as she placed her hands over Aiden's tiny ears. The governor looked like he might keel over in the platter of steaks.

"And you know that I'm, like, jacked-off crazy about you," he continued as audible gasps went around the table, and Mrs. Vindico's china plate hit the floor with a crash.

"Yeah," Lindley drawled as she laughed in delight.

"So, baby, I..." Tuttle reached in his back pocket, and Dan felt Fionna grasp his bicep and cast him. Tuttle fell to his knee, and Dan shook his head in horror. "I want to ask you if you'll marry me." He opened the jewelry box to reveal a silver ring that had a diamond that appeared to be encased in a thin silver banding.

Everyone studied it as Lindley jumped up and down.

Fionna's mouth dropped open. She was a half step ahead of Dan in figuring out that the odd oval-shaped diamond stood up from the band encased in what looked like twine. It was formed in a bizarrely phallic shape.

"It's a weewee ring," Lindley squealed. "Yes, I'll marry you!" She plucked the ring from the box and hoisted it on her own finger.

No one seemed able to formulate words as they tried to envision not only a wedding but a marriage between Lindley and Ryan Tuttle.

"Get up and hug me," Lindley ordered. Laughing in genuine delight, Tuttle stood and lifted Lindley off the ground in the exuberance of his embrace.

"Oh my God," Dan finally managed as Fionna tried to keep him calm. He turned to his wife with his eyes pleading as he continued to shake his head.

"It's okay." Fionna concentrated and forced her energy through his hands.

"Mommy." Aida tugged on Fionna's sleeve. "I think Grandma's tummy hurts." She sounded panicked. This had everyone turning toward Dan's mother.

"Marion, sit down," the governor ordered. Dan guided his pale-faced mother, who appeared to be in utter shock, down into a chair.

"Here, Mom." Meredith grabbed her water glass, dipped the cloth napkin in it, and began blotting Mrs. Vindico's face. She seemed to jolt back to life a moment later.

"I'm getting married!" Lindley announced once she and Tuttle stopped sucking each other's tongues vulgarly.

"Mrs. Vindico, would you like a glass of wine?" Fionna asked.

"That would be a good idea," the governor commanded.

"I'll help." Kara followed Fionna back into the kitchen. Shaking himself, Dan moved to the hutch in the dining room that held all of his prized bottles of Scotch and a few other bottles of liquor.

Fionna and Kara returned with a glass of strong red wine for Mrs. Vindico and the bottle to be served to everyone else. Dan poured his father a shot of bourbon and then one for himself.

"Well, uh, congratulations." Fionna remembered her manners before anyone else had yet recovered.

"Thanks," Lindley replied. Dan was shocked by her politeness. It was so unlike Lindley.

"That ring is hideous," Meredith spoke through her clenched teeth to Kara and Fionna.

"Oh, it's awful." Kara was still shaking her head. Mrs. Vindico began coming around, and the governor shot the bourbon like a pro.

Mrs. Vindico's recovery seemed to be accompanied by her ability to spin a situation to show off her family. "When would you like to have the ceremony? Ryan is an Elite Iodex Officer and your father is a governor. We could book the Meridian House or perhaps the Hay-Adams, or Vivi Beaumont's daughter, Lexi, just got married at the Anderson House. It was a lovely venue. We'll have the full Senate in attendance though, so I'm not certain it's large enough."

Dan shuddered to think of what Lindley had in mind for a wedding. Fionna rubbed her hands over her belly almost in a maternal need to protect Halia as Dan lifted Aida up in his arms. He shook himself again as he carried Aida into the kitchen to retrieve the broom and dust pan.

Meredith leaned to clean up the broken plate, but Tim stopped her. "I've got it." He took the broom from Dan.

"Thank you." Meredith almost cried as Dan slapped Tim on the back.

"Well, uh…let's eat." Fionna quickly summoned and reheated all the food. Tuttle kept Lindley's hand in his as they fixed their plates.

"You proposed on Grandparents' Day?" Dan was still in shock. The details came to him slowly. Fionna giggled, but Tuttle nodded.

"Right, so we'll never forget it."

It was then that Dan's world divided into two distinct camps, one on one end of the table and an entirely different reality on the other end.

"I know. I'll phone the Dumbarton House." Mrs. Vindico was suddenly ecstatic.

"I only have to work 'til noon next Saturday, Ry-Ry," Lindley seemed to speak only to Tuttle.

"Marion, we are not booking the Dumbarton." The governor rolled his eyes and dug in to his steak.

"Yeah, but I might not be able to get us reservations at that place in Jamaica," Tuttle lamented.

Dan, Fionna, Zach, Kara, Meredith, and Tim all continued to watch the two very different conversations taking place on each end of the table. Back and forth, back and forth. It was like watching some kind of bizarre tennis match.

"I'll phone Susan first thing tomorrow. She can handle all of the catering," Mrs. Vindico decided.

"Wait, let me see." Ryan pulled his cell phone from his pocket and began searching. Dan leaned to see what came up. His eyes goggled as Tuttle tapped a link to Hedon Island Weddings.

"The gown will be bespoke from Lucia." Mrs. Vindico rushed to her purse and pulled out a day planner. Dan doubted his mother's dress designer would want to design something suitable for a Hedon wedding.

She continued on with her planning while Lindley and Ryan went on with their own. "I don't want Lillian Haydenshire hosting the shower on that farm. I'll phone Judy Willow. We'll have it at Willow Estate. It won't be the Crown, but it'll do."

"Hey, look." Tuttle handed Lindley his phone. "They have a wedding package and then you just stay for your honeymoon."

"Aww, I like your package," Lindley sassed.

"Well, you'll get to see lots of it there."

Mrs. Vindico tapped her pen on the side of her mouth. "Nordstrom and William-Sonoma can handle the registries. Of course, I'll need to make certain Nordstrom is still carrying Wedgwood. Blanche Bettencourt said they weren't carrying it anymore. Can you imagine?"

"Oh yes, I'm sure Wedgwood's spring line will be an ode to male anatomy that Lindley will love," Kara whispered to Fionna. She bit her lips together to keep from laughing.

"We can do the Adam and Eve package, or they have an au naturel option on the Anaconda River," Ryan explained to Lindley.

Kara and Fionna shot each other a horrified expression, but Mrs. Vindico carried on as usual. "I've still got the contact information of the florists who handled Rainer and Emily's wedding. Though, I should phone Tad and Nathan Anderson. I'm certain they handled all of the arranging."

"I'll get Portwood to give me a week off. We can fly into Sangster Friday night in time for the King of Hedon Island contest." Ryan pointed to something on his phone. Dan shuddered.

"I'll need Lillian to tell me where she had the runner embroidered with the Haydenshire and Lawson crests." Mrs. Vindico made more notes in her planner. "Tuttle," she said his name though she didn't appear to be speaking to him, and he paid her no attention at all. "Seagull crest." She tsked. "No, we'll just go with the Vindico panther."

Dan, Kara, and Meredith all rolled their eyes.

"Let's do the au naturel." Lindley was almost as thrilled as her mother.

"Please don't let them use the wedding photos as Christmas cards," Meredith seemed to plead to any deity willing to listen.

"We'll serve Maine lobster and lamb skewers. We'll need a green and maybe foie gras."

"We're not serving lobster, Marion." The governor served himself another steak.

Tuttle continued to plan on the other end of the table. "We have to choose a drink for the party. Do you want the legspreader or the screaming orgasm?"

"I want both." Linley preened.

Dan turned his gaze back to his parents' end of the table. "I threw Greer Donnelley's daughter, Brittany, a shower a few months ago, so I'll have Greer handle the bridesmaid's champagne breakfast. Kara, you'll be the maid of honor. You'll need to lose a little more weight before I speak to Lucia about making your gown."

Kara's eyes closed, and she rubbed her temples. Zach looked ready to maim.

Fionna grasped Dan's hand. "What do we do?" she mouthed.

"Two forces of nature in direct opposition." Dan shook his head. "We take cover."

CHAPTER 33

INNOCENT INDISCRETIONS

By Tuesday evening, Dan could no longer put off working on the information Jeff had gotten for him from Chancellor Wilshire's computers or his cloned cell phone.

He helped Fionna put Aida to bed and then fixed her a large cup of tea before settling them on the couch with his laptop between them.

"A few rules," he warned. "I checked the WhatsApp account, and there's nothing much in it. It appears most of their communication was actually via text. There are numerous texted videos between Wilshire and Bryant." He tried not to gag. "But we will not be watching anything physical that they might have decided to perform for one another. I may have to fast forward through them in case there is discussion before or after, but I cannot let you see them like that."

"I don't want to see it, but if it's her, I'll fast forward." Fionna drew a restorative sip of tea. Dan nodded his understanding.

"We're really looking for evidence that either of them took money from the school or participated in any other illegal activity. I have to figure out what else he might've let break to construct this web of lies like Sam said."

"I know."

"If I take notes, which you are welcome to read, it will just be about that," he assured her. Fionna's terror over his investigating the affair still haunted him.

Caught somewhere between desperate desire to get this over with and desire to put it off a little longer, Dan drew a deep breath and turned on his computer. He plugged in the external drive. "The way I would have handled this at Iodex would be for me to go through several things just long enough to give them a cursory overview, then I would go back through them in detail. I like to try to get a feel for the case before I jump in with both feet. That helps my shield know what we're ultimately searching for."

The way he worked seemed to fascinate Fionna.

"Should we put on our crime fighting suits?" She laid her head on Dan's shoulder.

Chuckling and kissing her head, Dan ran his hand over her belly. He needed to cling to his heavenly angels before he watched a man give in to Satan's tempting powers.

"If you put on your Catwoman costume, baby doll, the computer goes away."

Dan fought the desperate urge to carry her upstairs, to tuck her in the safety of their bed, to scoop up Aida and cradle her and Halia between them. He just wanted to push the rest of the world away. All he wanted was his girls safe and sound in his arms. He *was* a Shield.

"Let's just get it over with." Fionna patted his arm.

He started with their personal Facebook pages and Bryant's Instagram account. Mentor Bryant hadn't made any posts on either in the past few days.

Scrolling through her posts, Dan's dinner swirled in his gut as he read a birthday wish from Katherine to her husband at the end of May. "Happy Birthday to the man that still makes me smile each and every day. Hope you have a great night, baby!"

Shaking his head, Dan switched to her husband, Terry's, page. His last three posts contained pictures of large mixed drinks he was about to consume. Fionna pointed to an information block that informed everyone that he'd changed his relationship status to separated.

He'd commented, "I thought it was forever. She apparently thought something else." Dan continued to read another comment from Terry, after he'd consumed several of the beverages. "Life sucks and then you die. Looking forward to that last part."

Fionna's hand clutched her chest. "Oh my gosh." She shook her head. "I don't know, though. Something feels off."

"Wait. What feels off?"

"His post about dying. The energy in that post isn't how suicidal people feel."

Dan cringed. "You mean like he posted that for attention maybe."

She nodded.

"I guess he deserves the sympathy." Dan didn't know how people did this. How do you look your husband in the eye? How do you make love to him that night when you've been with someone else that morning. How do you interact with your children after something like that?

"Look at how many people commented on the one." Fionna pointed to the post with all of the drinks. Dan began reading the dozens of well wishes from Terry's friends and family.

"You know that means that each and every one of those people haven't just seen what he said, but once they commented on it, their friends can see it and then their friends and it just goes on and on. Everyone suspected she was having an affair. He just confirmed it for the entire Realm."

"Then they shouldn't have done it, should they?" Dan huffed.

Dan continued reading Terry Bryant's page. He was a Duco Predilect, and it appeared fifteen years before he'd been employed at a large chain bank in DC. When their son had been born, Terry decided to stay home with their children, making Katherine the family breadwinner. Venton Mentors made excellent money. Dan was certainly aware of that. They wanted the best and were willing to pay to get the people they felt could best teach the students of Venton Academy.

Fionna reached and clicked on the photographs from Terry Bryant. "They had it all." She shook her head. "Nice house, a pool, two beautiful kids, vacations at the beach in the summer, and skiing in Colorado in the winter." There were shots of her and her husband embracing, smiling, laughing, being affectionate with each other and their children.

Simply unable to look at those pictures any longer, Dan opened the emails from Wilshire's computer. He summoned to have the computer show him only the ones between Wilshire and Bryant. The first was two and a half years before. Fionna continued sipping her tea as they studied the email from Mentor Bryant. *Just wanted to thank you again for helping me with that mentor evaluation. I guess I took it a little too seriously. Some people are never happy.* Dan's brow furrowed.

Each Venton student filled out a mentor evaluation at the end of the year. He wondered what the complaints had been that upset Bryant enough to go to the chancellor when appropriate protocol would have been for her to go to the Head of Adminis Order as that was the area she primarily taught in.

"What did he say?" Fionna asked. Dan clicked on Wilshire's response. *Glad to be of help, Katherine. You are a bright, diligent mentor with a heart for the students. I assured Mr. and Mrs. Jensen that I did feel that your decision to fail Christopher was a sound one. You'd been available to help him all year and he had not responded in any way other than to give you a poor review following his failing grade. I will not allow my mentors to be bullied by parents or students. Please feel free to contact me if there is anything else I can do to help. -Dean*

"He defended her," Fionna whispered. Dan nodded. It was like watching a very slow-moving train wreck, one he was powerless to stop. "You see, this is what I was telling you. It can all start so innocently, but just think. If Tim and Meredith, both feeling the way they've been feeling about their marriage lately. Imagine if someone sent Meredith an email like that, someone at work that she admires, or if a woman Tim thought was attractive complimented his work when all Meredith has been doing is complaining about him *to* him."

"Do you want me to put this up, sweetheart?" He wasn't certain how to help his father and reassure his wife at the same time.

"No, I want to do this case with you. I never got to work with you when you were in Iodex because everything was so dangerous. You're amazing. I want to see you in action. And I kind of hate both of them right now, so I want to see how this went down."

"Okay, but if this is going to make you doubt me or doubt what I feel for you, then I'll turn it over to Portwood."

Fionna offered him his smile before wrinkling her nose. "I know I was super hormonal the other night, but I don't doubt us. I was just a little worried you were going to get consumed with this."

"I'm going to prove to you that I'm not," he vowed.

The next email had come from Chancellor Wilshire and was date stamped over a month later.

Katherine, I've decided to have a few select mentors from the different Predilects involved in a kind of task force. I'd like us to meet every few weeks to discuss ways we might improve Venton. You were the first mentor I thought of. If you'd be interested, stop by my office after lunch. -Dean

"Does that task force still exist?" Fionna asked.

"Not that I've ever heard of." They could both see the beginnings of lies between the seemingly innocent words of an email. "And why couldn't she have responded via email? He could have informed her when the meetings would be held a thousand other ways. Hell, he could have installed a comment box in the teachers' lounge if he really wanted to hear what mentors thought. He wanted to see her. He wanted her to come to his office, to come to him, and right there is where he should have stopped it. He should have realized that something was very, very wrong, gone home, and fixed it."

Fionna looked impressed as she watched Dan's secondary Predilect come into power. There was a response less than a minute later. "See, she was still feeling whatever she felt from him defending her. The obsession for more already had her," Fionna pointed out.

Chancellor Wilshire, I'm so honored you thought of me. I've always greatly admired your work here at the academy. It's an honor to teach for a man like you. I'll see you after lunch-Katherine

"Stroked his ego." Dan rolled his eyes as Fionna nodded. There was no other email contact until the meeting of the task force, which was apparently a week later.

Katherine, I wanted to thank you again for your wisdom and insight this afternoon at our first task force meeting. I will try to get a few more mentors to join. I've had several turn down the idea. Not everyone wants to put in the time the way that you're willing to. Your idea that we should look into visiting the Gifted academy seminars around the Realm over the breaks and summer was ingenious. Thank you for providing me with the brochures for so many. That certainly shows a great deal of thought and preparation on your part. I'm planning on registering for the convention in Baltimore over spring break that you seemed so enthused about. They will be hosting numerous speakers that I feel could enlighten us all. -Dean

"Stroked her ego and went for one of her ideas," Fionna breathed. "She goes home at night. Her husband and her kids have this thing going on that she might've felt left out of because she's working and he's there with them. She makes an offhanded suggestion or wants to tell him about work, and he shuts her down, or doesn't react the way Chancellor Wilshire did."

Dan nodded. "Yeah, and I'm not saying that dads can't do a phenomenal job staying home. Most guys I know who stay home are kickass fathers. They love staying home. I try to emulate them. But I wonder if in this situation her working made him resentful."

Fionna nodded. "Remember, I told you when we first started dating, tons of guys I went out with couldn't handle how much money I made challenging for the Angels."

"Well, I'm not sorry those didn't work out," Dan teased.

"Even if it hadn't been the money, it would have been something because you, Mr. Vindico, are my one and only," she vowed adamantly. It made him feel like a king.

He realized immediately that it was a good feeling. However, it was a problem if another woman began making a man that was not her husband feel that way.

"But, I do seem to recall Dan Vindico holding me on the couch in our suite all tucked up in his luscious muscles," she sassed, only broadening his grin, "telling me that when he'd said he wanted me to be his girlfriend exclusively that he meant that he could buy me things and when we went out that he paid."

300

Unable to argue that as he had in fact said those very words, Dan nodded his admittance.

"Just try to imagine if you hadn't had that option. If you hadn't been Chief of Iodex with all of the money and power that you had. What if you'd had to rely on my paychecks?"

"I hear you, and I'll say this. If the resentment has been building for the past fifteen years, if he's angry and feeling like he's just falling further and further behind because he's at home, and that resentment builds, and they never talk about it, then the very last thing he'll want to hear about when she gets home will be her work."

"Not to be unsupportive or anything, but you are never, ever going on one of these convention things," she demanded.

Dan chuckled. "It has long been my opinion that nothing at all goes on at shit like that other than a bunch of people patting each other on the back and telling each other how great they are. They gather around the bar to whine about how other people just don't know how hard they work, or how bad they all have it, because of whatever profession they're convening about, while the marauding band of motivational speakers blows buzzwords and flattery out their pie holes to anyone who'll listen to them. And then they flock to the lobby to purchase the full gift set of their awe-inspiring books for the low, low price of your soul. Give me a fucking break. If you need somebody to lick your ass, tell you how great you are, and listen to you whine about how hard your life is, get a damn dog."

Fionna cracked up. "I love you."

"I love you too, Mrs. Vindico." He winked at her before going on.

They went on to read Wilshire inviting Mentor Bryant to sit at his table at the convention in Baltimore. "See, he had so many chances to stop this before he let it get this far, to put on the brakes, to figure out why he was thinking about her so much, to reconnect with his wife, and he didn't."

"Yeah, but she went into that first meeting with him basically planning on getting him out of town."

Dan skipped down a little ways until he landed on a series of emails that were dated the week after the conference. Drawing a deep breath and bracing himself, Dan opened the email. This was much longer and was formed like a more personal letter rather than an electronic message. *Katherine, Where do I begin?* The opening line had Fionna scowling and huffing furiously.

Revulsion washed through Dan's rhythms. His shield seemed to know what was coming. He forced himself to go on. *Seems we fought quite the good fight and desire vanquished our best efforts.*

"Your best efforts, my ass," Dan snarled before continuing.

I suppose I should feel at least a modicum of guilt over what we shared though I cannot seem to. When you asked me up to your room Friday evening, I couldn't have told you no if my wife had been in the room beside me. And yet the only guilt I feel is due to the fact that I seemed unable to go further.

Dan's mouth fell open as he realized what that meant. "He couldn't do it," he gasped as he continued to read.

You made me feel things I haven't felt in decades. Your energy draws were intoxicating, and the taste of you still lingers on my tongue. I need to feel you again to absolve myself and feel you coursing through me. As Shakespeare says, "Speak low if you speak love" I do hope to see you again soon and that I'll have a chance to redeem myself. Seems neither of us were at the top of our game. ~Dean

"I suppose only Shakespearean sonnets will do if you can't get it to stand up and cheat for you!" Dan shouted. He slammed the laptop shut and shoved it away from him.

"Oh, gross." Fionna was still gagging and convulsing beside him.

"His own freaking body tried to warn him off. Told him to go home and make things right with the woman that has been married to him for forty freaking years and bore him five children." All Dan could see was the red haze of his infuriated energy.

Fionna hoisted herself off the couch with no help whatsoever as she began a heated pace. "And I wonder how long it's been since he sent his wife love notes with Shakespearean quotes. I guess he saves all of that for his mistress. You know, the one who has children of her own who will never really get over this!" she fumed. "Ugh!" Fionna sank back down on the couch and reopened the laptop. She clicked on the reply. Her eyes narrowed in utter hatred.

Dean, I'm so relieved I'm not the only one who wants another chance. I couldn't seem to get my mind and body in sync that night either. At least with you there was a reason, unlike with Terry. He seems to have that same trouble with regularity. As for quotes from Shakespeare, I much prefer, "She's beautiful, and therefore to be wooed; She is woman and therefore to be won."

"Oh, gag me. She really thinks she's something, doesn't she? You homewrecking whore," Fionna shouted at the laptop.

"Fi," Dan tried to soothe her but she was inconsolable.

She stood again and jerked her purse off the coat rack at their front door. "I am going over to Wilshire's house and I am telling him that he is a low-life shit-sack that deserves to have his tiny, nonfunctioning, shriveled old man tool cut off and hung on a wall. And then I am taking Ellen out and finding her a real man that will love and adore her."

"Fi." Dan moved toward her carefully. "Honey." He took her hands and forcefully removed the death grip she had on her bag. "Come here." He guided her into his chest and wrapped his arms around her. The emotional energy she was feeling and the case were threatening to pull her under.

She began to sob.

"Okay, it's okay," he whispered as he drew the emotional energy pulsing through her out into his shield. "I've got you, and I love you so much. What's done is done. We can't save them now," he lamented.

"Ellen loved him. I could feel that when I was around them. They were supposed to be married forever." She broke down completely.

"I know, baby." He held her tightly and let her ruin his shirt. She calmed after several minutes of Dan keeping her cosseted in his shield. "Let's go on to bed. You curl up in your ball, and I'll hold you all night long. I'll never let you go."

She nodded against him but then lifted her head. "He told the Angels to come watch me challenge. He invited them out, told them that I was worth seeing." She tried desperately to rectify the two individuals that were held inside one man.

"I know, sweetheart. He signed me into special ops when I was a senior. He wrote the recommendation for me himself. He came to Amelia's funeral," Dan explained how he understood the bitter disappointment she felt.

With a heavy heart and a weary soul, Dan led his Maylea up to their bed and soothed her to sleep.

CHAPTER 34

REPERCUSSIONS AND RECEIVERS

Feeling vicious, Dan threw the Ferrari into park in the faculty parking lot the next morning. He began a cadenced march toward his office.

"Sir, are you okay?" Jeff sounded somewhat frightened when he approached.

"Oh, hey." Dan shook himself from his single-minded drive. He drew a deep breath and slowed his pace. "I was hoping to get in my office before I see Wilshire. I'm very likely to give him a big piece of my mind if he crosses my path this morning."

"I take it you started going through the stuff we found." It was awfully humble of Jeff to say *we* when he had provided Dan with all of the evidence he was currently in possession of.

"How's work?" Dan asked. He desperately needed a subject change.

"It's great. I've learned a ton, and Bec's doing okay with everything. She has an interview today at that preschool she's been wanting to work for."

"Great." Dan forced a smile. The desperate desire to protect his baby girls from the world itself had him driving Aida to school and walking her in to class after dragging his brother-in-law on a six-mile run.

"I...uh...I was wondering if you heard what happened last night," Jeff asked.

Dan's brow furrowed. He wasn't certain how much more he could hear without marching into Wilshire's office and backhanding him. "Mentor Bryant's husband showed up at the Wilshires' mansion last night. Iodex was called in. Ericcson took him back home, told him to chill out, that he needed to work it out in court not with his fists. He decided to take it public. He lit up Facebook last night with all of his suspicions, named Wilshire, called him out. It was a bunch of stuff. I was going to see if you and Mrs. Vindico and Aida might like to come over. Becca wants to make you dinner for all you did, and I could show you the new stuff."

Dan shook his head. "You don't need to be making us dinner. I think Fi and I both need a break this week. We're taking Aida to her first Angels challenge tomorrow night. Why don't you and Becca come over Monday after work. After we eat and I get Aida to bed, we can go over anything new."

"If you're sure."

"It'll be fine. That way we'll have a better grasp on the repercussions of what happened last night."

As Dan unlocked his office, he recalled his promise to Fionna that he'd negated Monday. He threw his laptop and briefcase on his desk and marched toward the administration building.

"Uh, Mentor Vindico, where are you going?" Deep concern thrummed in Jeff's rhythms.

"To rectify a situation that I should never have gotten myself into."

"Okay, but before you go tell him off, maybe think about what will happen if he fires you. Your dad kind of needs you to stay employed."

"I'm not telling him off...yet," he quipped. "I'll see you in class."

Dan continued his infuriated march to the chancellor's office. Fury built in his veins with every step. He stomped past Vivian Lamb's desk and all of the accountants' desks. He pounded on the vast cherrywood door.

Dan's eyes goggled when the door finally opened a full five minutes later. Dan had continued to pound out his frustration via his hammering fist. None other than Katherine Bryant, wearing dark

306

sunglasses and keeping her head down, proceeded out of the chancellor's office.

"Are you fucking kidding me?" Dan snarled.

"Let's go in my office, Dan," the chancellor commanded.

"Let's." Forcing himself to remember that he hadn't come near to finishing his investigation and that he wanted to nail Wilshire with every possible offense he could find, Dan forced himself to swallow down the long hate-fueled diatribe forming rapidly on his tongue.

But the look in Dean Wilshire's eyes had Dan reeling momentarily. He'd been crying. Dan blinked several times, unable to believe the images he was seeing with his own eyes. Shaking his head slightly, he went on with what he'd come to say.

"Have you found a replacement for the sub-freshman creative writing class yet? Because after this week I won't be teaching it anymore."

Wilshire drew a deep breath as he nodded his understanding. "I'm sorry, I haven't yet." He sounded weary and dejected.

"When I took this job, I signed on for five upper-level classes and two labs. That's full time. My wife," he spat the words vengefully, "is having a difficult time with the end of her pregnancy. I need to be home more, like I said I would be. I keep my promises."

Wilshire looked like Dan had just slapped him across the face, but he nodded his defeat.

"I'm sorry Fionna's having a difficult time. If there's anything I can do, let me know. Don't worry about the sub-freshman class. I'll find someone else."

"Thank you." Dan turned to leave.

"You know, I never meant to hurt anyone," the chancellor pled suddenly.

Turning back, Dan narrowed his eyes. He gave the chancellor a single nod. "The smartest man I've ever known said bad is bad, and wrong is wrong. No matter how you want to slice this cake, you had a choice." Dan slammed the door shut behind him.

. . .

Dan arrived home Wednesday afternoon to find Fionna in the bathroom methodically applying makeup. There were at least ten entire outfits on the bed that it appeared she'd tried on and discarded. He cringed. He knew this was going to be tough on her. This was the first Angels challenge she'd attended since she'd retired.

"Hey, sweetheart. How are we feeling about tonight?" He tried to get her to talk.

She offered him a weary smile. "I'm all right. How was your day?"

Dan shook his head. "You're not all right."

"Nervous," she admitted. "I don't know…how to feel. I don't know how to do this. I don't even know what to wear. What do you wear to a challenge when you don't wear a uniform anymore?" He heard the unspoken echo. *I don't know who I am anymore.*

Since he'd been feeling quite a bit of that himself lately, he drew her into his arms. "I'll be right beside you the entire time. Believe me, I get how hard this is. There are no wrong answers to any of the questions you just asked."

She managed a quick nod. "I know." She pulled away from him and went back to her eyeliner.

"If you're not feeling up to this, we don't have to go."

"I want to go. I want to show my support, and Aida's really excited to see all of the Angels. I just don't want to overshadow Emily or their new Junior Receiver. I know the press won't be kind."

Dan was certain that was true. "Is there anything I can do to make this easier on you?"

That earned him a real smile. "I don't think so. It's just a lot harder than I ever imagined. I love the life we've made. I just…" She shrugged. "I don't know."

"It's okay to miss parts of the one you had before." He tried desperately to remember that advice himself.

When Emily had been moved up to become the Angels' new Senior Receiver, Rachel Carson had been recruited out of Venton to become their Junior Receiver. She was struggling. Emily had asked Fionna for advice several times.

Fionna had done a phenomenal job of guiding Emily and teaching her when she'd been the Angels' newest Receiver, but Fionna had been on the team for seven years when Emily was recruited. Emily had only challenged one.

Their collective inexperience was showing. They'd lost three of the four challenges so far in the season. At the last meeting Dan and Fionna had attended as owners, there'd been talks of replacing Rachel midseason. Fionna had been adamant that they had to give her time to learn. But the team had gotten accustomed to Fionna's astounding powers. Dan wasn't certain how much longer Medio Sawyer, the team's primary owner, was going to be patient.

CHAPTER 35

DUALITY DICHOTOMY

Dan and Fionna were able to sneak in the team entrance to the arena, avoiding the press at the front entrances. Dan waited outside while his girls were exuberantly welcomed into the locker room by a gaggle of Angels.

He didn't like being alone in the arena. Too many memories. Too much of his and Fionna's parallel past that hadn't converged until Dan was already a mere shell of the man he should've been.

Relief eased the tense set of his shield when Rainer approached. He gave him a kind smile. "Emily's thrilled Fionna's here."

"Fi's a little nervous. She doesn't want to overshadow."

Rainer shook his head. "Emily and Rachel will both feel that she doesn't want that, and they'll trust their own feelings more than anything any press outlet might report."

Rainer was an endless source of wisdom about Receivers. Dan hadn't really thought that through yet, but he was right.

"Do you think Rachel will settle in? Fi's worried they're already looking to replace her."

Rainer nodded. "I watched her challenge with Emily all through school. They were on the Venton Vixens together. She's much better than her past few performances. Emily says her nerves are killing her confidence."

"Seems like the coaches could help with that."

"They've tried. According to Em, she does brilliantly in practice, but every challenge she chokes. Knowing that Sawyer's getting antsy can't be helping, and Receivers pick up on stuff like that. She'll sense it."

"So, everyone calming down and easing up would probably do a lot of good."

"Yeah, but good luck convincing the fans, the coaches, the press, and Sawyer. They all want Receivers to navigate the world the way they do. No one really gets it."

Dan and Fionna moved through a barrage of press in an effort to get to the Angels' box.

"Fionna, what are your feelings on Rachel Carson's performances in the last four challenges?"

"Fionna, do you believe Emily will be able to pick up Rachel's slack?"

"As team owners, what do you want to see the ladies do here today?"

"The team clearly misses your power and agility, Fionna. Any regrets on your retirement?"

"Do you feel you've let your teammates and the fans down, Fionna?"

Dan batted a boom mic out of her face. "Get the hell away from her. Now."

Mercifully, they neared the door to the box seats. Dan rushed Aida and Fionna inside. Garrett took the seat beside them a few moments later. "I was behind you but couldn't get to you." He explained as he hugged Aida and then Fionna. "You okay?" Dan heard Garrett whisper.

Fionna shook her head and buried it farther in his neck. Garrett shared a heartbroken look with Dan. "Hey, look at me," Garrett guided. "You're allowed to have a life outside of the Angels even if that isn't what other people wanted from you. You don't owe anybody anything."

"I know," she choked. "I just...hate this so bad for Rachel and Emily."

"They'll get it figured out. She'll simmer down. As I recall, your first season wasn't a winning season either. You had to figure it out too. The talking heads like to forget that because then they might have to admit that they're making bank off making you feel guilty and Rachel feel inept. They're assholes."

Aida crawled up in Garrett's lap as the drumroll echoed in the stadium and the field aegis was set.

"What's going to happen?" she asked him. She looked amazed at everything going on around her.

"In just a minute they'll announce all of the Angels and you can cheer for them, and then we'll watch them try to move energy around the field. I'll explain it to you once I see what kind of course it is." She nodded and kept a tight hold of Garrett.

"The Arlington Angels are proud to welcome you to Angels Arena for tonight's challenge against the Boston Bombers," boomed from the announcer. The names of both teams' challengers were called. They all raced onto the field, waving to their fans. Aida and Garrett cheered.

"The Angels have a new Junior Receiver, Miss Rachel Carson. Despite Rachel's stellar performances at Venton Academy, she's struggled to find her footing in the vast chasm left by former Senior Receiver Fionna Styler."

Fionna's head dropped. "Do they have to do that?"

Both Dan and Garrett tried to console her.

The course was revealed, and her eyes goggled. "Oh no."

Dan and Garrett grimaced. It was a Duality Division Duel. They were one of the most difficult challenge courses in Summation, and they were particularly hard on the teams' Receivers.

Garrett pointed to the four sources of energy along each side of the field as he began explaining the course to Aida. "Each of those things has two different kinds of energy inside of it. A light has heat and electricity. Once one of the challengers gets that engine to crank and turn, it will produce mechanical energy and heat. That's a magnetron right there. It has heat and electricity just like the light. And that last thing is a wind turbine. It produces wind energy and electricity. When the challenge starts, the captains on the teams will send out players one or two at a time. They'll have to make the object produce both kinds of energy, and then they'll hand it off to one of the team's Receivers. That's like you and Mommy." Aida nodded.

"The Receivers will have to separate the two kinds of energy. One will hold the heat energy and one will hold the electricity. The Angels' coaches will probably get Emily to convert the wind and the mechanical energy into electricity. Once Emily has all of the electricity and Rachel has all of the heat, they release it into those big iodes at the end of the field there. And once both of those are released, they'll made the even bigger one explode, and it'll blow confetti everywhere like a party. Does that sound fun?"

"It sounds hard for Emily."

Garrett cringed slightly. "You're not wrong, Aida Mae."

"They shouldn't do what they're going to do," Fionna whimpered. "They need to let Rachel convert either the mechanical or the wind. It's incredibly draining to convert while you're also holding."

"They need to do the conversions first," Garrett pointed out.

The buzzer sounded, and Dan hoped against hope. He wasn't certain how Fionna would take another Angels loss.

The Angels' coaches sent Emily out. She started on the windmill, which would be the most difficult to convert. She got it to spin and then moved it faster and faster until she was able to draw out enough wind energy to make the conversion including what she would lose as she did it. She pulled it in her own bands and converted it to electricity.

Dan looked at the Bomber side of the field. They'd decided to do the conversions last, it seemed. Their captain and their Senior Shield were working on separating the electricity and heat from the lamp.

"Oh good!" Fionna pointed to Rachel racing toward the engine. She cheered her on.

Dan, Rainer, Garrett, and Aida joined in.

Rachel got the engine to spin quickly.

Garrett elbowed Fionna. "See, she's settling in."

"That was the easy part," she reminded him.

Before Rachel had the engine producing mechanical energy, the Bombers had pulled and separated the energy from both the lamp and the magnetron. Their Senior Receiver was holding the heat and their Junior was holding the electricity. They were both more seasoned challengers than either Rachel or Emily.

As Rachel pulled the mechanical energy from the engine, she glanced up into the stands. It was like watching an oncoming train wreck you couldn't stop. Her face fell. She lost a great deal of the energy she was trying to convert. But a second later, she shook her head and seemed to refocus.

Fionna squeezed her eyes shut. Dan wasn't certain if it was in prayer or if she couldn't bear to watch anymore.

"She's got it. She's doing it!" Garrett urged. Fionna's eyes sprung back open. Rachel had managed to gather enough mechanical energy to make the conversion to heat.

Chloe Sawyer, the Angels' captain, and Sasha Cohen, their Senior Shield, took the field. They pulled the light and electricity from the lamp in less than a second and handed it off to the Receivers. Rachel managed the load. Emily gave her an encouraging smile.

"Come on, Rachel! You've got this!" Garrett shouted.

"You can do it!" Aida cheered. Fionna and Dan beamed as Garrett kissed her cheek.

Dana Mathers, the Angels' Senior Enforcer, and Jaya Yadav, their new Junior, took the field and performed the magnetron conversion.

But the Bombers' Receivers were already loading the heat and electricity into the individual iodes.

"Please, please, please," Fionna begged the air around her.

Rachel and Emily began loading energy into the iodes.

"It's not enough!" Garrett pointed to the Bombers' Receiver who'd been holding the heat. He was out, and the iode wasn't full. The Angels fans were on their feet. Garrett put Aida on his shoulders so she could see.

The Bombers sent out two more challengers to force the engine to produce more heat.

Emily's iode was full. She turned to cheer on Rachel who was trying to load in enough heat without any loss. It was going to be close.

"You can do it," Fionna spoke between her clenched teeth.

Dan cringed. "She's losing too much."

Suddenly, both of the Angels' smaller iodes lit. The box roared. Two seconds later, the Angels' iode exploded, covering the field in confetti.

"She did it!" Fionna was ecstatic.

Emily and Rachel raced to one another to hug and jump up and down. The Angels poured onto the field to cheer them on.

CHAPTER 36

CONSTANTS

Garrett carried Aida out to the car after they all heartily congratulated the Angels on their victory.

"Will you come to my house and have a spend-the-night party, pretty please?" Aida begged Garrett.

He chuckled, but Fionna gave him a pleading look as well. Dan reminded himself that his girls loved Garrett. Hell, *he* loved Garrett, even if having a house guest hadn't really been his plan.

"Sure. Maybe you can help me look over the stuff about Venton for Dad," Dan encouraged.

"There's clean sheets on the bed, and I'll make you my blueberry French toast for breakfast," Fionna promised.

"All right, let me go by my apartment and grab my stuff. I have a shift tomorrow at ten."

"Yay!" Aida was ecstatic.

"You want to come with me to the apartment and help me pack, Aida Mae?"

"Yes!"

"We'll see you two in a little while."

"Have fun," Dan called.

. . .

Dan followed Fionna into their bedroom to change. Tension and confusion still swam in her rhythms.

"Hey,"—he pulled her into his arms—"listen to me for just a minute. Believe me, I know what you're feeling. I know how hard this is. I just want you to hear me. I *know* who you are, and it doesn't have anything to do with the Angels or the uniform you used to wear."

She managed a broken smile. "I know."

"I'm not so sure you do, so listen to me. You are Maylea. You are a woman who loves her family, and her friends, and her island, and her little girls so much you would do anything in the world for them. And that makes this all the more difficult. You are terrified that you're letting people you love down, and I need you to understand that even if that is true, it doesn't mean that you don't love them with everything that you are. You are so accustomed to putting everyone's wants above your needs, and that's got to stop, sweetheart.

"You will always be Maylea. You will always make any space that you are in beautiful, but those spaces are going to change throughout our lives. People are going to have to be okay with that. Your evolution cannot be predicated on making other people happy." He brushed a kiss on her forehead. "I honestly can't wait to see you in every single stage we go through. I can't wait to show you that I'm going to love you through every single transformation." He lifted her chin so he could stare into the depths of her tearstained, sienna eyes. "You aren't an Arlington Angel anymore, and I promise you that's okay because you are always, always *my* angel."

She managed a haggard nod. "Thank you, but you need to hear me as well." She wiped away a few of her own tears. "I know how much you miss being Chief of Elite. You miss it more than you've even allowed yourself to acknowledge. It's okay to miss it. It's okay to mourn it. You deserve a chance to understand all you've lost."

He nodded and tried to swallow down the knot of regret and devastation that closed his throat. "It's also okay for you to really mourn the child we lost. It's okay to be devastated about that and to be excited about Halia. *You* deserve a chance to acknowledge all we lost, and we deserve the chance to be excited about what's to come. It is...life."

Her chin trembled, and his shield pulsed with the loss of it all. "I know, but I feel like I'm being torn apart at the seams."

"Then come here to me and let me hold you so tight we put each other back together."

He crushed her lips to his own. Her tears soaked his cheeks and cascaded over his jaw. His shield sought her in earnest. He pulled the sweater she'd worn to the challenge over her head, dispensing with the Realm-approved façade she'd donned to pretend to be what they wanted.

He wanted only her. His shield longed for *Maylea.*

She untucked his shirt and pushed it up his chest, seeking his skin, seeking him. He tore it over his head and dispensed with both of their jeans, socks, and boots. "All mine, baby doll. All fucking mine. My good girl."

She gasped out his name.

"That's it," he groaned. "Close your eyes. Just feel me. Be right here with me." He left her in the lacy bra and dipped his hand down the back of the satin panties to grip her ripe ass. He guided her body in rhythmic circles around his strain. "Do you feel what you do to me? That's all you. So fucking perfect."

Her rhythms tensed in needy, desperate arcs. She stared him down and splayed her hand across the center of his chest, the approximate location of where his badge used to hang. She drew from his chest, pulling his protective energy and his all-consuming love deep into her rhythms.

He groaned from the sensation as he lifted her into his arms and laid her out in their bed. Her head shook and her body rolled as the soft, cool sheets surrounded her.

He slipped the panties, with the satin now marked from her hunger, down her long legs and fell to his knees to worship his angel. His cock throbbed and wept for her as he licked up her slit. He was sloppy with need but so was she. He devoured everything she gave up for him. "Such a good girl," he moaned against her.

"Yes," echoed from the depth of her soul. He heard the cry from the emptiness she would no longer endure alone. He would fill her. He would save her. It was who he was.

His tongue circled her clit as her hips undulated with his moves. He clamped his hands around her waist. "Be still and let me enjoy you. Let me fill my mouth with you."

Her legs trembled from the order. "It feels so good," she groaned.

"I know it does, baby doll. I know it's so needy. That tight little pussy is so wet, crying all for me. I'm gonna fill it full. I'll show you who you belong to."

He had her. Her heated rhythms spun tight a second before they released her, and she cried out all for him. Her body tensed and writhed. Her thighs tightened against his jaw as he devoured the very essence of her. He licked and sucked until his chin was soaked in her juices, and she was writhing in desperation. The deep musk of her and of sex scent clung to him.

"Such a good, good girl for me."

Giving her no time to recover from the first of what he planned to be many orgasms that night, he plunged his fingers deep into her, hot and fast. He fucked her with his hand, preparing her for his cock. He pressed his palm to her mound, pushing her G-spot to his seeking fingers and providing her something to grind against.

"Yes...yes," gasped from her.

He smirked. She was so wet as he pounded into her with his fingers he could hear the slick cries of her body. "You're so fucking needy for me, baby doll. Pouring that sweet cum all over me. Are you showing me, honey? Showing me who I belong to."

A deep, frantic moan escaped her lungs.

"Makes me want to mark you with my cum, cover you in it."

"Do it. Please. I need it," she begged in earnest.

"What you need is to come for me again first like my good girl. Come so sweet for me and then I'll mark you." Heat and need rose from her in frantic pulses with each rhythm that formed from her body. "That's it," he urged. "Let it go for me."

It tore through her in a tidal wave of release that freed her from the memories, the ties, the past that was gone, and the future that was yet to be revealed. She came so hard he almost lost it all just watching her let him absorb the sobs of her body deep in his shield.

He stood and lifted her ass with his hands. Her calves spread around his waist, and he plunged her depths. He watched his cock, slick with her juices, pound into her and pull away in deep, desperate requisition.

He had to close his eyes. It was too much. She was too good, too perfect, all his. He would never deserve such unadulterated nirvana, and yet she gave more and he took with greed. He took it all—everything she ever was, everything she would ever be, everything she was in that moment, and he worshipped her in every possible way.

Her pussy clenched so tight around him he was certain he would lose it all. He dammed back the release his shield craved. Their fused rhythms surrounded them, moving in one arc of pure, constant, unshakeable love.

She cried out his name. Her head shook. Her ass tightened in his hands. The orgasm rose from her mound, and he sank into her one last time as he baptized her pussy with his release. He pulled out a second later and milked the rest out over her mound, covering her in thick spurts of him.

After he cleaned her up, he cradled her in their bed. She lifted her head from his chest. Her hair was in a wild mane on her shoulders. Her eyes were heavy and her lips were kiss swollen. "Thank you," she whispered.

He chuckled. "Trust me, baby doll, the pleasure was all mine."

She smirked. "For that, too, but thank you for always, always being *my* Shield."

CHAPTER 37

WINDOWS AND MIRRORS

Thursday night, just before Dan was about to settle in with the Venton disaster, his father phoned. "Dan, I need some help."

"What's wrong?"

"I know you've got a lot going on. I was just wondering if you'd gotten anywhere with the information on Wilshire. People are calling for my head. Some Facebook posting. I don't know."

"Yeah, Katherine Bryant's husband apparently let the world know just what he thought of what Wilshire did with his wife," Dan explained.

"What a class act," the governor quipped sarcastically.

"He's pissed. Rightfully so."

"I give the guy all the sympathy in the world, but what did putting something like that up on Facebook really do for him? It certainly didn't improve his life in any way. It might've gained him false sympathies, because, trust me, son, most people will tell you how sorry they are, so they can hear more of the story."

"I was just about to dive into it all. Garrett helped me go through some of it last night."

"If you want me to open it up as a full-blown Iodex and Senate affair, I will. I don't want you making yourself or my daughter-in-law sick over this."

"No, it's okay. I will not let you take the fall for Wilshire's lack of ethics."

The governor sighed. "This Realm elected me to govern and guide them, and I should have delved deeper when I thought something was going on at Venton instead of letting Wilshire assure me that all was well. I trusted him, and obviously, I shouldn't have. But the buck has to stop somewhere. If I lose my governorship over this then so be it, I suppose."

Governor Vindico was an excellent Realm governor. He was wise and fair. Dan was determined to save his father from the fallout of everything going on at Venton. His dad had certainly saved him on numerous occasions.

"I'm not going to let that happen," he vowed.

"Can you tell me how I can see for myself what Terry Bryant put on Facebook? I've had it screamed at me multiple times today on my telephone. I'd like to see what I'm actually dealing with."

"You know, the Senate has a Facebook page. Maybe the governors should get one," Dan teased.

Governor Vindico laughed. Dan could almost hear his eye roll. "Son, I'm trying to govern real people with real problems and trying to discern the best way to lead our nation. I do not have time to deal with what other people want you to believe about their lives, or whether or not they either like or hate a television show based on what they feel will get them the most attention. Beyond that, I personally feel it's more important for the Gifted Realm to help those in the Non-Gifted Realm figure out where their next meal is coming from, not when their crops are due in on a virtual farm."

Chuckling, Dan instructed his father on how to log onto Facebook. To his shock, his father was able to open Terry Bryant's page without summoning at all. He'd dropped all of the security measures and opened it to the world. In the scorching gall of his heartbreak and vengeful disdain, Dan sincerely hoped that he didn't find himself burned.

"All right, if I find anything tonight, I'll call you back," Dan promised.

"Just tell me tomorrow. I have a great desire to crawl in my bed with my wife and pretend this is all some kind of horrible dream."

Dan didn't really have any desire to think about his parents in bed together. "I'll talk to you in the morning." His cell rang again and he sighed. "Hello." Dan wondered what had the Crown Governor calling him that evening.

"You know, I still can't get used to your not barking, 'this is Vindico' whenever you answer the phone," Governor Haydenshire admitted.

"You took my badge so I figured it was time for a new greeting."

"You didn't seem to mind at the time, but if you'd like to try on the Crown Governor hat for a while, believe me, I'll share."

"Bad day, I take it."

"No," the governor stated thoughtfully. "My baby girl is asleep on my chest, my kids are healthy and happy as far as I know. Patrick and Lucy just left. The baby's kicking up a storm. They're both over the moon. Lillian's holding my hand, so no, not a bad day at all."

"I heard Levi asked Sarah Watson to marry him and that she accepted." Dan recalled seeing the announcement in the Realm Times earlier in the week.

"She did, but I don't really believe they'll ever make it down the aisle. Please never tell Levi I shared this, but I don't think they should. Lillian and I are waiting on Levi to figure that out."

Dan wasn't certain how to respond, but Governor Haydenshire was an outstanding judge of character. He had no doubt that he was correct. "I'm sorry to hear that. Let Levi know if I can do anything, I will." That seemed an odd thing to say, but Dan thought he should offer. He and Levi had been friends through childhood and the academy. Dan was far closer with Will and Garrett, but Levi usually tagged along.

"I'm worried about my son, so I appreciate that." The governor drew a deep, audible breath. "Listen, I did have a reason for calling. I need some questions answered. Terry Bryant has filed for separation, and he wants full custody of their children along with most of

Katherine's paychecks and half of their savings. Katherine showed up here in tears a few hours ago begging me not to take her kids away."

"Wow." Revulsion washed through Dan's veins. He wondered what Katherine Bryant thought of all that she'd done now. His heart broke for their children.

"Houses don't burn down slowly, Daniel," the governor vowed again. Letting that potent piece of wisdom sear into his mind and into his soul, Dan continued to listen. "I set a temporary custody trial at eight tomorrow morning. I plan to order counseling for the entire family with the Auxiliary department, but before I do something that will inevitably upend those kids' lives for something they had absolutely nothing to do with, I need you to tell me if she and Dean did have an affair and if that affair led to either of them doing anything that affected Venton. Was this affair the foundation for all of the insanity going on at the academy? I need to know how destructive this was outside of the families involved."

Dan drew a deep breath. How had an email from a colleague twisted and spun to ruin so many lives? He wondered if the debris could be resuscitated back into a recognizable life form.

"Truthfully sir, an emotional affair, yes, they did. As for a physical one, I'm not a hundred percent certain yet."

"One isn't any better than the other. Don't ever forget that."

"I know, sir. Fi and I started going through it the other night, and it made me sick. Can I pick it back up now? I'll call you back as soon as I have some answers for you. I'm sorry—I should have gone back to it sooner."

"Believe me, I do understand. Just let me know everything you find. We have to root out the problem before anyone can heal from this."

He sounded as sick as Dan felt. "Let me put Aida to bed, and then I'll figure this out."

"Let me know in the morning. I want to spend a little more time with Abigail, and then I want to spend some time with my wife."

"Yes sir, I understand."

"Give Fionna and Aida our love."

"What's an emotional affair, Daddy?" Aida asked. Dan spun. Panic shot through his shield.

Aida was in her Moana nightgown. She'd come downstairs to have a cup of Aida tea with Fionna.

Fionna's eyes closed as she swallowed.

"That's not something you ever, ever have to worry about, baby," Dan vowed.

Aida nodded. She studied him. "I love you." She reached her hands up.

Emotion tightened in his throat. Dan laid his phone on the counter and lifted her up into his embrace. "I love you too, baby girl."

Dan tucked Aida in before he retrieved his laptop.

"I just can't imagine. I couldn't do it. I couldn't go on." Fionna had been trying desperately not to cry since Dan had explained Governor Haydenshire's request.

CHAPTER 38

FROM THE OUTSIDE

Dan extended his feet out on the coffee table as he switched on his laptop. Fionna handed him a beer as she joined him with a large mug of tea.

"I just can't imagine going to sleep at night with my girls not in my home with me. Not kissing Aida good night or just going for weeks at a time not seeing them." Tears began to flow rapidly down her cheeks. Dan let his eyes close as he pulled her close.

"Baby, why don't you go on to bed? I'll find what I need for Governor Haydenshire and then I'll be up."

"No, I'll be okay." Fionna wiped away her tears. "The more we get through the faster we can get this out of our house." She shook her head as Dan opened the copy of the chancellor's computer along with the logins for the Venton banking accounts his father had provided him. "Didn't she ever think that this could all blow up in her face? I mean the governors could take her kids away from her."

Dan kissed her forehead. "I don't think either of them thought at all, sweetheart. It's all about the very next moment. The next time they can see each other. So, no, it never really occurred to her that anything bad could happen because she'd convinced herself that she wasn't hurting anyone. Honestly, I've lived that way," he admitted.

Fionna's brow furrowed.

"I went on for years in the state I was in, miserable, awful, hateful to everyone, and I convinced myself that I wasn't hurting anyone but myself. I constantly told myself that I deserved the pain. It took me meeting you and you showing me how to live for me to realize that I was hurting all of the people who cared about me." He shook his head, still disgusted with himself.

Her soothing cast worked through his arm. "We're all connected. If you hurt one part of the web of life, it affects the whole thing. It takes a really strong person to understand that, to internalize it. I'm so proud of you." She brushed a kiss on his cheek.

Certain he did not deserve her pride, he went on with the task at hand. He decided to start with the bad and move to the gruesome. Dan pulled up Terry Bryant's Facebook feed.

"Wow!" Fionna's mouth hung open as Dan stared at his own computer in shock. Terry had posted screenshots of a home computer outlining the dates that Katherine had been out of town, presumably with Chancellor Wilshire, and what she'd missed in her children's lives while she was being an—as Terry typed in all caps—adulterous slut.

Ballet recitals along with pictures of their daughter flying in the air in pointe shoes. Ball games, barbecues, their son being named ninth grade class vice president at Langley High School. He'd included photographs of receipts from lingerie shops in the cities that Katherine had traveled to under the guise of attending yet another seminar or convention. There were three photographed together from one of Fionna's favorite lingerie shops in DC.

Dan recognized the pink heart-shaped handwritten receipts. Each ticket totaled well over a hundred dollars. The totals of each receipt were highlighted. There was another from the sex shop where Lindley was currently employed. "Funny, I only saw one of these purchases. The day I came home from dropping Brad off at soccer practice and found my wife posed on the bed slamming her laptop shut. Guess I should have investigated a little further," was Terry's quip above the photographed receipts.

"Damn." Fionna's gasp shocked Dan into laughter. "So, she bought all of that stuff for another man, and then kept the receipts so her husband could find them? Look, those are dated over a year ago." She pointed to one of the pictures. "Why would she do that?"

Concentrating and tapping in to his additional Predilect again, Dan shook his head. "Everything becomes a memento. It's just like you said, she was utterly consumed. Her only thoughts became when she would get the next fix. So, each and every thing that reminded her of the chancellor and their time together, she kept like some kind of sick treasure. I overheard a few teachers talking. One of them said Katherine had gotten an apartment. I'm sure he kicked her out and then tore their place up, but honestly, I bet they weren't even that well-hidden."

Fionna shook her head and willed composure as Dan scrolled down the page.

Once she allowed herself to really focus on the situation enough to read the emotions, she nodded. "She kept those mementos because in some way that meant he was hers and she was his. She couldn't have a wedding band or a marriage license, so she kept those as her proof that she had something important. And really, she had nothing at all. Nothing but the tangled web of lies she kept telling herself, and her kids, and her husband."

"She had nothing at all," he echoed. There were hundreds of comments including outcries from Katherine's students both in her defense and blasting her actions attached to all of the photos. Several male students urged Terry Bryant to post the videos from Mentor Bryant's laptop.

The next photograph was of Katherine and Terry talking with Chancellor Wilshire and Ellen at the Venton picnic that had been at the beginning of the summer.

"Hungry for a little more than fried chicken, Chancellor?" was the sneering tag on the photo. Dan shook his head as he enlarged the photograph. The chancellor's arm was around his wife, but his ravenous eyes were undeniably locked on to Katherine Bryant's cleavage.

"Good grief." He rolled his eyes. "Is he twelve?"

"Consumed," Fionna reminded. Dan continued to scroll down as

Fionna grew thoughtful. She closed her eyes to tap into the full power of her abilities. "This isn't going to work."

"What isn't going to work?"

"If Governor Haydenshire wants you to say yes, sir, they most definitely had an emotional and a physical affair, and she knowingly broke her marriage vows, then that isn't going to be in their emails and it certainly isn't going to be on Facebook. How many times have we emailed about the amazing sex we had? I don't think I've ever emailed, 'hey baby, thanks for the O's last night. You rock my world,'" she giggled. Raising her eyebrows, she grabbed the cloned copy of the chancellor's phone.

"Texts are far more intimate. You feel like it's this sweet, special message between the two of you. An email has too much business in its energy." She summoned and turned on the phone. Dan and Fionna did send rather overt, lusty text messages throughout the day most every day. She was right. The phone held the evidence, not the laptop.

Dan was approaching it too logistically. It was a more passionate crime.

"We're going to have to watch at least some of these videos." She grimaced. Before Dan could try desperately to come up with a way for the videos to remain unseen, his own cell phone chirped.

Jeff texted—

Wasn't certain if you were still up. If you are, you might want to check out Mentor Bryant's husband's latest post. Becca's phone is ringing off the hook. Everyone's seeing this.

"What now?" Dan quickly refreshed Terry Bryant's Facebook page.

"Oh my word," fell from Fionna's mouth as she took in the newest update. Dan wanted desperately to look away. On the screen in front of them was an uploaded video window. Katherine was in the opening screenshot. She was dressed in a long, silk negligee, seated on what Dan assumed was her bed. Dan handed Fionna the laptop. He didn't want to see any woman dressed that way besides his wife.

"Just tell me what you think."

"Uh, well…" Fionna seemed hesitant to study the video upload as well. Suddenly, she gasped.

"What?"

"I know why he posted this one," she whimpered.

"Why?"

"Because the way she had her laptop positioned so they could video chat..." Fionna grimaced in horror. Dan willed patience. "You can see the laptop screen in the dresser mirror behind her. He enhanced the picture. I can see Chancellor Wilshire. It looks like he's at his desk in his office at the academy.

"So, is this cheating? Is this an affair? Is this what Governor Haydenshire wants? I mean, where is the line?" Fionna demanded. "Is a kiss too far, touching someone, making them orgasm, where does the line begin and end? If he finishes, and she doesn't, does that not count? To me, anything above a handshake or a polite hug would have me ending you violently. You know, like in a car explosion or something."

"You don't have to threaten me, honey. I completely agree. I guess that depends on the couples in question. What Governor Haydenshire really wants to know is how badly did their actions affect the academy? How many other people are in the fallout of this?"

"I'm gonna watch it." She cringed.

"You don't have to."

"The entire school is watching it, so here goes." She clicked the arrow in the center of the video window. Dan braced, not certain what to say or do. Fionna's face was twisted into a horrified scowl as the video loaded. Dan heard Mentor Bryant greet the chancellor.

"Hey angel," he replied.

"Ugh, angel straight from hell, you pig," Fionna sneered.

"Fi." Dan tried not to laugh.

"Sorry." She rewound the video and began it again.

Forcing herself to think about it abstractly, Fionna paused the video. "She's very uncomfortable. Her emotions are hard lined. She isn't sure of what she's doing."

"She's cheating on her husband, so she should be uncomfortable."

"That's true, but I meant she's very uncomfortable in the lingerie. She's not used to wearing stuff like that. It's kind of a stiff on her, like she's never worn it before. It's almost like she's trying to appear just a little older, but still sexy."

"You're a pretty damn good detective, Catwoman."

Fionna adored lingerie. It was by far her favorite thing to buy seconded only by shoes and purses. Dan added this to the lengthy list of things he loved about his wife. He always made certain to tell her repeatedly how stunningly gorgeous she was whenever she donned anything from her vast collection of silk, satin, leather, and lace.

It made her feel sexy, and to Dan, there was nothing more devastatingly delicious than when Fionna Vindico felt like the sex goddess he'd always known she was. If anyone could read the emotions off of a woman dressed up for an evening of sensual pleasure, it was his wife.

"You look beautiful, Kate," Dan heard the chancellor vow. His tone was low and hungry, certainly not an intonation Dan had ever heard him use. "I wish I was there to take it off you."

Fionna stuck her finger in her mouth, pretending to gag herself. Dan nodded his adamant agreement.

"Maybe I could do that for you. Or we could just wait until tomorrow night in Chicago," she attempted to flirt, but Fionna was right—she was uncomfortable. She wasn't confident in what she was doing. Dan could hear it in her voice. He didn't have to see it on the screen.

"I get tired of waiting to be with you, sweetheart," the chancellor urged.

"Gross, gross, gross! Someone should castrate him," Fionna shrieked. "NO," she went on vengefully, "we should cut it off and staple it to his forehead so everyone knows what a dickhead he is."

Dan doubled over laughing.

"I am serious," Fionna huffed though she was fighting laughter with every fiber of her being.

"Baby doll, I'll hold him down for you, but I really think Ellen should get to do the removal and the stapling." Suddenly, they both seemed to realize that what they were watching wasn't in any way funny. It was an example of a raw, inflicted, horrible pain.

At the end of the evening, Dan could turn off the computer and place it in his briefcase, but the Wilshires and the Bryants couldn't put it away. They couldn't gawk, shake their heads, spout their judgment, and then go to bed with their spouses. They'd taken that simple act for granted, and it had cost them a lifetime.

"Why now?" fell from Dan's lips suddenly. Fionna's brow furrowed as she paused the video. "Why is he posting all of this now?" Dan stood and began to pace as his Visium Predilection pulsed constantly. "He walked in on her in lingerie on her laptop months ago."

"I thought it was because of the custody hearing?"

"Yeah, and what made him push for that all of a sudden? What changed for him? He clearly suspected this for a lot longer than the Realm has known about it." He pulled the laptop back from Fionna and went back to the emails. "Something pushed him this far. What was it?"

"Maybe he thought she was having an affair but didn't know with whom. Maybe once he figured out it was Chancellor Wilshire, something changed for him."

Dan considered that. "Maybe, but what? Why would it matter who it was?"

"I don't know. Chancellor Wilshire has a lot of money."

"Yeah, but Bryant's certainly not blackmailing him. He not only laid all of his cards on the table, he put them up on a freaking billboard."

She nodded. "You're right. Him posting that on Facebook has a lot of panic and vengeance to it. It was an emotional decision. I don't think he thought it through." Fionna went back to the phone and began reading texts with intensity. Dan stared at the last email sent before Jeff cloned the laptop.

"What are these?" Fionna leaned toward Dan. "Every couple of dozen texts are just numbers."

Dan gave it a cursory glance and sighed. "Room numbers."

"Should've thought of that myself." She continued reading. "Dan, look!" She showed him a text from Wilshire to Bryant.

I'm so sorry, baby. I promise I'll take care of it. No one will find out.

"No one will find out what?" Fionna demanded.

"I'm assuming about the affair. What's the date on that text?" Dan asked.

"December fourth of last year." Dan opened every email near that date and began reading.

"Baby, look." He pointed to an email from Mentor Bryant. *Dean, I think this is more than I can handle. We've let this get completely out of hand. I don't know what to do. But maybe we should go back to being employer and employee. Maybe I should tell Terry. He suspects something anyway. There is no way to fix this. I need to talk to you. ~Kate*

"She tried to end it."

"Not only did she try to end it, but she did it via email. She was trying to go back and erase the mistakes, to take them back to employer and employee. But look at the texts right before that email." She showed Dan the phone.

There were numerous texts leading up to that email, and they were all decidedly flirtatious and even counting down the days until they'd be out of town together again.

"She went from 'meet me in my room' via text to 'we have to end this' via email in like two hours' time." Fionna looked as dumbfounded as Dan felt. He clicked on Wilshire's response to the email.

Katie, baby, no. I can't make it without you. You're everything to me. I'll figure out a way to take care of this. I won't allow our love to be threatened. Your beauty and your wisdom have become my life's blood, and without them I'm certain I will perish. Love, Dean

"What are they talking about? What happened? What's he going to take care of? What was threatening their love?" Fionna demanded.

Clenching his jaw, Dan picked up his phone and touched Jeff's name on his contact list.

"Mentor Vindico?" Jeff quizzed.

"I'm sorry it's so late. I need your help if you don't mind."

"Sure. What can I do?"

"Would you mind coming over and helping me dig into several things involving the Venton bank accounts? I may need you to break a heavy-duty encrypted code. Something tells me Wilshire used Venton money to cover something up. I don't know what, and I have to figure this out tonight."

"Sure." Jeff sounded thrilled.

"Becca's welcome to come with you."

"We'll be there in just a few."

CHAPTER 39
LOOKING IN

"What do you want him to do?" Fionna asked as Dan ended the call.

"Break into the Venton accounts via Chancellor Wilshire's passcode without leaving a trace. Dad only gave me his login information. I need Wilshire's."

"What are you reading in these messages?" Fionna tapped into his emotion instantly.

"Between you being the most incredible Receiver on the planet and my mediocre Visium Predilection, we make a damn good team."

"We'd make a damn good team even if we weren't Gifted. And your Visium Predilection is just as strong as your shield. I of all people know that. Now, what do you know?"

"I really don't know anything yet. I just suspect that whatever it is that Wilshire fixed, whatever threat he ended, he used Venton money to do it, and that's why he refused to show Dad the books for so long."

"You mean like someone found out about the affair and blackmailed him, and he used Venton money to pay them off?"

"I'm thinking so."

A quiet knock sounded on the front door several minutes later. Jeff guided Becca inside.

Nervous energy swam in the air around them.

Jeff sat down with Dan's computer.

Dan explained to him what he needed. "Can you do that? I know it's going to be heavily encrypted."

"I can do it," Jeff assured him. "Just give me a minute. I have to work my way through about a dozen firewalls."

Shaking his head, Jeff sighed. "They're still using ACLs," he huffed, clearly thinking that was a poor choice.

"The kind of good thing about all of this is that no one is talking about me being pregnant anymore," Becca confessed to Fionna who chuckled and patted her hand.

Dan fixed everyone drinks and began pacing.

"I'm trying. It'll just be a few more minutes," Jeff promised.

"It's fine. You have until eight tomorrow morning."

"Okay," Jeff whispered almost an hour later. Becca and Fionna were both asleep. "They're broken up into quarters."

"The last quarter of last year," Dan guided in a pained whisper.

With a single nod, Jeff slid the laptop to Dan. Every withdrawal and deposit made by Wilshire was there. Every charge to his company credit card along with salary and stock displays.

"You're amazing, you know that?"

"Thank you, sir. What are we looking for exactly?" Jeff studied the screen.

"Anything that can prove that Wilshire took money from the school to pay someone off to keep them quiet about the affair."

"But he makes a ton of money. Why would he risk his job using Venton accounts?"

"We don't know how much the blackmailer was asking for, and he wouldn't have wanted his wife to suspect anything. Him pulling a large chunk out of their personal accounts would probably have alerted Ellen to something going on."

"You're sure he was being blackmailed?" Jeff asked.

"No, but Wilshire said in an email that he wouldn't let their love be threatened. I can't think of what else that could possibly mean."

Jeff nodded. "I can write a script to run on all of his banking account entries that would weed out anything unusual. That would save us from having to go line by line."

Dan smirked and handed back the laptop. "Is Portwood aware that he's literally holding a gold mine in his hands?"

Heat stained Jeff's cheeks as he scoffed and set to work. He typed rapidly for several long minutes. His brow furrowed, and then he started in again. "There can't be nothing," he huffed. He started typing again, narrowed his eyes, and summoned and threw data up into his shield. He studied the coding floating all around him. Dan was still in awe.

"Wait a second," Jeff gasped and went back to the computer. "What the...?"

"What are you seeing?" Dan demanded.

Jeff turned the screen toward Dan. "He didn't take any money, sir. He deposited a ton of it. And the deposits started a week after that email you showed me." He pointed to a lengthy list of deposits in the Venton general fund in varying amounts from twenty-five hundred to five thousand dollars. "But the really weird part is that these came from his savings account. I can see that. Only he made sure that they're listed on the Venton books as being deposited only by an account number, not his name. And not only that, but normally if someone makes a contribution to the academy, it goes into a specific account for donations so that tax credit documentation can be distributed from that account. After it's recorded in this one account, then it can be moved to whatever account the donor specified. But Wilshire didn't deposit it in the donation account. There is no tax record of it. He just deposited all of that money directly into the primary checking account. Why would he do that? Why wouldn't you take the tax write-off?"

"You're absolutely certain there's nothing that went out from a Venton account? The only weird thing are the deposits?"

"Yeah, see, those are the mentors' and admins' paychecks." He scrolled through months and months of those. "Payouts to textbook companies, equipment companies, food suppliers, the company that provides the laptops, all of the normal things a school would pay for. Here are a few more random ones. That looks like stuff for the chem and physics labs. A seven-thousand-dollar purchase for Occamist Creation labs. Here's one for the Shield training courses. The training weapons purchases, stuff like that. But even the random ones are from companies that have been being paid by Venton for the past decade. Long before the affair started."

"How much money was deposited from Wilshire's savings accounts?"

"Give me just a second. I'm not a Duco Pred."

"I can give Will Haydenshire a call if that helps," Dan offered.

"I can at least give you an estimate, but Will could be more exact because he can see what's happening at the Senate bank moment to moment." Jeff opened the calculator app on the computer and began inputting numbers. He shook his head. Disbelief widened his eyes. "Well over four hundred thousand dollars, sir."

"Holy shit."

"Yeah." He nodded. "What do we do now? Donating money to the school isn't illegal."

"No, but if he's trying to broker his guilt or he's covering something up with money, that is illegal. I don't know what the governors will decide, but we present them the evidence. I'm going to have to cancel my morning classes."

"Senior defense is my only class tomorrow. I could work all day. Is it okay if I'm in the hearing?"

"As long as Portwood says it's okay, it's fine."

Dan went back to the emails and texts. Two days after the email where the chancellor reassured Bryant, they seemed to be back to their old tricks. The texts turned flirty again. Plans for out-of-town rendezvous were made. He found one where Wilshire had vividly described what he planned to do to her in their hotel room that night. He took a screenshot and printed that for the governors before he began studying the bank accounts again. "What the hell did you do?" Dan asked the ether, and to no one's shock, it had no answers either.

"Dan?" Fionna sat up off the couch. She rubbed her eyes. "What did you find?"

"Can you look over this information and explain anything to me? Neither of us understand it. Is there any emotion in the numbers? Wilshire has donated four hundred thousand dollars to the academy, without using any of it to lessen his taxes, and I need to know why."

Fionna studied the laptop but then shook her head. "Numbers don't have emotional energy. That's why Receivers usually aren't so great at math. I can't feel anything from any of this. I'd have to be around Wilshire as he thought about this to tell you what you want to know."

Dan had assumed that would be the case.

CHAPTER 40

DOLLARS AND SENSE

an moved from the bed at a quarter to five. He hadn't slept. The gnawing questions had permeated his soul, and the bitter disappointment ate at him in the inky blackness of night. He perked a fresh pot of coffee, casting it to stay warm without burning. What the hell was Wilshire covering up?

He poured a cup of the coffee and called his father at 5:01.

"Dan?" the governor sounded panicked. "Fionna hasn't gone into labor?"

"No, she's fine," he assured. "I need you to get up and meet me in your office."

"Is it that bad?"

"More bizarre than bad, but Wilshire is definitely up to no good. I don't yet know how much his mistress knew." He drew another restorative sip of coffee and phoned Governor Haydenshire.

"This can't be good," the Crown Governor sighed.

Dan could hear little Abigail's sweet suckles on the bottle. The governor must have been up feeding her.

"How quickly can you meet me in my dad's office?"

"Good grief. Let me shower and dress. I'll get Lillian up. I'll be there before six."

Easing back upstairs, Dan peeked in on Aida. He kissed her cheek, pulled the covers up to her chin, and sealed heat in their fibers. His heart ached as he moved back to Fionna. Performing the same task, Dan ran his hands over Halia's bump as he heated the quilts.

"I love you," Fionna whispered.

"I love you too, sweetheart. I'll be home as soon as I can."

"Be careful."

"I'll be fine."

Aida appeared at their door carrying her blanket. "Mommy is sad." She yawned. Dan lifted her into the bed beside Fionna. "It's okay, Mommy," Aida vowed before falling asleep curled up in Fionna's arms.

"It is now." Fionna kissed her cheek.

Governor Haydenshire shook his head in abject confusion as he read everything Dan had presented him. "This doesn't make any sense." They were standing outside Governor Vindico's office awaiting his arrival.

"I know, sir. All I can definitively tell you is that he's doing something with the books, just maybe not what we all suspected. I still say it's sketchy though. He's up to something."

"Sorry," Governor Vindico lamented as he rushed toward them. "I had to stop and get gas."

Governor Haydenshire offered no greeting but simply handed the file to Governor Vindico. He summoned and allowed everyone into his stately office as he started a pot of coffee. He sat on one of the leather couches and opened the file.

"What am I looking at?"

"I wish I could tell you. Wilshire has donated a significant amount of money to the school, without reporting it on his taxes, immediately after he expressed in an email to Katherine Bryant that he would not allow their love to be threatened. Makes no sense to me, but I will figure it out eventually," Dan assured him.

"I don't think you should have to figure it out, son. I think Dean can tell us himself."

Having to remind himself that he was in fact thirty-two years old, and a father himself, so that he wouldn't cower beneath his dad's infuriated scowl, Dan watched the man that had raised him stomp to his office phone.

"Dean, this is Arthur," he growled. "You have less than a half hour to be in my office, or I'm calling out Iodex." He slammed down the phone.

"What are you going to do, Arthur?" Governor Haydenshire asked.

"I'm suspending him first and foremost, but if I suspend him without pay then I'm punishing Ellen as well," he stated the difficulty in the reprimand. "What was he thinking?"

"Do you want me to leave?" Dan asked.

"You know what?" Governor Vindico spat. "He quite literally made this bed, so he can lie in it. He can know that you're there at the school on my orders checking out each and every thing. And he won't be there to fire you, because I'm taking over as chancellor of Venton Academy." He paced in his fury.

In under fifteen minutes, there was a weak knock on the governor's door. Governor Vindico slung it open with gall burning in his eyes.

"Sit down, Dean," he snarled.

"Well, now I know where you learned to do that," Governor Haydenshire spoke under his breath as he and Dan shared a slight grin.

"What's this about?" Chancellor Wilshire glanced nervously from Dan to Governor Haydenshire. Exhaustion and stress etched the man's face and rhythms.

He appeared to have aged decades in the last minute.

"Why don't you tell us?" Governor Vindico slung the file to the chancellor. Dan watched Wilshire pale dramatically as he sank down in a seat in front of the substantial polished oak desk that belonged to his father.

His eyes goggled as he swallowed harshly.

"Where did you find this?"

"Really, Dean." Governor Haydenshire reached the end of his notoriously short rope quickly. "That's where you're going to start?"

"What do you want me to say?" Wilshire quipped.

"I want some kind of plausible explanation of why you've been depositing a rather large sum of money into the Venton accounts? I want to know what it has to do with your mistress who is fourteen years younger than you! And I want to know now!"

"I donate to the school because I believe in the academy." It was very apparent to Dan that Wilshire had become rather skilled at lying. He did it well.

"I don't think so." Governor Vindico shook his head. "If that were the case, you wouldn't have balked every single time I asked to see the books. So, last chance. What the hell are you covering up?"

"Nothing," he lied again.

Dan rolled his eyes.

Governor Vindico managed a nod. "You have ruined not only your and Ellen's lives, but hers and her husband's as well, not to mention their children," he roared. "If you were willing to do that, then I don't believe for a moment that whatever you've done here isn't either some kind of negotiation with your conscience, or you're in something so deep you can't see your way out."

Governor Haydenshire nodded. "Yes, and now we get to go in that chamber in an hour and decide which parent gets to try and put those kids' lives back together."

It was distinctly odd to be in an office where anger permeated the very air and to not be the one shouting.

"Stephen, please," Wilshire began begging. "Please don't take her kids away from her."

"Are you seriously sitting there after all of this,"—Governor Haydenshire hit the file folder with the back of his hand—"and asking me for favors for your mistress when you just lied to my face?"

Dan understood very well that Governor Haydenshire would have loved to have hit the man holding the file instead of the file that for all intents and purposes held the man.

"My God, what happened to you?" Governor Vindico demanded. "What were you thinking?"

He rubbed his hands over his face. "What do you want me to say?"

"I want you to explain why you are depositing more than half of your yearly paychecks back into Venton."

"I believe in the school."

Governor Vindico shook his head. "Stop lying to me. You're suspended until further notice. Do not return to Venton Campus until you've been given written permission from me. And I think until you're actually terminated from the position, I'll see to it that your paychecks are made out to Ellen."

Wilshire turned to Governor Haydenshire. His expression was pleading. "Stephen, please." He begged the only man with the power to overturn another governor's decision.

"Sounds good to me." Governor Haydenshire stared Wilshire down.

Wilshire shook his head in disbelief. "How am I supposed to pay for the hotel where I'm currently staying?"

"Quite honestly, Dean, I might have Lillian give Ellen a call and give her a little advice. Because I assure you—although I would never, ever do something like this—that if I even thought about it, all of my belongings would be in a smoldering pile of ash in my front yard, and every single penny that had our names on it would be hers and hers alone. Rightfully so.

"I don't give a damn how you pay for your hotel room. I don't care if you end up living in a tent on one of your kids' lawns. You know, one of the five children that she gave you, who by the way, I don't know how you look in the eye anymore after what you've done to their mother."

"So, that's it then." Chancellor Wilshire stood in a fitful huff. Dan edged closer. He wasn't going to let his father or the Crown be threatened. "You just stand there in your indignation and blame me for everything. And then you get to decide my punishment. That how it works now? You're the Crown Governor, so you get to be judge, jury, and executioner?" He snarled as Dan rolled his eyes.

Governor Haydenshire's eyes narrowed in abject fury. His

Adminis bands tensed viciously. Dan and Governor Vindico stepped back as Governor Haydenshire leaned in. "You are an employee of this Realm and of the Senate that governs this Realm. The Realm I run," he seethed. "And no, I don't just blame you. It seems Katherine Bryant, who is by the way also an employee of this Realm and of the Senate, should bear half the burden. But don't you stand there playing the martyr, and playing the victim. Do not try to tell me that things weren't good at home, and you never meant to hurt anyone," the governor spit the words like venom from his lips.

"If things aren't good with your wife, then get off your lazy ass and fix it. If you'd spent half the energy and the time you spent wooing Katherine Bryant and lying to us, plus all of the money it took you to cover up the little den of cobras that you knowingly leapt in with both feet, trying to work on your marriage instead, then you'd still have a job, and a paycheck, and a home. Most importantly, you'd still have the heart of a woman that adored you and took care of you and bore your children. So yes"—the governor nodded—"I will stand here and I will back up Governor Vindico because he is your boss, though you never really liked the idea that you had anyone to report to.

"Arthur made numerous trips to the academy last year and numerous phone calls to make certain everything was all right, because once the foundation begins to give way, the entire house is gone in an instant. We knew something wasn't right. Yet, you looked him in the eye and lied over and over. And you're still lying to us now. You've told so many lies at this point, you couldn't see the truth if you fell over it.

"So, you can drown in the mess you're swimming in. Get out of my face."

Chancellor Wilshire swallowed harshly as he turned from the governors. He narrowed his eyes at Dan as he made his exit. "Don't think I don't know who found all of that for them," he threatened as he moved toward the door.

Dan shook his head with a derisive chuckle. "You know, my dad used to say to me, everyone makes mistakes. You're not a failure until you start blaming other people for them. So, Chancellor Wilshire, let me be the first to say, you're a complete and utter failure." The chancellor flung open the door and let it slam behind him.

Checking his watch, the Crown Governor vibrated in his fury. "We have to know what is going on at that academy. That has to be some kind of hush money cover-up."

"That's precisely what I intend to find out," Governor Vindico assured him.

CHAPTER 41

REMAINS AND REMNANTS

Dan followed his father and Governor Haydenshire into the Senate prep room. He took a seat in the back of the chamber room while the governors donned their robes.

Tucking himself in the back corner, Dan took in the room. Katherine Bryant was seated with a woman Dan assumed must be her lawyer. Her eyes were nearly swollen shut. She was slunk forward. Her depression was evident to everyone in the room. Her husband was scowling from the opposite bench. Two lawyers sat on either side of him.

Dan knew one, Martin Westfield. He was cutthroat and as vicious as they came. Moving back a few rows, Dan's eyes landed on the Bryants' son and daughter. They were seated behind their father. Dan wondered if that was a sign of their allegiance. The daughter, Elise, Dan recalled from the photos of her in pointe shoes the evening before, had her head on her brother's shoulder.

Dan drew a deep breath. He considered speaking to the kids, trying to offer them a little comfort, but couldn't come up with much to offer them other than *I'm so sorry your mother has no morals and your father is an idiot.*

No one else was in the courtroom. It was a civil case and didn't require the Senteon's involvement. The laws that had been compromised or broken were already in place. There was no need for interpretation.

Portwood, Ericcson, Logan, Rainer, and Jeff followed in behind four Non-Elite Iodex officers that were there to make certain that the civil case remained civil.

Understanding that Dan needed to remain as inconspicuous as possible, they all offered him a slight nod. Dan returned the gesture. The governors entered and everyone stood.

It was the first governing board in two decades that hosted two female governors. Dan wondered if that would sway things either for or against Katherine Bryant.

As the board made their entrance, Dan heard a slight squeak of a shoe near the door. His eyes goggled at Wilshire making a stealthy entrance. He'd donned glasses and a baseball cap and took a seat almost underneath the flag of the American Realm in the opposite corner.

It was then that Dan understood. Wilshire was truly worried about Katherine as the ramifications of all that they'd done began to crash down around them. If actions spoke louder than words or than texts, it appeared that Wilshire and Bryant were in love.

Governor Haydenshire looked sick as he glanced from Terry to Katherine. "I have an entered plea from Terrance Lyle Bryant to obtain full custody of Bradley Lyle Bryant, age fourteen, and Elise Madison Bryant, age twelve. He also requests that the banking accounts once belonging to him and Katherine Elise Bryant be divided in half, along with half of Katherine's current salary as a mentor at Venton Academy. Terry also requests that he be given the deed and full ownership of the family home in Alexandria. His request comes with an additional addendum that Bradley and Elise be kept from any visitation from their mother, Katherine. Is that correct, Mr. Bryant?"

Terry stood. "Yes, sir. That's correct."

Mentor Bryant began to weep audibly.

"Clerk, please give Mrs. Bryant a tissue," Governor Haydenshire requested. "Now, Mentor Katherine Elise Bryant has entered a plea for joint custody of Bradley and Elise. She would also like the family home in Alexandria. She offers Terrance half of her salary upon her returning to work and half of their savings accounts. She requests primary custody with Terrance being able to see the children throughout the week and every other weekend," the governor explained. "Is that correct, Mentor Bryant?"

Mentor Bryant grasped the bench in front of her to help her stand and offered a slight nod.

"Is there anything else either of you would like to inform the board of before I make my suggested ruling and the board votes?" Governor Haydenshire asked.

"You could talk to her lover. He's sitting right back there," Terry outed Wilshire.

Katherine gasped as everyone turned to see Chancellor Wilshire seated on the back row.

Shaking his head, Governor Haydenshire drew a deep breath. "That won't be necessary, Mr. Bryant. I feel certain most of us were subjected to the nauseating display you chose to smear all over the Internet last evening in effort to sway our votes. I am not impressed. It seems neither you nor your wife have the capability to make remotely decent decisions. Truthfully, I've half a mind to take Bradley and Elise from you both."

Terry's rhythms reeled visibly. His eyes goggled, as the fire he'd ignited and stirred all night long began to overtake him.

"Did either of you stop to consider even for a moment what your despicable actions"—he gestured his hand to Katherine before turning his glare to Terry—"and your unnecessary classless retaliation was doing to your children?"

In what Dan was certain was one of the first truths to exit Katherine Bryant's mind in a number of years, she shook her head as she succumbed to tears once again.

"Answer me," the governor demanded of Terry.

"No, sir." He glanced back at Brad who refused to meet his gaze as he kept his sister tucked on his chest. She was sobbing.

"I assumed as much. I'll lay out my suggested plans and we'll vote. It will take three governors' approval to decree my plan. If we do not reach consensus, we will take a brief intermission until we decide how to proceed." He explained the way the governing board of the American Realm and in this particular case also the board of the commonwealth of Virginia worked. Terry and Katherine both managed a nod.

"First of all, Mr. Bryant, I do understand the desperate desire to fight for and protect your children. It is something my wife and I have done together for the last thirty-three years," the governor huffed as Terry's eyes closed in defeat. "Every single posting that you've made about your wife's adultery will be removed from any social media site that you can access," the governor gave his first command.

"Yes, sir," Terry agreed immediately.

"Now, in terms of the entered pleas, I'd like to request that both of you try to understand the position that you have not only put me in but also this board. Mentor Bryant, when you decided to have an extramarital affair, that decision did not only affect you, as much as you tried desperately to convince yourself that it did. When you throw a rock in a pond, Katherine, the entire pond feels the rippling effects. Therefore,"—the governor sighed—"my recommendation is that Katherine Bryant return to her post as a mentor at Venton Academy bright and early Monday morning. A family needs money to live, and since your esteemed partner in crime,"—he threw a glare at Wilshire—"has been suspended, I see no reason for you not to provide for your family.

"Everyone is an example, either a good one or a bad one, and right now, you can show the students at Venton the ultimate outcome of cheating. Cheating your children, and your husband, cheating your work, and cheating yourself, because you didn't really give your all to any of those over the last few years. You were too busy at wells that brought no water.

"Half of your pay will be given to your husband." Katherine broke down completely. "However, I will not throw your children's lives into complete chaos. You and Terry will have joint, divided custody. You will switch back and forth each Sunday at five o'clock.

"The house, however, I am assigning to Bradley and Elise. I will not have these children, who are the victims in all of this, jerked back and forth every other week. During the week when Terry is their primary caregiver, he will live in the home with his children. You will not be in the home or intrude on their time in any way, Katherine."

"During your weeks, Katherine, you will stay there. Terry, you'll have to find somewhere to stay during Katherine's weeks. For now, the savings accounts will be divided in half. The entire family will begin counseling twice a week here at the Senate in the Auxiliary Department. Do not miss a session."

Dan watched the governing board back the Crown's suggestions unanimously.

After the slam of the gavel, Katherine hesitantly approached her children.

"You ruined everything! I hate you!" Elise spat and rushed from the courtroom.

Terry glared at Katherine. "Do not show up before five o'clock Sunday night." Wilshire had made his escape just as Governor Eleanor voted for the Crown Governor's plan, sealing in the third vote.

Governor Vindico and Governor Haydenshire shook hands with the members of the board. Governor Haydenshire was complimented by every other governor for the way he'd handled the Bryants.

They made their way to Dan. Portwood, Logan, and Rainer were shaking their heads as they all began discussing what everyone had viewed online and what was likely to happen with Mentor Bryant returning to work Monday. Jeff, however, stealthily snuck out of the courtroom. Dan wondered what he was up to.

"I'll be there to make certain that it doesn't get too out of hand," Governor Vindico announced.

"Are you sure this is how you want to handle this, Arthur? That's going to be quite an undertaking along with your duties here," Governor Haydenshire eased.

"It's ultimately my fault that Venton is in the state that it's in. I intend to return it to the bastion of education it used to be, and I'm kind of hoping I'll have a little help." Governor Vindico nodded to Dan.

"We'll get everything put back to rights, and then my beautiful daughter-in-law is going to have me another grandbaby, so my son and I will be busy with something much more pleasant."

Dan was impressed with his father's willingness to step in personally rather than assigning the cleanup to someone else.

"Great. I have a few suggestions," Dan teased, making everyone laugh. "First of all, how many freaking faculty meetings do I really need to sit through?"

"Mentor Vindico." Jeff rushed back in with a cell phone clutched in his palm. "Wilshire made a phone call when he left here. I cloned the phone while he was talking. You've got to see this."

ABOUT THE AUTHOR

J.E. Neal (aka Jillian) vastly prefers coffee to tea, guac to salsa, the beach over anywhere else, and the world inside her head over the one outside her front door. She also loves not having to choose.

Driven by the question 'what if,' J.E. Neal's world began to manifest. What if there were people with powers the rest of us couldn't see? What if the energy of our world could be summoned and used at their will? Characters with these amazing abilities took shape in her mind. She created—and continues to create—an endless number of stories full of delicious escape from our reality where emotions are visible, desire is palpable, and danger is universal.

Learn more about J.E. Neal at JillianNeal.com

facebook.com/jilliannealauthor
twitter.com/JillianNeal_
instagram.com/jilliannealauthor

ALSO BY J.E. NEAL

TANGLE OF MAGIC

Tangle of Magic Boxed Set (Books 1-6)

Tangle of Lies (Book 1)

Tangle of Chaos (Book 2)

Tangle of Desires (Book 3)

Tangle of Fates (Book 4)

Tangle of Trust (Book 5)

Tangle of Ruin (Book 6)

ENERGY OF MAGIC

Shield and Shattered Cages (Book 1)

Shield and Faltered Steps (Book 2)

Shield and Splintered Oaths (Book 3)

Shield and Humbled Crown (Book 4)

Shield and Vile Serpents (Book 5)

Shield and Coveted Splendor (Book 6)

Shield and Guarded Shadow (Book 7)

Shield and Worthy Sinner (Book 8)

Shield and Sacrificial Heirs (Book 9)

www.ingramcontent.com/pod-product-compliance
Lightning Source LLC
Chambersburg PA
CBHW060736190726
48285CB00001B/235